Quatermain

D1596691

Quatermain

The Complete Adventures: 2

Allan's Wife
★
Maiwa's Revenge
★
Marie

H. Rider Haggard

LEONAUR

Quatermain : the Complete Adventures: 2—
Allan's Wife, Maiwa's Revenge & Marie
by H. Rider Haggard

Leonaur is an imprint of Oakpast Ltd

ISBN: 978-1-84677-532-1 (hardcover)
ISBN: 978-1-84677-531-4 (softcover)

http://www.leonaur.com

Publisher's Notes

The views expressed in this book are not necessarily
those of the publisher.

Contents

Publisher's Note

Suggested reading sequence for the Allan Quatermain stories:

Allan's Wife

Dedication

My Dear Macumazahn,

It was your native name which I borrowed at the christening of that Allen who has become as well known to me as any other friend I have. It is therefore fitting that I should dedicate to you this, his last tale—the story of his wife, and the history of some further adventures which befell him. They will remind you of many an African yarn—that with the baboons may recall an experience of your own which I did not share. And perhaps they will do more than this. Perhaps they will bring back to you some of the long past romance of days that are lost to us. The country of which Allan Quatermain tells his tale is now, for the most part, as well known and explored as are the fields of Norfolk. Where we shot and trekked and galloped, scarcely seeing the face of civilized man, there the gold-seeker builds his cities. The shadow of the flag of Britain has, for a while, ceased to fall on the Transvaal plains; the game has gone; the misty charm of the morning has become the glare of day. All is changed. The blue gums that we planted in the garden of the Palatial must be large trees by now, and the Palatial itself has passed from us. Jess sat in it waiting for her love after we were gone. There she nursed him back to life. But Jess is dead, and strangers own it, or perhaps it is a ruin.

For us too, Macumazahn, as for the land we loved, the mystery and promise of the morning are outworn; the mid-day sun burns overhead, and at times the way is weary. Few of those we knew are left. Some are victims to battle and murder, their bones strew the veldt; death has taken some in a more gentle fashion; others are hidden from us, we know not where. We might well fear to return to that land lest we also should see ghosts. But though we walk apart to-day, the past yet looks upon us with its unalterable eyes. Still we can remember many a boyish enterprise and adventure, lightly undertaken, which now would strike us as hazardous indeed. Still we can recall the long familiar line of the Pretoria Horse, the face of war and panic, the weariness of midnight patrols; aye, and hear the roar of guns echoed from the Shameful Hill.

To you then, Macumazahn, in perpetual memory of those eventful years of youth which we passed together in the African towns and on the African veldt, I dedicate these pages, subscribing myself now as always,

Your sincere friend,

Indanda

To Arthur H. D. Cochrane, Esq.

CHAPTER 1

Early Days

It may be remembered that in the last pages of his diary, written just before his death, Allan Quatermain makes allusion to his long dead wife, stating that he has written of her fully elsewhere.

When his death was known, his papers were handed to myself as his literary executor. Among them I found two manuscripts, of which the following is one. The other is simply a record of events wherein Mr. Quatermain was not personally concerned—a Zulu novel, the story of which was told to him by the hero many years after the tragedy had occurred. But with this we have nothing to do at present.

I have often thought (Mr. Quatermain's manuscript begins) that I would set down on paper the events connected with my marriage, and the loss of my most dear wife. Many years have now passed since that event, and to some extent time has softened the old grief, though Heaven knows it is still keen enough. On two or three occasions I have even begun the record. Once I gave it up because the writing of it depressed me beyond bearing, once because I was suddenly called away upon a journey, and the third time because a *Kaffir* boy found my manuscript convenient for lighting the kitchen fire.

But now that I am at leisure here in England, I will make a fourth attempt. If I succeed, the story may serve to interest someone in after years when I am dead and gone; before that I should not wish it to be published. It is a wild tale enough, and suggests some curious reflections.

I am the son of a missionary. My father was originally curate in charge of a small parish in Oxfordshire. He had already been some ten years married to my dear mother when he went there, and he had four children, of whom I was the youngest. I remember faintly the place where we lived. It was an ancient long grey house, facing the road. There was a very large tree of some sort in the garden. It was hollow, and we children used to play about inside of it, and knock knots of wood from the rough bark. We all slept in a kind of attic, and my mother always came and kissed us when we were in bed. I used to wake up and see her bending over me, a candle in her hand. There was a curious kind of pole projecting from the wall over my bed. Once I was dreadfully frightened because my eldest brother made me hang to it by my hands. That is all I remember about our old home. It has been pulled down long ago, or I would journey there to see it.

A little further down the road was a large house with big iron gates to it, and on the top of the gate pillars sat two stone lions, which were so hideous that I was afraid of them. Perhaps this sentiment was prophetic. One could see the house by peeping through the bars of the gates. It was a gloomy-looking place, with a tall yew hedge round it; but in the summer-time some flowers grew about the sun-dial in the grass plat. This house was called the Hall, and Squire Carson lived there. One Christmas—it must have been the Christmas before my father emigrated, or I should not remember it—we children went to a Christmas-tree festivity at the Hall. There was a great party there, and footmen wearing red waistcoats stood at the door. In the dining-room, which was panelled with black oak, was the Christmas-tree. Squire Carson stood in front of it. He was a tall, dark man, very quiet in his manners, and he wore a bunch of seals on his waistcoat. We used to think him old, but as a matter of fact he was then not more than forty. He had been, as I afterwards learned, a great traveller in his youth, and some six or seven years before this date he married a lady who was half a Spaniard—a papist, my father called her. I can remember her well. She was small and very pretty, with a rounded figure, large black eyes, and glittering teeth. She spoke English with a curious accent. I suppose that I must have been a funny child to look at, and I know that my hair stood up on my head then as it does now, for I still have a sketch of myself that my mother made of me, in which this peculiarity is strongly marked. On this occasion of the Christmas-tree I remember that Mrs. Carson turned to a tall, foreign-looking gentleman who stood beside her, and, tapping him affectionately on the shoulder with her gold eye-glasses, said—

"Look, cousin—look at that droll little boy with the big brown eyes; his hair is like a—what you call him?—scrubbing-brush. Oh, what a droll little boy!"

The tall gentleman pulled at his moustache, and, taking Mrs. Carson's hand in his, began to smooth my hair down with it till I heard her whisper—

"Leave go my hand, cousin. Thomas is looking like—like the thunderstorm."

Thomas was the name of Mr. Carson, her husband.

After that I hid myself as well as I could behind a chair, for I was shy, and watched little Stella Carson, who was the squire's only child, giving the children presents off the tree. She was dressed as Father Christmas, with some soft white stuff round her lovely little face, and she had large dark eyes, which I thought more beautiful than anything I had ever seen. At last it came to my turn to receive a present—oddly enough, considered in the light of future events, it was a large monkey. Stella reached it down from one of the lower boughs of the tree and handed it to me, saying—

"Dat is my Christmas present to you, little Allan Quatermain."

As she did so her sleeve, which was covered with cotton wool, spangled over with something that shone, touched one of the tapers and caught fire—how I do not know—and the flame ran up her arm towards her throat. She stood quite still. I suppose that she was paralysed with fear; and the ladies who were near screamed very loud, but did nothing. Then some impulse seized me—perhaps instinct would be a better word to use, considering my age. I threw myself upon the child, and, beating at the fire with my hands, mercifully succeeded in extinguishing it before it really got hold. My wrists were so badly scorched that they had to be wrapped up in wool for a long time afterwards, but with the exception of a single burn upon her throat, little Stella Carson was not much hurt.

This is all that I remember about the Christmas-tree at the Hall. What happened afterwards is lost to me, but to this day in my sleep I sometimes see little Stella's sweet face and the stare of terror in her dark eyes as the fire ran up her arm. This, however, is not wonderful, for I had, humanly speaking, saved the life of her who was destined to be my wife.

The next event which I can recall clearly is that my mother and three brothers all fell ill of fever, owing, as I afterwards learned, to the poisoning of our well by some evil-minded person, who threw a dead sheep into it.

It must have been while they were ill that Squire Carson came one day to the vicarage. The weather was still cold, for there was a fire in the study, and I sat before the fire writing letters on a piece of paper with a pencil, while my father walked up and down the room talking to himself. Afterwards I knew that he was praying for the lives of his wife and children. Presently a servant came to the door and said that someone wanted to see him.

"It is the squire, sir," said the maid, "and he says he particularly wishes to see you."

"Very well," answered my father, wearily, and presently Squire Carson came in. His face was white and haggard, and his eyes shone so fiercely that I was afraid of him.

"Forgive me for intruding on you at such a time, Quatermain," he said, in a hoarse voice, "but Tomorrow I leave this place for ever, and I wish to speak to you before I go—indeed, I must speak to you."

"Shall I send Allan away?" said my father, pointing to me.

"No; let him bide. He will not understand." Nor, indeed, did I at the time, but I remembered every word, and in after years their meaning grew on me.

"First tell me," he went on, "how are they?" and he pointed upwards with his thumb.

"My wife and two of the boys are beyond hope," my father answered, with a groan. "I do not know how it will go with the third. The Lord's will be done!"

"The Lord's will be done," the squire echoed, solemnly. "And now, Quatermain, listen—my wife's gone."

"Gone!" my father answered. "Who with?"

"With that foreign cousin of hers. It seems from a letter she left me that she always cared for him, not for me. She married me because she thought me a rich English milord. Now she has run through my property, or most of it, and gone. I don't know where. Luckily, she did not care to encumber her new career with the child; Stella is left to me."

"That is what comes of marrying a papist, Carson," said my father. That was his fault; he was as good and charitable a man as ever lived, but he was bigoted. "What are you going to do—follow her?"

He laughed bitterly in answer.

"Follow her!" he said; "why should I follow her? If I met her I might kill her or him, or both of them, because of the disgrace they have brought upon my child's name. No, I never want to look upon her face again. I trusted her, I tell you, and she has betrayed me. Let her go and find her fate. But I am going too. I am weary of my life."

"Surely, Carson, surely," said my father, "you do not mean——"

"No, no; not that. Death comes soon enough. But I will leave this civilized world which is a lie. We will go right away into the wilds, I and my child, and hide our shame. Where? I don't know where. Anywhere, so long as there are no white faces, no smooth educated tongues——"

"You are mad, Carson," my father answered. "How will you live? How can you educate Stella? Be a man and wear it down."

"I will be a man, and I will wear it down, but not here, Quatermain. Education! Was not she—that woman who was my wife—was not she highly educated?—the cleverest woman in the country forsooth. Too clever for me, Quatermain—too clever by half! No, no, Stella shall be brought up in a different school; if it be possible, she shall forget her very name. Goodbye, old friend, goodbye forever. Do not try to find me out, henceforth I shall be like one dead to you, to you and all I knew," and he was gone.

"Mad," said my father, with a heavy sigh. "His trouble has turned his brain. But he will think better of it."

At that moment the nurse came hurrying in and whispered something in his ear. My father's face turned deadly pale. He clutched at the table to support himself, then staggered from the room. My mother was dying!

It was some days afterwards, I do not know exactly how long, that my father took me by the hand and led me upstairs into the big room which had been my mother's bedroom. There she lay, dead in her coffin, with flowers in her hand. Along the wall of the room were arranged three little white beds, and on each of the beds lay one of my brothers. They all looked as though they were asleep, and they all had flowers in their hands. My father told me to kiss them, because I should not see them anymore, and I did so, though I was very frightened. I did not know why. Then he took me in his arms and kissed me.

"The Lord hath given," he said, "and the Lord hath taken away; blessed be the name of the Lord."

I cried very much, and he took me downstairs, and after that I have only a confused memory of men dressed in black carrying heavy burdens towards the grey churchyard!

Next comes a vision of a great ship and wide tossing waters. My father could no longer bear to live in England after the loss that had fallen on him, and made up his mind to emigrate to South Africa. We must have been poor at the time—indeed, I believe that a large portion of our income went from my father on my mother's death. At any rate we travelled with the steerage passengers, and the intense discomfort of the journey with the rough ways of our fellow emigrants still remain upon my mind. At last it came to an end, and we reached Africa, which I was not to leave again for many, many years.

In those days civilization had not made any great progress in Southern Africa. My father went up the country and became a missionary among the *Kaffirs*, near to where the town of Cradock now stands, and here I grew to manhood. There were a few Boer farmers in the neighbourhood, and gradually a little settlement of whites gathered round our mission station—a drunken Scotch blacksmith and wheelwright was about the most interesting character, who, when he was sober, could quote the Scottish poet Burns and the *Ingoldsby Legends*, then recently published, literally by the page. It was from that I contracted a fondness for the latter amusing writings, which has never left me. Burns I never cared for so much, probably because of the Scottish dialect which repelled me. What little education I got was from my father, but I never had much leaning towards books, nor he much time to teach them to me. On the other hand, I was always a keen observer of the ways of men and nature. By the time that I was twenty I could speak Dutch and three or four *Kaffir* dialects perfectly, and I doubt if there was anybody in South Africa who understood native ways of thought and action more completely than I did. Also I was really a very good shot and horseman, and I think—as, indeed, my subsequent career proves to have been the case—a great deal tougher than the majority of men. Though I was then, as now, light and small, nothing seemed to tire me. I could bear any amount of exposure and privation, and I never met the native who was my master in feats of endurance. Of course, all that is different now, I am speaking of my early manhood.

It may be wondered that I did not run absolutely wild in such surroundings, but I was held back from this by my father's society. He was one of the gentlest and most refined men that I ever met; even the most savage *Kaffir* loved him, and his influence was a very good one for me. He used to call himself one of the world's failures. Would that there were more such failures. Every morning when his work was done he would take his prayer-book and, sitting on the little *stoep* or veranda of our station, would read the evening psalms to himself. Sometimes there was not light enough for this, but it made no difference, he knew them all by heart. When he had finished he would look out across the cultivated lands where the mission *Kaffirs* had their huts.

But I knew it was not these he saw, but rather the grey English church, and the graves ranged side by side before the yew near the wicket gate.

It was there on the *stoep* that he died. He had not been well, and one evening I was talking to him, and his mind went back to Oxfordshire and my mother. He spoke of her a good deal, saying that she had never been out of his mind for a single day during all these years, and that he rejoiced to think he was drawing near that land wither she

16

had gone. Then he asked me if I remembered the night when Squire Carson came into the study at the vicarage, and told him that his wife had run away, and that he was going to change his name and bury himself in some remote land.

I answered that I remembered it perfectly.

"I wonder where he went to," said my father, "and if he and his daughter Stella are still alive. Well, well! I shall never meet them again. But life is a strange thing, Allan, and you may. If you ever do, give them my kind love."

After that I left him. We had been suffering more than usual from the depredations of the *Kaffir* thieves, who stole our sheep at night, and, as I had done before, and not without success, I determined to watch the *kraal* and see if I could catch them. Indeed, it was from this habit of mine of watching at night that I first got my native name of Macumazahn, which may be roughly translated as "he who sleeps with one eye open." So I took my rifle and rose to go. But he called me to him and kissed me on the forehead, saying, "God bless you, Allan! I hope that you will think of your old father sometimes, and that you will lead a good and happy life."

I remember that I did not much like his tone at the time, but set it down to an attack of low spirits, to which he grew very subject as the years went on. I went down to the *kraal* and watched till within an hour of sunrise; then, as no thieves appeared, returned to the station. As I came near I was astonished to see a figure sitting in my father's chair. At first I thought it must be a drunken *Kaffir*, then that my father had fallen asleep there.

And so he had,—for he was dead!

CHAPTER 2

The Fire-Fight

When I had buried my father, and seen a successor installed in his place—for the station was the property of the Society—I set to work to carry out a plan which I had long cherished, but been unable to execute because it would have involved separation from my father. Put shortly, it was to undertake a trading journey of exploration right through the countries now known as the Free State and the Transvaal, and as much further North as I could go. It was an adventurous scheme, for though the emigrant Boers had begun to occupy positions in these territories, they were still to all practical purposes unexplored. But I was now alone in the world, and it mattered little what became of me; so, driven on by the overmastering love of adventure, which, old as I am, will perhaps still be the cause of my death, I determined to undertake the journey.

Accordingly I sold such stock and goods as we had upon the station, reserving only the two best wagons and two spans of oxen. The proceeds I invested in such goods as were then in fashion, for trading purposes, and in guns and ammunition. The guns would have moved any modern explorer to merriment; but such as they were I managed to do a good deal of execution with them. One of them was a single-barrelled, smooth bore, fitted for percussion caps—a *roer* we called it—which threw a three-ounce ball, and was charged with a handful of coarse black powder. Many is the elephant that I killed with that *roer*, although it generally knocked me backwards when I fired it, which I only did under compulsion. The best of the lot, perhaps, was a double-barrelled No. 12 shot-gun, but it had flint locks. Also there were some old tower muskets, which might or might not throw straight at seventy yards. I took six *Kaffirs* with me, and three good horses, which were supposed to be salted—that is, proof against the sickness. Among the *Kaffirs* was an old fellow named Indaba-zimbi, which, being translated, means "tongue of iron." I suppose he got this name from his strident voice and exhaustless eloquence. This man was a great character in his way. He had been a noted witch-doctor among a neighbouring tribe, and came to the station under the following circumstances, which, as he plays a considerable part in this history, are perhaps worth recording.

Two years before my father's death I had occasion to search the country round for some lost oxen. After a long and useless quest it occurred to me that I had better go to the place where the oxen were bred by a *Kaffir* chief, whose name I forget, but whose *kraal* was about fifty miles from our station. There I journeyed, and found the oxen safe at home. The chief entertained me handsomely, and on the following morning I went to pay my respects to him before leaving, and was somewhat surprised to find a collection of some hundreds of men and women sitting round him anxiously watching the sky in which the thunder-clouds were banking up in a very ominous way.

"You had better wait, white man," said the chief, "and see the rain-doctors fight the lightning."

I inquired what he meant, and learned that this man, Indaba-zimbi, had for some years occupied the position of wizard-in-chief to the tribe, although he was not a member of it, having been born in the country now known as Zululand. But a son of the chief's, a man of about thirty, had lately set up as a rival in supernatural powers. This irritated Indaba-zimbi beyond measure, and a quarrel ensued between the two witch-doctors that resulted in a challenge to trial by lightning being given and accepted. These were the conditions. The rivals must await the coming of a serious thunderstorm, no ordinary tempest would serve their turn. Then, carrying assegais in their hands, they must take their stand within fifty paces of each other upon a certain patch of ground where the big thunderbolts were observed to strike continually, and by the exercise of their occult powers and invocations to the lightning, must strive to avert death from themselves and bring it on their rival. The terms of this singular match had been arranged a month previously, but no storm worthy of the occasion had arisen. Now the local weather-prophets believed it to be brewing.

I inquired what would happen if neither of the men were struck, and was told that they must then wait for another storm. If they escaped the second time, however, they would be held to be equal in power, and be jointly consulted by the tribe upon occasions of importance.

The prospect of being a spectator of so unusual a sight overcame my desire to be gone, and I accepted the chief's invitation to see it out.

Before mid-day I regretted it, for though the western heavens grew darker and darker, and the still air heralded the coming of the storm, yet it did not come. By four o'clock, however, it became obvious that it must burst soon—at sunset, the old chief said, and in the company of the whole assembly I moved down to the place of combat. The *kraal* was built on the top of a hill, and below it the land sloped gently to the banks of a river about half a mile away. On the hither side of the bank was the piece of land that was, the natives said, "loved of the lightning." Here the magicians took up their stand, while the spectators grouped themselves on the hillside about two hundred yards away—which was, I thought, rather too near to be pleasant. When we had sat there for a while my curiosity overcame me, and I asked leave of the chief to go down and inspect the arena. He said I might do so at my own risk. I told him that the fire from above would not hurt white men, and went to find that the spot was a bed of iron ore, thinly covered with grass, which of course accounted for its attracting the lightning from the storms as they travelled along the line of the river. At each end of this iron-stone area were placed the combatants, Indaba-zimbi facing the east, and his rival the west, and before each there burned a little fire made of some scented root. Moreover they were dressed in all the paraphernalia of their craft, snakeskins, fish-bladders, and I know not what beside, while round their necks hung circlets of baboons' teeth and bones from human hands. First I went to the western end where the chief's son stood. He was pointing with his *assegai* towards the advancing storm, and invoking it in a voice of great excitement.

"Come, fire, and lick up Indaba-zimbi!

"Hear me, Storm Devil, and lick Indaba-zimbi with your red tongue!

"Spit on him with your rain!

"Whirl him away in your breath!

"Make him as nothing—melt the marrow in his bones!

"Run into his heart and burn away the lies!

"Show all the people who is the true Witch Finder!

"Let me not be put to shame in the eyes of this white man!"

Thus he spoke, or rather chanted, and all the while rubbed his broad chest—for he was a very fine man—with some filthy compound of medicine or *mouti*.

After a while, getting tired of his song, I walked across the iron-stone, to where Indaba-zimbi sat by his fire. He was not chanting at all, but his performance was much more impressive. It consisted in staring at the eastern sky, which was perfectly clear of cloud, and every now and again beckoning at it with his finger, then turning round to point with the *assegai* towards his rival. For a while I looked at him in silence. He was a curious wizened man, apparently over fifty years of age, with thin hands that looked as tough as wire. His nose was much sharper than is usual among these races, and he had a queer habit of holding his head sideways like a bird when he spoke, which, in addition to the humour that lurked in his eye, gave him a most comical appearance. Another strange thing about him was that he had a single white lock of hair among his black wool. At last I spoke to him:

"Indaba-zimbi, my friend," I said, "you may be a good witch-doctor, but you are certainly a fool. It is no good beckoning at the blue sky while your enemy is getting a start with the storm."

"You may be clever, but don't think you know everything, white man," the old fellow answered, in a high, cracked voice, and with something like a grin.

"They call you Iron-tongue," I went on; "you had better use it, or the Storm Devil won't hear you."

"The fire from above runs down iron," he answered, "so I keep my tongue quiet. Oh, yes, let him curse away, I'll put him out presently. Look now, white man."

I looked, and in the eastern sky there grew a cloud. At first it was small, though very black, but it gathered with extraordinary rapidity.

This was odd enough, but as I had seen the same thing happen before it did not particularly astonish me. It is by no means unusual in Africa for two thunderstorms to come up at the same time from different points of the compass.

"You had better get on, Indaba-zimbi," I said, "the big storm is coming along fast, and will soon eat up that baby of yours," and I pointed to the west.

"Babies sometimes grow to giants, white man," said Indaba-zimbi, beckoning away vigorously. "Look now at my cloud-child."

I looked; the eastern storm was spreading itself from earth to sky, and in shape resembled an enormous man. There was its head, its shoulders, and its legs; yes, it was like a huge giant travelling across the heavens. The light of the setting sun escaping from beneath the lower edge of the western storm shot across the intervening space in a sheet of splendour, and, lighting upon the advancing figure of cloud, wrapped its middle in hues of glory too wonderful to be described; but beneath and above this glowing belt his feet and head were black as jet. Presently, as I watched, an awful flash of light shot from the head of the cloud, circled it about as though with a crown of living fire, and vanished.

"Aha," chuckled old Indaba-zimbi, "my little boy is putting on his man's ring," and he tapped the gum ring on his own head, which natives assume when they reach a certain age and dignity. "Now, white man, unless you are a bigger wizard than either of us you had better clear off, for the fire-fight is about to begin."

I thought this sound advice.

"Good luck go with you, my black uncle," I said. "I hope you don't feel the iniquities of a misspent life weighing on you at the last."

"You look after yourself, and think of your own sins, young man," he answered, with a grim smile, and taking a pinch of snuff, while at that very moment a flash of lightning, I don't know from which storm, struck the ground within thirty paces of me. That was enough for me, I took to my heels, and as I went I heard old Indaba-zimbi's dry chuckle of amusement.

I climbed the hill till I came to where the chief was sitting with his *indunas*, or headmen, and sat down near to him. I looked at the man's face and saw that he was intensely anxious for his son's safety, and by no means confident of the young man's powers to resist the magic of Indaba-zimbi. He was talking in a low voice to the *induna* next to him. I affected to take no notice and to be concentrating my attention on the novel scene before me; but in those days I had very quick ears, and caught the drift of the conversation.

"Hearken!" the chief was saying, "if the magic of Indaba-zimbi prevails against my son I will endure him no more. Of this I am sure, that when he has slain my son he will slay me, me also, and make himself chief in my place. I fear Indaba-zimbi. *Ou!*"

"Black One," answered the *induna*, "wizards die as dogs die, and, once dead, dogs bark no more."

"And once dead," said the chiefs, "wizards work no more spells," and he bent and whispered in the *induna's* ear, looking at the *assegai* in his hand as he whispered.

"Good, my father, good!" said the *induna*, presently. "It shall be done tonight, if the lightning does not do it first."

"A bad look-out for old Indaba-zimbi," I said to myself. "They mean to kill him." Then I thought no more of the matter for a while, the scene before me was too tremendous.

The two storms were rapidly rushing together. Between them was a gulf of blue sky, and from time to time flashes of blinding light passed across this gulf, leaping from cloud to cloud. I remember that they reminded me of the story of the heathen god Jove and his thunderbolts. The storm that was shaped like a giant and ringed with the glory of the sinking sun made an excellent Jove, and I am sure that the bolts which leapt from it could not have been surpassed even in mythological times. Oddly enough, as yet the flashes were not followed by thunder. A deadly stillness lay upon the place, the cattle stood silently on the hillside, even the natives were awed to silence. Dark shadows crept along the bosom of the hills, the river to the right and left was hidden in wreaths of cloud, but before us and beyond the combatants it shone like a line of silver beneath the narrowing space of open sky. Now the western tempest was scrawled all over with lines of intolerable light, while the inky head of the cloud-giant to the east was continually suffused with a white and deadly glow that came and went in pulses, as though a blood of flame was being pumped into it from the heart of the storm.

The silence deepened and deepened, the shadows grew blacker and blacker, then suddenly all nature began to moan beneath the breath of an icy wind. On sped the wind; the smooth surface of the river was ruffled by it into little waves, the tall grass bowed low before it, and in its wake came the hissing sound of furious rain.

Ah! the storms had met. From each there burst an awful blaze of dazzling flame, and now the hill on which we sat rocked at the noise of the following thunder. The light went out of the sky, darkness fell suddenly on the land, but not for long. Presently the whole landscape grew vivid in the flashes, it appeared and disappeared, now everything was visible for miles, now even the men at my side vanished in the blackness. The thunder rolled and cracked and pealed like the trump of doom, whirlwinds tore round, lifting dust and even stones high into the air, and in a low, continuous undertone rose the hiss of the rushing rain.

I put my hand before my eyes to shield them from the terrible glare, and looked beneath it towards the lists of iron-stone. As flash followed flash, from time to time I caught sight of the two wizards. They were slowly advancing towards one another, each pointing at his foe with the *assegai* in his hand. I could see their every movement, and it seemed to me that the chain lightning was striking the iron-stone all round them.

Suddenly the thunder and lightning ceased for a minute, everything grew black, and, except for the rain, silent.

"It is over one way or the other, chief," I called out into the darkness.

"Wait, white man, wait!" answered the chief, in a voice thick with anxiety and fear.

Hardly were the words out of his mouth when the heavens were lit up again till they literally seemed to flame. There were the men, not ten paces apart. A great flash fell between them, I saw them stagger beneath the shock. Indaba-zimbi recovered himself first—at any rate when the next flash came he was standing bolt upright, pointing with his *assegai* towards his enemy. The chief's son was still on his legs, but he was staggering like a drunken man, and the *assegai* had fallen from his hand.

Darkness! then again a flash, more fearful, if possible, than any that had gone before. To me it seemed to come from the east, right over the head of Indaba-zimbi. At that instant I saw the chief's son wrapped, as it were, in the heart of it. Then the thunder pealed, the rain burst over us like a torrent, and I saw no more.

The worst of the storm was done, but for a while the darkness was so dense that we could not move, nor, indeed, was I inclined to leave the safety of the hillside where the lightning was never known to strike, and venture down to the iron-stone. Occasionally there still came flashes, but, search as we would, we could see no trace of either of the wizards. For my part, I believed that they were both dead. Now the clouds slowly rolled away down the course of the river, and with them went the rain; and now the stars shone in their wake.

"Let us go and see," said the old chief, rising and shaking the water from his hair. "The fire-fight is ended, let us go and see who has conquered."

I rose and followed him, dripping as though I had swum a hundred yards with my clothes on, and after me came all the people of the *kraal*.

We reached the spot; even in that light I could see where the iron-stone had been split and fused by the thunderbolts. While I was staring about me, I suddenly heard the chief, who was on my right, give a low moan, and saw the people cluster round him. I went up and looked. There, on the ground, lay the body of his son. It was a dreadful sight. The hair was burnt off his head, the copper rings upon his arms were fused, the *assegai* handle which lay near was literally shivered into threads, and, when I took hold of his arm, it seemed to me that every bone of it was broken.

The men with the chief stood gazing silently, while the women wailed.

"Great is the magic of Indaba-zimbi!" said a man, at length. The chief turned and struck him a heavy blow with the *kerrie* in his hand.

"Great or not, thou dog, he shall die," he cried, "and so shalt thou if thou singest his praises so loudly."

I said nothing, but thinking it probable that Indaba-zimbi had shared the fate of his enemy, I went to look. But I could see nothing of him, and at length, being thoroughly chilled with the wet, started back to my wagon to change my clothes. On reaching it, I was rather surprised to see a strange *Kaffir* seated on the driving-box wrapped up in a blanket.

"Hullo! come out of that," I said.

The figure on the box slowly unrolled the blanket, and with great deliberation took a pinch of snuff.

"It was a good fire-fight, white man, was it not?" said Indaba-zimbi, in his high, cracked voice. "But he never had a chance against me, poor boy. He knew nothing about it. See, white man, what becomes of presumption in the young. It is sad, very sad, but I made the flashes fly, didn't I?"

"You old humbug," I said, "unless you are careful you will soon learn what comes of presumption in the old, for your chief is after you with an *assegai*, and it will take all your magic to dodge that."

"Now you don't say so," said Indaba-zimbi, clambering off the wagon with rapidity; "and all because of this wretched upstart. There's gratitude for you, white man. I expose him, and they want to kill me. Well, thank you for the hint. We shall meet again before long," and he was gone like a shot, and not too soon, for just then some of the chief's men came up to the wagon.

On the following morning I started homewards. The first face I saw on arriving at the station was that of Indaba-zimbi.

"How do you do, Macumazahn?" he said, holding his head on one side and nodding his white lock. "I hear you are Christians here, and I want to try a new religion. Mine must be a bad one seeing that my people wanted to kill me for exposing an impostor."

Chapter 3

Northwards

I make no apology to myself, or to anybody who may happen to read this narrative in future, for having set out the manner of my meeting with Indaba-zimbi: first, because it was curious, and secondly, because he takes some hand in the subsequent events. If that old man was a humbug, he was a very clever one. What amount of truth there was in his pretensions to supernatural powers it is not for me to determine, though I may have my own opinion on the subject. But there was no mistake as to the extraordinary influence he exercised over his fellow-natives. Also he quite got round my poor father. At first the old gentleman declined to have him at the station, for he had a great horror of these *Kaffir* wizards or witch-finders. But Indaba-zimbi persuaded him that he was anxious to investigate the truths of Christianity, and challenged him to a discussion. The argument lasted two years—to the time of my father's death, indeed. At the conclusion of each stage Indaba-zimbi would remark, in the words of the Roman Governor, "Almost, praying white man, thou persuadest me to become a Christian," but he never quite became one—indeed, I do not think he ever meant to. It was to him that my father addressed his "Letters to a Native Doubter." This work, which, unfortunately, remains in manuscript, is full of wise saws and learned instances. It ought to be published together with a *précis* of the doubter's answers, which were verbal.

So the talk went on. If my father had lived I believe it would be going on now, for both the disputants were quite inexhaustible. Meanwhile Indaba-zimbi was allowed to live on the station on condition that he practised no witchcraft, which my father firmly believed to be a wile of the devil. He said that he would not, but for all that there was never an ox lost, or a sudden death, but he was consulted by those interested.

When he had been with us a year, a deputation came to him from the tribe he had left, asking him to return. Things had not gone well with them since he went away, they said, and now the chief, his enemy, was dead. Old Indaba-zimbi listened to them till they had done, and, as he listened, raked sand into a little heap with his toes. Then he spoke, pointing to the little heap, "There is your tribe to-day," he said. Then he lifted his heel and stamped the heap flat. "There is your tribe before three moons are gone. Nothing is left of it. You drove me away: I will have no more to do with you; but when you are being killed think of my words."

The messengers went. Three months afterwards I heard that the whole community had been wiped out by an *Impi* of raiding Pondos.

When I was at length ready to start upon my expedition, I went to old Indaba-zimbi to say goodbye to him, and was rather surprised to find him engaged in rolling up medicine, assegais, and other sundries in his blankets.

"Goodbye, Indaba-zimbi," I said, "I am going to trek north."

"Yes, Macumazahn," he answered, with his head on one side; "and so am I—I want to see that country. We will go together."

"Will we!" I said; "wait till you are asked, you old humbug."

"You had better ask me, then, Macumazahn, for if you don't you will never come back alive. Now that the old chief (my father) is gone to where the storms come from," and he nodded to the sky, "I feel myself getting into bad habits again. So last night I just threw up the bones and worked out about your journey, and I can tell you this, that if you don't take me you will die, and, what is more, you will lose one who is dearer to you than life in a strange fashion. So just because you gave me that hint a couple of years ago, I made up my mind to come with you."

"Don't talk stuff to me," I said.

"Ah, very well, Macumazahn, very well; but what happened to my own people six months ago, and what did I tell the messengers would happen? They drove me away, and they are gone. If you drive me away you will soon be gone too," and he nodded his white lock at me and smiled. Now I was not more superstitious than other people, but somehow old Indaba-zimbi impressed me. Also I knew his extraordinary influence over every class of native, and bethought me that he might be useful in that way.

"All right," I said: "I appoint you witch-finder to the expedition without pay."

"First serve, then ask for wages," he answered. "I am glad to see

27

that you have enough imagination not to be altogether a fool, like most white men, Macumazahn. Yes, yes, it is want of imagination that makes people fools; they won't believe what they can't understand. You can't understand my prophecies any more than the fool at the *kraal* could understand that I was his master with the lightning. Well, it is time to trek, but if I were you, Macumazahn, I should take one wagon, not two."

"Why?" I said.

"Because you will lose your wagons, and it is better to lose one than two."

"Oh, nonsense!" I said.

"All right, Macumazahn, live and learn." And without another word he walked to the foremost wagon, put his bundle into it, and climbed on to the front seat.

So having bid an affectionate adieu to my white friends, including the old Scotchman who got drunk in honour of the event, and quoted Burns till the tears ran down his face, at length I started, and travelled slowly northwards. For the first three weeks nothing very particular befell me. Such *Kaffirs* as we came in contact with were friendly, and game literally swarmed. Nobody living in those parts of South Africa nowadays can have the remotest idea of what the veldt was like even thirty years ago.

Often and often I have crept shivering on to my wagon-box just as the sun rose and looked out. At first one would see nothing but a vast field of white mist suffused towards the east by a tremulous golden glow, through which the tops of stony *koppies* stood up like gigantic beacons. From the dense mist would come strange sounds—snorts, gruntings, bellows, and the thunder of countless hoofs. Presently this great curtain would grow thinner, then it would melt, as the smoke from a pipe melts into the air, and for miles on miles the wide rolling country interspersed with bush opened to the view. But it was not tenantless as it is now, for as far as the eye could reach it would be literally black with game. Here to the right might be a herd of *vilderbeeste* that could not number less than two thousand. Some were grazing, some gambolled, whisking their white tails into the air, while all round the old bulls stood upon hillocks sniffing suspiciously at the breeze. There, in front, a hundred yards away, though to the unpractised eye they looked much closer, because of the dazzling clearness of the atmosphere, was a great herd of springbok trekking along in single file. Ah, they have come to the wagon-track and do not like the look of it. What will they do?—go back? Not a bit of it. It is nearly thirty feet wide, but that is nothing to a springbok. See, the first of them bounds into the air like a ball. How beautifully the sunshine gleams upon his golden hide! He has cleared it, and the others come after him in numberless succession, all except the fawns, who cannot jump so far, and have to scamper over the doubtful path with a terrified *bah*. What is that yonder, moving above the tops of the mimosa, in the little dell at the foot of the *koppie*? Giraffes, by George! three of them; there will be marrow-bones for supper tonight. Hark! the ground shakes behind us, and over the brow of the rise rush a vast herd of *blesbock*. On they come at full gallop, their long heads held low, they look like so many bearded goats. I thought so—behind them is a pack of wild dogs, their fur draggled, their tongues lolling. They are in full cry; the giraffes hear them and are away, rolling round the *koppie* like a ship in a heavy sea. No marrow-bones after all. See! the foremost dogs are close on a buck. He has galloped far and is outworn. One springs at his flank and misses him. The buck gives a kind of groan, looks wildly round and sees the wagon. He seems to hesitate a moment, then in his despair rushes up to it, and falls exhausted among the oxen. The dogs pull up some thirty paces away, panting and snarling. Now, boy, the gun—no, not the rifle, the shot-gun loaded with loopers.

Bang! bang! there, my friends, two of you will never hunt buck again. No, don't touch the buck, for he has come to us for shelter, and he shall have it.

Ah, how beautiful is nature before man comes to spoil it!

Such a sight as this have I seen many a hundred times, and I hope to see it again before I die.

The first real adventure that befell me on this particular journey was with elephants, which I will relate because of its curious termination. Just before we crossed the Orange River we came to a stretch of forest-land some twenty miles broad. The night we entered this forest we camped in a lovely open glade. A few yards ahead *tambouki* grass was growing to the height of a man, or rather it had been; now, with the exception of a few stalks here and there, it was crushed quite flat. It was already dusk when we camped; but after the moon got up I walked from the fire to see how this had happened. One glance was enough for me; a great herd of elephants had evidently passed over the tall grass not many hours before. The sight of their spoor rejoiced me exceedingly, for though I had seen wild elephants, at that time I had never shot one. Moreover, the sight of elephant spoor to the African hunter is what "colour in the pan" is to the prospector of gold. It is by the ivory that he lives, and to shoot it or trade it is his chief aim in life. My resolution was soon taken. I would camp the wagons for a while in the forest, and start on horseback after the elephants.

I communicated my decision to Indaba-zimbi and the other *Kaffirs*. The latter were not loth, for your *Kaffir* loves hunting, which means plenty of meat and congenial occupation, but Indaba-zimbi would express no opinion. I saw him retire to a little fire that he had lit for himself, and go through some mysterious performances with bones and clay mixed with ashes, which were watched with the greatest interest by the other *Kaffirs*. At length he rose, and, coming forward, informed me that it was all right, and that I did well to go and hunt the elephants, as I should get plenty of ivory; but he advised me to go on foot. I said I should do nothing of the sort, but meant to ride. I am wiser now; this was the first and last time that I ever attempted to hunt elephants on horseback.

Accordingly we started at dawn, I, Indaba-zimbi, and three men; the rest I left with the wagons. I was on horseback, and so was my driver, a good rider and a skilful shot for a *Kaffir*, but Indaba-zimbi and the others walked. From dawn till mid-day we followed the trail of the herd, which was as plain as a high road. Then we off-saddled to let the horses rest and feed, and about three o'clock started on again. Another hour or so passed, and still there was no sign of elephants. Evidently the herd had travelled fast and far, and I began to think that we should have to give it up, when suddenly I caught sight of a brown mass moving through the thorn-trees on the side of a slope about a quarter of a mile away. My heart seemed to jump into my mouth. Where is the hunter who has not felt like this at the sight of his first elephant?

I called a halt, and then the wind being right, we set to work to stalk the bull. Very quietly I rode down the hither side of the slope till we came to the bottom, which was densely covered with bush. Here I saw the elephants had been feeding, for broken branches and up-turned trees lay all about. I did not take much notice, however, for all my thoughts were fixed upon the bull I was stalking, when suddenly my horse gave a violent start that nearly threw me from the saddle, and there came a mighty rush and upheaval of something in front of me. I looked: there was the hinder part of a second bull elephant not four yards off. I could just catch sight of its outstretched ears projecting on either side. I had disturbed it sleeping, and it was running away.

Obviously the best thing to do would have been to let it run, but I was young in those days and foolish, and in the excitement of the moment I lifted my *roer* or elephant gun and fired at the great brute over my horse's head. The recoil of the heavy gun nearly knocked me off the horse. I recovered myself, however, and, as I did so, saw the bull lurch forward, for the impact of a three-ounce bullet in the flank will quicken the movement even of an elephant. By this time I had realized the folly of the shot, and devoutly hoped that the bull would take no further notice of it. But he took a different view of the matter. Pulling himself up in a series of plunges, he spun round and came for me with outstretched ears and uplifted trunk, scream-ing terribly. I was quite defenceless, for my gun was empty, and my first thought was of escape. I dug my heels into the sides of my horse, but he would not move an inch. The poor animal was paralyzed with terror, and he simply stood still, his fore-legs outstretched, and quivering all over like a leaf.

On rushed the elephant, awful to see; I made one more vain effort to stir the horse. Now the trunk of the great bull swung aloft above my head. A thought flashed through my brain. Quick as light I rolled from the saddle. By the side of the horse lay a fallen tree, as thick through as a man's body. The tree was lifted a little off the ground by the broken boughs which took its weight, and with a single move-ment, so active is one in such necessities, I flung myself beneath it. As I did so, I heard the trunk of the elephant descend with a mighty thud on the back of my poor horse, and the next instant I was almost in darkness, for the horse, whose back was broken, fell over across the tree under which I lay ensconced. But he did not stop there long. In ten seconds more the bull had wound his trunk about my dead nag's neck, and, with a mighty effort, hurled him clear of the tree. I wrig-gled backwards as far as I could towards the roots of the tree, for I knew what he was after. Presently I saw the red tip of the bull's trunk stretching itself towards me. If he could manage to hook it round any part of me I was lost. But in the position I occupied, that was just what he could not do, although he knelt down to facilitate his operations. On came the snapping tip like a great open-mouthed snake; it closed upon my hat, which vanished. Again it was thrust down, and a scream of rage was bellowed through it within four inches of my head. Now it seemed to elongate itself. Oh, heavens! now it had me by the hair, which, luckily for myself, was not very long. Then it was my turn to scream, for next instant half a square inch of hair was dragged from my scalp by the roots. I was being plucked alive, as I have seen cruel *Kaffir* kitchen boys pluck a fowl.

The elephant, however, disappointed with these moderate results, changed his tactics. He wound his trunk round the fallen tree and lifted. The tree stirred, but fortunately the broken branches embedded in the spongy soil, and some roots, which still held, prevented it from being turned over, though he lifted it so much that, had it occurred to him, he could now easily have drawn me out with his trunk. Again he hoisted with all his mighty strength, and I saw that the tree was coming, and roared aloud for help. Some shots were fired close by in answer, but if they hit the bull, their only effect was to stir his energies to more active life. In another few seconds my shelter would be torn away, and I should be done for. A cold perspiration burst out over me as I realized that I was lost. Then of a sudden I remembered that I had a pistol in my belt, which I often used for despatching wounded game. It was loaded and capped. By this time the tree was lifted so much that I could easily get my hand down to my middle and draw the pistol from its case. I drew and cocked it. Now the tree was coming over, and there, within three feet of my head, was the great brown trunk of the elephant. I placed the muzzle of the pistol within an inch of it and fired. The result was instantaneous. Down sunk the tree again, giving one of my legs a considerable squeeze, and next instant I heard a crashing sound. The elephant had bolted.

By this time, what between fright and struggling, I was pretty well tired. I cannot remember how I got from under the fallen tree, or indeed anything, until I found myself sitting on the ground drinking some peach brandy from a flask, and old Indaba-zimbi opposite to me nodding his white lock sagely, while he fired off moral reflections on the narrowness of my escape, and my unwisdom in not having taken his advice to go on foot. That reminded me of my horse—I got up and went to look at it. It was quite dead, the blow of the elephant's trunk had fallen on the saddle, breaking the framework, and rendering it useless. I reflected that in another two seconds it would have fallen on *me*. Then I called to Indaba-zimbi and asked which way the elephants had gone.

"There!" he said, pointing down the gully, "and we had better go after them, Macumazahn. We have had the bad luck, now for the good."

There was philosophy in this, though, to tell the truth, I did not feel particularly sharp set on elephants at the moment. I seemed to have had enough of them. However, it would never do to show the white feather before the boys, so I assented with much outward readiness, and we started, I on the second horse, and the others on foot. When we had travelled for the best part of an hour down the valley, all of a sudden we came upon the whole herd, which numbered a little more than eighty. Just in front of them the bush was so thick that they seemed to hesitate about entering it, and the sides of the valley were so rocky and steep at this point that they could not climb them.

They saw us at the same moment as we saw them, and inwardly I was filled with fears lest they should take it into their heads to charge back up the gully. But they did not; trumpeting aloud, they rushed at the thick bush which went down before them like corn before a sickle. I do not think that in all my experiences I ever heard anything to equal the sound they made as they crashed through and over the shrubs and trees. Before them was a dense forest belt from a hundred to a hundred and fifty feet in width. As they rushed on, it fell, so that behind them was nothing but a level roadway strewed with fallen trunks, crushed branches, and here and there a tree, too strong even for them, left stranded amid the wreck. On they went, and, notwithstanding the nature of the ground over which they had to travel, they kept their distance ahead of us. This sort of thing continued for a mile or more, and then I saw that in front of the elephants the valley opened into a space covered with reeds and grass—it might have been five or six acres in extent—beyond which the valley ran on again.

The herd reached the edge of this expanse, and for a moment pulled up, hesitating—evidently they mistrusted it. My men yelled aloud, as only *Kaffirs* can, and that settled them. Headed by the wounded bull, whose martial ardour, like my own, was somewhat cooled, they spread out and dashed into the treacherous swamp—for such it was, though just then there was no water to be seen. For a few yards all went well with them, though they clearly found it heavy going; then suddenly the great bull sank up to his belly in the stiff peaty soil, and remained fixed. The others, mad with fear, took no heed of his struggles and trumpetings, but plunged on to meet the same fate. In five minutes the whole herd of them were hopelessly bogged, and the more they struggled to escape, the deeper they sank. There was one exception, indeed, a cow managed to win back to firm shore, and, lifting her trunk, prepared to charge us as we came up. But at that moment she heard the scream of her calf, and rushed back to its assistance, only to be bogged with the others.

Such a scene I never saw before or since. The swamp was spotted all over with the large forms of the elephants, and the air rang with their screams of rage and terror as they waved their trunks wildly to and fro. Now and then a monster would make a great effort and drag his mass from its peaty bed, only to stick fast again at the next step. It was a most pitiable sight, though one that gladdened the hearts of my men. Even the best natives have little compassion for the sufferings of animals.

Well, the rest was easy. The marsh that would not bear the elephants carried our weight well enough. Before midnight all were dead, for we shot them by moonlight. I would gladly have spared the young ones and some of the cows, but to do so would only have meant leaving them to perish of hunger; it was kinder to kill them at once. The wounded bull I slew with my own hand, and I cannot say that I felt much compunction in so doing. He knew me again, and made a desperate effort to get at me, but I am glad to say that the peat held him fast.

The pan presented a curious sight when the sun rose next morning. Owing to the support given by the soil, few of the dead elephants had fallen: there they stood as though they were asleep.

I sent back for the wagons, and when they arrived on the morrow, formed a camp, about a mile away from the pan. Then began the work of cutting out the elephants' tusks; it took over a week, and for obvious reasons was a disgusting task. Indeed, had it not been for the help of some wandering bushmen, who took their pay in elephant meat, I do not think we could ever have managed it.

At last it was done. The ivory was far too cumbersome for us to carry, so we buried it, having first got rid of our bushmen allies. My boys wanted me to go back to the Cape with it and sell it, but I was too much bent on my journey to do this. The tusks lay buried for five years. Then I came and dug them up; they were but little harmed. Ultimately I sold the ivory for something over twelve hundred pounds—not bad pay for one day's shooting.

This was how I began my career as an elephant hunter. I have shot many hundreds of them since, but have never again attempted to do so on horseback.

CHAPTER 4

The Zulu Impi

After burying the elephant tusks, and having taken careful notes of
the bearings and peculiarities of the country so that I might be able
to find the spot again, we proceeded on our journey. For a month or
more I trekked along the line which now divides the Orange Free
State from Griqualand West, and the Transvaal from Bechuanaland.
The only difficulties met with were such as are still common to African travellers—occasional want of water and troubles about crossing
sluits and rivers. I remember that I outspanned on the spot where
Kimberley now stands, and had to press on again in a hurry because
there was no water. I little dreamed then that I should live to see Kimberley a great city producing millions of pounds worth of diamonds
annually, and old Indaba-zimbi's magic cannot have been worth so
much after all, or he would have told me.

I found the country almost entirely depopulated. Not very long
before Mosilikatze the Lion, Chaka's General had swept across it in
his progress towards what is now Matabeleland. His footsteps were
evident enough. Time upon time I trekked up to what had evidently
been the sites of *Kaffir kraals*. Now the *kraals* were ashes and piles
of tumbled stones, and strewn about among the rank grass were the
bones of hundreds of men, women, and children, all of whom had
kissed the Zulu *assegai*. I remember that in one of these desolate places
I found the skull of a child in which a ground-lark had built its nest. It
was the twittering of the young birds inside that first called my attention to it. Shortly after this we met with our second great adventure,
a much more serious and tragic one than the first.

We were trekking parallel with the Kolong river when a herd of
blesbock crossed the track. I fired at one of them and hit it behind. It
galloped about a hundred yards with the rest of the herd, then lay
down. As we were in want of meat, not having met with any game for

a few days past, I jumped on to my horse, and, telling Indaba-zimbi that I would overtake the wagons or meet them on the further side of a rise about an hour's trek away, I started after the wounded buck. As soon as I came within a hundred yards of it, however, it jumped up and ran away as fast as though it were untouched, only to lie down again at a distance. I followed, thinking that strength would soon fail it. This happened three times. On the third occasion it vanished behind a ridge, and, though by now I was out of both temper and patience, I thought I might as well ride to the crest and see if I could get a shot at it on the further side.

I reached the ridge, which was strewn with stones, looked over it, and saw—a Zulu *Impi*!

I rubbed my eyes and looked again. Yes, there was no doubt of it. They were halted about a thousand yards away, by the water; some were lying down, some were cooking at fires, others were stalking about with spears and shields in their hands; there might have been two thousand or more of them in all. While I was wondering—and that with no little uneasiness—what on earth they could be doing there, suddenly I heard a wild cry to the right and left of me. I glanced first one way, then the other. From either side a great Zulu was bearing down on me, their broad stabbing assegais aloft, and black shields in their left hands. The man to the right was about fifteen yards away, he to the left was not more than ten. On they came, their fierce eyes almost starting out of their heads, and I felt, with a cold thrill of fear, that in another three seconds those broad *bangwans* might be buried in my vitals. On such occasions we act, I suppose, more from instinct than from anything else—there is no time for thought. At any rate, I dropped the reins and, raising my gun, fired point blank at the left-hand man. The bullet struck him in the middle of his shield, pierced it, and passed through him, and over he rolled upon the veldt. I swung round in the saddle; most happily my horse was accustomed to standing still when I fired from his back, also he was so surprised that he did not know which way to shy. The other savage was almost on me; his outstretched shield reached the muzzle of my gun as I pulled the trigger of the left barrel. It exploded, the warrior sprung high into the air, and fell against my horse dead, his spear passing just in front of my face.

Without waiting to reload, or even to look if the main body of the Zulus had seen the death of their two scouts, I turned my horse and drove my heels into his sides. As soon as I was down the slope of the rise I pulled a little to the right in order to intercept the wagons before the Zulus saw them. I had not gone three hundred yards in this new direction when, to my utter astonishment, I struck a trail marked with wagon-wheels and the hoofs of oxen. Of wagons there must have been at least eight, and several hundred cattle. Moreover, they had passed within twelve hours; I could tell that by the spoor. Then I understood; the *Impi* was following the track of the wagons, which, in all probability, belonged to a party of emigrant Boers.

The spoor of the wagons ran in the direction I wished to go, so I followed it. About a mile further on I came to the crest of a rise, and there, about five furlongs away, I saw the wagons drawn up in a rough *laager* upon the banks of the river. There, too, were my own wagons trekking down the slope towards them.

In another five minutes I was there. The Boers—for Boers they were—were standing about outside the little *laager* watching the approach of my two wagons. I called to them, and they turned and saw me. The very first man my eyes fell on was a Boer named Hans Botha, whom I had known well years ago in the Cape. He was not a bad specimen of his class, but a very restless person, with a great objection to authority, or, as he expressed it, "a love of freedom." He had joined a party of the emigrant Boers some years before, but, as I learned presently, had quarrelled with its leader, and was now trekking away into the wilderness to found a little colony of his own. Poor fellow! It was his last trek.

"How do you do, *Meinheer* Botha?" I said to him in Dutch.

The man looked at me, looked again, then, startled out of his Dutch stolidity, cried to his wife, who was seated on the box of the wagon—

"Come here, *Frau*, come. Here is Allan Quatermain, the Englishman, the son of the Predicant. How goes it, *Heer* Quatermain, and what is the news down in the Cape yonder?"

"I don't know what the news is in the Cape, Hans," I answered, solemnly; "but the news here is that there is a Zulu *Impi* upon your spoor and within two miles of the wagons. That I know, for I have just shot two of their sentries," and I showed him my empty gun.

For a moment there was a silence of astonishment, and I saw the bronzed faces of the men turn pale beneath their tan, while one or two of the women gave a little scream, and the children crept to their sides.

"Almighty!" cried Hans, "that must be the Umtetwa Regiment that Dingaan sent against the Basutus, but who could not come at them because of the marshes, and so were afraid to return to Zululand, and struck north to join Mosilikatze."

"*Laager* up, Carles! *Laager* up for your lives, and one of you jump on a horse and drive in the cattle."

At this moment my own wagons came up. Indaba-zimbi was sitting on the box of the first, wrapped in a blanket. I called him and told him the news.

"Ill tidings, Macumazahn," he said; "there will be dead Boers about Tomorrow morning, but they will not attack till dawn, then they will wipe out the *laager so!*" and he passed his hand before his mouth.

"Stop that croaking, you white-headed crow," I said, though I knew his words were true. What chance had a *laager* of ten wagons all told against at least two thousand of the bravest savages in the world?

"Macumazahn, will you take my advice this time?" Indaba-zimbi said, presently.

"What is it?" I asked.

"This. Leave your wagons here, jump on that horse, and let us two run for it as hard as we can go. The Zulus won't follow us, they will be looking after the Boers."

"I won't leave the other white men," I said; "it would be the act of a coward. If I die, I die."

"Very well, Macumazahn, then stay and be killed," he answered, taking a pinch of snuff. "Come, let us see about the wagons," and we walked towards the *laager*.

Here everything was in confusion. However, I got hold of Hans Botha and put it to him if it would not be best to desert the wagons and make a run for it.

"How can we do it?" he answered; "two of the women are too fat to go a mile, one is sick in childbed, and we have only six horses among us. Besides, if we did we should starve in the desert. No, *Heer* Allan, we must fight it out with the savages, and God help us!"

"God help us, indeed. Think of the children, Hans!"

"I can't bear to think," he answered, in a broken voice, looking at his own little girl, a sweet, curly-haired, blue-eyed child of six, named Tota, whom I had often nursed as a baby. "Oh, *Heer* Allan, your father, the Predicant, always warned me against trekking north, and I never would listen to him because I thought him a cursed Englishman; now I see my folly. *Heer* Allan, if you can, try to save my child from those black devils; if you live longer than I do, or if you can't save her, kill her," and he clasped my hand.

"It hasn't come to that yet, Hans," I said.

Then we set to work on the *laager*. The wagons, of which, including my two, there were ten, were drawn into the form of a square,

38

and the *disselboom* of each securely lashed with *reims* to the under-works of that in front of it. The wheels also were locked, and the space between the ground and the bed-planks of the wagons was stuffed with branches of the "wait-a-bit" thorn that fortunately grew near in considerable quantities. In this way a barrier was formed of no mean strength as against a foe unprovided with firearms, places being left for the men to fire from. In a little over an hour everything was done that could be done, and a discussion arose as to the disposal of the cattle, which had been driven up close to the camp. Some of the Boers were anxious to get them into the *laager*, small as it was, or at least as many of them as it would hold. I argued strongly against this, pointing out that the brutes would probably be seized with panic as soon as the firing began, and trample the defenders of the *laager* under foot. As an alternative plan I suggested that some of the native servants should drive the herd along the valley of the river till they reached a friendly tribe or some other place of safety. Of course, if the Zulus saw them they would be taken, but the nature of the ground was favourable, and it was possible that they might escape if they started at once. The proposition was promptly agreed to, and, what is more, it was settled that one Dutchman and such of the women and children as could travel should go with them. In half an hour's time twelve of them started with the natives, the Boer in charge, and the cattle. Three of my own men went with the latter, the three others and Indaba-zimbi stopped with me in the *laager*.

The parting was a heart-breaking scene, upon which I do not care to dwell. The women wept, the men groaned, and the children looked on with scared white faces. At length they were gone, and I for one was thankful of it. There remained in the *laager* seventeen white men, four natives, the two Boer *fraus* who were too stout to travel, the woman in childbed and her baby, and Hans Bother's lit-tle daughter Tota, whom he could not make up his mind to part with. Happily her mother was already dead. And here I may state that ten of the women and children, together with about half of the cattle, escaped. The Zulu *Impi* never saw them, and on the third day of travel they came to the fortified place of a Griqua chief, who sheltered them on receiving half the cattle in payment. Thence by slow degrees they journeyed down to the Cape Colony, reaching a civilized region within a little more than a year from the date of the attack on the *laager*.

The afternoon was now drawing towards evening, but still there were no signs of the *Impi*. A wild hope struck us that they might have gone on about their business. Ever since Indaba-zimbi had heard that the regiment was supposed to belong to the Umtetwa tribe, he had, I noticed, been plunged in deep thought. Presently he came to me and volunteered to go out and spy upon their movements. At first Hans Botha was against this idea, saying that he was a *"verdomde swart-zel"*—an accursed black creature—and would betray us. I pointed out that there was nothing to betray. The Zulus must know where the wagons were, but it was important for us to gain information of their movements. So it was agreed that Indaba-zimbi should go. I told him this. He nodded his white lock, said "All right, Macumazahn," and started. I noticed with some surprise, however, that before he did so he went to the wagon and fetched his *mouti*, or medicine, which, to-gether with his other magical apparatus, he always carried in a skin bag. I asked him why he did this. He answered that it was to make himself invulnerable against the spears of the Zulus. I did not in the least believe his explanation, for in my heart I was sure that he meant to take the opportunity to make a bolt of it, leaving me to my fate. I did not, however, interfere to prevent this, for I had an affection for the old fellow, and sincerely hoped that he might escape the doom which overshadowed us.

So Indaba-zimbi sauntered off, and as I looked at his retreating form I thought I should never see it again. But I was mistaken, and lit-tle knew that he was risking his life, not for the Boers whom he hated one and all, but for me whom in his queer way he loved.

When he had gone we completed our preparations for defence, strengthening the wagons and the thorns beneath with earth and stones. Then at sunset we ate and drank as heartily as we could un-der the circumstances, and when we had done, Hans Botha, as head of the party, offered up prayer to God for our preservation. It was a touching sight to see the burly Dutchman, his hat off, his broad face lit up by the last rays of the setting sun, praying aloud in homely, simple language to Him who alone could save us from the spears of a cruel foe. I remember that the last sentence of his prayer was, "Almighty, if we must be killed, save the women and children and my little girl Tota from the accursed Zulus, and do not let us be tortured."

I echoed the request very earnestly in my own heart, that I know, for in common with the others I was dreadfully afraid, and it must be admitted not without reason.

Then the darkness came on, and we took up our appointed places each with a rifle in his hands and peered out into the gloom in silence.

Occasionally one of the Boers would light his pipe with a brand from the smouldering fire, and the glow of it would shine for a few moments on his pale, anxious face.

Behind me one of the stout "*fraus*" lay upon the ground. Even the terror of our position could not keep her heavy eyes from their accustomed sleep, and she snored loudly. On the further side of her, just by the fire, lay little Tota, wrapped in a *kaross*. She was asleep also, her thumb in her mouth, and from time to time her father would come to look at her.

So the hours wore on while we waited for the Zulus. But from my intimate knowledge of the habits of natives I had little fear that they would attack us at night, though, had they done so, they could have compassed our destruction with but small loss to themselves. It is not the habit of this people, they like to fight in the light of day—at dawn for preference.

About eleven o'clock, just as I was nodding a little at my post, I heard a low whistle outside the *laager*. Instantly I was wide awake, and all along the line I heard the clicking of locks as the Boers cocked their guns.

"Macumazahn," said a voice, the voice of Indaba-zimbi, "are you there?"

"Yes," I answered.

"Then hold a light so that I can see how to climb into the *laager*," he said.

"Yah! yah! hold a light," put in one of the Boers. "I don't trust that black *schepsel* of yours, *Heer* Quatermain; he may have some of his countrymen with him." Accordingly a lantern was produced and held towards the voice. There was Indaba-zimbi alone. We let him into the *laager* and asked him the news.

"This is the news, white men," he said. "I waited till dark, and creeping up to the place where the Zulus are encamped, hid myself behind a stone and listened. They are a great regiment of Umtetwas as Baas Botha yonder thought. They struck the spoor of the wagons three days ago and followed it. Tonight they sleep upon their spears, Tomorrow at daybreak they will attack the *laager* and kill everybody. They are very bitter against the Boers, because of the battle at Blood River and the other fights, and that is why they followed the wagons instead of going straight north after Mosilikatze."

A kind of groan went up from the group of listening Dutchmen.

"I tell you what it is, *Heeren*," I said, "instead of waiting to be butchered here like buck in a pitfall, let us go out now and fall upon the *Impi* while it sleeps."

41

This proposition excited some discussion, but in the end only one man could be found to vote for it. Boers as a rule lack that dash which makes great soldiers; such forlorn hopes are not in their line, and rather than embark upon them they prefer to take their chance in a *laager*, however poor that chance may be. For my own part I firmly believe that had my advice been taken we should have routed the Zulus. Seventeen desperate white men, armed with guns, would have produced no small effect upon a camp of sleeping savages. But it was not taken, so it is no use talking about it.

After that we went back to our posts, and slowly the weary night wore on towards the dawn. Only those who have watched under similar circumstances while they waited the advent of almost certain and cruel death, can know the torturing suspense of those heavy hours. But they went somehow, and at last in the far east the sky began to lighten, while the cold breath of dawn stirred the tilts of the wagons and chilled me to the bone. The fat Dutchwoman behind me woke with a yawn, then, remembering all, moaned aloud, while her teeth chattered with cold and fear. Hans Botha went to his wagon and got a bottle of peach brandy, from which he poured into a tin *pannikin*, giving us each a stiff dram, and making attempts to be cheerful as he did so. But his affected jocularity only seemed to depress his comrades the more. Certainly it depressed me.

Now the light was growing, and we could see some way into the mist which still hung densely over the river, and now—ah! there it was. From the other side of the hill, a thousand yards or more from the *laager*, came a faint humming sound. It grew and grew till it gathered to a chant—the awful war chant of the Zulus. Soon I could catch the words. They were simple enough:

"We shall slay, we shall slay! Is it not so, my brothers? Our spears shall blush blood-red. Is it not so, my brothers? For we are the sucklings of Chaka, blood is our milk, my brothers. Awake, children of the Umtetwa, awake! The vulture wheels, the jackal sniffs the air; Awake, children of the Umtetwa—cry aloud, ye ringed men: There is the foe, we shall slay them. Is it not so, my brothers? *S'gee! S'gee! S'gee!*"

Such is a rough translation of that hateful chant which to this very day I often seem to hear. It does not look particularly imposing on paper, but if, while he waited to be killed, the reader could have heard it as it rolled through the still air from the throats of nearly three thousand warriors singing all to time, he would have found it impressive enough.

Now the shields began to appear over the brow of the rise. They came by companies, each company about ninety strong. Altogether there were thirty-one companies. I counted them. When all were over they formed themselves into a triple line, then trotted down the slope towards us. At a distance of a hundred and fifty yards or just out of the shot of such guns as we had in those days, they halted and began singing again—

"Yonder is the *kraal* of the white man—a little *kraal*, my brothers; We shall eat it up, we shall trample it flat, my brothers. But where are the white man's cattle—where are his oxen, my brothers?"

This question seemed to puzzle them a good deal, for they sang the song again and again. At last a herald came forward, a great man with ivory rings about his arm, and, putting his hands to his mouth, called out to us asking where our cattle were.

Hans Botha climbed on to the top of a wagon and roared out that they might answer that question themselves.

Then the herald called again, saying that he saw the cattle had been sent away.

"We shall go and find the cattle," he said, "then we shall come and kill you, because without cattle you must stop where you are, but if we wait to kill you before we get the cattle, they may have trekked too far for us to follow. And if you try to run away we shall easily catch you white men!"

This struck me as a very odd speech, for the Zulus generally attack an enemy first and take his cattle afterwards; still, there was a certain amount of plausibility about it. While I was still wondering what it all might mean, the Zulus began to run past us in companies towards the river. Suddenly a shout announced that they had found the spoor of the cattle, and the whole *Impi* of them started down it at a run till they vanished over a rise about a quarter of a mile away.

We waited for half an hour or more, but nothing could we see of them.

"Now I wonder if the devils have really gone," said Hans Botha to me. "It is very strange."

"I will go and see," said Indaba-zimbi, "if you will come with me, Macumazahn. We can creep to the top of the ridge and look over."

At first I hesitated, but curiosity overcame me. I was young in those days and weary with suspense.

"Very well," I said, "we will go."

So we started. I had my elephant gun and ammunition. Indaba-zimbi had his medicine bag and an *assegai*. We crept to the top of the rise like sportsmen stalking a buck. The slope on the other side was strewn with rocks, among which grew bushes and tall grass.

43

"They must have gone down the Donga," I said to Indaba-zimbi, "I can't see one of them."

As I spoke there came a roar of men all round me. From every rock, from every tuft of grass rose a Zulu warrior. Before I could turn, before I could lift a gun, I was seized and thrown.

"Hold him! Hold the White Spirit fast!" cried a voice. "Hold him, or he will slip away like a snake. Don't hurt him, but hold him fast. Let Indaba-zimbi walk by his side."

I turned on Indaba-zimbi. "You black devil, you have betrayed me!" I cried.

"Wait and see, Macumazahn," he answered, coolly. "Now the fight is going to begin."

CHAPTER 5

The End of the Laager

I gasped with wonder and rage. What did that scoundrel Indaba-zimbi mean? Why had I been drawn out of the *laager* and seized, and why, being seized, was I not instantly killed? They called me the White Spirit. Could it be that they were keeping me to make me into medicine? I had heard of such things being done by Zulus and kindred tribes, and my blood ran cold at the thought. What an end! To be pounded up, made medicine of, and eaten!

However, I had little time for further reflection, for now the whole *Impi* was pouring back from the donga and river-banks where it had hidden while their ruse was carried out, and once more formed up on the side of the slope. I was taken to the crest of the slope and placed in the centre of the reserve line in the especial charge of a huge Zulu named Bombyane, the same man who had come forward as a herald. This brute seemed to regard me with an affectionate curiosity. Now and again he poked me in the ribs with the handle of his *assegai*, as though to assure himself that I was solid, and several times he asked me to be so good as to prophesy how many Zulus would be killed before the *Amaboona*, as they called the Boers, were "eaten up."

At first I took no notice of him beyond scowling, but presently, goaded into anger, I prophesied that he would be dead in an hour!

He only laughed aloud. "Oh! White Spirit," he said, "is it so? Well, I've walked a long way from Zululand, and shall be glad of a rest."

And he got it shortly, as will be seen.

Now the Zulus began to sing again—

"We have caught the White Spirit, my brother! my brother! Iron-Tongue whispered of him, he smelt him out, my brother. Now the Maboona are ours—they are already dead, my brother."

So that treacherous villain Indaba-zimbi had betrayed me. Suddenly the chief of the *Impi*, a grey-haired man named Sususa, held

45

up his *assegai*, and instantly there was silence. Then he spoke to some *indunas* who stood near him. Instantly they ran to the right and left down the first line, saying a word to the captain of each company as they passed him. Presently they were at the respective ends of the line, and simultaneously held up their spears. As they did so, with an awful roar of *"Bulala Amaboona"*—"Slay the Boers," the entire line, numbering nearly a thousand men, bounded forward like a buck startled from its form, and rushed down upon the little *laager*. It was a splendid sight to see them, their assegais glittering in the sunlight as they rose and fell above their black shields, their war-plumes bending back upon the wind, and their fierce faces set intently on the foe, while the solid earth shook beneath the thunder of their rushing feet. I thought of my poor friends the Dutchmen, and trembled. What chance had they against so many?

Now the Zulus, running in the shape of a bow so as to wrap the *laager* round on three sides, were within seventy yards, and now from every wagon broke tongues of fire. Over rolled a number of the Umtetwa, but the rest cared little. Forward they sped straight to the *laager*, striving to force a way in. But the Boers plied them with volley after volley, and, packed as the Zulus were, the elephant guns loaded with slugs and small shot did frightful execution. Only one man even got on to a wagon, and as he did so I saw a Boer woman strike him on the head with an axe. He fell down, and slowly, amid howls of derision from the two lines on the hill-side, the Zulus drew back.

"Let us go, father!" shouted the soldiers on the slope, among whom I was, to their chief, who had come up. "You have sent out the little girls to fight, and they are frightened. Let us show them the way."

"No, no!" the chief Sususa answered, laughing. "Wait a minute and the little girls will grow to women, and women are good enough to fight against Boers!"

The attacking Zulus heard the mockery of their fellows, and rushed forward again with a roar. But the Boers in the *laager* had found time to load, and they met with a warm reception. Reserving their fire till the Zulus were packed like sheep in a *kraal*, they loosed into them with the *roers*, and the warriors fell in little heaps. But I saw that the blood of the Umtetwas was up; they did not mean to be beaten back this time, and the end was near. See! six men had leapt on to a wagon, slain the man behind it, and sprung into the *laager*. They were killed there, but others followed, and then I turned my head. But I could not shut my ears to the cries of rage and death, and the terrible *S'gee! S'gee!* of the savages as they did their work of murder. Once only I looked up and saw poor Hans Botha standing on a wagon smiting down men with the butt of his rifle. The assegais shot up towards him like tongues of steel, and when I looked again he was gone.

I turned sick with fear and rage. But alas! what could I do? They were all dead now, and probably my own turn was coming, only my death with not be so swift.

The fight was ended, and the two lines on the slope broke their order, and moved down to the *laager*. Presently we were there, and a dreadful sight it was. Many of the attacking Zulus were dead—quite fifty I should say, and at least a hundred and fifty were wounded, some of them mortally. The chief Sususa gave an order, the dead men were picked up and piled in a heap, while those who were slightly hurt walked off to find someone to tie up their wounds. But the more serious cases met with a different treatment. The chief or one of his *indunas* considered each case, and if it was in any way bad, the man was taken up and thrown into the river which ran near. None of them offered any objection, though one poor fellow swam to shore again. He did not stop there long, however, for they pushed him back and drowned him by force.

The strangest case of all was that of the chief's own brother. He had been captain of the line, and his ankle was smashed by a bullet. Sususa came up to him, and, having examined the wound, rated him soundly for failing in the first onslaught.

The poor fellow made the excuse that it was not his fault, as the Boers had hit him in the first rush. His brother admitted the truth of this, and talked to him amicably.

"Well," he said at length, offering him a pinch of snuff, "you cannot walk again."

"No, chief," said the wounded man, looking at his ankle.

"And Tomorrow we must walk far," went on Sususa.

"Yes, chief."

"Say, then, will you sit here on the veldt, or——" and he nodded towards the river.

The man dropped his head on his breast for a minute as though in thought. Presently he lifted it and looked Sususa straight in the face.

"My ankle pains me, my brother," he said; "I think I will go back to Zululand, for there is the only *kraal* I wish to see again, even if I creep about it like a snake."[1]

---

1. The Zulus believe that after death their spirits enter into the bodies of large green snakes, which glide about the *kraals*. To kill these snakes is sacrilege.

"It is well, my brother," said the chief. "Rest softly," and having shaken hands with him, he gave an order to one of the *indunas*, and turned away.

Then men came, and, supporting the wounded man, led him down to the banks of the stream. Here, at his request, they tied a heavy stone round his neck, and then threw him into a deep pool. I saw the whole sad scene, and the victim never even winced. It was impossible not to admire the extraordinary courage of the man, or to avoid being struck with the cold-blooded cruelty of his brother the chief. And yet the act was necessary from his point of view. The man must either die swiftly, or be left to perish of starvation, for no Zulu force will encumber itself with wounded men. Years of merciless warfare had so hardened these people that they looked on death as nothing, and were, to do them justice, as willing to meet it themselves as to inflict it on others. When this very *Impi* had been sent out by the Zulu King Dingaan, it consisted of some nine thousand men. Now it numbered less than three; all the rest were dead. They, too, would probably soon be dead. What did it matter? They lived by war to die in blood. It was their natural end. *Kill till you are killed.* That is the motto of the Zulu soldier. It has the merit of simplicity.

Meanwhile the warriors were looting the wagons, including my own, having first thrown all the dead Boers into a heap. I looked at the heap; all of them were there, including the two stout *fraus*, poor things. But I missed one body, that of Hans Botha's daughter, little Tota. A wild hope came into my heart that she might have escaped; but no, it was not possible. I could only pray that she was already at rest.

Just then the great Zulu, Bombyane, who had left my side to indulge in the congenial occupation of looting, came out of a wagon crying that he had got the "little white one." I looked; he was carrying the child Tota, gripping her frock in one of his huge black hands. He stalked up to where we were, and held the child before the chief. "Is it dead, father?" he said, with a laugh.

Now, as I could well see, the child was not dead, but had been hidden away, and fainted with fear.

The chief glanced at it carelessly, and said—

"Find out with your *kerrie*."

Acting on this hint the black devil held up the child, and was about to kill it with his *knobstick*. This was more than I could bear. I sprang at him and struck him with all my force in the face, little caring if I was speared or not. He dropped Tota on the ground.

"*Ou!*" he said, putting his hand to his nose, "the White Spirit has a hard fist. Come, Spirit, I will fight you for the child."

The soldiers cheered and laughed. "Yes! yes!" they said, "let Bomby-ane fight the White Spirit for the child. Let them fight with assegais."

For a moment I hesitated. What chance had I against this black giant? But I had promised poor Hans to save the child if I could, and what did it matter? As well die now as later. However, I had wit enough left to make a favour of it, and intimated to the chief through Indaba-zimbi that I was quite willing to condescend to kill Bomby-ane, on condition that if I did so the child's life should be given to me. Indaba-zimbi interpreted my words, but I noticed that he would not look on me as he spoke, but covered his face with his hands and spoke of me as "the ghost" or the "son of the spirit." For some reason that I have never quite understood, the chief consented to the duel. I fancy it was because he believed me to be more than mortal, and was anxious to see the last of Bombyane.

"Let them fight," he said. "Give them assegais and no shields; the child shall be to him who conquers."

"Yes! yes!" cried the soldiers. "Let them fight. Don't be afraid, Bombyane; if he is a spirit, he's a very small one."

"I never was frightened of man or beast, and I am not going to run away from a White Ghost," answered the redoubtable Bombyane, as he examined the blade of his great *bangwan* or stabbing *assegai*.

Then they made a ring round us, gave me a similar *assegai*, and set us some ten paces apart. I kept my face as calm as I could, and tried to show no signs of fear, though in my heart I was terribly afraid. Humanly speaking, my doom was on me. The giant warrior before me had used the *assegai* from a child—I had no experience of the weapon. Moreover, though I was quick and active, he must have been at least twice as strong as I am. However, there was no help for it, so, setting my teeth, I grasped the great spear, breathed a prayer, and waited.

The giant stood awhile looking at me, and, as he stood, Indaba-zimbi walked across the ring behind me, muttering as he passed, "Keep cool, Macumazahn, and wait for him. I will make it all right."

As I had not the slightest intention of commencing the fray, I thought this good advice, though how Indaba-zimbi could "make it all right" I failed to see.

Heavens! how long that half-minute seemed! It happened many years ago, but the whole scene rises up before my eyes as I write. There behind us was the blood-stained *laager*, and near it lay the piles of dead; round us was rank upon rank of plumed savages, standing in silence to wait the issue of the duel, and in the centre stood the grey-haired chief and general, Sususa, in all his war finery, a cloak

49

of leopard skin upon his shoulders. At his feet lay the senseless form of little Tota, to my left squatted Indaba-zimbi, nodding his white lock and muttering something—probably spells; while in front was my giant antagonist, his spear aloft and his plumes wavering in the gentle wind. Then over all, over grassy slope, river, and *koppie*, over the wagons of the *laager*, the piles of dead, the dense masses of the living, the swooning child, over all shone the bright impartial sun, looking down like the indifferent eye of Heaven upon the loveliness of nature and the cruelty of man. Down by the river grew thorn-trees, and from them floated the sweet scent of the mimosa flower, and came the sound of cooing turtle-doves. I never smell the one or hear the other without the scene flashing into my mind again, complete in its every detail.

Suddenly, without a sound, Bombyane shook his *assegai* and rushed straight at me. I saw his huge form come; like a man in a dream, I saw the broad spear flash on high; now he was on me! Then, prompted to it by some providential impulse—or had the spells of Indaba-zimbi anything to do with the matter?—I dropped to my knee, and quick as light stretched out my spear. He drove at me: the blade passed over my head. I felt a weight on my *assegai*; it was wrenched from my hand; his great limbs knocked against me. I glanced round. Bombyane was staggering along with head thrown back and outstretched arms from which his spear had fallen. His spear had fallen, but the blade of mine stood out between his shoulders—I had transfixed him. He stopped, swung slowly round as though to look at me: then with a sigh the giant sank down—*dead*.

For a moment there was silence; then a great cry rose—a cry of "Bombyane is dead. The White Spirit has slain Bombyane. Kill the wizard, kill the ghost who has slain Bombyane by witchcraft."

Instantly I was surrounded by fierce faces, and spears flashed before my eyes. I folded my arms and stood calmly waiting the end. In a moment it would have come, for the warriors were mad at seeing their champion overthrown thus easily. But presently through the tumult I heard the high, cracked voice of Indaba-zimbi.

"Stand back, you fools!" it cried; "can a spirit then be killed?"

"Spear him! spear him!" they roared in fury. "Let us see if he is a spirit. How did a spirit slay Bombyane with an *assegai*? Spear him, rain-maker, and we shall see."

"Stand back," cried Indaba-zimbi again, "and I will show you if he can be killed. I will kill him myself, and call him back to life again before your eyes."

"Macumazahn, trust me," he whispered in my ear in the Sisutu tongue, which the Zulus did not understand. "Trust me; kneel on the grass before me, and when I strike at you with the spear, roll over like one dead; then, when you hear my voice again, get up. Trust me—it is your only hope."

Having no choice I nodded my head in assent, though I had not the faintest idea of what he was about to do. The tumult lessened somewhat, and once more the warriors drew back.

"Great White Spirit—Spirit of victory," said Indaba-zimbi, addressing me aloud, and covering his eyes with his hand, "hear me and forgive me. These children are blind with folly, and think thee mortal because thou hast dealt death upon a mortal who dared to stand against thee. Deign to kneel down before me and let me pierce thy heart with this spear, then when I call upon thee, arise unhurt."

I knelt down, not because I wished to, but because I must. I had not overmuch faith in Indaba-zimbi, and thought it probable that he was in truth about to make an end of me. But really I was so worn out with fears, and the horrors of the night and day had so shaken my nerves, that I did not greatly care what befell me. When I had been kneeling thus for about half a minute Indaba-zimbi spoke.

"People of the Umtetwa, children of T'Chaka," he said, "draw back a little way, lest an evil fall on you, for now the air is thick with ghosts."

They drew back a space, leaving us in a circle about twelve yards in diameter.

"Look on him who kneels before you," went on Indaba-zimbi, "and listen to my words, to the words of the witch-finder, the words of the rain-maker, Indaba-zimbi, whose fame is known to you. He seems to be a young man, does he not? I tell you, children of the Umtetwa, he is no man. He is the Spirit who gives victory to the white men, he it is who gave them assegais that thunder and taught them how to slay. Why were the *Impis* of Dingaan rolled back at the Blood River? Because *he* was there. Why did the *Amaboona* slay the people of Mosilikatze by the thousand? Because *he* was there. And so I say to you that, had I not drawn him from the *laager* by my magic but three hours ago, you would have been conquered—yes, you would have been blown away like the dust before the wind; you would have been burnt up like the dry grass in the winter when the fire is awake among it. Ay, because he had but been there many of your bravest were slain in overcoming a few—a pinch of men who could be counted on the fingers. But because I loved you, because your chief Sususa is my half-brother—for had we not one father?—I came to you, I warned you. Then you prayed me and I drew the Spirit forth. But you were not satisfied when the victory was yours, when the Spirit, of all you had taken asked but one little thing—a white child to take away and sacrifice to himself, to make the medicine of his magic of——"

Here I could hardly restrain myself from interrupting, but thought better of it.

"You said him nay; you said, 'Let him fight with our bravest man, let him fight with Bombyane the giant for the child.' And he deigned to slay Bombyane as you have seen, and now you say, 'Slay him; he is no spirit.' Now I will show you if he is a spirit, for I will slay him before your eyes, and call him to life again. But you have brought this upon yourselves. Had you believed, had you offered no insult to the Spirit, he would have stayed with you, and you should have become unconquerable. Now he will arise and leave you, and woe be on you if you try to stay him.

"Now all men," he went on, "look for a space upon this *assegai* that I hold up," and he lifted the *bangwan* of the deceased Bombyane high above his head so that all the multitude could see it. Every eye was fixed upon the broad bright spear. For a while he held it still, then he moved it round and round in a circle, muttering as he did so, and still their gaze followed it. For my part, I watched his movements with the greatest anxiety. That *assegai* had already been nearer my person than I found at all pleasant, and I had no desire to make a further acquaintance with it. Nor, indeed, was I sure that Indaba-zimbi was not really going to kill me. I could not understand his proceedings at all, and at the best I did not relish playing the *corpus vile* to his magical experiments.

"Look! look! look!" he screamed.

Then suddenly the great spear flashed down towards my breast. I felt nothing, but, to my sight, it seemed as though it had passed through me.

"See!" roared the Zulus. "Indaba-zimbi has speared him; the red *assegai* stands out behind his back."

"Roll over, Macumazahn," Indaba-zimbi hissed in my ear, "roll over and pretend to die—quick! quick!"

I lost no time in following these strange instructions, but falling on to my side, threw my arms wide, kicked my legs about, and died as artistically as I could. Presently I gave a stage shiver and lay still.

"See!" said the Zulus, "he is dead, the Spirit is dead. Look at the blood upon the *assegai*!"

"Stand back! stand back!" cried Indaba-zimbi, "or the ghost will haunt you. Yes, he is dead, and now I will call him back to life again. Look!" and putting down his hand, he plucked the spear from wherever it was fixed, and held it aloft. "The spear is red, is it not? Watch, men, watch! *It grows white!*"

"Yes, it grows white," they said. "*Ou!* it grows white."

"It grows white because the blood returns to whence it came," said Indaba-zimbi. "Now, great Spirit, hear me. Thou art dead, the breath has gone out of thy mouth. Yet hear me and arise. Awake, White Spirit, awake and show thy power. Awake! arise unhurt!"

I began to respond cheerfully to this imposing invocation.

"Not so fast, Macumazahn," whispered Indaba-zimbi.

I took the hint, and first held up my arm, then lifted my head and let it fall again.

"He lives! by the head of T'Chaka he lives!" roared the soldiers, stricken with mortal fear.

Then slowly and with the greatest dignity I gradually arose, stretched my arms, yawned like one awaking from heavy sleep, turned and looked upon them unconcernedly. While I did so, I noticed that old Indaba-zimbi was almost fainting from exhaustion. Beads of perspiration stood upon his brow, his limbs trembled, and his breast heaved.

As for the Zulus, they waited for no more. With a howl of terror the whole regiment turned and fled across the rise, so that presently we were left alone with the dead, and the swooning child.

"How on earth did you do that, Indaba-zimbi?" I asked in amaze.

"Do not ask me, Macumazahn," he gasped. "You white men are very clever, but you don't quite know everything. There are men in the world who can make people believe they see things which they do not see. Let us be going while we may, for when those Umtetwas have got over their fright, they will come back to loot the wagons, and then perhaps *they* will begin asking questions that I can't answer."

And here I may as well state that I never got any further information on this matter from old Indaba-zimbi. But I have my theory, and here it is for whatever it may be worth. I believe that Indaba-zimbi *mesmerized* the whole crowd of onlookers, myself included, making them believe that they saw the *assegai* in my heart, and the blood upon the blade. The reader may smile and say, *impossible*; but I would ask him how the Indian jugglers do their tricks unless it is by mesmerism. The spectators *seem* to see the boy go under the basket and there pierced with daggers, they *seem* to see women in a trance

53

supported in mid-air upon the point of a single sword. In themselves these things are not possible, they violate the laws of nature, as those laws are known to us, and therefore must surely be illusion. And so through the glamour thrown upon them by Indaba-zimbi's will, that Zulu *Impi* seemed to see me transfixed with an *assegai* which never touched me. At least, that is my theory; if anyone has a better, let him adopt it. The explanation lies between illusion and magic of a most imposing character, and I prefer to accept the first alternative.

CHAPTER 6

Stella

I was not slow to take Indaba-zimbi's hint. About a hundred and fifty yards to the left of the *laager* was a little dell where I had hidden my horse, together with one belonging to the Boers, and my saddle and bridle. Thither we went, I carrying the swooning Tota in my arms. To our joy we found the horses safe, for the Zulus had not seen them. Now, of course, they were our only means of locomotion, for the oxen had been sent away, and even had they been there we could not have found time to inspan them. I laid Tota down, caught my horse, undid his knee halter, and saddled up. As I was doing so a thought struck me, and I told Indaba-zimbi to run to the *laager* and see if he could find my double-barrelled gun and some powder and shot, for I had only my elephant *roer* and a few charges of powder and ball with me.

He went, and while he was away, poor little Tota came to herself and began to cry, till she saw my face.

"Ah, I have had such a bad dream," she said, in Dutch: "I dreamed that the black *Kaffirs* were going to kill me. Where is my papa?"

I winced at the question. "Your papa has gone on a journey, dear," I said, "and left me to look after you. We shall find him one day. You don't mind going with *Heer* Allan, do you?"

"No," she said, a little doubtfully, and began to cry again. Presently she remembered that she was thirsty, and asked for water. I led her to the river and she drank. "Why is my hand red, *Heer* Allan?" she asked, pointing to the smear of Bombyane's blood-stained fingers.

At this moment I felt very glad that I had killed Bombyane.

"It is only paint, dear," I said; "see, we will wash it and your face."

As I was doing this, Indaba-zimbi returned. The guns were all gone; he said the Zulus had taken them and the powder. But he had found some things and brought them in a sack. There was a thick blanket, about twenty pounds weight of biltong or sun-dried meat, a few double-handfuls of biscuits, two water-bottles, a tin *pannikin*, some matches and sundries.

"And now, Macumazahn," he said, "we had best be going, for those Umtetwas are coming back. I saw one of them on the brow of the rise."

That was enough for me. I lifted little Tota on to the bow of my saddle, climbed into it, and rode off, holding her in front of me. Indaba-zimbi slipped a *reim* into the mouth of the best of the Boer horses, threw of the sack of sundries on to its back and mounted also, holding the elephant gun in his hand. We went eight or nine hundred yards in silence till we were quite out of range of sight from the wagons, which were in a hollow. Then I pulled up, with such a feeling of thankfulness in my heart as cannot be told in words; for now I knew that, mounted as we were, those black demons could never catch us. But where were we to steer for? I put the question to Indaba-zimbi, asking him if he thought that we had better try and follow the oxen which we had sent away with the *Kaffirs* and women on the preceding night. He shook his head.

"The Umtetwas will go after the oxen presently," he answered, "and we have seen enough of them."

"Quite enough," I answered, with enthusiasm; "I never want to see another; but where are we to go? Here we are alone with one gun and a little girl in the vast and lonely veldt. Which way shall we turn?"

"Our faces were towards the north before we met the Zulus," answered Indaba-zimbi; "let us still keep them to the north. Ride on, Macumazahn; tonight when we off-saddle I will look into the matter."

So all that long afternoon we rode on, following the course of the river. From the nature of the ground we could only go slowly, but before sunset I had the satisfaction of knowing that there must be at least twenty-five miles between us and those accursed Zulus. Little Tota slept most of the way, the motion of the horse was easy, and she was worn out.

At last the sunset came, and we off-saddled in a dell by the river. There was not much to eat, but I soaked some biscuit in water for Tota, and Indaba-zimbi and I made a scanty meal of biltong. When we had done I took off Tota's frock, wrapped her up in a blanket near the fire we had made, and lit a pipe. I sat there by the side of the sleeping orphaned child, and from my heart thanked Providence for saving her life and mine from the slaughter of that day. What a horrible experience it had been! It seemed like a nightmare to look back upon. And yet it was sober fact, one among those many tragedies which dotted the paths of the emigrant Boers with the bones of men, women, and children. These horrors are almost forgotten now; people living in Natal now, for instance, can scarcely realize that some forty years ago six hundred white people, many of them women and children, were thus massacred by the *Impis* of Dingaan. But it was so, and the name of the district, *Weenen*, or the Place of Weeping, will commemorate them forever.

Then I fell to reflecting on the extraordinary adroitness old Indaba-zimbi had shown in saving my life. It appeared that he himself had lived among the Umtetwa Zulus in his earlier manhood, and was a noted rain-doctor and witch-finder. But when T'Chaka, Dingaan's brother, ordered a general massacre of the witch-finders, he alone had saved his life by his skill in magic, and ultimately fled south for reasons too long to set out here. When he heard, therefore, that the regiment was an Umtetwa regiment, which, leaving their wives and children, had broken away from Zululand to escape the cruelties of Dingaan; under pretence of spying on them, he took the bold course of going straight up to the chief, Sususa, and addressing him as his brother, which he was. The chief knew him at once, and so did the soldiers, for his fame was still great among them. Then he told them his cock and bull story about my being a white spirit, whose presence in the *laager* would render it invincible, and with the object of saving my life in the slaughter which he knew must ensue, agreed to charm me out of the *laager* and deliver me into their keeping. How the plan worked has already been told; it was a risky one; still, but for it my troubles would have been done with these many days.

So I lay and thought with a heart full of gratitude, and as I did so saw old Indaba-zimbi sitting by the fire and going through some mysterious performances with bones which he produced from his bag, and ashes mixed with water. I spoke to him and asked what he was about. He replied that he was tracing out the route that we should follow. I felt inclined to answer *bosh!* but remembering the very remarkable instances which he had given of his prowess in occult matters I held my tongue, and taking little Tota into my arms, worn out with toil and danger and emotion, I went to sleep.

I awoke just as the dawn was beginning to flame across the sky in sheets of primrose and of gold, or rather it was little Tota who woke me by kissing me as she lay between sleep and waking, and calling me "papa." It wrung my heart to hear her, poor orphaned child. I got up, washed and dressed her as best I could, and we breakfasted as we had supped, on biltong and biscuit. Tota asked for milk, but I had none to give her. Then we caught the horses, and I saddled mine.

"Well, Indaba-zimbi," I said, "now what path do your bones point to?"

"Straight north," he said. "The journey will be hard, but in about four days we shall come to the *kraal* of a white man, an Englishman, not a Boer. His *kraal* is in a beautiful place, and there is a great peak behind it where there are many baboons."

I looked at him. "This is all nonsense, Indaba-zimbi," I said. "Whoever heard of an Englishman building a house in these wilds, and how do you know anything about it? I think that we had better strike east towards Port Natal."

"As you like, Macumazahn," he answered, "but it will take us three months' journey to get to Port Natal, if we ever get there, and the child will die on the road. Say, Macumazahn, have my words come true heretofore, or have they not? Did I not tell you not to hunt the elephants on horseback? Did I not tell you to take one wagon with you instead of two, as it is better to lose one than two?"

"You told me all these things," I answered.

"And so I tell you now to ride north, Macumazahn, for there you will find great happiness—yes, and great sorrow. But no man should run away from happiness because of the sorrow. As you will, as you will!"

Again I looked at him. In his divinations I did not believe, yet I came to the conclusion that he was speaking what he knew to be the truth. It struck me as possible that he might have heard of some white man living like a hermit in the wilds, but preferring to keep up his prophetic character would not say so.

"Very well, Indaba-zimbi," I said, "let us ride north."

Shortly after we started, the river we had followed hitherto turned off in a westerly direction, so we left it. All that day we rode across rolling uplands, and about an hour before sunset halted at a little stream which ran down from a range of hills in front of us. By this time I was heartily tired of the biltong, so taking my elephant rifle—for I had nothing else—I left Tota with Indaba-zimbi, and started to try if I could shoot something. Oddly enough we had seen no game all the day, nor did we see any on the subsequent days. For some mysterious reason they had temporarily left the district. I crossed the little streamlet in order to enter the belt of thorns which grew upon the hill-side beyond, for there I hoped to find buck. As I did so I was rather disturbed to see the spoor of two lions in the soft sandy edge of a pool. Breathing a hope that they might not still be in the neighbourhood, I went on into the belt of scattered thorns. For a long while I hunted about without seeing anything, except one duiker buck, which bounded off with a crash from the other side of a stone without giving me a chance. At length, just as it grew dusk, I spied a Petie buck, a graceful little creature, scarcely bigger than a large hare, standing on a stone, about forty yards from me. Under ordinary circumstances I should never have dreamed of firing at such a thing, especially with an elephant gun, but we were hungry. So I sat down with my back against a rock, and aimed steadily at its head. I did this because if I struck it in the body the three-ounce ball would have knocked it to bits. At last I pulled the trigger, the gun went off with the report of a small cannon, and the buck disappeared. I ran to the spot with more anxiety than I should have felt in an ordinary way over a *koodoo* or an eland. To my delight there the little creature lay—the huge bullet had decapitated it. Considering all the circumstances I do not think I have often made a better shot than this, but if any one doubts, let him try his hand at a rabbit's head fifty yards away with an elephant gun and a three-ounce ball.

I picked up the Petie in triumph, and returned to the camp. There we skinned him and toasted his flesh over the fire. He just made a good meal for us, though we kept the hind legs for breakfast.

There was no moon this night, and so it chanced that when I suddenly remembered about the lion spoor, and suggested that we had better tie up the horses quite close to us, we could not find them, though we knew they were grazing within fifty yards. This being so we could only make up the fire and take our chance. Shortly afterwards I went to sleep with little Tota in my arms. Suddenly I was awakened by hearing that peculiarly painful sound, the scream of a horse, quite close to the fire, which was still burning brightly. Next second there came a noise of galloping hoofs, and before I could even rise my poor horse appeared in the ring of firelight. As in a flash of lightning I saw his staring eyes and wide-stretched nostrils, and the broken *reim* with which he had been knee-haltered, flying in the air. Also I saw something else, for on his back was a great dark form with glowing eyes, and from the form came a growling sound. It was a lion.

The horse dashed on. He galloped right through the fire, for which he had run in his terror, fortunately, however, without treading on us, and vanished into the night. We heard his hoofs for a hundred yards or more, then there was silence, broken now and again by distant growls. As may be imagined, we did not sleep any more that night, but waited anxiously till the dawn broke, two hours later.

As soon as there was sufficient light we rose, and, leaving Tota still asleep, crept cautiously in the direction in which the horse had vanished. When we had gone fifty yards or so, we made out its remains lying on the veldt, and caught sight of two great cat-like forms slinking away in the grey light.

To go any further was useless; we knew all about it now, so we turned to look for the other horse. But our cup of misfortune was not yet full; the horse was nowhere to be found. Terrified by the sight and smell of the lions, it had with a desperate effort also burst the *reim* with which it had been knee-haltered, and galloped far away. I sat down, feeling as though I could cry like a woman. For now we were left alone in these vast solitudes without a horse to carry us, and with a child who was not old enough to walk for more than a little way at a time.

Well, it was no use giving in, so with a few words we went back to our camp, where I found Tota crying because she had woke to find herself alone. Then we ate a little food and prepared to start. First we divided such articles as we must take with us into two equal parts, rejecting everything that we could possibly do without. Then, by an afterthought, we filled our water-bottles, though at the time I was rather against doing so, because of the extra weight. But Indaba-zimbi overruled me in the matter, fortunately for all three of us. I settled to look after Tota for the first march, and to give the elephant gun to Indaba-zimbi. At length all was ready, and we set out on foot. By the help of occasional lifts over rough places, Tota managed to walk up the slope of the hill-side where I had shot the Petie buck. At length we reached it, and, looking at the country beyond, I gave an exclamation of dismay. To say that it was desert would be saying too much; it was more like the Karroo in the Cape—a vast sandy waste, studded here and there with low shrubs and scattered rocks. But it was a great expanse of desolate land, stretching further than the eye could reach, and bordered far away by a line of purple hills, in the centre of which a great solitary peak soared high into the air.

"Indaba-zimbi," I said, "we can never cross this if we take six days."

"As you will, Macumazahn," he answered; "but I tell you that there"—and he pointed to the peak—"there the white man lives. Turn which way you like, but if you turn you will perish."

I reflected for a moment, Our case was, humanly speaking, almost hopeless. It mattered little which way we went. We were alone, almost without food, with no means of transport, and a child to carry. As well perish in the sandy waste as on the rolling veldt or among the trees of the hill-side. Providence alone could save us, and we must trust to Providence.

"Come on," I said, lifting Tota on to my back, for she was already tired. "All roads lead to rest."

How am I to describe the misery of the next four days? How am I to tell how we stumbled on through that awful desert, almost without food, and quite without water, for there were no streams, and we saw no springs? We soon found how the case was, and saved almost all the water in our bottles for the child. To look back on it is like a nightmare. I can scarcely bear to dwell on it. Day after day, by turns carrying the child through the heavy sand; night after night lying down in the scrub, chewing the leaves, and licking such dew as there was from the scanty grass! Not a spring, not a pool, not a head of game! It was the third night; we were nearly mad with thirst. Tota was in a comatose condition. Indaba-zimbi still had a little water in his bottle—perhaps a wine-glassful. With it we moistened our lips and blackened tongues. Then we gave the rest to the child. It revived her. She awoke from her swoon to sink into sleep.

See, the dawn was breaking. The hills were not more than eight miles or so away now, and they were green. There must be water there.

"Come," I said.

Indaba-zimbi lifted Tota into the kind of sling that we had made out of the blanket in which to carry her on our backs, and we staggered on for an hour through the sand. She awoke crying for water, and alas! we had none to give her; our tongues were hanging from our lips, we could scarcely speak.

We rested awhile, and Tota mercifully swooned away again. Then Indaba-zimbi took her. Though he was so thin the old man's strength was wonderful.

Another hour; the slope of the great peak could not be more than two miles away now. A couple of hundred yards off grew a large baobab tree. Could we reach its shade? We had done half the distance when Indaba-zimbi fell from exhaustion. We were now so weak that neither of us could lift the child on to our backs. He rose again, and we each took one of her hands and dragged her along the road. Fifty yards—they seemed to be fifty miles. Ah, the tree was reached at last; compared with the heat outside, the shade of its dense foliage seemed like the dusk and cool of a vault. I remember thinking that it was a good place to die in. Then I remember no more.

* * * * * * * *

I woke with a feeling as though the blessed rain were falling on my face and head. Slowly, and with great difficulty, I opened my eyes, then shut them again, having seen a vision. For a space I lay thus, while the rain continued to fall; I saw now that I must be asleep, or off my head with thirst and fever. If I were not off my head how came I to imagine that a lovely dark-eyed girl was bending over me sprinkling water on my face? A white girl, too, not a *Kaffir* woman. However, the dream went on.

"Hendrika," said a voice in English, the sweetest voice that I had ever heard; somehow it reminded me of wind whispering in the trees at night. "Hendrika, I fear he dies; there is a flask of brandy in my saddle-bag; get it."

"Ah! ah!" grunted a harsh voice in answer; "let him die, Miss Stella. He will bring you bad luck—let him die, I say." I felt a movement of air above me as though the woman of my vision turned swiftly, and once again I opened my eyes. She had risen, this dream woman. Now I saw that she was tall and graceful as a reed. She was angry, too; her dark eyes flashed, and she pointed with her hand at a female who stood before her, dressed in nondescript kind of clothes such as might be worn by either a man or a woman. The woman was young, of white blood, very short, with bowed legs and enormous shoulders. In face she was not bad-looking, but the brow receded, the chin and ears were prominent—in short, she reminded me of nothing so much as a very handsome monkey. She might have been the missing link.

The lady was pointing at her with her hand. "How dare you?" she said. "Are you going to disobey me again? Have you forgotten what I told you, Babyan?"[1]

"Ah! ah!" grunted the woman, who seemed literally to curl and shrivel up beneath her anger. "Don't be angry with me, Miss Stella, because I can't bear it. I only said it because it was true. I will fetch the brandy."

Then, dream or no dream, I determined to speak.

"Not brandy," I gasped in English as well as my swollen tongue would allow; "give me water."

"Ah, he lives!" cried the beautiful girl, "and he talks English. See, sir, here is water in your own bottle; you were quite close to a spring, it is on the other side of the tree."

I struggled to a sitting position, lifted the bottle to my lips, and drank from it. Oh! that drink of cool, pure water! never had I tasted anything so delicious. With the first gulp I felt life flow back into me.

---

1. Baboon.

But wisely enough she would not let me have much. "No more! no more!" she said, and dragged the bottle from me almost by force.

"The child," I said—"is the child dead?"

"I do not know yet," she answered. "We have only just found you, and I tried to revive you first."

I turned and crept to where Tota lay by the side of Indaba-zimbi. It was impossible to say if they were dead or swooning. The lady sprinkled Tota's face with the water, which I watched greedily, for my thirst was still awful, while the woman Hendrika did the same office for Indaba-zimbi. Presently, to my vast delight, Tota opened her eyes and tried to cry, but could not, poor little thing, because her tongue and lips were so swollen. But the lady got some water into her mouth, and, as in my case, the effect was magical. We allowed her to drink about a quarter of a pint, and no more, though she cried bitterly for it. Just then old Indaba-zimbi came to with a groan. He opened his eyes, glanced round, and took in the situation.

"What did I tell you, Macumazahn?" he gasped, and seizing the bottle, he took a long pull at it.

Meanwhile I sat with my back against the trunk of the great tree and tried to realize the situation. Looking to my left I saw too good horses—one bare-backed, and one with a rudely made lady's saddle on it. By the side of the horses were two dogs, of a stout greyhound breed, that sat watching us, and near the dogs lay a dead *oribe* buck, which they had evidently been coursing.

"Hendrika," said the lady presently, "they must not eat meat just yet. Go look up the tree and see if there is any ripe fruit on it."

The woman ran swiftly into the plain and obeyed. Presently she returned. "I see some ripe fruit," she said, "but it is high, quite at the top."

"Fetch it," said the lady.

"Easier said than done," I thought to myself; but I was much mistaken. Suddenly the woman bounded at least three feet into the air and caught one of the spreading boughs in her large flat hands; then came a swing that would have filled an acrobat with envy—and she was on it.

"Now there is an end," I thought again, for the next bough was beyond her reach. But again I was mistaken. She stood up on the bough, gripping it with her bare feet, and once more sprang at the one above, caught it and swung herself into it.

I suppose that the lady saw my expression of astonishment. "Do not wonder, sir," she said, "Hendrika is not like other people. She will not fall."

I made no answer, but watched the progress of this extraordinary person with the most breathless interest. On she went, swinging herself from bough to bough, and running along them like a monkey. At last she reached the top, and began to swarm up a thin branch towards the ripe fruit. When she was near enough she shook the branch violently. There was a crack—a crash—it broke. I shut my eyes, expecting to see her crushed on the ground before me.

"Don't be afraid," said the lady again, laughing gently. "Look, she is quite safe."

I looked, and so she was. She had caught a bough as she fell, clung to it, and was now calmly dropping to another. Old Indaba-zimbi had also watched this performance with interest, but it did not seem to astonish him over-much. "Baboon-woman?" he said, as though such people were common, and then turned his attention to soothing Tota, who was moaning for more water. Meanwhile Hendrika came down the tree with extraordinary rapidity, and swinging by one hand from a bough, dropped about eight feet to the ground.

In another two minutes we were all three sucking the pulpy fruit. In an ordinary way we should have found it tasteless enough: as it was I thought it the most delicious thing I had ever tasted. After three days spent without food or water, in the desert, one is not particular. While we were still eating the fruit, the lady of my vision set her companion to work to partially flay the *oribe* which her dogs had killed, and busied herself in making a fire of fallen boughs. As soon as it burned brightly she took strips of the *oribe* flesh, toasted them, and gave them to us on leaves. We ate, and now were allowed a little more water. After that she took Tota to the spring and washed her, which she sadly needed, poor child! Next came our turn to wash, and oh, the joy of it!

I came back to the tree, walking painfully, indeed, but a changed man. There sat the beautiful girl with Tota on her knees. She was lulling her to sleep, and held up her finger to me enjoining silence. At last the child went off into a sound natural slumber—an example that I should have been glad to follow had it not been for my burning curiosity. Then I spoke.

"May I ask what your name is?" I said.

"Stella," she answered.

"Stella what?" I said.

"Stella nothing," she answered, in some pique; "Stella is my name; it is short and easy to remember at any rate. My father's name is Thomas, and we live up there," and she pointed round the base of the great peak. I looked at her astonished. "Have you lived there long?" I asked.

64

"Ever since I was seven years old. We came there in a wagon. Before that we came from England—from Oxfordshire; I can show you the place on a big map. It is called Garsingham."

Again I thought I must be dreaming. "Do you know, Miss Stella," I said, "it is very strange—so strange that it almost seems as though it could not be true—but I also came from Garsingham in Oxfordshire many years ago."

She started up. "Are you an English gentleman?" she said. "Ah, I have always longed to see an English gentleman. I have never seen but one Englishman since we lived here, and he certainly was not a gentleman—no white people at all, indeed, except a few wandering Boers. We live among black people and baboons—only I have read about English people—lots of books—poetry and novels. But tell me what is your name? Macumazahn the black man called you, but you must have a white name, too."

"My name is Allan Quatermain," I said.

Her face turned quite white, her rosy lips parted, and she looked at me wildly with her beautiful dark eyes.

"It is wonderful," she said, "but I have often heard that name. My father has told me how a little boy called Allan Quatermain once saved my life by putting out my dress when it was on fire—see!"—and she pointed to a faint red mark upon her neck—"here is the scar of the burn."

"I remember it," I said. "You were dressed up as Father Christmas. It was I who put out the fire; my wrists were burnt in doing so."

Then for a space we sat silent, looking at each other, while Stella slowly fanned herself with her wide felt hat, in which some white ostrich plumes were fixed.

"This is God's doing," she said at last. "You saved my life when I was a child; now I have saved yours and the little girl's. Is she your own daughter?" she added, quickly.

"No," I answered; "I will tell you the tale presently."

"Yes," she said, "you shall tell me as we go home. It is time to be starting home, it will take us three hours to get there. Hendrika, Hendrika, bring the horses here!"

CHAPTER 7

The Baboon-Woman

Hendrika obeyed, leading the horses to the side of the tree.

"Now, Mr. Allan," said Stella, "you must ride on my horse, and the old black man must ride on the other. I will walk, and Hendrika will carry the child. Oh, do not be afraid, she is very strong, she could carry you or me."

Hendrika grunted assent. I am sorry that I cannot express her method of speech by any more polite term. Sometimes she grunted like a monkey, sometimes she clicked like a Bushman, and sometimes she did both together, when she became quite unintelligible.

I expostulated against this proposed arrangement, saying that we could walk, which was a fib, for I do not think that I could have done a mile; but Stella would not listen, she would not even let me carry my elephant gun, but took it herself. So we mounted with some difficulty, and Hendrika took up the sleeping Tota in her long, sinewy arms.

"See that the 'Baboon-woman' does not run away into the mountains with the little white one," said Indaba-zimbi to me in *Kaffir*, as he climbed slowly on to the horse.

Unfortunately Hendrika understood his speech. Her face twisted and grew livid with fury. She put down Tota and literally sprang at Indaba-zimbi as a monkey springs. But weary and worn as he was, the old gentleman was too quick for her. With an exclamation of genuine fright he threw himself from the horse on the further side, with the somewhat ludicrous result that all in a moment Hendrika was occupying the seat which he had vacated. Just then Stella realized the position.

"Come down, you savage, come down!" she said, stamping her foot.

The extraordinary creature flung herself from the horse and literally grovelled on the ground before her mistress and burst into tears.

"Pardon, Miss Stella," she clicked and grunted in villainous English, "but he called me *'Babyan-frau'* (Baboon-woman)."

"Tell your servant that he must not use such words to Hendrika, Mr. Allan," Stella said to me. "If he does," she added, in a whisper, "Hendrika will certainly kill him."

I explained this to Indaba-zimbi, who, being considerably frightened, deigned to apologize. But from that hour there was hate and war between these two.

Harmony having been thus restored, we started, the dogs following us. A small strip of desert intervened between us and the slope of the peak—perhaps it was two miles wide. We crossed it and reached rich grass lands, for here a considerable stream gathered from the hills; but it did not flow across the barren lands, it passed to the east along the foot of the hills. This stream we had to cross by a ford. Hendrika walked boldly through it, holding Tota in her arms. Stella leapt across from stone to stone like a roebuck; I thought to myself that she was the most graceful creature that I had ever seen. After this the track passed around a pleasantly-wooded shoulder of the peak, which was, I found, known as Babyan Kap, or Baboon Head. Of course we could only go at a foot pace, so our progress was slow. Stella walked for some way in silence, then she spoke.

"Tell me, Mr. Allan," she said, "how it was that I came to find you dying in the desert?"

So I began and told her all. It took an hour or more to do so, and she listened intently, now and again asking a question.

"It is all very wonderful," she said when I had done, "very wonderful indeed. Do you know I went out this morning with Hendrika and the dogs for a ride, meaning to get back home by mid-day, for my father is ill, and I do not like to leave him for long. But just as I was going to turn, when we were about where we are now—yes, that was the very bush—an *oribe* got up, and the dogs chased it. I followed them for the gallop, and when we came to the river, instead of turning to the left as bucks generally do, the *oribe* swam the stream and took to the Bad Lands beyond. I followed it, and within a hundred yards of the big tree the dogs killed it. Hendrika wanted to turn back at once, but I said that we would rest under the shade of the tree, for I knew that there was a spring of water near. Well, we went; and there I saw you all lying like dead; but Hendrika, who is very clever in some ways, said no—and you know the rest. Yes, it is very wonderful."

"It is indeed," I said. "Now tell me, Miss Stella, who is Hendrika?"

She looked round before answering to see that the woman was not near.

"Hers is a strange story, Mr. Allan. I will tell you. You must know that all these mountains and the country beyond are full of baboons. When I was a girl of about ten I used to wander a great deal alone in the hills and valleys, and watch the baboons as they played among the rocks. There was one family of baboons that I watched especially—they used to live in a *kloof* about a mile from the house. The old man baboon was very large, and one of the females had a grey face. But the reason why I watched them so much was because I saw that they had with them a creature that looked like a girl, for her skin was quite white, and, what was more, that she was protected from the weather when it happened to be cold by a fur belt of some sort, which was tied round her throat. The old baboons seemed to be especially fond of her, and would sit with their arms round her neck. For nearly a whole summer I watched this particular white-skinned baboon till at last my curiosity quite overmastered me. I noticed that, though she climbed about the cliffs with the other monkeys, at a certain hour a little before sundown they used to put her with one or two other much smaller ones into a little cave, while the family went off somewhere to get food, to the *mealie* fields, I suppose. Then I got an idea that I would catch this white baboon and bring it home. But of course I could not do this by myself, so I took a Hottentot—a very clever man when he was not drunk—who lived on the stead, into my confidence. He was called Hendrik, and was very fond of me; but for a long while he would not listen to my plan, because he said that the *babyans* would kill us. At last I bribed him with a knife that had four blades, and one afternoon we started, Hendrik carrying a stout sack made of hide, with a rope running through it so that the mouth could be drawn tight.

"Well, we got to the place, and, hiding ourselves carefully in the trees at the foot of the *kloof*, watched the baboons playing about and grunting to each other, till at length, according to custom, they took the white one and three other little babies and put them in the cave. Then the old man came out, looked carefully round, called to his family, and went off with them over the brow of the *kloof*. Now very slowly and cautiously we crept up over the rocks till we came to the mouth of the cave and looked in. All the four little baboons were fast asleep, with their backs towards us, and their arms round each other's necks, the white one being in the middle. Nothing could have been better for our plans. Hendrik, who by this time had quite entered into the spirit of the thing, crept along the cave like a snake, and suddenly dropped the mouth of the hide bag over the head of the white baboon. The poor little thing woke up and gave a violent jump which caused it to vanish right into the bag. Then Hendrik pulled the string tight, and together we knotted it so that it was impossible for our captive to escape. Meanwhile the other baby baboons had rushed from the cave screaming, and when we got outside they were nowhere to be seen.

"'Come on, Missie,' said Hendrik; 'the *babyans* will soon be back.' He had shouldered the sack, inside of which the white baboon was kicking violently, and screaming like a child. It was dreadful to hear its shrieks.

"We scrambled down the sides of the *kloof* and ran for home as fast as we could manage. When we were near the waterfall, and within about three hundred yards of the garden wall, we heard a voice behind us, and there, leaping from rock to rock, and running over the grass, was the whole family of baboons headed by the old man.

"'Run, Missie, run!' gasped Hendrik, and I did, like the wind, leaving him far behind. I dashed into the garden, where some *Kaffirs* were working, crying, 'The *babyans*! The *babyans*!' Luckily the men had their sticks and spears by them and ran out just in time to save Hendrik, who was almost overtaken. The baboons made a good fight for it, however, and it was not till the old man was killed with an *assegai* that they ran away.

"Well, there is a stone hut in the *kraal* at the stead where my father sometimes shuts up natives who have misbehaved. It is very strong, and has a barred window. To this hut Hendrik carried the sack, and, having untied the mouth, put it down on the floor, and ran from the place, shutting the door behind him. In another moment the poor little thing was out and dashing round the stone hut as though it were mad. It sprung at the bars of the window, clung there, and beat its head against them till the blood came. Then it fell to the floor, and sat upon it crying like a child, and rocking itself backwards and forwards. It was so sad to see it that I began to cry too.

"Just then my father came in and asked what all the fuss was about. I told him that we had caught a young white baboon, and he was angry, and said that it must be let go. But when he looked at it through the bars of the window he nearly fell down with astonishment.

"'Why!' he said, 'this is not a baboon, it is a white child that the baboons have stolen and brought up!'

"Now, Mr. Allan, whether my father is right or wrong, you can judge for yourself. You see Hendrika—we named her that after Hendrik, who caught her—she is a woman, not a monkey, and yet she has many of the ways of monkeys, and looks like one too. You saw how she can climb, for instance, and you hear how she talks. Also she is very savage, and when she is angry or jealous she seems to go mad, though she is as clever as anybody. I think that she must have been stolen by the baboons when she was quite tiny and nurtured by them, and that is why she is so like them.

"But to go on. My father said that it was our duty to keep Hendrika at any cost. The worst of it was, that for three days she would eat nothing, and I thought that she would die, for all the while she sat and wailed. On the third day, however, I went to the bars of the window place, and held out a cup of milk and some fruit to her. She looked at it for a long while, then crept up moaning, took the milk from my hand, drank it greedily, and afterwards ate the fruit. From that time forward she took food readily enough, but only if I would feed her.

"But I must tell you of the dreadful end of Hendrik. From the day that we captured Hendrika the whole place began to swarm with baboons which were evidently employed in watching the *kraals*. One day Hendrik went out towards the hills alone to gather some medicine. He did not come back again, so the next day search was made. By a big rock which I can show you, they found his scattered and broken bones, the fragments of his *assegai*, and four dead baboons. They had set upon him and torn him to pieces.

"My father was very much frightened at this, but still he would not let Hendrika go, because he said that she was human, and that it was our duty to reclaim her. And so we did—to a certain extent, at least. After the murder of Hendrik, the baboons vanished from the neighbourhood, and have only returned quite recently, so at length we ventured to let Hendrika out. By this time she had grown very fond of me; still, on the first opportunity she ran away. But in the evening she returned again. She had been seeking the baboons, and could not find them. Shortly afterwards she began to speak—I taught her—and from that time she has loved me so that she will not leave me. I think it would kill her if I went away from her. She watches me all day, and at night sleeps on the floor of my hut. Once, too, she saved my life when I was swept down the river in flood; but she is jealous, and hates everybody else. Look, how she is glaring at you now because I am talking to you!"

I looked. Hendrika was tramping along with the child in her arms and staring at me in a most sinister fashion out of the corners of her eyes.

While I was reflecting on the Baboon-woman's strange story, and thinking that she was an exceedingly awkward customer, the path took a sudden turn.

"Look!" said Stella, "there is our home. Is it not beautiful?"

It was beautiful indeed. Here on the western side of the great peak a bay had been formed in the mountain, which might have measured eight hundred or a thousand yards across by three-quarters of a mile in depth. At the back of this indentation the sheer cliff rose to the height of several hundred feet, and behind it and above it the great Babyan Peak towered up towards the heavens. The space of ground, embraced thus in the arms of the mountain, as it were, was laid out, as though by the cunning hand of man, in three terraces that rose one above the other. To the right and left of the topmost terrace were chasms in the cliff, and down each chasm fell a waterfall, from no great height, indeed, but of considerable volume. These two streams flowed away on either side of the enclosed space, one towards the north, and the other, the course of which we had been following, round the base of the mountain. At each terrace they made a cascade, so that the traveller approaching had a view of eight waterfalls at once. Along the edge of the stream to our left were placed *Kaffir kraals*, built in orderly groups with verandas, after the Basutu fashion, and a very large part of the entire space of land was under cultivation. All of this I noted at once, as well as the extraordinary richness and depth of the soil, which for many ages past had been washed down from the mountain heights. Then following the line of an excellent wagon road, on which we now found ourselves, that wound up from terrace to terrace, my eye lit upon the crowning wonder of the scene. For in the centre of the topmost platform or terrace, which may have enclosed eight or ten acres of ground, and almost surrounded by groves of orange trees, gleamed buildings of which I had never seen the like. There were three groups of them, one in the middle, and one on either side, and a little to the rear, but, as I afterwards discovered, the plan of all was the same. In the centre was an edifice constructed like an ordinary Zulu hut—that is to say, in the shape of a beehive, only it was five times the size of any hut I ever saw, and built of blocks of hewn white marble, fitted together with extraordinary knowledge of the principles and properties of arch building, and with so much accuracy and finish that it was often difficult to find the joints of the massive blocks. From this centre hut ran three covered passages, leading to other buildings of an exactly similar character, only smaller, and each whole block was enclosed by a marble wall about four feet in height.

Of course we were as yet too far off to see all these details, but the general outline I saw at once, and it astonished me considerably. Even old Indaba-zimbi, whom the Baboon-woman had been unable to move, deigned to show wonder.

"*Ou!*" he said; "this is a place of marvels. Who ever saw *kraals* built of white stone?"

Stella watched our faces with an expression of intense amusement, but said nothing.

"Did your father build those *kraals*?" I gasped, at length.

"My father! no, of course not," she answered. "How would it have been possible for one white man to do so, or to have made this road? He found them as you see."

"Who built them, then?" I said again.

"I do not know. My father thinks that they are very ancient, for the people who live here now do not know how to lay one stone upon another, and these huts are so wonderfully constructed that, though they must have stood for ages, not a stone of them had fallen. But I can show you the quarry where the marble was cut; it is close by and behind it is the entrance to an ancient mine, which my father thinks was a silver mine. Perhaps the people who worked the mine built the marble huts. The world is old, and no doubt plenty of people have lived in it and been forgotten."[1]

Then we rode on in silence. I have seen many beautiful sights in Africa, and in such matters, as in others, comparisons are odious and worthless, but I do not think that I ever saw a lovelier scene. It was no one thing—it was the combination of the mighty peak looking forth on to the everlasting plains, the great cliffs, the waterfalls that sparkled in rainbow hues, the rivers girdling the rich cultivated lands, the gold-specked green of the orange trees, the flashing domes of the marble huts, and a thousand other things. Then over all brooded the peace of evening, and the infinite glory of the sunset that filled heaven with changing hues of splendour, that wrapped the mountain and cliffs in cloaks of purple and of gold, and lay upon the quiet face of the water like the smile of a god.

Perhaps also the contrast, and the memory of those three awful days and nights in the hopeless desert, enhanced the charm, and perhaps the beauty of the girl who walked beside me completed it. For of this I am sure, that of all sweet and lovely things that I looked on then, she was the sweetest and the loveliest.

Ah, it did not take me long to find my fate. How long will it be before I find her once again?

---

1. *Kraals* of a somewhat similar nature to those described by Mr. Quatermain have been discovered in the Marico district of the Transvaal, and an illustration of them is to be found in Mr. Anderson's *Twenty-five Years in a Wagon*, vol. ii. p. 55. Mr. Anderson says, "In this district are the ancient stone *kraals* mentioned in an early chapter; but it requires a fuller description to show that these extensive *kraals* must have been erected by a white race who understood building in stone and at right angles, with door-posts, lintels, and sills, and it required more than *Kaffir* skill to erect the stone huts, with stone circular roofs, beautifully formed and most substantially erected; strong enough, if not disturbed, to last a thousand years."—Editor.

CHAPTER 8

The Marble Kraals

At length the last platform, or terrace, was reached, and we pulled up outside the wall surrounding the central group of marble huts—for so I must call them, for want of a better name. Our approach had been observed by a crowd of natives, whose race I have never been able to determine accurately; they belonged to the Basutu and peaceful section of the Bantu peoples rather than to the Zulu and warlike. Several of these ran up to take the horses, gazing on us with astonishment, not unmixed with awe. We dismounted—speaking for myself, not without difficulty—indeed, had it not been for Stella's support I should have fallen.

"Now you must come and see my father," she said. "I wonder what he will think of it, it is all so strange. Hendrika, take the child to my hut and give her milk, then put her into my bed; I will come presently."

Hendrika went off with a somewhat ugly grin to do her mistress's bidding, and Stella led the way through the narrow gateway in the marble wall, which may have enclosed nearly half an *erf*, or three-quarters of an acre of ground in all. It was beautifully planted as a garden, many European vegetables and flowers were growing in it, besides others with which I was not acquainted. Presently we came to the centre hut, and it was then that I noticed the extraordinary beauty and finish of the marble masonry. In the hut, and facing the gateway, was a modern door, rather rudely fashioned of *buckenhout*, a beautiful reddish wood that has the appearance of having been sedulously pricked with a pin. Stella opened it, and we entered. The interior of the hut was the size of a large and lofty room, the walls being formed of plain polished marble. It was lighted somewhat dimly, but quite effectively, by peculiar openings in the roof, from which the rain was excluded by overhanging eaves. The marble floor was strewn with native mats and skins of animals. Bookcases filled with books were placed against the walls, there was a table in the centre, chairs seated with *rimpi* or strips of hide stood about, and beyond the table was a couch on which a man was lying reading.

"Is that you, Stella?" said a voice, that even after so many years seemed familiar to me. "Where have you been, my dear? I began to think that you had lost yourself again."

"No, father, dear, I have not lost myself, but I have found somebody else."

At that moment I stepped forward so that the light fell on me. The old gentleman on the couch rose with some difficulty and bowed with much courtesy. He was a fine-looking old man, with deep-set dark eyes, a pale face that bore many traces of physical and mental suffering, and a long white beard.

"Be welcome, sir," he said. "It is long since we have seen a white face in these wilds, and yours, if I am not mistaken, is that of an Englishman. There has been but one Englishman here for twelve years, and he, I grieve to say, was an outcast flying from justice," and he bowed again and stretched out his hand.

I looked at him, and then of a sudden his name flashed back into my mind. I took his hand.

"How do you do, Mr. Carson?" I said.

He started as though he had been stung.

"Who told you that name?" he cried. "It is a dead name. Stella, is it you? I forbade you to let it pass your lips."

"I did not speak it, father. I have never spoken it," she answered.

"Sir," I broke in, "if you will allow me I will show you how I came to know your name. Do you remember many years ago coming into the study of a clergyman in Oxfordshire and telling him that you were going to leave England forever?"

He bowed his head.

"And do you remember a little boy who sat upon the hearthrug writing with a pencil?"

"I do," he said.

"Sir, I was that boy, and my name is Allan Quatermain. Those children who lay sick are all dead, their mother is dead, and my father, your old friend, is dead also. Like you he emigrated, and last year he died in the Cape. But that is not all the story. After many adventures, I, one *Kaffir*, and a little girl, lay senseless and dying in the Bad Lands, where we had wandered for days without water, and there we should have perished, but your daughter, Miss——"

"Call her Stella," he broke in, hastily. "I cannot bear to hear that name. I have forsworn it."

"Miss Stella found us by chance and saved our lives."

"By chance, did you say, Allan Quatermain?" he answered. "There is little chance in all this; such chances spring from another will than ours. Welcome, Allan, son of my old friend. Here we live as it were in a hermitage, with Nature as our only friend, but such as we have is yours, and for as long as you will take it. But you must be starving; talk no more now. Stella, it is time to eat. Tomorrow we will talk."

To tell the truth I can recall very little of the events of that evening. A kind of dizzy weariness overmastered me. I remember sitting at a table next to Stella, and eating heartily, and then I remember nothing more.

I awoke to find myself lying on a comfortable bed in a hut built and fashioned on the same model as the centre one. While I was wondering what time it was, a native came bringing some clean clothes on his arm, and, luxury of luxuries, produced a bath hollowed from wood. I rose, feeling a very different man, my strength had come back again to me; I dressed, and following a covered passage found myself in the centre hut. Here the table was set for breakfast with all manner of good things, such as I had not seen for many a month, which I contemplated with healthy satisfaction. Presently I looked up, and there before me was a more delightful sight, for standing in one of the doorways which led to the sleeping huts was Stella, leading little Tota by the hand.

She was very simply dressed in a loose blue gown, with a wide collar, and girdled in at the waist by a little leather belt. In the bosom of her robe was a bunch of orange blooms, and her rippling hair was tied in a single knot behind her shapely head. She greeted me with a smile, asking how I had slept, and then held Tota up for me to kiss. Under her loving care the child had been quite transformed. She was neatly dressed in a garment of the same blue stuff that Stella wore, her fair hair was brushed; indeed, had it not been for the sun blisters on her face and hands, one would scarcely have believed that this was the same child whom Indaba-zimbi and I had dragged for hour after hour through the burning, waterless desert.

"We must breakfast alone, Mr. Allan," she said; "my father is so upset by your arrival that he will not get up yet. Oh, you cannot tell how thankful I am that you have come. I have been so anxious about him of late. He grows weaker and weaker; it seems to me as though the strength were ebbing away from him. Now he scarcely leaves the *kraal*, I have to manage everything about the farm; he does nothing but read and think."

Just then Hendrika entered, bearing a jug of coffee in one hand and of milk in the other, which she set down upon the table, casting a look of little love at me as she did so.

"Be careful, Hendrika; you are spilling the coffee," said Stella. "Don't you wonder how we come to have coffee here, Mr. Allan? I will tell you—we grow it. That was my idea. Oh, I have lots of things to show you. You don't know what we have managed to do in the time that we have been here. You see we have plenty of labour, for the people about look upon my father as their chief."

"Yes," I said, "but how do you get all these luxuries of civilization?" and I pointed to the books, the crockery, and the knives and forks.

"Very simply. Most of the books my father brought with him when we first trekked into the wilds; there was nearly a wagon load of them. But every few years we have sent an expedition of three wagons right down to Port Natal. The wagons are loaded with ivory and other goods, and come back with all kinds of things that been sent out from England for us. So you see, although we live in this wild place, we are not altogether cut off. We can send runners to Natal and back in three months, and the wagons get there and back in a year. The last lot arrived quite safe about three months ago. Our servants are very faithful, and some of them speak Dutch well."

"Have you ever been with the wagons?" I asked.

"Since I was a child I have never been more than thirty miles from Babyan's Peak," she answered. "Do you know, Mr. Allan, that you are, with one exception, the first Englishman that I have known out of a book. I suppose that I must seem very wild and savage to you, but I have had one advantage—a good education. My father has taught me everything, and perhaps I know some things that you don't. I can read French and German, for instance. I think that my father's first idea was to let me run wild altogether, but he gave it up."

"And don't you wish to go into the world?" I asked.

"Sometimes," she said, "when I get lonely. But perhaps my father is right—perhaps it would frighten and bewilder me. At any rate he would never return to civilization; it is his idea, you know, although I am sure I do not know where he got it from, nor why he cannot bear that our name should be spoken. In short, Mr. Quatermain, we do not make our lives, we must take them as we find them. Have you done your breakfast? Let us go out, and I will show you our home."

I rose and went to my sleeping-place to fetch my hat. When I returned, Mr. Carson—for after all that was his name, though he would never allow it to be spoken—had come into the hut. He felt better now, he said, and would accompany us on our walk if Stella would give him an arm.

So we started, and after us came Hendrika with Tota and old Indaba-zimbi whom I found sitting outside as fresh as paint. Nothing could tire that old man.

The view from the platform was almost as beautiful as that from the lower ground looking up to the peak. The marble *kraals*, as I have said, faced west, consequently all the upper terrace lay in the shadow of the great peak till nearly eleven o'clock in the morning—a great advantage in that warm latitude. First we walked through the garden, which was beautifully cultivated, and one of the most productive that I ever saw. There were three or four natives working in it, and they all saluted my host as "Baba," or father. Then we visited the other two groups of marble huts. One of these was used for stables and outbuildings, the other as storehouses, the centre hut having been, however, turned into a chapel. Mr. Carson was not ordained, but he earnestly tried to convert the natives, most of whom were refugees who had come to him for shelter, and he had practised the more elementary rites of the church for so long that I think he began to believe that he really was a clergyman. For instance, he always married those of his people who would consent to a monogamous existence, and baptized their children.

When we had examined those wonderful remains of antiquity, the marble huts, and admired the orange trees, the vines and fruits which thrive like weeds in this marvellous soil and climate, we descended to the next platform, and saw the farming operations in full swing. I think that it was the best farm I have ever seen in Africa. There was ample water for purposes of irrigation, the grass lands below gave pasturage for hundreds of head of cattle and horses, and, for natives, the people were most industrious. Moreover, the whole place was managed by Mr. Carson on the co-operative system; he only took a tithe of the produce—indeed, in this land of teeming plenty, what was he to do with more? Consequently the tribesmen, who, by the way, called themselves the Children of Thomas, were able to accumulate considerable wealth. All their disputes were referred to their *father*, and he also was judge of offences and crimes. Some were punished by imprisonment, whipping, and loss of goods, other and graver transgressions by expulsion from the community, a *fiat* which to one of these favoured natives must have seemed as heavy as the decree that drove Adam from the Garden of Eden.

Old Mr. Carson leaned upon his daughter's arm and contemplated the scene with pride.

"I have done all this, Allan Quatermain," he said. "When renouncing civilization, I wandered here by chance; seeking a home in the remotest places of the world, I found this lonely spot a wilderness. Nothing was to be seen except the site, the domes of the marble huts, and the waterfalls. I took possession of the huts. I cleared the path of garden land and planted the orange grove. I had only six natives then, but by degrees others joined me, now my tribe is a thousand strong. Here we live in profound peace and plenty. I have all I need, and I seek no more. Heaven has prospered me so far—may it do so to the end, which for me draws nigh. And now I am tired and will go back. If you wish to see the old quarry and the mouth of the ancient mines, Stella will show them to you. No, my love, you need not trouble to come, I can manage. Look! some of the headmen are waiting to see me."

So he went; but still followed by Hendrika and Indaba-zimbi, we turned, and, walking along the bank of one of the rivers, passed up behind the marble *kraals*, and came to the quarry, whence the material of which they were built had been cut in some remote age. The pit opened up a very thick seam of the whitest and most beautiful marble. I know another like it in Natal. But by whom it had been worked I cannot say; not by natives, that is certain, though the builders of these *kraals* had condescended to borrow the shape of native huts for their model. By the way, the only relic of those builders that I ever saw was a highly finished bronze pick-axe which Stella had found one day in the quarry.

After we had examined this quarry we climbed the slope of the hill till we came to the mouth of the ancient mines which were situated in a gorge. I believe them to have been silver mines. The gorge was long and narrow, and the moment we entered it there rose from every side a sound of groaning and barking that was almost enough to deafen us. I knew what it was at once: the whole place was filled with baboons, which clambered down the rocks towards us from every direction, and in a manner that struck me as being unnaturally fearless. Stella turned a little pale and clung to my arm.

"It is very silly of me," she whispered. "I am not at all nervous, but ever since they killed Hendrik I cannot bear the sight of those animals. I always think that there is something human about them."

Meanwhile the baboons drew nearer, talking to each other as they came. Tota began to cry, and clung to Stella. Stella clung to me, while I and Indaba-zimbi put as bold a front on the matter as we could. Only Hendrika stood looking at the brutes with an unconcerned smile on her monkey face. When the great apes were quite near, she suddenly called aloud. Instantly they stopped their hideous clamour as though at a word of command. Then Hendrika addressed them: I can only describe it so. That is to say, she began to make a noise such as baboons do when they converse with each other. I have known Hottentots and Bushmen who said that they could talk with the baboons and understand their language, but I confess I never heard it done before or since.

From the mouth of Hendrika came a succession of grunts, groans, squeals, clicks, and every other abominable noise that can be conceived, conveying to my mind a general idea of expostulation. At any rate the baboons listened. One of them grunted back some answer, and then the whole mob drew off to the rocks.

I stood astonished, and without a word we turned back to the *kraal*, for Hendrika was too close to allow me to speak. When we reached the dining hut Stella went in, followed by Hendrika. But Indaba-zimbi plucked me by the sleeve, and I stopped outside.

"Macumazahn," he said. "Baboon-woman—devil-woman. Be careful, Macumazahn. She loves that Star (the natives aptly enough called Stella the Star), and is jealous. Be careful, Macumazahn, or the Star will set!"

CHAPTER 9

Let Us Go In, Allan!

It is very difficult for me to describe the period of time which elapsed between my arrival at Babyan's Peak and my marriage with Stella. When I look back on it, it seems sweet as with the odour of flowers, and dim as with the happy dusk of summer eves, while through the sweetness comes the sound of Stella's voice, and through the gloom shines the starlight of her eyes. I think that we loved each other from the first, though for a while we said no word of love. Day by day I went about the place with her, accompanied by little Tota and Hendrika only, while she attended to the thousand and one matters which her father's ever-growing weakness had laid upon her; or rather, as time drew on, I attended to the business, and she accompanied me. All day through we were together. Then after supper, when the night had fallen, we would walk together in the garden and come at length to hear her father read aloud sometimes from the works of a poet, sometimes from history. Or, if he did not feel well, Stella would read, and when this was done, Mr. Carson would celebrate a short form of prayer, and we would separate till the morning once more brought our happy hour of meeting.

So the weeks went by, and with every week I grew to know my darling better. Often, I wonder now, if my fond fancy deceives me, or if indeed there are women as sweet and dear as she. Was it solitude that had given such depth and gentleness to her? Was it the long years of communing with Nature that had endowed her with such peculiar grace, the grace we find in opening flowers and budding trees? Had she caught that murmuring voice from the sound of the streams which fall continually about her rocky home? was it the tenderness of the evening sky beneath which she loved to walk, that lay like a shadow on her face, and the light of the evening stars that shone in her quiet eyes? At the least to me she was the realization of that dream which haunts the sleep of sin-stained men; so my memory paints her, so I hope to find her when at last the sleep has rolled away and the fevered dreams are done.

At last there came a day—the most blessed of my life, when we told our love. We had been together all the morning, but after dinner Mr. Carson was so unwell that Stella stopped in with him. At supper we met again, and after supper, when she had put little Tota, to whom she had grown much attached, to bed, we went out, leaving Mr. Carson dozing on the couch.

The night was warm and lovely, and without speaking we walked up the garden to the orange grove and sat down upon a rock. There was a little breeze which shook the petals of the orange blooms over us in showers, and bore their delicate fragrance far and wide. Silence reigned around, broken only by the sound of the falling waterfalls that now died to a faint murmur, and now, as the wavering breeze turned, boomed loudly in our ears. The moon was not yet visible, but already the dark clouds which floated through the sky above us—for there had been rain—showed a glow of silver, telling us that she shone brightly behind the peak. Stella began to talk in her low, gentle voice, speaking to me of her life in the wilderness, how she had grown to love it, how her mind had gone on from idea to idea, and how she pictured the great rushing world that she had never seen as it was reflected to her from the books which she had read. It was a curious vision of life that she had: things were out of proportion to it; it was more like a dream than a reality—a mirage than the actual face of things. The idea of great cities, and especially of London, had a kind of fascination for her: she could scarcely realize the rush, the roar and hurry, the hard crowds of men and women, strangers to each other, feverishly seeking for wealth and pleasure beneath a murky sky, and treading one another down in the fury of their competition.

"What is it all for?" she asked earnestly. "What do they seek? Having so few years to live, why do they waste them thus?"

I told her that in the majority of instances it was actual hard necessity that drove them on, but she could barely understand me. Living as she had done, in the midst of the teeming plenty of a fruitful earth, she did not seem to be able to grasp the fact that there were millions who from day to day know not how to stay their hunger.

"I never want to go there," she went on; "I should be bewildered and frightened to death. It is not natural to live like that. God put Adam and Eve in a garden, and that is how he meant their children to live—in peace, and looking always on beautiful things. This is my idea of perfect life. I want no other."

"I thought you once told me that you found it lonely," I said.

"So I did," she answered, innocently, "but that was before you came. Now I am not lonely any more, and it is perfect—perfect as the night."

Just then the full moon rose above the elbow of the peak, and her rays stole far and wide down the misty valley, gleaming on the water, brooding on the plain, searching out the hidden places of the rocks, wrapping the fair form of nature as in a silver bridal veil through which her beauty shone mysteriously.

Stella looked down the terraced valley; she turned and looked up at the scarred face of the golden moon, and then she looked at me. The beauty of the night was about her face, the scent of the night was on her hair, the mystery of the night shone in her shadowed eyes. She looked at me, I looked on her, and all our hearts' love blossomed within us. We spoke no word—we had no words to speak, but slowly we drew near, till lips were pressed to lips as we kissed our eternal troth.

It was she who broke that holy silence, speaking in a changed voice, in soft deep notes that thrilled me like the lowest chords of a smitten harp.

"Ah, now I understand," she said, "now I know why we are lonely, and how we can lose our loneliness. Now I know what it is that stirs us in the beauty of the sky, in the sound of water and in the scent of flowers. It is Love who speaks in everything, though till we hear his voice we understand nothing. But when we hear, then the riddle is answered and the gates of our heart are opened, and, Allan, we see the way that wends through death to heaven, and is lost in the glory of which our love is but a shadow.

"Let us go in, Allan. Let us go before the spell breaks, so that whatever overtakes us, sorrow, death, or separation, we may always have this perfect memory to save us. Come, dearest, let us go!"

I rose like a man in a dream, still holding her by the hand. But as I rose my eye fell upon something that gleamed white among the foliage of the orange bush at my side. I said nothing, but looked. The breeze stirred the orange leaves, the moonlight struck for a moment full upon the white object.

It was the face of Hendrika, the Babyan-woman, as Indaba-zimbi had called her, and on it was a glare of hate that made me shudder.

I said nothing; the face vanished, and just then I heard a baboon bark in the rocks behind.

Then we went down the garden, and Stella passed into the centre hut. I saw Hendrika standing in the shadow near the door, and went up to her.

"Hendrika," I said, "why were you watching Miss Stella and myself in the garden?"

She drew her lips up till her teeth gleamed in the moonlight.

"Have I not watched her these many years, Macumazahn? Shall I cease to watch because a wandering white man comes to steal her? Why were you kissing her in the garden, Macumazahn? How dare you kiss her who is a star?"

"I kissed her because I love her, and because she loves me," I answered. "What has that to do with you, Hendrika?"

"Because you love her," she hissed in answer; "and do I not love her also, who saved me from the *babyans*? I am a woman as she is, and you are a man, and they say in the *kraals* that men love women better than women love women. But it is a lie, though this is true, that if a woman loves a man she forgets all other love. Have I not seen it? I gather her flowers—beautiful flowers; I climb the rocks where you would never dare to go to find them; you pluck a piece of orange bloom in the garden and give it to her. What does she do?—she takes the orange bloom, she puts it in her breast, and lets my flowers die. I call to her—she does not hear me—she is thinking. You whisper to someone far away, and she hears and smiles. She used to kiss me sometimes; now she kisses that white brat you brought, because you brought it. Oh, I see it all—all; I have seen it from the first; you are stealing her from us, stealing her to yourself, and those who loved her before you came are forgotten. Be careful, Macumazahn, be careful, lest I am revenged upon you. You, you hate me; you think me half a monkey; that servant of yours calls me Baboon-woman. Well, I have lived with baboons, and they are clever—yes, they can play tricks and know things that you don't, and I am cleverer than they, for I have learnt the wisdom of white people also, and I say to you, Walk softly, Macumazahn, or you will fall into a pit," and with one more look of malice she was gone.

I stood for a moment reflecting. I was afraid of this strange creature who seemed to combine the cunning of the great apes that had reared her with the passions and skill of human kind. I foreboded evil at her hands. And yet there was something almost touching in the fierceness of her jealousy. It is generally supposed that this passion only exists in strength when the object loved is of another sex from the lover, but I confess that, both in this instance and in some others which I have met with, this has not been my experience. I have known men, and especially uncivilized men, who were as jealous of the affection of their friend or master as any lover could be of that of his mistress; and who has not seen cases of the same thing where parents and their children are concerned? But the lower one gets in the scale of humanity, the more readily this passion thrives; indeed, it may be said to come to its intensest perfection in brutes. Women are more jealous than men, small-hearted men are more jealous than those of larger mind and wider sympathy, and animals are the most jealous of all. Now Hendrika was in some ways not far removed from animal, which may perhaps account for the ferocity of her jealousy of her mistress's affection.

Shaking off my presentiments of evil, I entered the centre hut. Mr. Carson was resting on the sofa, and by him knelt Stella holding his hand, and her head resting on his breast. I saw at once that she had been telling him of what had come about between us; nor was I sorry, for it is a task that a would-be son-in-law is generally glad to do by deputy.

"Come here, Allan Quatermain," he said, almost sternly, and my heart gave a jump, for I feared lest he might be about to require me to go about my business. But I came.

"Stella tells me," he went on, "that you two have entered into a marriage engagement. She tells me also that she loves you, and that you say that you love her."

"I do indeed, sir," I broke in; "I love her truly; if ever a woman was loved in this world, I love her."

"I thank Heaven for it," said the old man. "Listen, my children. Many years ago a great shame and sorrow fell upon me, so great a sorrow that, as I sometimes think, it affected my brain. At any rate, I determined to do what most men would have considered the act of a madman, to go far away into the wilderness with my only child, there to live remote from civilization and its evils. I did so; I found this place, and here we have lived for many years, happily enough, and perhaps not without doing good in our generation, but still in a way unnatural to our race and status. At first I thought I would let my daughter grow up in a state of complete ignorance, that she should be Nature's child. But as time went on, I saw the folly and the wickedness of my plan. I had no right to degrade her to the level of the savages around me, for if the fruit of the tree of knowledge is a bitter fruit, still it teaches good from evil. So I educated her as well as I was able, till in the end I knew that in mind, as in body, she was in no way inferior to her sisters, the children of the civilized world. She grew up and entered into womanhood, and then it came into my mind that I was doing her a bitter wrong, that I was separating her from her kind and keeping her in a wilderness where she could find neither mate nor companion. But though I knew this, I could not yet make up my mind to return to active life; I had grown to love this place. I dreaded to return into the world I had abjured. Again and again I put my resolutions aside. Then at the commencement of this year I fell ill. For a while I waited, hoping that I might get better, but at last I realized that I should never get better, that the hand of Death was upon me."

"Ah, no, father, not that!" Stella said, with a cry.

"Yes, love, that, and it is true. Now you will be able to forget our separation in the happiness of a new meeting," and he glanced at me and smiled. "Well, when this knowledge came home to me, I determined to abandon this place and trek for the coast, though I well knew that the journey would kill me. I should never live to reach it. But Stella would, and it would be better than leaving her here alone with savages in the wilderness. On the very day that I had made up my mind to take this step Stella found you dying in the Bad Lands, Allan Quatermain, and brought you here. She brought you, of all men in the world, you, whose father had been my dear friend, and who once with your baby hands had saved her life from fire, that she might live to save yours from thirst. At the time I said little, but I saw the hand of Providence in this, and I determined to wait and see what came about between you. At the worst, if nothing came about, I soon learned that I could trust you to see her safely to the coast after I was gone. But many days ago I knew how it stood between you, and now things are determined as I prayed they might be. God bless you both, my children; may you be happy in your love; may it endure till death and beyond it. God bless you both!" and he stretched out his hand towards me.

I took it, and Stella kissed him.

Presently he spoke again—

"It is my intention," he said, "if you two consent, to marry you next Sunday. I wish to do so soon, for I do not know how much longer will be allowed to me. I believe that such a ceremony, solemnly celebrated and entered into before witnesses, will, under the circumstances, be perfectly legal; but of course you will repeat it with every formality the first moment it lies in your power so to do. And now, there is one more thing: when I left England my fortunes were in a shattered condition; in the course of years they have recovered themselves, the accumulated rents, as I heard but recently, when the wagons last returned from Port Natal, have sufficed to pay off all charges, and there is a considerable balance over. Consequently you will not marry on nothing, for of course you, Stella, are my heiress, and I wish to make a stipulation. It is this. That so soon as my death occurs you should leave this place and take the first opportunity of returning to England. I do not ask you to live there always; it might prove too much for people reared in the wilds, as both of you have been; but I do ask you to make it your permanent home. Do you consent and promise this?"

"I do," I answered.

"And so do I," said Stella.

"Very well," he answered; "and now I am tired out. Again God bless you both, and good-night."

Chapter 10

Hendrika Plots Evil

On the following morning I had a conversation with Indaba-zimbi. First of all I told him that I was going to marry Stella.

"Oh!" he said, "I thought so, Macumazahn. Did I not tell you that you would find happiness on this journey? Most men must be content to watch the Star from a long way off, to you it is given to wear her on your heart. But remember, Macumazahn, remember that stars set."

"Can you not stop your croaking even for a day?" I answered, angrily, for his words sent a thrill of fear through me.

"A true prophet must tell the ill as well as the good, Macumazahn. I only speak what is on my mind. But what of it? What is life but loss, loss upon loss, till life itself be lost? But in death we may find all the things that we have lost. So your father taught, Macumazahn, and there was wisdom in his gentleness. *Ou!* I do not believe in death; it is change, that is all, Macumazahn. Look now, the rain falls, the drops of rain that were one water in the clouds fall side by side. They sink into the ground; presently the sun will come out, the earth will be dry, the drops will be gone. A fool looks and says the drops are dead, they will never be one again, they will never again fall side by side. But I am a rain-maker, and I know the ways of rain. It is not true. The drops will drain by many paths into the river, and will be one water there. They will go up to the clouds again in the mists of morning, and there will again be as they have been. We are the drops of rain, Macumazahn. When we fall that is our life. When we sink into the ground that is death, and when we are drawn up again to the sky, what is that, Macumazahn? No! no! when we find we lose, and when we seem to lose, then we shall really find. I am not a Christian, Macumazahn, but I am old, and have watched and seen things that perhaps Christians do not see. There, I have spoken. Be happy with your star, and if it sets, wait, Macumazahn, wait till it rises again. It will not be long; one day you will go to sleep, then your eyes will open on another sky, and there your star will be shining, Macumazahn."

I made no answer at the time. I could not bear to talk of such a thing. But often and often in the after years I have thought of Indabazimbi and his beautiful simile and gathered comfort from it. He was a strange man, this old rain-making savage, and there was more wisdom in him than in many learned atheists—those spiritual destroyers who, in the name of progress and humanity, would divorce hope from life, and leave us wandering in a lonesome, self-consecrated hell.

"Indaba-zimbi," I said, changing the subject, "I have something to say," and I told him of the threats of Hendrika.

He listened with an unmoved face, nodding his white lock at intervals as the narrative went on. But I saw that he was disturbed by it.

"Macumazahn," he said at length, "I have told you that this is an evil woman. She was nourished on baboon milk, and the baboon nature is in her veins. Such creatures should be killed, not kept. She will make you mischief if she can. But I will watch her, Macumazahn. Look, the Star is waiting for you; go, or she will hate me as Hendrika hates you."

So I went, nothing loth, for attractive as was the wisdom of Indabazimbi, I found a deeper meaning in Stella's simplest word. All the rest of that day I passed in her company, and the greater part of the two following days. At last came Saturday night, the eve of our marriage. It rained that night, so we did not go out, but spent the evening in the hut. We sat hand in hand, saying little, but Mr. Carson talked a good deal, telling us tales of his youth, and of countries that he had visited. Then he read aloud from the Bible, and bade us goodnight. I also kissed Stella and went to bed. I reached my hut by the covered way, and before I undressed opened the door to see what the night was like. It was very dark, and rain was still falling, but as the light streamed out into the gloom I fancied that I caught sight of a dusky form gliding away. The thought of Hendrika flashed into my mind; could she be skulking about outside there? Now I had said nothing of Hendrika and her threats either to Mr. Carson or Stella, because I did not wish to alarm them. Also I knew that Stella was attached to this strange person, and I did not wish to shake her confidence in her unless it was absolutely necessary. For a minute or two I stood hesitating, then, reflecting that if it was Hendrika, there she should stop, I went in and put up the stout wooden bar that was used to secure the door. For the last few nights old Indaba-zimbi had made a habit of sleeping in the covered passage, which was the only other possible way of access. As I came to bed I had stepped over him rolled up in his blanket, and to all appearances fast asleep. So it being evident that I had nothing to fear, I promptly dismissed the matter from my mind, which, as may be imagined, was indeed fully occupied with other thoughts.

I got into bed, and for awhile lay awake thinking of the great happiness in store for me, and of the providential course of events that had brought it within my reach. A few weeks since and I was wandering in the desert a dying man, bearing a dying child, and with scarcely a possession left in the world except a store of buried ivory that I never expected to see again. And now I was about to wed one of the sweetest and loveliest women on the whole earth—a woman whom I loved more than I could have thought possible, and who loved me back again. Also, as though that were not good fortune enough, I was to acquire with her very considerable possessions, quite sufficiently large to enable us to follow any plan of life we found agreeable. As I lay and reflected on all this I grew afraid of my good fortune. Old Indaba-zimbi's melancholy prophecies came into my mind. Hitherto he had always prophesied truly. What if these should be true also? I turned cold as I thought of it, and prayed to the Power above to preserve us both to live and love together. Never was prayer more needed. While its words were still upon my lips I dropped asleep and dreamed a most dreadful dream.

I dreamed that Stella and I were standing together to be married. She was dressed in white, and radiant with beauty, but it was a wild, spiritual beauty which frightened me. Her eyes shone like stars, a pale flame played about her features, and the wind that blew did not stir her hair. Nor was this all, for her white robes were death wrappings, and the altar at which we stood was formed of the piled-up earth from an open grave that yawned between us. So we stood waiting for one to wed us, but no one came. Presently from the open grave sprang the form of Hendrika. In her hand was a knife, with which she stabbed at me, but pierced the heart of Stella, who, without a cry, fell backwards into the grave, still looking at me as she fell. Then Hendrika leaped after her into the grave. I heard her feet strike heavily.

"Awake, Macumazahn! awake!" cried the voice of Indaba-zimbi.

I awoke and bounded from the bed, a cold perspiration pouring from me. In the darkness on the other side of the hut I heard sounds of furious struggling. Luckily I kept my head. Just by me was a chair on which were matches and a rush taper. I struck a match and held it to the taper. Now in the growing light I could see two forms rolling one over the other on the floor, and from between them came the flash of steel. The fat melted and the light burnt up. It was Indaba-zimbi and the woman Hendrika who were struggling, and, what is more, the woman was getting the better of the man, strong as he was. I rushed towards them. Now she was uppermost, now she had wrenched herself from his fierce grip, and now the great knife she had in her hand flashed up.

But I was behind her, and, placing my hands beneath her arms, jerked with all my strength. She fell backwards, and, in her effort to save herself, most fortunately dropped the knife. Then we flung ourselves upon her. Heavens! the strength of that she-devil! Nobody who has not experienced it could believe it. She fought and scratched and bit, and at one time nearly mastered the two of us. As it was she did break loose. She rushed at the bed, sprung on it, and bounded thence straight up at the roof of the hut. I never saw such a jump, and could not conceive what she meant to do. In the roof were the peculiar holes which I have described. They were designed to admit light, and covered with overhanging eaves. She sprung straight and true like a monkey, and, catching the edge of the hole with her hands, strove to draw herself through it. But here her strength, exhausted with the long struggle, failed her. For a moment she swung, then dropped to the ground and fell senseless.

"*Ou!*" gasped Indaba-zimbi. "Let us tie the devil up before she comes to life again."

I thought this a good counsel, so we took a *reim* that lay in the corner of the room, and lashed her hands and feet in such a fashion that even she could scarcely escape. Then we carried her into the passage, and Indaba-zimbi sat over her, the knife in his hand, for I did not wish to raise an alarm at that hour of the night.

"Do you know how I caught her, Macumazahn?" he said. "For several nights I have slept here with one eye open, for I thought she had made a plan. Tonight I kept wide awake, though I pretended to be asleep. An hour after you got into the blankets the moon rose, and I saw a beam of light come into the hut through the hole in the roof. Presently I saw the beam of light vanish. At first I thought that a cloud was passing over the moon, but I listened and heard a noise as though someone was squeezing himself through a narrow space. Presently he was through, and hanging by his hands. Then the light came in again, and in the middle of it I saw the *Babyan-frau* swinging from the roof, and about to drop into the hut. She clung by both hands, and in her mouth was a great knife. She dropped, and I ran forward to seize her as she dropped, and gripped her round the middle. But she heard me come, and, seizing the knife, struck at me in the dark and missed me. Then we struggled, and you know the rest. You were very nearly dead tonight, Macumazahn."

"Very nearly indeed," I answered, still panting, and arranging the rags of my night-dress round me as best I might. Then the memory of my horrid dream flashed into my mind. Doubtless it had been conjured up by the sound of Hendrika dropping to the floor—in my dream it had been a grave that she dropped into. All of it, then, had been experienced in that second of time. Well, dreams are swift; perhaps Time itself is nothing but a dream, and events that seem far apart really occur simultaneously.

We passed the rest of the night watching Hendrika. Presently she came to herself and struggled furiously to break the *reim*. But the untanned buffalo hide was too strong even for her, and, moreover, Indaba-zimbi unceremoniously sat upon her to keep her quiet. At last she gave it up.

In due course the day broke—my marriage day. Leaving Indaba-zimbi to watch my would-be murderess, I went and fetched some natives from the stables, and with their aid bore Hendrika to the prison hut—that same hut in which she had been confined when she had been brought a baboon-child from the rocks. Here we shut her up, and, leaving Indaba-zimbi to watch outside, I returned to my sleeping-place and dressed in the best garments that the Babyan *Kraals* could furnish. But when I looked at the reflection of my face, I was horrified. It was covered with scratches inflicted by the nails of Hendrika. I doctored them up as best I could, then went out for a walk to calm my nerves, which, what between the events of the past night, and of those pending that day, were not a little disturbed.

When I returned it was breakfast time. I went into the dining hut, and there Stella was waiting to greet me, dressed in simple white and with orange flowers on her breast. She came forward to me shyly enough; then, seeing the condition of my face, started back.

"Why, Allan! what have you been doing to yourself?" she asked.

As I was about to answer, her father came in leaning on his stick, and, catching sight of me, instantly asked the same question.

Then I told them everything, both of Hendrika's threats and of her fierce attempt to carry them into execution. But I did not tell my horrid dream.

Stella's face grew white as the flowers on her breast, but that of her father became very stern.

"You should have spoken of this before, Allan," he said. "I now see that I did wrong to attempt to civilize this wicked and revengeful creature, who, if she is human, has all the evil passions of the brutes that reared her. Well, I will make an end of it this very day."

"Oh, father," said Stella, "don't have her killed. It is all dreadful enough, but that would be more dreadful still. I have been very fond of her, and, bad as she is, she has loved me. Do not have her killed on my marriage day."

"No," her father answered, "she shall not be killed, for though she deserves to die, I will not have her blood upon our hands. She is a brute, and has followed the nature of brutes. She shall go back whence she came."

No more was said on the matter at the time, but when breakfast—which was rather a farce—was done, Mr. Carson sent for his headman and gave him certain orders.

We were to be married after the service which Mr. Carson held every Sunday morning in the large marble hut set apart for that purpose. The service began at ten o'clock, but long before that hour all the natives on the place came up in troops, singing as they came, to be present at the wedding of the "Star." It was a pretty sight to see them, the men dressed in all their finery, and carrying shields and sticks in their hands, and the women and children bearing green branches of trees, ferns, and flowers. At length, about half-past nine, Stella rose, pressed my hand, and left me to my reflections. A few minutes to ten she reappeared again with her father, dressed in a white veil, a wreath of orange flowers on her dark curling hair, a bouquet of orange flowers in her hand. To me she seemed like a dream of loveliness. With her came little Tota in a high state of glee and excitement. She was Stella's only bridesmaid. Then we all passed out towards the church hut. The bare space in front of it was filled with hundreds of natives, who set up a song as we came. But we went on into the hut, which was crowded with such of the natives as usually worshipped there. Here Mr. Carson, as usual, read the service, though he was obliged to sit down in order to do so. When it was done—and to me it seemed interminable—Mr. Carson whispered that he meant to marry us outside the hut in sight of all the people. So we went out and took our stand under the shade of a large tree that grew near the hut facing the bare space where the natives were gathered.

Mr. Carson held up his hand to enjoin silence. Then, speaking in the native dialect, he told them that he was about to make us man and wife after the Christian fashion and in the sight of all men. This done, he proceeded to read the marriage service over us, and very solemnly and beautifully he did it. We said the words, I placed the ring—it was her father's signet ring, for we had no other—upon Stella's finger, and it was done.

Then Mr. Carson spoke. "Allan and Stella," he said, "I believe that the ceremony which has been performed makes you man and wife in the sight of God and man, for all that is necessary to make a marriage binding is, that it should be celebrated according to the custom of the country where the parties to it reside. It is according to the custom that has been in force here for fifteen years or more that you have been married in the face of all the people, and in token of it you will both sign the register that I have kept of such marriages, among those of my people who have adopted the Christian Faith. Still, in case there should be any legal flaw I again demand the solemn promise of you both that on the first opportunity you will cause this marriage to be re-celebrated in some civilized land. Do you promise?"

"We do," we answered.

Then the book was brought out and we signed our names. At first my wife signed hers "Stella" only, but her father bade her write it Stella Carson for the first and last time in her life. Then several of the *indunas*, or headmen, including old Indaba-zimbi, put their marks in witness. Indaba-zimbi drew his mark in the shape of a little star, in humorous allusion to Stella's native name. That register is before me now as I write. That, with a lock of my darling's hair which lies between its leaves, is my dearest possession. There are all the names and marks as they were written many years ago beneath the shadow of the tree at Babyan *kraals* in the wilderness, but alas! and alas! where are those who wrote them?

"My people," said Mr. Carson, when the signing was done, and we had kissed each other before them all—"My people, Macumazahn and the Star, my daughter, are now man and wife, to live in one *kraal*, to eat of one bowl, to share one fortune till they reach the grave. Hear now, my people, you know this woman," and turning he pointed to Hendrika, who, unseen by us, had been led out of the prison hut.

"Yes, yes, we know her," said a little ring of headmen, who formed the primitive court of justice, and after the fashion of natives had squatted themselves in a circle on the ground in front of us. "We know her, she is the white Babyan-woman, she is Hendrika, the body servant of the Star."

"You know her," said Mr. Carson, "but you do not know her altogether. Stand forward, Indaba-zimbi, and tell the people what came about last night in the hut of Macumazahn."

Accordingly old Indaba-zimbi came forward, and, squatting down, told his moving tale with much descriptive force and many gestures, finishing up by producing the great knife from which his watchfulness had saved me.

Then I was called upon, and in a few brief words substantiated his story: indeed my face did that in the sight of all men.

Then Mr. Carson turned to Hendrika, who stood in sullen silence, her eyes fixed upon the ground, and asked her if she had anything to say.

She looked up boldly and answered—

"Macumazahn has robbed me of the love of my mistress. I would have robbed him of his life, which is a little thing compared to that which I have lost at his hands. I have failed, and I am sorry for it, for had I killed him and left no trace the Star would have forgotten him and shone on me again."

"Never," murmured Stella in my ear; but Mr. Carson turned white with wrath.

"My people," he said, "you hear the words of this woman. You hear how she pays me back, me and my daughter whom she swears she loves. She says that she would have murdered a man who has done her no evil, the man who is the husband of her mistress. We saved her from the *babyans*, we tamed her, we fed her, we taught her, and this is how she pays us back. Say, my people, what reward should be given to her?"

"Death," said the circle of *indunas*, pointing their thumbs downwards, and all the multitude beyond echoed the word "Death."

"Death," repeated the head *induna*, adding, "If you save her, my father, we will slay her with our own hands. She is a Babyan-woman, a devil-woman; ah, yes, we have heard of such before; let her be slain before she works more evil."

Then it was that Stella stepped forward and begged for Hendrika's life in moving terms. She pleaded the savagery of the woman's nature, her long service, and the affection that she had always shown towards herself. She said that I, whose life had been attempted, forgave her, and she, my wife, who had nearly been left a widow before she was made a bride, forgave her; let them forgive her also, let her be sent away, not slain, let not her marriage day be stained with blood.

Now her father listened readily enough, for he had no intention of killing Hendrika—indeed, he had already promised not to do so. But the people were in a different humour, they looked upon Hendrika as a devil, and would have torn her to pieces there and then, could they have had their way. Nor were matters mended by Indaba-zimbi, who had already gained a great reputation for wisdom and magic in the place. Suddenly the old man rose and made quite an impassioned speech, urging them to kill Hendrika at once or mischief would come of it.

At last matters got very bad, for two of the *Indunas* came forward to drag her off to execution, and it was not until Stella burst into tears that the sight of her grief, backed by Mr. Carson's orders and my own remonstrances, carried the day.

All this while Hendrika had been standing quite unmoved. At last the tumult ceased, and the leading *induna* called to her to go, promising that if ever she showed her face near the *kraals* again she should be stabbed like a jackal. Then Hendrika spoke to Stella in a low voice and in English—

"Better let them kill me, mistress, better for all. Without you to love I shall go mad and become a *babyan* again."

Stella did not answer, and they loosed her. She stepped forward and looked at the natives with a stare of hate. Then she turned and walked past me, and as she passed whispered a native phrase in my ear, that, being literally translated, means, "Till another moon," but which has the same significance as the French *au revoir*.

It frightened me, for I knew she meant that she had not done with me, and saw that our mercy was misplaced. Seeing my face change she ran swiftly from me, and as she passed Indaba-zimbi, with a sudden movement snatched her great knife from his hand. When she had gone about twenty paces she halted, looked long and earnestly on Stella, gave one loud cry of anguish, and fled. A few minutes later we saw her far away, bounding up the face of an almost perpendicular cliff—a cliff that nobody except herself and the baboons could possibly climb.

"Look," said Indaba-zimbi in my ear—"Look, Macumazahn, there goes the *Babyan-frau*. But, Macumazahn, *she will come back again*. Ah, why will you not listen to my words. Have they not always been true words, Macumazahn?" and he shrugged his shoulders and turned away.

For a while I was much disturbed, but at any rate Hendrika was gone for the present, and Stella, my dear and lovely wife, was there at my side, and in her smiles I forgot my fears.

For the rest of that day, why should I write of it?—there are things too happy and too sacred to be written of.

At last I had, if only for a little while, found that rest, that perfect joy which we seek so continually and so rarely clasp.

CHAPTER 11

Gone!

I wonder if many married couples are quite as happy as we found ourselves. Cynics, a growing class, declare that few illusions can survive a honeymoon. Well, I do not know about it, for I only married once, and can but speak from my limited experience. But certainly our illusion, or rather the great truth of which it is the shadow, did survive, as to this day it survives in my heart across all the years of utter separation, and across the unanswering gulf of gloom.

But complete happiness is not allowed in this world even for an hour. As our marriage day had been shadowed by the scene which has been described, so our married life was shadowed by its own sorrow.

Three days after our wedding Mr. Carson had a stroke. It had been long impending, now it fell. We came into the centre hut to dinner and found him lying speechless on the couch. At first I thought that he was dying, but this was not so. On the contrary, within four days he recovered his speech and some power of movement. But he never recovered his memory, though he still knew Stella, and sometimes myself. Curiously enough he remembered little Tota best of all three, though occasionally he thought that she was his own daughter in her childhood, and would ask her where her mother was. This state of affairs lasted for some seven months. The old man gradually grew weaker, but he did not die. Of course his condition quite precluded the idea of our leaving Babyan *Kraals* till all was over. This was the more distressing to me because I had a nervous presentiment that Stella was incurring danger by staying there, and also because the state of her health rendered it desirable that we should reach a civilized region as soon as possible. However, it could not be helped.

At length the end came very suddenly. We were sitting one evening by Mr. Carson's bedside in his hut, when to our astonishment he sat up and spoke in a strong, full voice.

"I hear you," he said. "Yes, yes, I forgive you. Poor woman! you too have suffered," and he fell back dead.

I have little doubt that he was addressing his lost wife, some vision of whom had flashed across his dying sense. Stella, of course, was overwhelmed with grief at her loss. Till I came her father had been her sole companion, and therefore, as may be imagined, the tie between them was much closer than is usual even in the case of father and daughter. So deeply did she mourn that I began to fear for the effect upon her health. Nor were we the only ones to grieve; all the natives on the settlement called Mr. Carson *father*, and as a father they lamented him. The air resounded with the wailing of women, and the men went about with bowed heads, saying that "the sun had set in the heavens, now only the Star (Stella) remained." Indaba-zimbi alone did not mourn. He said that it was best that the *Inkoos* should die, for what was life worth when one lay like a log?—moreover, that it would have been well for all if he had died sooner.

On the following day we buried him in the little graveyard near the waterfall. It was a sad business, and Stella cried very much, in spite of all I could do to comfort her.

That night as I sat outside the hut smoking—for the weather was hot, and Stella was lying down inside—old Indaba-zimbi came up, saluted, and squatted at my feet.

"What is it, Indaba-zimbi?" I said.

"This, Macumazahn. When are you going to trek towards the coast?"

"I don't know," I answered. "The Star is not fit to travel now, we must wait awhile."

"No, Macumazahn, you must not wait, you must go, and the Star must take her chance. She is strong. It is nothing. All will be well."

"Why do you say so? why must we go?"

"For this reason, Macumazahn," and he looked cautiously round and spoke low. "The baboons have come back in thousands. All the mountain is full of them."

"I did not know that they had gone," I said.

"Yes," he answered, "they went after the marriage, all but one or two; now they are back, all the baboons in the world, I think. I saw a whole cliff back with them."

"Is that all?" I said, for I saw that he had something behind. "I am not afraid of a pack of baboons."

"No, Macumazahn, it is not all. The *Babyan-frau*, Hendrika, is with them."

Now nothing had been heard or seen of Hendrika since her ex-

pulsion, and though at first she and her threats had haunted me somewhat, by degrees she to a great extent had passed out of my mind,
which was fully preoccupied with Stella and my father-in-law's illness.
I started violently. "How do you know this?" I asked.

"I know it because I saw her, Macumazahn. She is disguised, she is
dressed up in baboon skins, and her face is stained dark. But though
she was a long way off, I knew her by her size, and I saw the white
flesh of her arm when the skins slipped aside. She has come back,
Macumazahn, with all the baboons in the world, and she has come
back to do evil. Now do you understand why you should trek?"

"Yes," I said, "though I don't see how she and the baboons can
harm us, I think that it will be better to go. If necessary we can camp
the wagons somewhere for a while on the journey. Hearken, Indaba-
zimbi: say nothing of this to the Star; I will not have her frightened.
And hearken again. Speak to the headmen, and see that watchers are
set all round the huts and gardens, and kept there night and day. To-
morrow we will get the wagons ready, and next day we will trek."

He nodded his white lock and went to do my bidding, leaving me
not a little disturbed—unreasonably so, indeed. It was a strange story.
That this woman had the power of conversing with baboons I knew.[1]
That was not so very wonderful, seeing that the Bushmen claim to
be able to do the same thing, and she had been nurtured by them.
But that she had been able to muster them, and by the strength of
her human will and intelligence muster them in order to forward her
ends of revenge, seemed to me so incredible that after reflection my
fears grew light. Still I determined to trek. After all, a journey in an
ox wagon would not be such a very terrible thing to a strong woman
accustomed to roughing it, whatever her state of health. And when all
was said and done I did not like this tale of the presence of Hendrika
with countless hosts of baboons.

So I went in to Stella, and without saying a word to her of the baboon story, told her I had been thinking matters over, and had come to
the conclusion that it was our duty to follow her father's instructions
to the letter, and leave Babyan *Kraals* at once. Into all our talk I need
not enter, but the end of it was that she agreed with me, and declared
that she could quite well manage the journey, saying, moreover, that
now that her dear father was dead she would be glad to get away.

Nothing happened to disturb us that night, and on the following

---

1. For an instance of this, see Anderson's *Twenty-five Years in a Wagon*, vol. i. p. 262.—
Editor.

morning I was up early making preparations. The despair of the people when they learned that we were going to leave them was something quite pitiable. I could only console them by declaring that we were but on a journey, and would return the following year.

"They had lived in the shadow of their father, who was dead," they declared; "ever since they were little they had lived in his shadow. He had received them when they were outcasts and wanderers without a mat to lie on, or a blanket to cover them, and they had grown fat in his shadow. Then he had died, and the Star, their father's daughter, had married me, Macumazahn, and they had believed that I should take their father's place, and let them live in my shadow. What should they do when there was no one to protect them? The tribes were kept from attacking them by fear of the white man. If we went they would be eaten up," and so on. Alas! there was but too much foundation for their fears.

I returned to the huts at mid-day to get some dinner. Stella said that she was going to pack during the afternoon, so I did not think it necessary to caution her about going out alone, as I did not wish to allude to the subject of Hendrika and the baboons unless I was obliged to. I told her, however, that I would come back to help her as soon as I could get away. Then I went down to the native *kraals* to sort out such cattle as had belonged to Mr. Carson from those which belonged to the *Kaffirs*, for I proposed to take them with us. It was a large herd, and the business took an incalculable time. At length, a little before sundown, I gave it up, and leaving Indaba-zimbi to finish the job, got on my horse and rode homewards.

Arriving, I gave the horse to one of the stable boys, and went into the central hut. There was no sign of Stella, though the things she had been packing lay about the floor. I passed first into our sleeping hut, thence one by one into all the others, but still saw no sign of her. Then I went out, and calling to a *Kaffir* in the garden asked him if he had seen his mistress.

He answered "yes." He had seen her carrying flowers and walking towards the graveyard, holding the little white girl—my daughter—as he called her, by the hand, when the sun stood "there," and he pointed to a spot on the horizon where it would have been about an hour and a half before. "The two dogs were with them," he added. I turned and ran towards the graveyard, which was about a quarter of a mile from the huts. Of course there was no reason to be anxious—evidently she had gone to lay the flowers on her father's grave. And yet I was anxious.

When I got near the graveyard I met one of the natives, who, by my orders, had been set round the *kraals* to watch the place, and noticed that he was rubbing his eyes and yawning. Clearly he had been asleep. I asked him if he had seen his mistress, and he answered that he had not, which under the circumstances was not wonderful. Without stopping to reproach him, I ordered the man to follow me, and went on to the graveyard. There, on Mr. Carson's grave, lay the drooping flowers which Stella had been carrying, and there in the fresh mould was the spoor of Tota's *veldschoon*, or hide slipper. But where were they?

I ran from the graveyard and called aloud at the top of my voice, but no answer came. Meanwhile the native was more profitably engaged in tracing their spoor. He followed it for about a hundred yards till he came to a clump of mimosa bush that was situated between the stream and the ancient marble quarries just over the waterfall, and at the mouth of the ravine. Here he stopped, and I heard him give a startled cry. I rushed to the spot, passed through the trees, and saw this. The little open space in the centre of the glade had been the scene of a struggle. There, in the soft earth, were the marks of three pairs of human feet—two shod, one naked—Stella's, Tota's, and *Hendrika's*. Nor was this all. There, close by, lay the fragments of the two dogs—they were nothing more—and one baboon, not yet quite dead, which had been bitten in the throat by the dogs. All round was the spoor of numberless baboons. The full horror of what had happened flashed into my mind.

My wife and Tota had been carried off by the baboons. As yet they had not been killed, for if so their remains would have been found with those of the dogs. They had been carried off. The brutes, acting under the direction of that woman-monkey, Hendrika, had dragged them away to some secret den, there to keep them till they died—or kill them!

For a moment I literally staggered beneath the terror of the shock. Then I roused myself from my despair. I bade the native run and alarm the people at the *kraals*, telling them to come armed, and bring me guns and ammunition. He went like the wind, and I turned to follow the spoor. For a few yards it was plain enough—Stella had been dragged along. I could see where her heels had struck the ground; the child had, I presumed, been carried—at least there were no marks of her feet. At the water's edge the spoor vanished. The water was shallow, and they had gone along in it, or at least Hendrika and her victim had, in order to obliterate the trail. I could see where a moss-grown stone had been freshly turned over in the water-bed. I ran along the bank some way up the ravine, in the vain hope of catching a sight of them. Presently I heard a bark in the cliffs above me; it was answered by another, and then I saw that scores of baboons were hidden about among the rocks on either side, and were softly swinging themselves down to bar the path. To go on unarmed as I was would be useless. I should only be torn to pieces as the dogs had been. So I turned and fled back towards the huts. As I drew near I could see that my messenger had roused the settlement, for natives with spears and *kerries* in their hands were running up towards the *kraals*. When I reached the hut I met old Indaba-zimbi, who wore a very serious face.

"So the evil has fallen, Macumazahn," he said.

"It has fallen," I answered.

"Keep a good heart, Macumazahn," he said again. "She is not dead, nor is the little maid, and before they die we shall find them. Remember this, Hendrika loves her. She will not harm her, or allow the *babyans* to harm her. She will try to hide her away from you, that is all."

"Pray God that we may find her," I groaned. "The light is going fast."

"The moon rises in three hours," he answered; "we will search by moonlight. It is useless to start now; see, the sun sinks. Let us get the men together, eat, and make things ready. *Hamba gachla*. Hasten slowly, Macumazahn."

As there was no help, I took his advice. I could eat no food, but I packed some up to take with us, and made ready ropes, and a rough kind of litter. If we found them they would scarcely be able to walk. Ah! if we found them! How slowly the time passed! It seemed hours before the moon rose. But at last it did rise.

Then we started. In all we were about a hundred men, but we only mustered five guns between us, my elephant *roer* and four that had belonged to Mr. Carson.

CHAPTER 12

The Magic of Indaba-Zimbi

We gained the spot by the stream where Stella had been taken. The natives looked at the torn fragments of the dogs, and at the marks of violence, and I heard them swearing to each other, that whether the Star lived or died they would not rest till they had exterminated every baboon on Babyan's Peak. I echoed the oath, and, as shall be seen, we kept it.

We started on along the stream, following the spoor of the baboons as we best could. But the stream left no spoor, and the hard, rocky banks very little. Still we wandered on. All night we wandered through the lonely moonlit valleys, startling the silence into a thousand echoes with our cries. But no answer came to them. In vain our eyes searched the sides of precipices formed of water-riven rocks fantastically piled one upon another; in vain we searched through endless dells and fern-clad crannies. There was nothing to be found. How could we expect to find two human beings hidden away in the recesses of this vast stretch of mountain ground, which no man yet had ever fully explored. They were lost, and in all human probability lost forever.

To and fro we wandered hopelessly, till at last dawn found us foot-sore and weary nearly at the spot whence we had started. We sat down waiting for the sun to rise, and the men ate of such food as they had brought with them, and sent to the *kraals* for more.

I sat upon a stone with a breaking heart. I cannot describe my feelings. Let the reader put himself in my position and perhaps he may get some idea of them. Near me was old Indaba-zimbi, who sat staring straight before him as though he were looking into space, and taking note of what went on there. An idea struck me. This man had some occult power. Several times during our adventures he had prophesied, and in every case his prophecies had proved true. He it was who, when we escaped from the Zulu *Impi*, had told me to steer north, because there we should find the place of a white man who lived under the shadow of a great peak that was full of baboons. Perhaps he could help in this extremity—at any rate it was worth trying.

"Indaba-zimbi," I said, "you say that you can send your spirit through the doors of space and see what we cannot see. At the least I know that you can do strange things. Can you not help me now? If you can, and will save her, I will give you half the cattle that we have here."

"I never said anything of the sort, Macumazahn," he answered. "I do things, I do not talk about them. Neither do I seek reward for what I do like a common witch-doctor. It is well that you have asked me to use my wisdom, Macumazahn, for I should not have used it again without being asked—no, not even for the sake of the Star and yourself, whom I love, for if so my Spirit would have been angry. In the other matters I had a part, for my life was concerned as well as yours; but in this matter I have no part, and therefore I might not use my wisdom unless you thought well to call upon my Spirit. However, it would have been no good to ask me before, for I have only just found the herb I want," and he produced a handful of the leaves of a plant that was unfamiliar to me. It had prickly leaves, shaped very much like those of the common English nettle.

"Now, Macumazahn," he went on, "bid the men leave us alone, and then follow me presently to the little glade down there by the water."

I did so. When I reached the glade I found Indaba-zimbi kindling a small fire under the shadow of a tree by the edge of the water.

"Sit there, Macumazahn," he said, pointing to a stone near the fire, "and do not be surprised or frightened at anything you see. If you move or call out we shall learn nothing."

I sat down and watched. When the fire was alight and burning brightly, the old fellow stripped himself stark naked, and, going to the foot of the pool, dipped himself in the water. Then he came back shivering with the cold, and, leaning over the little fire, thrust leaves of the plant I have mentioned into his mouth and began to chew them, muttering as he chewed. Most of the remaining leaves he threw on to the fire. A dense smoke rose from them, but he held his head in this smoke and drew it down his lungs till I saw that he was exhibiting every sign of suffocation. The veins in his throat and chest swelled, he gasped loudly, and his eyes, from which tears were streaming, seemed as though they were going to start from his head. Presently he fell over on his side, and lay senseless. I was terribly alarmed, and my first impulse was to run to his assistance, but fortunately I remembered his caution, and sat quiet.

Indaba-zimbi lay on the ground like a person quite dead. His limbs had all the utter relaxation of death. But as I watched I saw them begin to stiffen, exactly as though *rigor mortis* had set in. Then, to my astonishment, I perceived them once more relax, and this time there appeared upon his chest the stain of decomposition. It spread and spread; in three minutes the man, to all appearance, was a livid corpse.

I sat amazed watching this uncanny sight, and wondering if any further natural process was about to be enacted. Perhaps Indaba-zimbi was going to fall to dust before my eyes. As I watched I observed that the discoloration was beginning to fade. First it vanished from the extremities, then from the larger limbs, and lastly from the trunk. Then in turn came the third stage of relaxation, the second stage of stiffness or *rigor*, and the first stage of after-death collapse. When all these had rapidly succeeded each other, Indaba-zimbi quietly woke up.

I was too astonished to speak; I simply looked at him with my mouth open.

"Well, Macumazahn," he said, putting his head on one side like a bird, and nodding his white lock in a comical fashion, "it is all right; I have seen her."

"Seen who?" I said.

"The Star, your wife, and the little maid. They are much frightened, but unharmed. The Babyan-frau watches them. She is mad, but the baboons obey her, and do not hurt them. The Star was sleeping from weariness, so I whispered in her ear and told her not to be frightened, for you would soon rescue her, and that meanwhile she must seem to be pleased to have Hendrika near her."

"You whispered in her ear?" I said. "How could you whisper in her ear?"

"*Bah!* Macumazahn. How could I seem to die and go rotten before your eyes? You don't know, do you? Well, I will tell you one thing. I had to die to pass the doors of space, as you call them. I had to draw all the healthy strength and life from my body in order to gather power to speak with the Star. It was a dangerous business, Macumazahn, for if I had let things go a little further they must have stopped so, and there would have been an end of Indaba-zimbi. Ah, you white men, you know so much that you think you know everything. But you don't! You are always staring at the clouds and can't see the things that lie at your feet. You hardly believe me now, do you, Macumazahn? Well, I will show you. Have you anything on you that the Star has touched or worn?"

I thought for a moment, and said that I had a lock of her hair in my pocket-book. He told me to give it him. I did so. Going to the fire, he lit the lock of hair in the flame, and let it burn to ashes, which he caught in his left hand. These ashes he mixed up in a paste with the juice of one of the leaves of the plant I have spoken of.

"Now, Macumazahn, shut your eyes," he said.

I did so, and he rubbed his paste on to my eyelids. At first it burnt me, then my head swam strangely. Presently this effect passed off, and my brain was perfectly clear again, but I could not feel the ground with my feet. Indaba-zimbi led me to the side of the stream. Beneath us was a pool of beautifully clear water.

"Look into the pool, Macumazahn," said Indaba-zimbi, and his voice sounded hollow and far away in my ears.

I looked. The water grew dark; it cleared, and in it was a picture. I saw a cave with a fire burning in it. Against the wall of the cave rested Stella. Her dress was torn almost off her, she looked dreadfully pale and weary, and her eyelids were red as though with weeping. But she slept, and I could almost think that I saw her lips shape my name in her sleep. Close to her, her head upon Stella's breast, was little Tota; she had a skin thrown over her to keep out the night cold. The child was awake, and appeared to be moaning with fear. By the fire, and in such a position that the light fell full upon her face, and engaged in cooking something in a rough pot shaped from wood, sat the Baboon-woman, Hendrika. She was clothed in baboon skins, and her face had been rubbed with some dark stain, which was, however, wearing off it. In the intervals of her cooking she would turn on Stella her wild eyes, in which glared visible madness, with an expression of tenderness that amounted to worship. Then she would stare at the child and gnash her teeth as though with hate. Clearly she was jealous of it. Round the entrance arch of the cave peeped and peered the heads of many baboons. Presently Hendrika made a sign to one of them; apparently she did not speak, or rather grunt, in order not to wake Stella. The brute hopped forward, and she gave it a second rude wooden pot which was lying by her. It took it and went. The last thing that I saw, as the vision slowly vanished from the pool, was the dim shadow of the baboon returning with the pot full of water.

Presently everything had gone. I ceased to feel strange. There beneath me was the pool, and at my side stood Indaba-zimbi, smiling.

"You have seen things," he said.

"I have," I answered, and made no further remark on the matter. What was there to say?[1] "Do you know the path to the cave?" I added.

He nodded his head. "I did not follow it all just now, because it winds," he said. "But I know it. We shall want the ropes."

"Then let us be starting; the men have eaten."

He nodded his head again, and going to the men I told them to make ready, adding that Indaba-zimbi knew the way. They said that was all right, if Indaba-zimbi had "smelt her out," they should soon find the Star. So we started cheerfully enough, and my spirits were so much improved that I was able to eat a boiled *mealie* cob or two as we walked.

We went up the valley, following the course of the stream for about a mile; then Indaba-zimbi made a sudden turn to the right, along another *kloof*, of which there were countless numbers in the base of the great hill.

On we went through *kloof* after *kloof*. Indaba-zimbi, who led us, was never at a loss, he turned up gullies and struck across necks of hills with the certainty of a hound on a hot scent. At length, after about three hours' march, we came to a big silent valley on the northern slope of the great peak. On one side of this valley was a series of stony *koppies*, on the other rose a sheer wall of rock. We marched along the wall for a distance of some two miles. Then suddenly Indaba-zimbi halted.

"There is the place," he said, pointing to an opening in the cliff. This opening was about forty feet from the ground, and ellipse-shaped. It cannot have been more than twenty feet high by ten wide, and was partially hidden by ferns and bushes that grew about it in the surface of the cliff. Keen as my eyes were, I doubt if I should ever have noticed it, for there were many such cracks and crannies in the rocky face of the great mountain.

We drew near and looked carefully at the place. The first thing I noticed was that the rock, which was not quite perpendicular, had been worn by the continual passage of baboons; the second, that something white was hanging on a bush near the top of the ascent.

It was a pocket-handkerchief.

Now there was no more doubt about the matter. With a beating heart I began the ascent. For the first twenty feet it was comparatively easy, for the rock shelved; the next ten feet was very difficult, but

---

1. For some almost equally remarkable instances of *Kaffir* magic the reader is referred to a work named *Among the Zulus*, by David Leslie.—Editor.

still possible to an active man, and I achieved it, followed by Indaba-zimbi. But the last twelve or fifteen feet could only be scaled by throwing a rope over the trunk of a stunted tree, which grew at the bottom of the opening. This we accomplished with some trouble, and the rest was easy. A foot or two above my head the handkerchief fluttered in the wind. Hanging to the rope, I grasped it. It was my wife's. As I did so I noticed the face of a baboon peering at me over the edge of the cleft, the first baboon we had seen that morning. The brute gave a bark and vanished. Thrusting the handkerchief into my breast, I set my feet against the cliff and scrambled up as hard as I could go. I knew that we had no time to lose, for the baboon would quickly alarm the others. I gained the cleft. It was a mere arched passage cut by water, ending in a gulley, which led to a wide open space of some sort. I looked through the passage and saw that the gulley was black with baboons. On they came by the hundred. I unslung my elephant gun from my shoulders and waited, calling to the men below to come up with all possible speed. The brutes streamed on down the gloomy gulf towards me, barking, grunting, and showing their huge teeth. I waited till they were within fifteen yards. Then I fired the elephant gun, which was loaded with slugs, right into the thick of them. In that narrow place the report echoed like a cannon shot, but its sound was quickly swallowed in the volley of piercing human-sounding groans and screams that followed. The charge of heavy slugs had ploughed through the host of baboons, of which at least a dozen lay dead or dying in the passage. For a moment they hesitated, then they came on again with a hideous clamour. Fortunately by this time Indaba-zimbi, who also had a gun, was standing by my side, otherwise I should have been torn to pieces before I could re-load. He fired both barrels into them, and again checked the rush. But they came on again, and notwithstanding the appearance of two other natives with guns, which they let off with more or less success, we should have been overwhelmed by the great and ferocious apes had I not by this time succeeded in re-loading the elephant gun. When they were right on us, I fired, with even more deadly effect than before, for at that distance every slug told on their long line. The howls and screams of pain and rage were now something inconceivable. One might have thought that we were doing battle with a host of demons; indeed in that light—for the overhanging arch of rock made it very dark—the gnashing snouts and sombre glowing eyes of the apes looked like those of devils as they are represented by monkish fancy. But the last shot was too much for them; they withdrew, dragging some of their wounded with them, and thus gave us time to get our men up the cliff. In a few minutes all were there, and we advanced down the passage, which presently opened into a rocky gulley with shelving sides. This gulley had a water-way at the bottom of it; it was about a hundred yards long, and the slopes on either side were topped by precipitous cliffs. I looked at these slopes; they literally swarmed with baboons, grunting, barking, screaming, and beating their breasts with their long arms, in fury. I looked up the water-way; along it, accompanied by a mob, or, as it were, a guard of baboons, ran Hendrika, her long hair flying, madness written on her face, and in her arms was the senseless form of little Tota.

She saw us, and a foam of rage burst from her lips. She screamed aloud. To me the sound was a mere inarticulate cry, but the baboons clearly understood it, for they began to roll rocks down on to us. One boulder leaped past me and struck down a *Kaffir* behind; another fell from the roof of the arch on to a man's head and killed him. Indaba-zimbi lifted his gun to shoot Hendrika; I knocked it up, so that the shot went over her, crying that he would kill the child. Then I shouted to the men to open out and form a line from side to side of the shelving gulley. Furious at the loss of their two comrades, they obeyed me, and keeping in the water-way myself, together with Indaba-zimbi and the other guns, I gave the word to charge.

Then the real battle began. It is difficult to say who fought the most fiercely, the natives or the baboons. The *Kaffirs* charged along the slopes, and as they came, encouraged by the screams of Hendrika, who rushed to and fro holding the wretched Tota before her as a shield, the apes bounded at them in fury. Scores were killed by the assegais, and many more fell beneath our gun-shots; but still they came on. Nor did we go scathless. Occasionally a man would slip, or be pulled over in the grip of a baboon. Then the others would fling themselves upon him like dogs on a rat, and worry him to death. We lost five men in this way, and I myself received a bite through the fleshy part of the left arm, but fortunately a native near me *assegaied* the animal before I was pulled down.

At length, and all of a sudden, the baboons gave up. A panic seemed to seize them. Notwithstanding the cries of Hendrika they thought no more of fight, but only of escape; some even did not attempt to get away from the assegais of the *Kaffirs*, they simply hid their horrible faces in their paws, and, moaning piteously, waited to be slain.

Hendrika saw that the battle was lost. Dropping the child from her arms, she rushed straight at us, a very picture of horrible insanity. I lifted my gun, but could not bear to shoot. After all she was but a mad thing, half ape, half woman. So I sprang to one side, and she landed full on Indaba-zimbi, knocking him down. But she did not stay to do any more. Wailing terribly, she rushed down the gulley and through the arch, followed by a few of the surviving baboons, and vanished from our sight.

Chapter 13

What Happened to Stella

The fight was over. In all we had lost seven men killed, and several more severely bitten, while but few had escaped without some tokens whereby he might remember what a baboon's teeth and claws are like. How many of the brutes we killed I never knew, because we did not count, but it was a vast number. I should think that the stock must have been low about Babyan's Peak for many years afterwards. From that day to this, however, I have always avoided baboons, feeling more afraid of them than any beast that lives.

The path was clear, and we rushed forward along the water-course. But first we picked up little Tota. The child was not in a swoon, as I had thought, but paralyzed by terror, so that she could scarcely speak. Otherwise she was unhurt, though it took her many a week to re-cover her nerve. Had she been older, and had she not remembered Hendrika, I doubt if she would have recovered it. She knew me again, and flung her little arms about my neck, clinging to me so closely that I did not dare to give her to anyone else to carry lest I should add to her terrors. So I went on with her in my arms. The fears that pierced my heart may well be imagined. Should I find Stella living or dead? Should I find her at all? Well, we should soon know now. We stumbled on up the stony watercourse; notwithstanding the weight of Tota I led the way, for suspense lent me wings. Now we were through, and an extraordinary scene lay before us. We were in a great natural amphitheatre, only it was three times the size of any amphi-theatre ever shaped by man, and the walls were formed of precipitous cliffs, ranging from one to two hundred feet in height. For the rest, the space thus enclosed was level, studded with park-like trees, bril-liant with flowers, and having a stream running through the centre of it, that, as I afterwards discovered, welled up from the ground at the head of the open space.

We spread ourselves out in a line, searching everywhere, for Tota was too overcome to be able to tell us where Stella was hidden away. For nearly half an hour we searched and searched, scanning the walls of rock for any possible openings to a cave. In vain, we could find none. I applied to old Indaba-zimbi, but his foresight was at fault here. All he could say was that this was the place, and that the "Star" was hidden somewhere in a cave, but where the cave was he could not tell. At last we came to the top of the amphitheatre. There before us was a wall of rock, of which the lower parts were here and there clothed in grasses, lichens, and creepers. I walked along it, calling at the top of my voice.

Presently my heart stood still, for I thought I heard a faint answer. I drew nearer to the place from which the sound seemed to come, and again called. Yes, there was an answer in my wife's voice. It seemed to come from the rock. I went up to it and searched among the creepers, but still could find no opening.

"Move the stone," cried Stella's voice, "the cave is shut with a stone."

I took a spear and prodded at the cliff whence the sound came. Suddenly the spear sunk in through a mass of lichen. I swept the lichen aside, revealing a boulder that had been rolled into the mouth of an opening in the rock, which it fitted so accurately that, covered as it was by the overhanging lichen, it might well have escaped the keenest eye. We dragged the boulder out; it was two men's work to do it. Beyond was a narrow, water-worn passage, which I followed with a beating heart. Presently the passage opened into a small cave, shaped like a pickle bottle, and coming to a neck at the top end. We passed through and found ourselves in a second, much larger cave, that I at once recognized as the one of which Indaba-zimbi had shown me a vision in the water. Light reached it from above—how I know not—and by it I could see a form half-sitting, half lying on some skins at the top end of the cave. I rushed to it. It was Stella! Stella bound with strips of hide, bruised, torn, but still Stella, and alive.

She saw me, she gave one cry, then, as I caught her in my arms, she fainted. It was happy indeed that she did not faint before, for had it not been for the sound of her voice I do not believe we should ever have found that cunningly hidden cave, unless, indeed, Indaba-zimbi's magic (on which be blessings) had come to our assistance.

We bore her to the open air, laid her beneath the shade of a tree, and cut the bonds loose from her ankles. As we went I glanced at the cave. It was exactly as I had seen it in the vision. There burnt the fire, there were the rude wooden vessels, one of them still half full of the water which I had seen the baboon bring. I felt awed as I looked, and marvelled at the power wielded by a savage who could not even read and write.

Now I could see Stella clearly. Her face was scratched, and haggard with fear and weeping, her clothes were almost torn off her, and her beautiful hair was loose and tangled. I sent for water, and we sprinkled her face. Then I forced a little of the brandy which we distilled from peaches at the *kraals* between her lips, and she opened her eyes, and throwing her arms about me clung to me as little Tota had done, sobbing, "Thank God! thank God!"

After a while she grew quieter, and I made her and Tota eat some food from the store that we had brought with us. I too ate and was thankful, for with the exception of the *mealie* cobs I had tasted nothing for nearly four-and-twenty hours. Then she washed her face and hands, and tidied her rags of dress as well as she was able. As she did so by degrees I drew her story from her.

It seemed that on the previous afternoon, being wearied with packing, she went out to visit her father's grave, taking Tota with her, and was followed there by the two dogs. She wished to lay some flowers on the grave and take farewell of the dust it covered, for as we had expected to trek early on the morrow she did not know if she would find a later opportunity. They passed up the garden, and gathering some flowers from the orange trees and elsewhere, went on to the little graveyard. Here she laid them on the grave as we had found them, and then sitting down, fell into a deep and sad reverie, such as the occasion would naturally induce. While she sat thus, Tota, who was a lively child and active as a kitten, strayed away without Stella observing it. With her went the dogs, who also had grown tired of inaction; a while passed, and suddenly she heard the dogs barking furiously about a hundred and fifty yards away. Then she heard Tota scream, and the dogs also yelling with fear and pain. She rose and ran as swiftly as she could towards the spot whence the sound came. Presently she was there. Before her in the glade, holding the screaming Tota in her arms, was a figure in which, notwithstanding the rough disguise of baboon skins and colouring matter, she had no difficulty in recognizing Hendrika, and all about her were numbers of baboons, rolling over and over in two hideous heaps, of which the centres were the unfortunate dogs now in process of being rent to fragments.

"Hendrika," Stella cried, "what does this mean? What are you doing with Tota and those brutes?"

The woman heard her and looked up. Then Stella saw that she was

112

mad; madness stared from her eyes. She dropped the child, which instantly flew to Stella for protection. Stella clasped it, only to be herself clasped by Hendrika. She struggled fiercely, but it was of no use—the *Babyan-frau* had the strength of ten. She lifted her and Tota as though they were nothing, and ran off with them, following the bed of the stream in order to avoid leaving a spoor. Only the baboons who came with her, minus the one the dogs had killed, would not take to the water, but kept pace with them on the bank.

Stella said that the night which followed was more like a hideous nightmare than a reality. She was never able to tell me all that occurred in it. She had a vague recollection of being borne over rocks and along *kloofs*, while around her echoed the horrible grunts and clicks of the baboons. She spoke to Hendrika in English and *Kaffir*, imploring her to let them go; but the woman, if I may call her so, seemed in her madness to have entirely forgotten these tongues. When Stella spoke she would kiss her and stroke her hair, but she did not seem to understand what it was she said. On the other hand, she could, and did, talk to the baboons, that seemed to obey her implicitly. Moreover, she would not allow them to touch either Stella or the child in her arms. Once one of them tried to do so, and she seized a dead stick and struck it so heavily on the head that it fell senseless. Thrice Stella made an attempt to escape, for sometimes even Hendrika's giant strength waned and she had to set them down. But on each occasion she caught them, and it was in these struggles that Stella's clothes were so torn. At length before daylight they reached the cliff, and with the first break of light the ascent began. Hendrika dragged them up the first stages, but when they came to the precipitous place she tied the strips of hide, of which she had a supply wound round her waist, beneath Stella's arms. Steep as the place was the baboons ascended it easily enough, springing from a knock of rock to the trunk of the tree that grew on the edge of the crevasse. Hendrika followed them, holding the end of the hide *reim* in her teeth, one of the baboons hanging down from the tree to assist her ascent. It was while she was ascending that Stella thought of letting fall her handkerchief in the faint hope that some searcher might see it.

By this time Hendrika was on the tree, and grunting out orders to the baboons which clustered about Stella below. Suddenly these seized her and little Tota who was in her arms, and lifted her from the ground. Then Hendrika above, aided by other baboons, put out all her great strength and pulled the two of them up the rock. Twice Stella swung heavily against the cliff. After the second blow she felt her senses going, and was consumed with terror lest she should drop Tota. But she managed to cling to her, and together they reached the cleft.

"From that time," Stella went on, "I remember no more till I woke to find myself in a gloomy cave resting on a bed of skins. My legs were bound, and Hendrika sat near me watching me, while round the edge of the cave peered the heads of those horrible baboons. Tota was still in my arms, and half dead from terror; her moans were pitiful to hear. I spoke to Hendrika, imploring her to release us; but either she has lost all understanding of human speech, or she pretends to have done so. All she would do was to caress me, and even kiss my hands and dress with extravagant signs of affection. As she did so, Tota shrunk closer to me. This Hendrika saw and glared so savagely at the child that I feared lest she was going to kill her. I diverted her attention by making signs that I wanted water, and this she gave me in a wooden bowl. As you saw, the cave was evidently Hendrika's dwelling-place. There are stores of fruit in it and some strips of dried flesh. She gave me some of the fruit and Tota a little, and I made Tota eat some. You can never know what I went through, Allan. I saw now that Hendrika was quite mad, and but little removed from the brutes to which she is akin, and over which she has such unholy power. The only trace of humanity left about her was her affection for me. Evidently her idea was to keep me here with her, to keep me away from you, and to carry out this idea she was capable of the exercise of every artifice and cunning. In this way she was sane enough, but in every other way she was mad. Moreover, she had not forgotten her horrible jealousy. Already I saw her glaring at Tota, and knew that the child's murder was only a matter of time. Probably within a few hours she would be killed before my eyes. Of escape, even if I had the strength, there was absolutely no chance, and little enough of our ever being found. No, we should be kept here guarded by a mad thing, half ape, half woman, till we perished miserably. Then I thought of you, dear, and of all that you must be suffering, and my heart nearly broke. I could only pray to God that I might either be rescued or die swiftly.

"As I prayed I dropped into a kind of doze from utter weariness, and then I had the strangest dream. I dreamed that Indaba-zimbi stood over me nodding his white lock, and spoke to me in *Kaffir*, telling me not to be frightened, for you would soon be with me, and that meanwhile I must humour Hendrika, pretending to be pleased to have her near me. The dream was so vivid that I actually seemed to see and hear him, as I see and hear him now."

Here I looked up and glanced at old Indaba-zimbi, who was sitting near. But it was not till afterwards that I told Stella of how her vision was brought about.

"At any rate," she went on, "when I awoke I determined to act on my dream. I took Hendrika's hand, and pressed it. She actually laughed in a wild kind of way with happiness, and laid her head upon my knee. Then I made signs that I wanted food, and she threw wood on the fire, which I forgot to tell you was burning in the cave, and began to make some of the broth that she used to cook very well, and she did not seem to have forgotten all about it. At any rate the broth was not bad, though neither Tota nor I could drink much of it. Fright and weariness had taken away our appetites.

"After the meal was done—and I prolonged it as much as possible—I saw Hendrika was beginning to get jealous of Tota again. She glared at her and then at the big knife which was tied round her own body. I knew the knife again, it was the one with which she had tried to murder you, dear. At last she went so far as to draw the knife. I was paralyzed with fear, then suddenly I remembered that when she was our servant, and used to get out of temper and sulk, I could always calm her by singing to her. So I began to sing hymns. Instantly she forgot her jealousy and put the knife back into its sheath. She knew the sound of the singing, and sat listening to it with a rapt face; the baboons, too, crowded in at the entrance of the cave to listen. I must have sung for an hour or more, all the hymns that I could remember. It was so very strange and dreadful sitting there singing to mad Hendrika and those hideous man-like apes that shut their eyes and nodded their great heads as I sang. It was a horrible nightmare; but I believe that the baboons are almost as human as the Bushmen.

"Well, this went on for a long time till my voice was getting exhausted. Then suddenly I heard the baboons outside raise a loud noise, as they do when they are angry. Then, dear, I heard the boom of your elephant gun, and I think it was the sweetest sound that ever came to my ears. Hendrika heard it too. She sprang up, stood for a moment, then, to my horror, swept Tota into her arms and rushed down the cave. Of course I could not stir to follow her, for my feet were tied. Next instant I heard the sound of a rock being moved, and presently the lessening of the light in the cave told me that I was shut in. Now the sound even of the elephant gun only reached me very faintly, and presently I could hear nothing more, straining my ears as I would.

"At last I heard a faint shouting that reached me through the wall of rock. I answered as loud as I could. You know the rest; and oh, my dear husband, thank God! thank God!" and she fell weeping into my arms.

CHAPTER 14

Fifteen Years After

Both Stella and Tota were too weary to be moved, so we camped that night in the baboons' home, but were troubled by no baboons. Stella would not sleep in the cave; she said the place terrified her, so I made her up a kind of bed under a thorn-tree. As this rock-bound valley was one of the hottest places I ever was in, I thought that this would not matter; but when at sunrise on the following morning I saw a veil of miasmatic mist hanging over the surface of the ground, I changed my opinion. However, neither Stella nor Tota seemed the worse, so as soon as was practical we started homewards. I had already on the previous day sent some of the men back to the *kraals* to fetch a ladder, and when we reached the cliff we found them waiting for us beneath. With the help of the ladder the descent was easy. Stella simply got out of her rough litter at the top of the cliff, for we found it necessary to carry her, climbed down the ladder, and got into it again at the bottom.

Well, we reached the *kraals* safely enough, seeing nothing more of Hendrika, and, were this a story, doubtless I should end it here with—"and lived happily ever after." But alas! it is not so. How am I to write it?

My dearest wife's vital energy seemed completely to fail her now that the danger was past, and within twelve hours of our return I saw that her state was such as to necessitate the abandonment of any idea of leaving Babyan *Kraals* at present. The bodily exertion, the anguish of mind, and the terror which she had endured during that dreadful night, combined with her delicate state of health, had completely broken her down. To make matters worse, also, she was taken with an attack of fever, contracted no doubt in the unhealthy atmosphere of that accursed valley. In time she shook the fever off, but it left her dreadfully weak, and quite unfit to face the trial before her.

I think she knew that she was going to die; she always spoke of my future, never of *our* future. It is impossible for me to tell how sweet she was; how gentle, how patient and resigned. Nor, indeed, do I wish to tell it, it is too sad. But this I will say, I believe that if ever a woman drew near to perfection while yet living on the earth, Stella Quatermain did so.

The fatal hour drew on. My boy Harry was born, and his mother lived to kiss and bless him. Then she sank. We did what we could, but we had little skill, and might not hold her back from death. All through one weary night I watched her with a breaking heart.

The dawn came, the sun rose in the east. His rays falling on the peak behind were reflected in glory upon the bosom of the western sky. Stella awoke from her swoon and saw the light. She whispered to me to open the door of the hut. I did so, and she fixed her dying eyes on the splendour of the morning sky. She looked on me and smiled as an angel might smile. Then with a last effort she lifted her hand, and, pointing to the radiant heavens, whispered:

"There, Allan, there!"

It was done, and I was broken-hearted, and broken-hearted I must wander to the end. Those who have endured my loss will know my sorrow; it cannot be written. In such peace and at such an hour may I also die!

Yes, it is a sad story, but wander where we will about the world we can never go beyond the sound of the passing bell. For me, as for my father before me, and for the millions who have been and who shall be, there is but one word of comfort. "The Lord hath given, and the Lord hath taken away." Let us, then, bow our heads in hope, and add with a humble heart, "Blessed be the name of the Lord."

* * * * * * * *

I buried her by her father's side, and the weeping of the people who had loved her went up to heaven. Even Indaba-zimbi wept, but I could weep no more.

On the second night from her burial I could not sleep. I rose, dressed myself, and went out into the night. The moon was shining brightly, and by its rays I shaped my course towards the graveyard. I drew near silently, and as I came I thought that I heard a sound of moaning on the further side of the wall. I looked over it. Crouched by Stella's grave, and tearing at its sods with her hands, as though she would unearth that which lay within, was *Hendrika*. Her face was wild and haggard, her form was so emaciated that when the pelts she wore slipped aside, the shoulder-blades seemed to project almost through her skin. Suddenly she looked up and saw me. Laughing a dreadful maniac laugh, she put her hand to her girdle and drew her great knife from it. I thought that she was about to attack me, and prepared to defend myself as I best could, for I was unarmed. But she made no effort to do so. Lifting the knife on high, for a moment she held it glittering in the moonlight, then plunged it into her own breast, and fell headlong to the ground.

I sprang over the wall and ran to her. She was not yet dead. Presently she opened her eyes, and I saw that the madness had gone out of them.

"Macumazahn," she said, speaking in English and in an thick difficult voice like one who half forgot and half remembered—"Macumazahn, I remember now. I have been mad. Is she really dead, Macumazahn?"

"Yes," I said, "she is dead, and you killed her."

"I killed her!" the dying woman faltered, "and I loved her. Yes, yes, I know now. I became a brute again and dragged her to the brutes, and now once more I am a woman, and she is dead, and I killed her—because I loved her so. I killed her who saved me from the brutes. I am not dead yet, Macumazahn. Take me and torture me to death, slowly, very slowly. It was jealousy of you that drove me mad, and I have killed her, and now she never can forgive me."

"Ask forgiveness from above," I said, for Hendrika had been a Christian, and the torment of her remorse touched me.

"I ask no forgiveness," she said. "May God torture me forever, because I killed her; may I become a brute for ever till she comes to find me and forgives me! I only want her forgiveness." And wailing in an anguish of the heart so strong that her bodily suffering seemed to be forgotten, Hendrika, the Baboon-woman, died.

I went back to the *kraals*, and, waking Indaba-zimbi, told him what had happened, asking him to send someone to watch the body, as I proposed to give it burial. But next morning it was gone, and I found that the natives, hearing of the event, had taken the corpse and thrown it to the vultures with every mark of hate. Such, then, was the end of Hendrika.

****

A week after Hendrika's death I left Babyan *Kraals*. The place was hateful to me now; it was a haunted place. I sent for old Indaba-zimbi and told him that I was going. He answered that it was well. "The place has served your turn," he said; "here you have won that joy which it was fated you should win, and have suffered those things that it was fated you should suffer. Yes, and though you know it not now, the joy and the suffering, like the sunshine and the storm, are the same thing, and will rest at last in the same heaven, the heaven from which they came. Now go, Macumazahn."

I asked him if he was coming with me.

"No," he answered, "our paths lie apart henceforth, Macumazahn. We met together for certain ends. Those ends are fulfilled. Now each one goes his own way. You have still many years before you, Macumazahn; my years are few. When we shake hands here it will be for the last time. Perhaps we may meet again, but it will not be in this world. Henceforth we have each of us a friend the less."

"Heavy words," I said.

"True words," he answered.

Well, I have little heart to write the rest of it. I went, leaving Indaba-zimbi in charge of the place, and making him a present of such cattle and goods as I did not want.

Tota, I of course took with me. Fortunately by this time she had almost recovered the shock to her nerves. The baby Harry, as he was afterwards named, was a fine healthy child, and I was lucky in getting a respectable native woman, whose husband had been killed in the fight with the baboons, to accompany me as his nurse.

Slowly, and followed for a distance by all the people, I trekked away from Babyan *Kraals*. My route towards Natal was along the edge of the Bad Lands, and my first night's outspan was beneath that very tree where Stella, my lost wife, had found us as we lay dying of thirst.

I did not sleep much that night. And yet I was glad that I had not died in the desert about eleven months before. I felt then, as from year to year I have continued to feel while I wander through the lonely wilderness of life, that I had been preserved to an end. I had won my darling's love, and for a little while we had been happy together. Our happiness was too perfect to endure. She is lost to me now, but she is lost to be found again.

Here on the following morning I bade farewell to Indaba-zimbi.

"Goodbye, Macumazahn," he said, nodding his white lock at me. "Goodbye for a while. I am not a Christian; your father could not make me that. But he was a wise man, and when he said that those who loved each other shall meet again, he did not lie. And I too am a wise man in my way, Macumazahn, and I say it is true that we shall meet again. All my prophecies to you have come true, Macumazahn,

119

and this one shall come true also. I tell you that you shall return to Babyan *Kraals* and shall not find me. I tell you that you shall journey to a further land than Babyan *Kraals* and shall find me. Farewell!" and he took a pinch of snuff, turned, and went.

* * * * * * * *

Of my journey down to Natal there is little to tell. I met with many adventures, but they were of an every-day kind, and in the end arrived safely at Port Durban, which I now visited for the first time. Both Tota and my baby boy bore the journey well. And here I may as well chronicle the destiny of Tota. For a year she remained under my charge. Then she was adopted by a lady, the wife of an English colonel, who was stationed at the Cape. She was taken by her adopted parents to England, where she grew up a very charming and pretty girl, and ultimately married a clergyman in Norfolk. But I never saw her again, though we often wrote to each other.

Before I returned to the country of my birth, she too had been gathered to the land of shadows, leaving three children behind her. Ah me! all this took place so long ago, when I was young who now am old.

Perhaps it may interest the reader to know the fate of Mr. Carson's property, which should of course have gone to his grandson Harry. I wrote to England to claim the estate on his behalf, but the lawyer to whom the matter was submitted said that my marriage to Stella, not having been celebrated by an ordained priest, was not legal according to English law, and therefore Harry could not inherit. Foolishly enough I acquiesced in this, and the property passed to a cousin of my father-in-law's; but since I have come to live in England I have been informed that this opinion is open to great suspicion, and that there is every probability that the courts would have declared the marriage perfectly binding as having been solemnly entered into in accordance with the custom of the place where it was contracted. But I am now so rich that it is not worthwhile to move in the matter. The cousin is dead, his son is in possession, so let him keep it.

Once, and once only, did I revisit Babyan *Kraals*. Some fifteen years after my darling's death, when I was a man in middle life, I undertook an expedition to the Zambezi, and one night outspanned at the mouth of the well-known valley beneath the shadow of the great peak. I mounted my horse, and, quite alone, rode up the valley, noticing with a strange prescience of evil that the road was overgrown, and, save for the music of the waterfalls, the place silent as death. The *kraals* that used to be to the left of the road by the river had vanished. I rode towards their site; the *mealie* fields were choked with weeds, the paths were dumb with grass. Presently I reached the place. There, overgrown with grass, were the burnt ashes of the *kraals*, and there among the ashes, gleaming in the moonlight, lay the white bones of men. Now it was clear to me. The settlement had been fallen on by some powerful foe, and its inhabitants put to the *assegai*. The forebodings of the natives had come true; Babyan *Kraals* were peopled by memories alone.

I passed on up the terraces. There shone the roofs of the marble huts. They would not burn, and were too strong to be easily pulled down. I entered one of them—it had been our sleeping hut—and lit a candle which I had with me. The huts had been sacked; leaves of books and broken mouldering fragments of the familiar furniture lay about. Then I remembered that there was a secret place hollowed in the floor and concealed by a stone, where Stella used to hide her little treasures. I went to the stone and dragged it up. There was something within wrapped in rotting native cloth. I undid it. It was the dress my wife had been married in. In the centre of the dress were the withered wreath and flowers she had worn, and with them a little paper packet. I opened it; it contained a lock of my own hair!

I remembered then that I had searched for this dress when I came away and could not find it, for I had forgotten the secret recess in the floor.

Taking the dress with me, I left the hut for the last time. Leaving my horse tied to a tree, I walked to the graveyard, through the ruined garden. There it was a mass of weeds, but over my darling's grave grew a self-sown orange bush, of which the scented petals fell in showers on to the mound beneath. As I drew near, there was a crash and a rush. A great baboon leapt from the centre of the graveyard and vanished into the trees. I could almost believe that it was the wraith of Hendrika doomed to keep an eternal watch over the bones of the woman her jealous rage had done to death.

I tarried there a while, filled with such thoughts as may not be written. Then, leaving my dead wife to her long sleep where the waters fall in melancholy music beneath the shadow of the everlasting mountain, I turned and sought that spot where first we had told our love. Now the orange grove was nothing but a tangled thicket; many of the trees were dead, choked with creepers, but some still flourished. There stood the one beneath which we had lingered, there was the rock that had been our seat, and there on the rock sat the wraith of *Stella*, the Stella whom I had wed! Ay! there she sat, and on her

121

upturned face was that same spiritual look which I saw upon it in the hour when we first had kissed. The moonlight shone in her dark eyes, the breeze wavered in her curling hair, her breast rose and fell, a gentle smile played about her parted lips. I stood transfixed with awe and joy, gazing on that lost loveliness which once was mine. I could not speak, and she spoke no word; she did not even seem to see me. Now her eyes fell. For a moment they met mine, and their message entered into me.

Then she was gone. She was gone; nothing was left but the tremulous moonlight falling where she had been, the melancholy music of the waters, the shadow of the everlasting mountain, and, in my heart, the sorrow and the hope.

Maiwa's Revenge

Preface

It may be well to state that the incident of the *Thing that Bites* recorded in this tale is not an effort of the imagination. On the contrary, it is *plagiarized*. Mandara, a well-known chief on the east coast of Africa, has such an article, *and uses it*. In the same way the wicked conduct attributed to Wambe is not without a precedent. T'Chaka, the Zulu Napoleon, never allowed a child of his to live. Indeed he went further, for on discovering that his mother, Unandi, was bringing up one of his sons in secret, like Nero he killed her, and with his own hand.

CHAPTER 1

Gobo Strikes

One day—it was about a week after Allan Quatermain told me his story of the "Three Lions," and of the moving death of Jim-Jim—he and I were walking home together on the termination of a day's shooting. He owned about two thousand acres of shooting round the place he had bought in Yorkshire, over a hundred of which were wood. It was the second year of his occupation of the estate, and already he had reared a very fair head of pheasants, for he was an all-round sportsman, and as fond of shooting with a shot-gun as with an eight-bore rifle. We were three guns that day, Sir Henry Curtis, Old Quatermain, and myself; but Sir Henry was obliged to leave in the middle of the afternoon in order to meet his agent, and inspect an outlying farm where a new shed was wanted. However, he was coming back to dinner, and going to bring Captain Good with him, for Brayley Hall was not more than two miles from the Grange.

We had met with very fair sport, considering that we were only going through outlying cover for cocks. I think that we had killed twenty-seven, a woodcock and a leash of partridges which we secured out of a driven covey. On our way home there lay a long narrow spinney, which was a very favourite *lie* for woodcocks, and generally held a pheasant or two as well.

"Well, what do you say?" said old Quatermain, "shall we beat through this for a finish?"

I assented, and he called to the keeper who was following with a little knot of beaters, and told him to beat the spinney.

"Very well, sir," answered the man, "but it's getting wonderful dark, and the wind's rising a gale. It will take you all your time to hit a woodcock if the spinney holds one."

"You show us the woodcocks, Jeffries," answered Quatermain

quickly, for he never liked being crossed in anything to do with sport, "and we will look after shooting them."

The man turned and went rather sulkily. I heard him say to the under-keeper, "He's pretty good, the master is, I'm not saying he isn't, but if he kills a woodcock in this light and wind, I'm a Dutchman."

I think that Quatermain heard him too, though he said nothing. The wind was rising every minute, and by the time the beat begun it blew big guns. I stood at the right-hand corner of the spinney, which curved round somewhat, and Quatermain stood at the left, about forty paces from me. Presently an old cock pheasant came rocketing over me, looking as though the feathers were being blown out of his tail. I missed him clean with the first barrel, and was never more pleased with myself in my life than when I doubled him up with the second, for the shot was not an easy one. In the faint light I could see Quatermain nodding his head in approval, when through the groaning of the trees I heard the shouts of the beaters, "Cock forward, cock to the right."

Then came a whole volley of shouts.

"Woodcock to the right."

"Cock to the left."

"Cock over."

I looked up, and presently caught sight of one of the woodcocks coming down the wind upon me like a flash. In that dim light I could not follow all his movements as he zigzagged through the naked tree-tops; indeed I could see him when his wings flitted up. Now he was passing me—*bang*, and a flick of the wing, I had missed him; *bang* again. Surely he was down; no, there he went to my left.

"Cock to you," I shouted, stepping forward so as to get Quatermain between me and the faint angry light of the dying day, for I wanted to see if he would "wipe my eye." I knew him to be a wonderful shot, but I thought that cock would puzzle him.

I saw him raise his gun ever so little and bend forward, and at that moment out flashed two woodcocks into the open, the one I had missed to his right, and the other to his left.

At the same time a fresh shout arose of, "Woodcock over," and looking down the spinney I saw a third bird high up in the air, being blown along like a brown and whirling leaf straight over Quatermain's head. And then followed the prettiest little bit of shooting that I ever saw. The bird to the right was flying low, not ten yards from the line of a hedgerow, and Quatermain took him first because he would become invisible the soonest of any. Indeed, nobody who had not his hawk's eyes could have seen to shoot at all. But he saw the bird well enough to kill it dead as a stone. Then turning sharply, he pulled on the second bird at about forty-five yards, and over he went. By this time the third woodcock was nearly over him, and flying very high, straight down the wind, a hundred feet up or more, I should say. I saw him glance at it as he opened his gun, threw out the right cartridge and slipped in another, turning round as he did so. By this time the cock was nearly fifty yards away from him, and travelling like a flash. Lifting his gun he fired after it, and, wonderful as the shot was, killed it dead. A tearing gust of wind caught the dead bird, and blew it away like a leaf torn from an oak, so that it fell a hundred and thirty yards off or more.

"I say, Quatermain," I said to him when the beaters were up, "do you often do this sort of thing?"

"Well," he answered, with a dry smile, "the last time I had to load three shots as quickly as that was at rather larger game. It was at elephants. I killed them all three as dead as I killed those woodcocks; but it very nearly went the other way, I can tell you; I mean that they very nearly killed me."

Just at that moment the keeper came up, "Did you happen to get one of them there cocks, sir?" he said, with the air of a man who did not in the least expect an answer in the affirmative.

"Well, yes, Jeffries," answered Quatermain; "you will find one of them by the hedge, and another about fifty yards out by the plough there to the left——"

The keeper had turned to go, looking a little astonished, when Quatermain called him back.

"Stop a bit, Jeffries," he said. "You see that pollard about one hundred and forty yards off? Well, there should be another woodcock down in a line with it, about sixty paces out in the field."

"Well, if that bean't the very smartest bit of shooting," murmured Jeffries, and departed.

After that we went home, and in due course Sir Henry Curtis and Captain Good arrived for dinner, the latter arrayed in the tightest and most ornamental dress-suit I ever saw. I remember that the waistcoat was adorned with five pink coral buttons.

It was a very pleasant dinner. Old Quatermain was in an excellent humour; induced, I think, by the recollection of his triumph over the doubting Jeffries. Good, too, was full of anecdotes. He told us a most miraculous story of how he once went shooting ibex in Kashmir. These ibex, according to Good, he stalked early and late for four entire days. At last on the morning of the fifth day he succeeded in getting within range of the flock, which consisted of a magnificent old ram with horns so long that I am afraid to mention their measure, and five or six females. Good crawled upon his stomach, painfully taking shelter behind rocks, till he was within two hundred yards; then he drew a fine bead upon the old ram. At this moment, however, a diversion occurred. Some wandering native of the hills appeared upon a distant mountain top. The females turned, and rushing over a rock vanished from Good's ken. But the old ram took a bolder course. In front of him stretched a mighty crevasse at least thirty feet in width. He went at it with a bound. Whilst he was in mid-air Good fired, and killed him dead. The ram turned a complete somersault in space, and fell in such fashion that his horns hooked themselves upon a big projection of the opposite cliffs. There he hung, till Good, after a long and painful detour, gracefully dropped a lasso over him and fished him up.

This moving tale of wild adventure was received with undeserved incredulity.

"Well," said Good, "if you fellows won't believe my story when I tell it—a perfectly true story mind—perhaps one of you will give us a better; I'm not particular if it is true or not." And he lapsed into a dignified silence.

"Now, Quatermain," I said, "don't let Good beat you, let us hear how you killed those elephants you were talking about this evening just after you shot the woodcocks."

"Well," said Quatermain, dryly, and with something like a twinkle in his brown eyes, "it is very hard fortune for a man to have to follow on Good's 'spoor.' Indeed if it were not for that running giraffe which, as you will remember, Curtis, we saw Good bowl over with a Martini rifle at three hundred yards, I should almost have said that this was an impossible tale."

Here Good looked up with an air of indignant innocence.

"However," he went on, rising and lighting his pipe, "if you fellows like, I will spin you a yarn. I was telling one of you the other night about those three lions and how the lioness finished my unfortunate *voorlooper*, Jim-Jim, the boy whom we buried in the bread-bag.

"Well, after this little experience I thought that I would settle down a bit, so I entered upon a venture with a man who, being of a speculative mind, had conceived the idea of running a store at Pretoria upon strictly cash principles. The arrangement was that I should find the capital and he the experience. Our partnership was not of a long duration. The Boers refused to pay cash, and at the end of four months my partner had the capital and I had the experience. After this I came to the conclusion that store-keeping was not in my line, and having four hundred pounds left, I sent my boy Harry to a school in Natal, and buying an outfit with what remained of the money, started upon a big trip.

"This time I determined to go further afield than I had ever been before; so I took a passage for a few pounds in a trading brig that ran between Durban and Delagoa Bay. From Delagoa Bay I marched inland accompanied by twenty porters, with the idea of striking up north, towards the Limpopo, and keeping parallel to the coast, but at a distance of about one hundred and fifty miles from it. For the first twenty days of our journey we suffered a good deal from fever, that is, my men did, for I think that I am fever proof. Also I was hard put to it to keep the camp in meat, for although the country proved to be very sparsely populated, there was but little game about. Indeed, during all that time I hardly killed anything larger than a waterbuck, and, as you know, waterbuck's flesh is not very appetising food. On the twentieth day, however, we came to the banks of a largish river, the Gonooroo it was called. This I crossed, and then struck inland towards a great range of mountains, the blue crests of which we could see lying on the distant heavens like a shadow, a continuation, as I believe, of the Drakensberg range that skirts the coast of Natal. From this main range a great spur shoots out some fifty miles or so towards the coast, ending abruptly in one tremendous peak. This spur I discovered separated the territories of two chiefs named Nala and Wambe, Wambe's territory being to the north, and Nala's to the south. Nala ruled a tribe of bastard Zulus called the Butiana, and Wambe a much larger tribe, called the Matuku, which presents marked Bantu characteristics. For instance, they have doors and verandas to their huts, work skins perfectly, and wear a waistcloth and not a *moocha*. At this time the Butiana were more or less subject to the Matuku, having been surprised by them some twenty years before and mercilessly slaughtered down. The tribe was now recovering itself, however, and as you may imagine, it did not love the Matuku.

"Well, I heard as I went along that elephants were very plentiful in the dense forests which lie upon the slopes and at the foot of the mountains that border Wambe's territory. Also I heard a very ill report of that worthy himself, who lived in a *kraal* upon the side of the mountain, which was so strongly fortified as to be practically impregnable. It was said that he was the most cruel chief in this part of Africa, and that he had murdered in cold blood an entire party of

English gentlemen, who, some seven years before, had gone into his country to hunt elephants. They took an old friend of mine with them as guide, John Every by name, and often had I mourned over his untimely death. All the same, Wambe or no Wambe, I determined to hunt elephants in his country. I never was afraid of natives, and I was not going to show the white feather now. I am a bit of a fatalist, as you fellows know, so I came to the conclusion that if it was fated that Wambe should send me to join my old friend John Every, I should have to go, and there was an end of it. Meanwhile, I meant to hunt elephants with a peaceful heart.

"On the third day from the date of our sighting the great peak, we found ourselves beneath its shadow. Still following the course of the river which wound through the forests at the base of the peak, we entered the territory of the redoubtable Wambe. This, however, was not accomplished without a certain difference of opinion between my bearers and myself, for when we reached the spot where Wambe's boundary was supposed to run, the bearers sat down and emphatically refused to go a step further. I sat down too, and argued with them, putting my fatalistic views before them as well as I was able. But I could not persuade them to look at the matter in the same light. 'At present,' they said, 'their skins were whole; if they went into Wambe's country without his leave they would soon be like a water-eaten leaf. It was very well for me to say that this would be Fate. Fate no doubt might be walking about in Wambe's country, but while they stopped outside they would not meet him.'

"'Well,' I said to Gobo, my head man, 'and what do you mean to do?'

"'We mean to go back to the coast, Macumazahn,' he answered insolently.

"'Do you?' I replied, for my bile was stirred. 'At any rate, Mr. Gobo, you and one or two others will never get there; see here, my friend,' and I took a repeating rifle and sat myself comfortably down, resting my back against a tree—'I have just breakfasted, and I had as soon spend the day here as anywhere else. Now if you or any of those men walk one step back from here, and towards the coast, I shall fire at you; and you know that I don't miss.'

"The man fingered the spear he was carrying—luckily all my guns were stacked against the tree—and then turned as though to walk away, the others keeping their eyes fixed upon him all the while. I rose and covered him with the rifle, and though he kept up a brave appearance of unconcern, I saw that he was glancing nervously at me all the time. When he had gone about twenty yards I spoke very quietly—

"'Now, Gobo,' I said, 'come back, or I shall fire.'

"Of course this was taking a very high hand; I had no real right to kill Gobo or anybody else because they objected to run the risk of death by entering the territory of a hostile chief. But I felt that if I wished to keep up any authority it was absolutely necessary that I should push matters to the last extremity short of actually shooting him. So I sat there, looking fierce as a lion, and keeping the sight of my rifle in a dead line for Gobo's ribs. Then Gobo, feeling that the situation was getting strained, gave in.

"'Don't shoot, Boss,' he shouted, throwing up his hand, 'I will come with you.'

"'I thought you would,' I answered quietly; 'you see Fate walks about outside Wambe's country as well as in it.'

"After that I had no more trouble, for Gobo was the ringleader, and when he collapsed the others collapsed also. Harmony being thus restored, we crossed the line, and on the following morning I began shooting in good earnest."

CHAPTER 2

A Morning's Sport

"Moving some five or six miles round the base of the great peak of which I have spoken, we came the same day to one of the fairest bits of African country that I have seen outside of Kukuanaland. At this spot the mountain spur that runs out at right angles to the great range, which stretches its cloud-clad length north and south as far as the eye can reach, sweeps inwards with a vast and splendid curve. This curve measures some five-and-thirty miles from point to point, and across its moon-like segment the river flashed, a silver line of light. On the further side of the river is a measureless sea of swelling ground, a natural park covered with great patches of bush—some of them being many square miles in extent. These are separated one from another by glades of grass land, broken here and there with clumps of timber trees; and in some instances by curious isolated *koppies*, and even by single crags of granite that start up into the air as though they were monuments carved by man, and not tombstones set by nature over the grave of ages gone. On the west this beautiful plain is bordered by the lonely mountain, from the edge of which it rolls down toward the fever coast; but how far it runs to the north I cannot say—eight days' journey, according to the natives, when it is lost in an untravelled morass.

"On the hither side of the river the scenery is different. Along the edge of its banks, where the land is flat, are green patches of swamp. Then comes a wide belt of beautiful grass land covered thickly with game, and sloping up very gently to the borders of the forest, which, beginning at about a thousand feet above the level of the plain, clothes the mountain-side almost to its crest. In this forest grow great trees, most of them of the yellow-wood species. Some of these trees are so lofty, that a bird in their top branches would be out of range of an ordinary shot gun. Another peculiar thing about them is, that they are for the most part covered with a dense growth of the Orchilla moss; and from this moss the natives manufacture a most excellent deep purple dye, with which they stain tanned hides and also cloth, when they happen to get any of the latter. I do not think that I ever saw anything more remarkable than the appearance of one of these mighty trees festooned from top to bottom with trailing wreaths of this sad-hued moss, in which the wind whispers gently as it stirs them. At a distance it looks like the gray locks of a Titan crowned with bright green leaves, and here and there starred with the rich bloom of orchids.

"The night of that day on which I had my little difference of opinion with Gobo, we camped by the edge of this great forest, and on the following morning at daylight I started out shooting. As we were short of meat I determined to kill a buffalo, of which there were plenty about, before looking for traces of elephants. Not more than half a mile from camp we came across a trail broad as a cart-road, evidently made by a great herd of buffaloes which had passed up at dawn from their feeding ground in the marshes, to spend the day in the cool air of the uplands. This trail I followed boldly; for such wind as there was blew straight down the mountain-side, that is, from the direction in which the buffaloes had gone, to me. About a mile further on the forest began to be dense, and the nature of the trail showed me that I must be close to my game. Another two hundred yards and the bush was so thick that, had it not been for the trail, we could scarcely have passed through it. As it was, Gobo, who carried my eight-bore rifle (for I had the .570-express in my hand), and the other two men whom I had taken with me, showed the very strongest dislike to going any further, pointing out that there was 'no room to run away.' I told them that they need not come unless they liked, but that I was certainly going on; and then, growing ashamed, they came.

"Another fifty yards, and the trail opened into a little glade. I knelt down and peeped and peered, but no buffalo could I see. Evidently the herd had broken up here—I knew that from the spoor—and penetrated the opposite bush in little troops. I crossed the glade, and choosing one line of spoor, followed it for some sixty yards, when it became clear to me that I was surrounded by buffaloes; and yet so dense was the cover that I could not see any. A few yards to my left I could hear one rubbing its horns against a tree, while from my right came an occasional low and throaty grunt which told me that I was uncomfortably near an old bull. I crept on towards him with my heart in my mouth, as gently as though I were walking upon eggs for a bet, lifting every little bit of wood in my path, and placing it behind me lest it should crack and warn the game. After me in single file came my three retainers, and I don't know which of them looked the most frightened. Presently Gobo touched my leg; I glanced round, and saw him pointing slantwise towards the left. I lifted my head a little and peeped over a mass of creepers; beyond the creepers was a dense bush of sharp-pointed aloes, of that kind of which the leaves project laterally, and on the other side of the aloes, not fifteen paces from us, I made out the horns, neck, and the ridge of the back of a tremendous old bull. I took my eight-bore, and getting on to my knee prepared to shoot him through the neck, taking my chance of cutting his spine. I had already covered him as well as the aloe leaves would allow, when he gave a kind of sigh and lay down.

"I looked round in dismay. What was to be done now? I could not see to shoot him lying down, even if my bullet would have pierced the intervening aloes—which was doubtful—and if I stood up he would either run away or charge me. I reflected, and came to the conclusion that the only thing to do was to lie down also; for I did not fancy wandering after other buffaloes in that dense bush. If a buffalo lies down, it is clear that he must get up again some time, so it was only a case of patience—'fighting the fight of sit down,' as the Zulus say.

"Accordingly I sat down and lighted a pipe, thinking that the smell of it might reach the buffalo and make him get up. But the wind was the wrong way, and it did not; so when it was done I lit another. Afterwards I had cause to regret that pipe.

"Well, we squatted like this for between half and three quarters of an hour, till at length I began to grow heartily sick of the performance. It was about as dull a business as the last hour of a comic opera. I could hear buffaloes snorting and moving all round, and see the red-beaked tic birds flying up off their backs, making a kind of hiss as they did so, something like that of the English misselthrush, but I could not see a single buffalo. As for my old bull, I think he must have slept the sleep of the just, for he never even stirred.

"Just as I was making up my mind that something must be done to save the situation, my attention was attracted by a curious grinding noise. At first I thought that it must be a buffalo chewing the cud, but was obliged to abandon the idea because the noise was too loud. I shifted myself round and stared through the cracks in the bush, in the direction whence the sound seemed to come, and once I thought that I saw something gray moving about fifty yards off, but could not make certain. Although the grinding noise still continued I could see nothing more, so I gave up thinking about it, and once again turned my attention to the buffalo. Presently, however, something happened. Suddenly from about forty yards away there came a tremendous snorting sound, more like that made by an engine getting a heavy train under weigh than anything else in the world.

"'By Jove,' I thought, turning round in the direction from which the grinding sound had come, 'that must be a rhinoceros, and he has got our wind.' For, as you fellows know, there is no mistaking the sound made by a rhinoceros when he gets wind of you.

"Another second, and I heard a most tremendous crashing noise. Before I could think what to do, before I could even get up, the bush behind me seemed to burst asunder, and there appeared not eight yards from us, the great horn and wicked twinkling eye of a charging rhinoceros. He had winded us or my pipe, I do not know which, and, after the fashion of these brutes, had charged up the scent. I could not rise, I could not even get the gun up, I had no time. All that I was able to do was to roll over as far out of the monster's path as the bush would allow. Another second and he was over me, his great bulk towering above me like a mountain, and, upon my word, I could not get his smell out of my nostrils for a week. Circumstances impressed it on my memory, at least I suppose so. His hot breath blew upon my face, one of his front feet just missed my head, and his hind one actually trod upon the loose part of my trousers and pinched a little bit of my skin. I saw him pass over me lying as I was upon my back, and next second I saw something else. My men were a little behind me, and therefore straight in the path of the rhinoceros. One of them flung himself backwards into the bush, and thus avoided him. The second with a wild yell sprung to his feet, and bounded like an India-rubber ball right into the aloe bush, landing well among the spikes. But the third, it was my friend Gobo, could not by any means get away. He managed to gain his feet, and that was all. The rhinoceros was charging with his head low; his horn passed between Gobo's legs, and feeling something on his nose, he jerked it up. Away went Gobo, high into the air. He turned a complete somersault at the apex of the curve, and as he did so, I caught sight of his face. It was gray with terror, and his mouth was wide open. Down he came, right on to the great brute's back, and that broke his fall. Luckily for him the rhinoceros never turned, but crashed straight through the aloe bush, only missing the man who had jumped into it by about a yard.

"Then followed a complication. The sleeping buffalo on the further side of the bush, hearing the noise, sprang to his feet, and for a second, not knowing what to do, stood still. At that instant the huge rhinoceros blundered right on to him, and getting his horn beneath his stomach gave him such a fearful dig that the buffalo was turned over on to his back, while his assailant went a most amazing cropper over his carcase. In another moment, however, the rhinoceros was up, and wheeling round to the left, crashed through the bush down-hill and towards the open country.

"Instantly the whole place became alive with alarming sounds. In every direction troops of snorting buffaloes charged through the forest, wild with fright, while the injured bull on the further side of the bush began to bellow like a mad thing. I lay quite still for a moment, devoutly praying that none of the flying buffaloes would come my way. Then when the danger lessened I got on to my feet, shook myself, and looked round. One of my boys, he who had thrown himself backward into the bush, was already half way up a tree—if heaven had been at the top of it he could not have climbed quicker. Gobo was lying close to me, groaning vigorously, but, as I suspected, quite unhurt; while from the aloe bush into which No. 3 had bounded like a tennis ball, issued a succession of the most piercing yells.

"I looked, and saw that this unfortunate fellow was in a very tight place. A great spike of aloe had run through the back of his skin waistbelt, though without piercing his flesh, in such a fashion that it was impossible for him to move, while within six feet of him the injured buffalo bull, thinking, no doubt, that he was the aggressor, bellowed and ramped to get at him, tearing the thick aloes with his great horns. That no time was to be lost, if I wished to save the man's life, was very clear. So seizing my eight-bore, which was fortunately uninjured, I took a pace to the left, for the rhinoceros had enlarged the hole in the bush, and aimed at the point of the buffalo's shoulder, since on account of my position I could not get a fair side shot for the heart. As I did so I saw that the rhinoceros had given the bull a tremendous wound in the stomach, and that the shock of the encounter had put his left hind-leg out of joint at the hip. I fired, and the bullet striking the shoulder broke it, and knocked the buffalo down. I knew that he could not get up any more, because he was now injured fore and aft, so notwithstanding his terrific bellows I scrambled round to where he was. There he lay glaring furiously and tearing up the soil with his horns. Stepping up to within two yards of him I aimed at the vertebra of his neck and fired. The bullet struck true, and with a thud he dropped his head upon the ground, groaned, and died.

"This little matter having been attended to with the assistance of Gobo, who had now found his feet, I went on to extricate our unfortunate companion from the aloe bush. This we found a thorny task, but at last he was dragged forth uninjured, though in a very pious and prayerful frame of mind. His 'spirit had certainly looked that way,' he said, or he would now have been dead. As I never like to interfere with true piety, I did not venture to suggest that his spirit had deigned to make use of my eight-bore in his interest.

"Having despatched this boy back to the camp to tell the bearers to come and cut the buffalo up, I bethought me that I owed that rhinoceros a grudge which I should love to repay. So without saying a word of what was in my mind to Gobo, who was now more than ever convinced that Fate walked about loose in Wambe's country, I just followed on the brute's spoor. He had crashed through the bush till he reached the little glade. Then moderating his pace somewhat, he had followed the glade down its entire length, and once more turned to the right through the forest, shaping his course for the open land that lies between the edge of the bush and the river. Having followed him for a mile or so further, I found myself quite on the open. I took out my glasses and searched the plain. About a mile ahead was something brown—as I thought, the rhinoceros. I advanced another quarter of a mile, and looked once more—it was not the rhinoceros, but a big antheap. This was puzzling, but I did not like to give it up, because I knew from his spoor that he must be somewhere ahead. But as the wind was blowing straight from me towards the line that he had followed, and as a rhinoceros can smell you for about a mile, it would not, I felt, be safe to follow his trail any further; so I made a detour of a mile and more, till I was nearly opposite the ant-heap, and then once more searched the plain. It was no good, I could see nothing of him, and was about to give it up and start after some oryx I saw on the skyline, when suddenly at a distance of about three hundred yards from the ant-heap, and on its further side, I saw my rhino stand up in a patch of grass.

"'Heavens!' I thought to myself, 'he's off again;' but no, after standing staring for a minute or two he once more lay down.

"Now I found myself in a quandary. As you know, a rhinoceros is a very short-sighted brute, indeed his sight is as bad as his scent is good. Of this fact he is perfectly aware, but he always makes the most of his natural gifts. For instance, when he lies down he invariably does so with his head down wind. Thus, if any enemy crosses his wind he will still be able to escape, or attack him; and if, on the other hand, the danger approaches up wind he will at least have a chance of seeing it. Otherwise, by walking delicately, one might actually kick him up like a partridge, if only the advance was made up wind.

"Well, the point was, how on earth should I get within shot of this rhinoceros? After much deliberation I determined to try a side approach, thinking that in this way I might get a shoulder shot. Accordingly we started in a crouching attitude, I first, Gobo holding on to my coat tails, and the other boy on to Gobo's *moocha*. I always adopt this plan when stalking big game, for if you follow any other system the bearers will get out of line. We arrived within three hundred yards safely enough, and then the real difficulties began. The grass had been so closely eaten off by game that there was scarcely any cover. Consequently it was necessary to go on to our hands and knees, which in my case involved laying down the eight-bore at every step and then lifting it up again. However, I wriggled along somehow, and if it had not been for Gobo and his friend no doubt everything would have gone well. But as you have, I dare say, observed, a native out stalking is always of that mind which is supposed to actuate an ostrich—so long as his head is hidden he seems to think that nothing else can be seen. So it was in this instance, Gobo and the other boy crept along on their hands and toes with their heads well down, but, though unfortunately I did not notice it till too late, bearing the fundamental portions of their frames high in the air. Now all animals are quite as suspicious of this end of mankind as they are of his face, and of that fact I soon had a proof. Just when we had got within about two hundred yards, and I was congratulating myself that I had not had this long crawl with the sun beating on the back of my neck like a furnace for nothing, I heard the hissing note of the rhinoceros birds, and up flew four or five of them from the brute's back, where they had been comfortably employed in catching tics. Now this performance on the part of the birds is to a rhinoceros what the word 'cave' is to a schoolboy—it puts him on the *qui vive* at once. Before the birds were well in the air I saw the grass stir.

"'Down you go,' I whispered to the boys, and as I did so the rhinoceros got up and glared suspiciously around. But he could see nothing, indeed if we had been standing up I doubt if he would have seen us at that distance; so he merely gave two or three sniffs and then lay down, his head still down wind, the birds once more settling on his back.

"But it was clear to me that he was sleeping with one eye open, being generally in a suspicious and unchristian frame of mind, and that it was useless to proceed further on this stalk, so we quietly withdrew to consider the position and study the ground. The results were not satisfactory. There was absolutely no cover about except the ant-heap, which was some three hundred yards from the rhinoceros upon his up-wind side. I knew that if I tried to stalk him in front I should fail, and so I should if I attempted to do so from the further side—he or the birds would see me; so I came to a conclusion: I would go to the ant-heap, which would give him my wind, and instead of stalking him I would let him stalk me. It was a bold step, and one which I should never advise a hunter to take, but somehow I felt as though rhino and I must play the hand out.

"I explained my intentions to the men, who both held up their arms in horror. Their fears for my safety were a little mitigated, however, when I told them that I did not expect them to come with me.

"Gobo breathed a prayer that I might not meet Fate walking about, and the other one sincerely trusted that my spirit might look my way when the rhinoceros charged, and then they both departed to a place of safety.

"Taking my eight-bore, and half-a-dozen spare cartridges in my pocket, I made a detour, and reaching the ant-heap in safety lay down. For a moment the wind had dropped, but presently a gentle puff of air passed over me, and blew on towards the rhinoceros. By the way, I wonder what it is that smells so strong about a man? Is it his body or his breath? I have never been able to make out, but I saw it stated the other day, that in the duck decoys the man who is working the ducks holds a little piece of burning turf before his mouth, and that if he does this they cannot smell him, which looks as though it were the breath. Well, whatever it was about me that attracted his attention, the rhinoceros soon smelt me, for within half a minute after the puff of wind had passed me he was on his legs, and turning round to get his head up wind. There he stood for a few seconds and sniffed, and then he began to move, first of all at a trot, then, as the scent grew stronger, at a furious gallop. On he came, snorting like a runaway engine, with his tail stuck straight up in the air; if he had seen me lie down there he could not have made a better line. It was rather nervous work, I can tell you, lying there waiting for his onslaught, for he looked like a mountain of flesh. I determined, however, not to fire till I could plainly see his eye, for I think that rule always gives one the right distance for big game; so I rested my rifle on the ant-heap and waited for him, kneeling. At last, when he was about forty yards away, I saw that the time had come, and aiming straight for the middle of the chest I pulled.

"*Thud* went the heavy bullet, and with a tremendous snort over rolled the rhinoceros beneath its shock, just like a shot rabbit. But if I had thought that he was done for I was mistaken, for in another second he was up again, and coming at me as hard as ever, only with his head held low. I waited till he was within ten yards, in the hope that he would expose his chest, but he would do nothing of the sort; so I just had to fire at his head with the left barrel, and take my chance. Well, as luck would have it, of course the animal put its horn in the way of the bullet, which cut clean through it about three inches above the root and then glanced off into space.

"After that things got rather serious. My gun was empty and the rhinoceros was rapidly arriving, so rapidly indeed that I came to the conclusion that I had better make way for him. Accordingly I jumped to my feet and ran to the right as hard as I could go. As I did so he arrived full tilt, knocked my friendly ant-heap flat, and for the third time that day went a most magnificent cropper. This gave me a few seconds' start, and I ran down wind—my word, I did run! Unfortunately, however, my modest retreat was observed, and the rhinoceros, as soon as he had found his legs again, set to work to run after me. Now no man on earth can run so fast as an irritated rhinoceros can gallop, and I knew that he must soon catch me up. But having some slight experience of this sort of thing, luckily for myself, I kept my head, and as I fled I managed to open my rifle, get the old cartridges out, and put in two fresh ones. To do this I was obliged to steady my pace a little, and by the time that I had snapped the rifle to I heard the beast snorting and thundering away within a few paces of my back. I stopped, and as I did so rapidly cocked the rifle and slued round upon my heel. By this time the brute was within six or seven yards of me, but luckily his head was up. I lifted the rifle and fired at him. It was a snap shot, but the bullet struck him in the chest within three inches of the first, and found its way into his lungs. It did not stop him, however, so all I could do was to bound to one side, which I did with surprising activity, and as he brushed past me to fire the other barrel into his side. That did for him. The ball passed in behind the shoulder and right through his heart. He fell over on to his side, gave one more awful squeal—a dozen pigs could not have made such a noise—and promptly died, keeping his wicked eyes wide open all the time.

"As for me, I blew my nose, and going up to the rhinoceros sat on his head, and reflected that I had done a capital morning's shooting."

CHAPTER 3

The First Round

"After this, as it was now midday, and I had killed enough meat, we marched back triumphantly to camp, where I proceeded to concoct a stew of buffalo beef and compressed vegetables. When this was ready we ate the stew, and then I took a nap. About four o'clock, however, Gobo woke me up, and told me that the head man of one of Wambe's *kraals* had arrived to see me. I ordered him to be brought up, and presently he came, a little, wizened, talkative old man, with a waistcloth round his middle, and a greasy, frayed *kaross* made of the skins of rock rabbits over his shoulders.

"I told him to sit down, and then abused him roundly. 'What did he mean,' I asked, 'by disturbing me in this rude way? How did he dare to cause a person of my quality and evident importance to be awakened in order to interview his entirely contemptible self?'

"I spoke thus because I knew that it would produce an impression on him. Nobody, except a really great man, he would argue, would dare to speak to him in that fashion. Most savages are desperate bullies at heart, and look on insolence as a sign of power.

"The old man instantly collapsed. He was utterly overcome, he said; his heart was split in two, and well realized the extent of his misbehaviour. But the occasion was very urgent. He heard that a mighty hunter was in the neighbourhood, a beautiful white man, how beautiful he could not have imagined had he not seen (this to me!), and he came to beg his assistance. The truth was, that three bull elephants such as no man ever saw had for years been the terror of their *kraal*, which was but a small place—a cattle *kraal* of the great chief Wambe's, where they lived to keep the cattle. And now of late these elephants had done them much damage; but last night they had destroyed a whole patch of *mealie* land, and he feared that if they came back they would all starve next season for want of food. Would the mighty white man then be pleased to come and kill the elephants? It would be easy for him to do—oh, most easy! It was only necessary that he should hide himself in a tree, for there was a full moon, and then when the elephants appeared he would speak to them with the gun, and they would fall down dead, and there would be an end of their troubling.

"Of course I hummed and hawed, and made a great favour of consenting to his proposal, though really I was delighted to have such a chance. One of the conditions that I made was that a messenger should at once be despatched to Wambe, whose *kraal* was two days' journey from where I was, telling him that I proposed to come and pay my respects to him in a few days, and to ask his formal permission to shoot in his country. Also I intimated that I was prepared to present him with *hongo*, that is, blackmail, and that I hoped to do a little trade with him in ivory, of which I heard he had a great quantity.

"This message the old gentleman promised to despatch at once, though there was something about his manner which showed me that he was doubtful as to how it would be received. After that we struck our camp and moved on to the *kraal*, which we reached about an hour before sunset. This *kraal* was a collection of huts surrounded by a slight thorn-fence, perhaps there were ten of them in all. It was situated in a *kloof* of the mountain down which a rivulet flowed. The *kloof* was densely wooded, but for some distance above the *kraal* it was free from bush, and here on the rich deep ground brought down by the rivulet were the cultivated lands, in extent somewhere about twenty or twenty-five acres. On the *kraal* side of these lands stood a single hut, that served for a *mealie* store, which at the moment was used as a dwelling-place by an old woman, the first wife of our friend the head man.

"It appears that this lady, having had some difference of opinion with her husband about the extent of authority allowed to a younger and more amiable wife, had refused to dwell in the *kraal* any more, and, by way of marking her displeasure, had taken up her abode among the *mealies*. As the issue will show, she was, it happened, cutting off her nose to spite her face.

"Close by this hut grew a large baobab tree. A glance at the *mealie* grounds showed me that the old head man had not exaggerated the mischief done by the elephants to his crops, which were now getting ripe. Nearly half of the entire patch was destroyed. The great brutes had eaten all they could, and the rest they had trampled down. I went up to their spoor and started back in amazement—never had I seen such a spoor before. It was simply enormous, more especially that of one old bull, that carried, so said the natives, but a single tusk. One might have used any of the footprints for a hip-bath.

"Having taken stock of the position, my next step was to make arrangements for the fray. The three bulls, according to the natives, had been spoored into the dense patch of bush above the *kloof*. Now it seemed to me very probable that they would return to-night to feed on the remainder of the ripening *mealies*. If so, there was a bright moon, and it struck me that by the exercise of a little ingenuity I might bag one or more of them without exposing myself to any risk, which, having the highest respect for the aggressive powers of bull elephants, was a great consideration to me.

"This then was my plan. To the right of the huts as you look up the *kloof*, and commanding the *mealie* lands, stands the baobab tree that I have mentioned. Into that baobab tree I made up my mind to go. Then if the elephants appeared I should get a shot at them. I announced my intentions to the head man of the *kraal*, who was delighted. 'Now,' he said, 'his people might sleep in peace, for while the mighty white hunter sat aloft like a spirit watching over the welfare of his *kraal* what was there to fear?'

"I told him that he was an ungrateful brute to think of sleeping in peace while, perched like a wounded vulture on a tree, I watched for his welfare in wakeful sorrow; and once more he collapsed, and owned that my words were 'sharp but just.'

"However, as I have said, confidence was completely restored; and that evening everybody in the *kraal*, including the superannuated victim of jealousy in the little hut where the *mealie* cobs were stored, went to bed with a sense of sweet security from elephants and all other animals that prowl by night.

"For my part, I pitched my camp below the *kraal*; and then, having procured a beam of wood from the head man—rather a rotten one, by the way—I set it across two boughs that ran out laterally from the baobab tree, at a height of about twenty-five feet from the ground, in such fashion that I and another man could sit upon it with our legs hanging down, and rest our backs against the bole of the tree. This done I went back to the camp and ate my supper. About nine o'clock, half-an-hour before the moon-rise, I summoned Gobo, who, thinking that he had seen about enough of the delights of big game hunting for that day, did not altogether relish the job; and, despite his remonstrances, gave him my eight-bore to carry, I having the .570-express. Then we set out for the tree. It was very dark, but we found it without difficulty, though climbing it was a more complicated matter. However, at last we got up and sat down, like two little boys on a form that is too high for them, and waited. I did not dare to smoke, because I remembered the rhinoceros, and feared that the elephants might wind the tobacco if they should come my way, and this made the business more wearisome, so I fell to thinking and wondering at the completeness of the silence.

"At last the moon came up, and with it a moaning wind, at the breath of which the silence began to whisper mysteriously. Lonely enough in the newborn light looked the wide expanse of mountain, plain, and forest, more like some vision of a dream, some reflection from a fair world of peace beyond our ken, than the mere face of garish earth made soft with sleep. Indeed, had it not been for the fact that I was beginning to find the log on which I sat very hard, I should have grown quite sentimental over the beautiful sight; but I will defy anybody to become sentimental when seated in the damp, on a very rough beam of wood, and half-way up a tree. So I merely made a mental note that it was a particularly lovely night, and turned my attention to the prospect of elephants. But no elephants came, and after waiting for another hour or so, I think that what between weariness and disgust, I must have dropped into a gentle doze. Presently I awoke with a start. Gobo, who was perched close to me, but as far off as the beam would allow—for neither white man nor black like the aroma which each vows is the peculiar and disagreeable property of the other—was faintly, very faintly clicking his forefinger against his thumb. I knew by this signal, a very favourite one among native hunters and gun-bearers, that he must have seen or heard something. I looked at his face, and saw that he was staring excitedly towards the dim edge of the bush beyond the deep green line of *mealies*. I stared too, and listened. Presently I heard a soft large sound as though a giant were gently stretching out his hands and pressing back the ears of standing corn. Then came a pause, and then, out into the open majestically stalked the largest elephant I ever saw or ever shall see. Heavens! what a monster he was; and how the moonlight gleamed upon his one splendid tusk—for the other was missing—as he stood among the *mealies* gently moving his enormous ears to and fro, and testing the wind with his trunk. While I was still marvelling at his girth, and speculating upon the weight of that huge tusk, which I swore should be my tusk before very long, out stepped a second bull and stood beside him. He was not quite so tall, but he seemed to me to be almost thicker-set than the first; and even in that light I could see that both his tusks were perfect. Another pause, and the third emerged. He was shorter than either of the others, but higher in the shoulder than No.

2; and when I tell you, as I afterwards learnt from actual measurement, that the smallest of these mighty bulls measured twelve feet one and a half inches at the shoulder, it will give you some idea of their size. The three formed into line and stood still for a minute, the one-tusked bull gently caressing the elephant on the left with his trunk.

"Then they began to feed, walking forward and slightly to the right as they gathered great bunches of the sweet *mealies* and thrust them into their mouths. All this time they were more than a hundred and twenty yards away from me (this I knew, because I had paced the distances from the tree to various points), much too far to allow of my attempting a shot at them in that uncertain light. They fed in a semicircle, gradually drawing round towards the hut near my tree, in which the corn was stored and the old woman slept.

"This went on for between an hour and an hour and a half, till, what between excitement and hope, that maketh the heart sick, I grew so weary that I was actually contemplating a descent from the tree and a moonlight stalk. Such an act in ground so open would have been that of a stark staring lunatic, and that I should even have been contemplating it will show you the condition of my mind. But everything comes to him who knows how to wait, and sometimes too to him who doesn't, and so at last those elephants, or rather one of them, came to me.

"After they had fed their fill, which was a very large one, the noble three stood once more in line some seventy yards to the left of the hut, and on the edge of the cultivated lands, or in all about eighty-five yards from where I was perched. Then at last the one with a single tusk made a peculiar rattling noise in his trunk, just as though he were blowing his nose, and without more ado began to walk deliberately toward the hut where the old woman slept. I made my rifle ready and glanced up at the moon, only to discover that a new complication was looming in the immediate future. I have said that a wind rose with the moon. Well, the wind brought rain-clouds along its track. Several light ones had already lessened the light for a little while, though without obscuring it, and now two more were coming up rapidly, both of them very black and dense. The first cloud was small and long, and the one behind big and broad. I remember noticing that the pair of them bore a most comical resemblance to a dray drawn by a very long raw-boned horse. As luck would have it, just as the elephant arrived within twenty-five yards or so of me, the head of the horse-cloud floated over the face of the moon, rendering it impossible for me to fire. In the faint twilight which remained, however, I could just make out the gray mass of the great brute still advancing towards the hut.

Then the light went altogether and I had to trust to my ears. I heard him fumbling with his trunk, apparently at the roof of the hut; next came a sound as of straw being drawn out, and then for a little while there was complete silence.

"The cloud began to pass; I could see the outline of the elephant; he was standing with his head quite over the top of the hut. But I could not see his trunk, and no wonder, for it was *inside the hut*. He had thrust it through the roof, and, attracted no doubt by the smell of the *mealies*, was groping about with it inside. It was growing light now, and I got my rifle ready, when suddenly there was a most awful yell, and I saw the trunk reappear, and in its mighty fold the old woman who had been sleeping in the hut. Out she came through the hole like a periwinkle on the point of a pin, still wrapped up in her blanket, and with her skinny arms and legs stretched to the four points of the compass, and as she did so, gave that most alarming screech. I really don't know who was the most frightened, she, or I, or the elephant. At any rate the last was considerably startled; he had been fishing for *mealies*—the old woman was a mere accident, and one that greatly discomposed his nerves. He gave a sort of trumpet, and threw her away from him right into the crown of a low mimosa tree, where she stuck shrieking like a metropolitan engine. The old bull lifted his tail, and flapping his great ears prepared for flight. I put up my eight-bore, and aiming hastily at the point of his shoulder (for he was broadside on), I fired. The report rang out like thunder, making a thousand echoes in the quiet hills. I saw him go down all of a heap as though he were stone dead. Then, alas! whether it was the kick of the heavy rifle, or the excited bump of that idiot Gobo, or both together, or merely an unhappy coincidence, I do not know, but the rotten beam broke and I went down too, landing flat at the foot of the tree upon a certain humble portion of the human frame. The shock was so severe that I felt as though all my teeth were flying through the roof of my mouth, but although I sat slightly stunned for a few seconds, luckily for me I fell light, and was not in any way injured.

"Meanwhile the elephant began to scream with fear and fury, and, attracted by his cries, the other two charged up. I felt for my rifle; it was not there. Then I remembered that I had rested it on a fork of the bough in order to fire, and doubtless there it remained. My position was now very unpleasant. I did not dare to try and climb the tree again, which, shaken as I was, would have been a task of some difficulty, because the elephants would certainly see me, and Gobo, who had clung to a bough, was still aloft with the other rifle. I could not run because there was no shelter near. Under these circumstances I did the only thing feasible, clambered round the trunk as softly as possible, and keeping one eye on the elephants, whispered to Gobo to bring down the rifle, and awaited the development of the situation. I knew that if the elephants did not see me—which, luckily, they were too enraged to do—they would not smell me, for I was up-wind. Gobo, however, either did not, or, preferring the safety of the tree, would not hear me. He said the former, but I believed the latter, for I knew that he was not enough of a sportsman to really enjoy shooting elephants by moon-light in the open. So there I was behind my tree, dismayed, unarmed, but highly interested, for I was witnessing a remarkable performance.

"When the two other bulls arrived the wounded elephant on the ground ceased to scream, but began to make a low moaning noise, and to gently touch the wound near his shoulder, from which the blood was literally spouting. The other two seemed to understand; at any rate, they did this. Kneeling down on either side, they placed their trunks and tusks underneath him, and, aided by his own efforts, with one great lift got him on to his feet. Then leaning against him on either side to support him, they marched off at a walk in the direction of the village.[1] It was a pitiful sight, and even then it made me feel a brute.

"Presently, from a walk, as the wounded elephant gathered himself together a little, they broke into a trot, and after that I could follow them no longer with my eyes, for the second black cloud came up over the moon and put her out, as an extinguisher puts out a dip. I say with my eyes, but my ears gave me a very fair notion of what was going on. When the cloud came up the three terrified animals were heading directly for the *kraal*, probably because the way was open and the path easy. I fancy that they grew confused in the darkness, for when they came to the *kraal* fence they did not turn aside, but crashed straight through it. Then there were 'times,' as the Irish servant-girl says in the American book. Having taken the fence, they thought that they might as well take the *kraal* also, so they just ran over it. One hive-shaped hut was turned quite over on to its top, and when I arrived upon the scene the people who had been sleeping there were bumbling about inside like bees disturbed at night, while two more were crushed flat, and a third had all its side torn out. Oddly enough, however, nobody was hurt, though several people had a narrow escape of being trodden to death.

---

1. The Editor would have been inclined to think that in relating this incident Mr. Quatermain was making himself interesting at the expense of the exact truth, did it not happen that a similar incident has come within his knowledge.—Editor.

"On arrival I found the old head man in a state painfully like that favoured by Greek art, dancing about in front of his ruined abodes as vigorously as though he had just been stung by a scorpion.

"I asked him what ailed him, and he burst out into a flood of abuse. He called me a Wizard, a Sham, a Fraud, a Bringer of bad luck! I had promised to kill the elephants, and I had so arranged things that the elephants had nearly killed him, etc.

"This, still smarting, or rather aching, as I was from that most terrific bump, was too much for my feelings, so I just made a rush at my friend, and getting him by the ear, I banged his head against the doorway of his own hut, which was all that was left of it.

"'You wicked old scoundrel,' I said, 'you dare to complain about your own trifling inconveniences, when you gave me a rotten beam to sit on, and thereby delivered me to the fury of the elephant' (*Bump! Bump! Bump!*), 'when your own wife' (*Bump!*) 'has just been dragged out of her hut' (*Bump!*) 'like a snail from its shell, and thrown by the Earth-shaker into a tree' (*Bump! Bump!*).

"'Mercy, my father, mercy!' gasped the old fellow. 'Truly I have done amiss—my heart tells me so.'

"'I should hope it did, you old villain' (*Bump!*).

"'Mercy, great white man! I thought the log was sound. But what says the unequalled chief—is the old woman, my wife, indeed dead? Ah, if she is dead all may yet prove to have been for the very best;' and he clasped his hands and looked up piously to heaven, in which the moon was once more shining brightly.

"I let go his ear and burst out laughing, the whole scene and his devout aspirations for the decease of the partner of his joys, or rather woes, were so intensely ridiculous.

"'No, you old iniquity,' I answered; 'I left her in the top of a thorn-tree, screaming like a thousand blue jays. The elephant put her there.'

"'Alas! alas!' he said, 'surely the back of the ox is shaped to the burden. Doubtless, my father, she will come down when she is tired;' and without troubling himself further about the matter, he began to blow at the smouldering embers of the fire.

"And, as a matter of fact, she did appear a few minutes later, considerably scratched and startled, but none the worse.

"After that I made my way to my little camp, which, fortunately, the elephants had not walked over, and wrapping myself up in a blanket, was soon fast asleep.

"And so ended my first round with those three elephants."

CHAPTER 4

The Last Round

"On the morrow I woke up full of painful recollections, and not without a certain feeling of gratitude to the Powers above that I was there to wake up. Yesterday had been a tempestuous day; indeed, what between buffalo, rhinoceros, and elephant, it had been very tempestuous. Having realized this fact, I next bethought me of those magnificent tusks, and instantly, early as it was, broke the tenth commandment. I coveted my neighbours tusks, if an elephant could be said to be my neighbour *de jure*, as certainly, so recently as the previous night, he had been *de facto*—a much closer neighbour than I cared for, indeed. Now when you covet your neighbour's goods, the best thing, if not the most moral thing, to do is to enter his house as a strong man armed, and take them. I was not a strong man, but having recovered my eight-bore I was armed, and so was the other strong man—the elephant with the tusks. Consequently I prepared for a struggle to the death. In other words, I summoned my faithful retainers, and told them that I was now going to follow those elephants to the edge of the world, if necessary. They showed a certain bashfulness about the business, but they did not gainsay me, because they dared not. Ever since I had prepared with all due solemnity to execute the rebellious Gobo they had conceived a great respect for me.

"So I went up to bid adieu to the old head man, whom I found alternately contemplating the ruins of his *kraal* and, with the able assistance of his last wife, thrashing the jealous lady who had slept in the *mealie* hut, because she was, as he declared, the fount of all his sorrows.

"Leaving them to work a way through their domestic differences, I levied a supply of vegetable food from the *kraal* in consideration of services rendered, and left them with my blessing. I do not know how they settled matters, because I have not seen them since.

"Then I started on the spoor of the three bulls. For a couple

151

of miles or so below the *kraal*—as far, indeed, as the belt of swamp that borders the river—the ground is at this spot rather stony, and clothed with scattered bushes. Rain had fallen towards the daybreak, and this fact, together with the nature of the soil, made *spooring* a very difficult business. The wounded bull had indeed bled freely, but the rain had washed the blood off the leaves and grass, and the ground being so rough and hard did not take the footmarks so clearly as was convenient. However, we got along, though slowly, partly by the spoor, and partly by carefully lifting leaves and blades of grass, and finding blood underneath them, for the blood gushing from a wounded animal often falls upon their inner surfaces, and then, of course, unless the rain is very heavy, it is not washed away. It took us something over an hour and a half to reach the edge of the marsh, but once there our task became much easier, for the soft soil showed plentiful evidences of the great brutes' passage. Threading our way through the swampy land, we came at last to a ford of the river, and here we could see where the poor wounded animal had lain down in the mud and water in the hope of easing himself of his pain, and could see also how his two faithful companions had assisted him to rise again. We crossed the ford, and took up the spoor on the further side, and followed it into the marsh-like land beyond. No rain had fallen on this side of the river, and the blood-marks were consequently much more frequent.

"All that day we followed the three bulls, now across open plains, and now through patches of bush. They seemed to have travelled on almost without stopping, and I noticed that as they went the wounded bull recovered his strength a little. This I could see from his spoor, which had become firmer, and also from the fact that the other two had ceased to support him. At last evening closed in, and having travelled some eighteen miles, we camped, thoroughly tired out.

"Before dawn on the following day we were up, and the first break of light found us once more on the spoor. About half-past five o'clock we reached the place where the elephants had fed and slept. The two unwounded bulls had taken their fill, as the condition of the neighbouring bushes showed, but the wounded one had eaten nothing. He had spent the night leaning against a good-sized tree, which his weight had pushed out of the perpendicular. They had not long left this place, and could not be very far ahead, especially as the wounded bull was now again so stiff after his night's rest that for the first few miles the other two had been obliged to support him. But elephants go very quick, even when they seem to be travelling slowly, for shrub and creepers that almost stop a man's progress are no hindrance to them. The three had now turned to the left, and were travelling back again in a semicircular line toward the mountains, probably with the idea of working round to their old feeding grounds on the further side of the river.

"There was nothing for it but to follow their lead, and accordingly we followed with industry. Through all that long hot day did we tramp, passing quantities of every sort of game, and even coming across the spoor of other elephants. But, in spite of my men's entreaties, I would not turn aside after these. I would have those mighty tusks or none.

"By evening we were quite close to our game, probably within a quarter of a mile, but the bush was dense, and we could see nothing of them, so once more we must camp, thoroughly disgusted with our luck. That night, just after the moon rose, while I was sitting smoking my pipe with my back against a tree, I heard an elephant trumpet, as though something had startled it, and not three hundred yards away. I was very tired, but my curiosity overcame my weariness, so, without saying a word to any of the men, all of whom were asleep, I took my eight-bore and a few spare cartridges, and steered toward the sound. The game path which we had been following all day ran straight on in the direction from which the elephant had trumpeted. It was narrow, but well trodden, and the light struck down upon it in a straight white line. I crept along it cautiously for some two hundred yards, when it opened suddenly into a most beautiful glade some hundred yards or more in width, wherein tall grass grew and flat-topped trees stood singly. With the caution born of long experience I watched for a few moments before I entered the glade, and then I saw why the elephant had trumpeted. There in the middle of the glade stood a large maned lion. He stood quite still, making a soft purring noise, and waving his tail to and fro. Presently the grass about forty yards on the hither side of him gave a wide ripple, and a lioness sprang out of it like a flash, and bounded noiselessly up to the lion. Reaching him, the great cat halted suddenly, and rubbed her head against his shoulder. Then they both began to purr loudly, so loudly that I believe that in the stillness one might have heard them two hundred yards or more away.

"After a time, while I was still hesitating what to do, either they got a whiff of my wind, or they wearied of standing still, and determined to start in search of game. At any rate, as though moved by a common impulse, they bounded suddenly away, leap by leap, and vanished in the depths of the forest to the left. I waited for a little while longer to see if there were any more yellow skins about, and seeing none, came to the conclusion that the lions must have frightened the elephants away, and that I had taken my stroll for nothing. But just as I was turning back I thought that I heard a bough break upon the further side of the glade, and, rash as the act was, I followed the sound. I crossed the glade as silently as my own shadow. On its further side the path went on. Albeit with many fears, I went on too. The jungle growth was so thick here that it almost met overhead, leaving so small a passage for the light that I could scarcely see to grope my way along. Presently, however, it widened, and then opened into a second glade slightly smaller than the first, and there, on the further side of it, about eighty yards from me, stood the three enormous elephants.

"They stood thus:—Immediately opposite and facing me was the wounded one-tusked bull. He was leaning his bulk against a dead thorn-tree, the only one in the place, and looked very sick indeed. Near him stood the second bull as though keeping a watch over him. The third elephant was a good deal nearer to me and broadside on. While I was still staring at them, this elephant suddenly walked off and vanished down a path in the bush to the right.

"There are now two things to be done—either I could go back to the camp and advance upon the elephants at dawn, or I could attack them at once. The first was, of course, by far the wiser and safer course. To engage one elephant by moonlight and single-handed is a sufficiently rash proceeding; to tackle three was little short of lunacy. But, on the other hand, I knew that they would be on the march again before daylight, and there might come another day of weary trudging before I could catch them up, or they might escape me altogether.

"'No,' I thought to myself, 'faint heart never won fair tusk. I'll risk it, and have a slap at them. But how?' I could not advance across the open, for they would see me; clearly the only thing to do was to creep round in the shadow of the bush and try to come upon them so. So I started. Seven or eight minutes of careful stalking brought me to the mouth of the path down which the third elephant had walked. The other two were now about fifty yards from me, and the nature of the wall of bush was such that I could not see how to get nearer to them without being discovered. I hesitated, and peeped down the path which the elephant had followed. About five yards in, it took a turn round a shrub. I thought that I would just have a look behind it, and advanced, expecting that I should be able to catch a sight of the elephant's tail. As it happened, however, I met his trunk coming

154

round the corner. It is very disconcerting to see an elephant's trunk when you expect to see his tail, and for a moment I stood paralyzed almost under the vast brute's head, for he was not five yards from me. He too halted, threw up his trunk and trumpeted preparatory to a charge. I was in for it now, for I could not escape either to the right or left, on account of the bush, and I did not dare turn my back. So I did the only thing that I could do—raised the rifle and fired at the black mass of his chest. It was too dark for me to pick a shot; I could only brown him, as it were.

"The shot rang out like thunder on the quiet air, and the elephant answered it with a scream, then dropped his trunk and stood for a second or two as still as though he had been cut in stone. I confess that I lost my head; I ought to have fired my second barrel, but I did not. Instead of doing so, I rapidly opened my rifle, pulled out the old cartridge from the right barrel and replaced it. But before I could snap the breech to, the bull was at me. I saw his great trunk fly up like a brown beam, and I waited no longer. Turning, I fled for dear life, and after me thundered the elephant. Right into the open glade I ran, and then, thank Heaven, just as he was coming up with me the bullet took effect on him. He had been shot right through the heart, or lungs, and down he fell with a crash, stone dead.

"But in escaping from Scylla I had run into the jaws of Charybdis. I heard the elephant fall, and glanced round. Straight in front of me, and not fifteen paces away, were the other two bulls. They were staring about, and at that moment they caught sight of me. Then they came, the pair of them—came like thunderbolts, and from different angles. I had only time to snap my rifle to, lift it, and fire, almost at haphazard, at the head of the nearest, the unwounded bull.

"Now, as you know, in the case of the African elephant, whose skull is convex, and not concave like that of the Indian, this is always a most risky and very frequently a perfectly useless shot. The bullet loses itself in the masses of bone, that is all. But there is one little vital place, and should the bullet happen to strike there, it will follow the channel of the nostrils—at least I suppose it is that of the nostrils—and reach the brain. And this was what happened in the present case—the ball struck the fatal spot in the region of the eye and travelled to the brain. Down came the great bull all of a heap, and rolled on to his side as dead as a stone. I swung round at that instant to face the third, the monster bull with one tusk that I had wounded two days before. He was already almost over me, and in the dim moonlight seemed to tower above me like a house. I lifted the rifle and pulled at his neck. It would not go off! Then, in a flash, as it were, I remembered that it was on the half-cock. The lock of this barrel was a little weak, and a few days before, in firing at a cow eland, the left barrel had jarred off at the shock of the discharge of the right, knocking me backwards with the recoil; so after that I had kept it on the half-cock till I actually wanted to fire it.

"I gave one desperate bound to the right, and, my lame leg notwithstanding, I believe that few men could have made a better jump. At any rate, it was none too soon, for as I jumped I felt the wind made by the tremendous downward stroke of the monster's trunk. Then I ran for it.

"I ran like a buck, still keeping hold of my gun, however. My idea, so far as I could be said to have any fixed idea, was to bolt down the pathway up which I had come, like a rabbit down a burrow, trusting that he would lose sight of me in the uncertain light. I sped across the glade. Fortunately the bull, being wounded, could not go full speed; but wounded or no, he could go quite as fast as I could. I was unable to gain an inch, and away we went, with just about three feet between our separate extremities. We were at the other side now, and a glance served to show me that I had miscalculated and overshot the opening. To reach it now was hopeless; I should have blundered straight into the elephant. So I did the only thing I could do: I swerved like a course hare, and started off round the edge of the glade, seeking for some opening into which I could plunge. This gave me a moment's start, for the bull could not turn as quickly as I could, and I made the most of it. But no opening could I see; the bush was like a wall. We were speeding round the edge of the glade, and the elephant was coming up again. Now he was within about six feet, and now, as he trumpeted or rather screamed, I could feel the fierce hot blast of his breath strike upon my head. Heavens! how it frightened me!

"We were three parts round the glade now, and about fifty yards ahead was the single large dead thorn-tree against which the bull had been leaning. I spurted for it; it was my last chance of safety. But spurt as I would, it seemed hours before I got there. Putting out my right hand, I swung round the tree, thus bringing myself face to face with the elephant. I had not time to lift the rifle to fire, I had barely time to cock it, and run sideways and backward, when he was on to me. *Crash!* He came, striking the tree full with his forehead. It snapped like a carrot about forty inches from the ground. Fortunately I was clear of the trunk, but one of the dead branches struck me on the chest as it went down and swept me to the ground. I fell upon my back, and the elephant blundered past me as I lay. More by instinct than anything else I lifted the rifle with one hand and pulled the trigger. It exploded, and, as I discovered afterwards, the bullet struck him in the ribs. But the recoil of the heavy rifle held thus was very severe; it bent my arm up, and sent the butt with a thud against the top of my shoulder and the side of my neck, for the moment quite paralyzing me, and causing the weapon to jump from my grasp. Meanwhile the bull was rushing on. He travelled for some twenty paces, and then suddenly he stopped. Faintly I reflected that he was coming back to finish me, but even the prospect of imminent and dreadful death could not rouse me into action. I was utterly spent; I could not move.

"Idly, almost indifferently, I watched his movements. For a moment he stood still, next he trumpeted till the welkin rang, and then very slowly, and with great dignity, he knelt down. At this point I swooned away.

"When I came to myself again I saw from the moon that I must have been insensible for quite two hours. I was drenched with dew, and shivering all over. At first I could not think where I was, when, on lifting my head, I saw the outline of the one-tusked bull still kneeling some five-and-twenty paces from me. Then I remembered. Slowly I raised myself, and was instantly taken with a violent sickness, the result of over-exertion, after which I very nearly fainted a second time. Presently I grew better, and considered the position. Two of the elephants were, as I knew, dead; but how about No. 3? There he knelt in majesty in the lonely moonlight. The question was, was he resting, or dead? I rose on my hands and knees, loaded my rifle, and painfully crept a few paces nearer. I could see his eye now, for the moonlight fell full upon it—it was open, and rather prominent. I crouched and watched; the eyelid did not move, nor did the great brown body, or the trunk, or the ear, or the tail—nothing moved. Then I knew that he must be dead.

"I crept up to him, still keeping the rifle well forward, and gave him a thump, reflecting as I did so how very near I had been to being thumped instead of thumping. He never stirred; certainly he was dead, though to this day I do not know if it was my random shot that killed him, or if he died from concussion of the brain consequent upon the tremendous shock of his contact with the tree. Anyhow, there he was. Cold and beautiful he lay, or rather knelt, as the poet nearly puts it. Indeed, I do not think that I have ever seen a sight more imposing in its way than that of the mighty beast crouched in majestic death, and shone upon by the lonely moon.

"While I stood admiring the scene, and heartily congratulating myself upon my escape, once more I began to feel sick. Accordingly, without waiting to examine the other two bulls, I staggered back to the camp, which in due course I reached in safety. Everybody in it was asleep. I did not wake them, but having swallowed a mouthful of brandy I threw off my coat and shoes, rolled myself up in a blanket, and was soon fast asleep.

"When I woke it was already light, and at first I thought that, like Joseph, I had dreamed a dream. At that moment, however, I turned my head, and quickly knew that it was no dream, for my neck and face were so stiff from the blow of the butt-end of the rifle that it was agony to move them. I collapsed for a minute or two. Gobo and another man, wrapped up like a couple of monks in their blankets, thinking that I was still asleep, were crouched over a little fire they had made, for the morning was damp and chilly, and holding sweet converse.

"Gobo said that he was getting tired of running after elephants which they never caught. Macumazahn (that is, myself) was without doubt a man of parts, and of some skill in shooting, but also he was a fool. None but a fool would run so fast and far after elephants which it was impossible to catch, when they kept cutting the spoor of fresh ones. He certainly was a fool, but he must not be allowed to continue in his folly; and he, Gobo, had determined to put a stop to it. He should refuse to accompany him any further on so mad a hunt.

"'Yes,' the other answered, 'the poor man certainly was sick in his head, and it was quite time that they checked his folly while they still had a patch of skin left upon their feet. Moreover, he for his part certainly did not like this country of Wambe's, which really was full of ghosts. Only the last night he had heard the spooks at work—they were out shooting, at least it sounded as though they were. It was very queer, but perhaps their lunatic of a master——'

"'Gobo, you scoundrel!' I shouted out at this juncture, sitting bolt upright on the blankets, 'stop idling there and make me some coffee.'

"Up sprang Gobo and his friend, and in half a moment were respectfully skipping about in a manner that contrasted well with the lordly contempt of their previous conversation. But all the time they were in earnest in what they said about hunting the elephants any further, for before I had finished my coffee they came to me in a body, and said that if I wanted to follow those elephants I must follow them myself, for they would not go.

"I argued with them, and affected to be much put out. The elephants were close at hand, I said; I was sure of it; I had heard them trumpet in the night.

"'Yes,' answered the men mysteriously, 'they too had heard things in the night, things not nice to hear; they had heard the spooks out shooting, and no longer would they remain in a country so vilely haunted.'

"'It was nonsense,' I replied. 'If ghosts went out shooting, surely they would use air-guns and not black powder, and one would not hear an air-gun. Well, if they were cowards, and would not come, of course I could not force them to, but I would make a bargain with them. They should follow those elephants for one half-hour more, then if we failed to come upon them I would abandon the pursuit, and we would go straight to Wambe, chief of the Matuku, and give him *hongo*.'

"To this compromise the men agreed readily. Accordingly about half-an-hour later we struck our camp and started, and notwithstanding my aches and bruises, I do not think that I ever felt in better spirits in my life. It is something to wake up in the morning and remember that in the dead of the night, single-handed, one has given battle to and overthrown three of the largest elephants in Africa, slaying them with three bullets. Such a feat to my knowledge had never been done before, and on that particular morning I felt a very 'tall man of my hands' indeed. The only thing I feared was, that should I ever come to tell the story nobody would believe it, for when a strange tale is told by a hunter, people are apt to think it is necessarily a lie, instead of being only probably so.[1]

"Well, we passed on till, having crossed the first glade where I had seen the lions, we reached the neck of bush that separated it from the second glade, where the dead elephants were. And here I began to take elaborate precautions, amongst others ordering Gobo to keep some yards ahead and look out sharp, as I thought that the elephants might be about. He obeyed my instructions with a superior smile, and pushed ahead. Presently I saw him pull up as though he had been shot, and begin to snap his fingers faintly.

"'What is it?' I whispered.

"'The elephant, the great elephant with one tusk kneeling down.'

"I crept up beside him. There knelt the bull as I had left him last night, and there too lay the other bulls.

---

1. For the satisfaction of any who may be so disbelieving as to take this view of Mr. Quatermain's story, the Editor may state that a gentleman with whom he is acquainted, and whose veracity he believes to be beyond doubt, not long ago described to him how he chanced to kill *four* African elephants with four consecutive bullets. Two of these elephants were charging him simultaneously, and out of the four three were killed with the head shot, a very uncommon thing in the case of the African elephant.—Editor.

"'Do these elephants sleep?' I whispered to the astonished Gobo.

"'Yes, Macumazahn, they sleep.'

"'Nay, Gobo, they are dead.'

"'Dead? How can they be dead? Who killed them?'

"'What do people call me, Gobo?'

"'They call you Macumazahn.'

"'And what does Macumazahn mean?'

"'It means the man who keeps his eyes open, the man who gets up in the night.'

"'Yes, Gobo, and I am that man. Look, you idle, lazy cowards; while you slept last night I rose, and alone I hunted those great elephants, and slew them by the moonlight. To each of them I gave one bullet and only one, and it fell dead. Look,' and I advanced into the glade, 'here is my spoor, and here is the spoor of the great bull charging after me, and there is the tree that I took refuge behind; see, the elephant shattered it in his charge. Oh, you cowards, you who would give up the chase while the blood spoor steamed beneath your nostrils, see what I did single-handed while you slept, and be ashamed.'

"'*Ou!*' said the men, '*Ou! Koos! Koos y umcool!*' (Chief, great Chief!) And then they held their tongues, and going up to the three dead beasts, gazed upon them in silence.

"But after that those men looked upon me with awe as being almost more than mortal. No mere man, they said, could have slain those three elephants alone in the night-time. I never had any further trouble with them. I believe that if I had told them to jump over a precipice and that they would take no harm, they would have believed me.

"Well, I went up and examined the bulls. Such tusks as they had I never saw and never shall see again. It took us all day to cut them out; and when they reached Delagoa Bay, as they did ultimately, though not in my keeping, the single tusk of the big bull scaled one hundred and sixty pounds, and the four other tusks averaged ninety-nine and a half pounds—a most wonderful, indeed an almost unprecedented, lot of ivory.[2] Unfortunately I was forced to saw the big tusk in two, otherwise we could not have carried it."

"Oh, Quatermain, you barbarian!" I broke in here, "the idea of spoiling such a tusk! Why, I would have kept it whole if I had been obliged to drag it myself."

"Oh yes, young man," he answered, "it is all very well for you to

---

2. The largest elephant tusk of which the Editor has any certain knowledge scaled one hundred and fifty pounds.

talk like that, but if you had found yourself in the position which it was my privilege to occupy a few hours afterwards, it is my belief that you would have thrown the tusks away altogether and taken to your heels."

"Oh," said Good, "so that isn't the end of the yarn? A very good yarn, Quatermain, by the way—I couldn't have made up a better one myself."

The old gentleman looked at Good severely, for it irritated him to be chaffed about his stories.

"I don't know what you mean, Good. I don't see that there is any comparison between a true story of adventure and the preposterous tales which you invent about ibex hanging by their horns. No, it is not the end of the story; the most exciting part is to come. But I have talked enough for tonight; and if you go on in that way, Good, it will be some time before I begin again."

"Sorry I spoke, I'm sure," said Good, humbly. "Let's have a split to show that there is no ill-feeling." And they did.

CHAPTER 5

The Message of Maiwa

On the following evening we once more dined together, and Quatermain, after some pressure, was persuaded to continue his story—for Good's remark still rankled in his breast.

"At last," he went on, "a few minutes before sunset, the task was finished. We had laboured at it all day, stopping only once for dinner, for it is no easy matter to hew out five such tusks as those which now lay before me in a white and gleaming line. It was a dinner worth eating, too, I can tell you, for we dined off the heart of the great one-tusked bull, which was so big that the man whom I sent inside the elephant to look for his heart was forced to remove it in two pieces. We cut it into slices and fried it with fat, and I never tasted heart to equal it, for the meat seemed to melt in one's mouth. By the way, I examined the jaw of the elephant; it never grew but one tusk; the other had not been broken off, nor was it present in a rudimentary form.

"Well, there lay the five beauties, or rather four of them, for Gobo and another man were engaged in sawing the grand one in two. At last with many sighs I ordered them to do this, but not until by practical experiment I had proved that it was impossible to carry it in any other way. One hundred and sixty pounds of solid ivory, or rather more in its green state, is too great a weight for two men to bear for long across a broken country. I sat watching the job and smoking the pipe of contentment, when suddenly the bush opened, and a very handsome and dignified native girl, apparently about twenty years of age, stood before me, carrying a basket of green *mealies* upon her head.

"Although I was rather surprised to see a native girl in such a wild spot, and, so far as I knew, a long way from any *kraal*, the matter did not attract my particular notice; I merely called to one of the men, and told him to bargain with the woman for the *mealies*, and ask her if there were any more to be bought in the neighbourhood. Then I turned my head and continued to superintend the cutting of the tusk. Presently a shadow fell upon me. I looked up, and saw that the girl was standing before me, the basket of *mealies* still on her head.

"'*Marême, Marême,*' she said, gently clapping her hands together. The word *Marême* among these Matuku (though she was no Matuku) answers to the Zulu *Koos*, and the clapping of hands is a form of salutation very common among the tribes of the Basutu race.

"'What is it, girl?' I asked her in Sisutu. 'Are those *mealies* for sale?'

"'No, great white hunter,' she answered in Zulu, 'I bring them as a gift.'

"'Good,' I replied; 'set them down.'

"'A gift for a gift, white man.'

"'Ah,' I grumbled, 'the old story—nothing for nothing in this wicked world. What do you want—beads?'

"She nodded, and I was about to tell one of the men to go and fetch some from one of the packs, when she checked me.

"'A gift from the giver's own hand is twice a gift,' she said, and I thought that she spoke meaningly.

"'You mean that you want me to give them to you myself?'

"'Surely.'

"I rose to go with her. 'How is it that, being of the Matuku, you speak in the Zulu tongue?' I asked suspiciously.

"'I am not of the Matuku,' she answered as soon as we were out of hearing of the men. 'I am of the people of Nala, whose tribe is the Butiana tribe, and who lives there,' and she pointed over the mountain. 'Also I am one of the wives of Wambe,' and her eyes flashed as she said the name.

"'And how did you come here?'

"'On my feet,' she answered laconically.

"We reached the packs, and undoing one of them, I extracted a handful of beads. 'Now,' I said, 'a gift for a gift. Hand over the *mealies*.'

"She took the beads without even looking at them, which struck me as curious, and setting the basket of *mealies* on the ground, emptied it.

"At the bottom of the basket were some curiously-shaped green leaves, rather like the leaves of the gutta-percha tree in shape, only somewhat thicker and of a more fleshy substance. As though by hazard, the girl picked one of these leaves out of the basket and smelt it. Then she handed it to me. I took the leaf, and supposing that she wished me to smell it also, was about to oblige her by doing so, when my eye fell upon some curious red scratches on the green surface of the leaf.

"'Ah,' said the girl (whose name, by the way, was Maiwa), speaking beneath her breath, 'read the signs, white man.'

"Without answering her I continued to stare at the leaf. It had been scratched or rather written upon with a sharp tool, such as a nail, and wherever this instrument had touched it, the acid juice oozing through the outer skin had turned a rusty blood colour. Presently I found the beginning of the scrawl, and read this in English, and covering the surface of the leaf and of two others that were in the basket.

"'I hear that a white man is hunting in the Matuku country. This is to warn him to fly over the mountain to Nala. Wambe sends an *impi* at daybreak to eat him up, because he has hunted before bringing *hongo*. For God's sake, whoever you are, try to help me. I have been the slave of this devil Wambe for nearly seven years, and am beaten and tortured continually. He murdered all the rest of us, but kept me because I could work iron. Maiwa, his wife, takes this; she is flying to Nala her father because Wambe killed her child. Try to get Nala to attack Wambe; Maiwa can guide them over the mountain. You won't come for nothing, for the stockade of Wambe's private *kraal* is made of elephants' tusks. For God's sake, don't desert me, or I shall kill myself. I can bear this no longer.

"'John Every.'

"'Great heavens!' I gasped. 'Every!—why, it must be my old friend.' The girl, or rather the woman Maiwa, pointed to the other side of the leaf, where there was more writing. It ran thus—'I have just heard that the white man is called Macumazahn. If so, it must be my friend Quatermain. Pray Heaven it is, for I know he won't desert an old chum in such a fix as I am. It isn't that I'm afraid of dying, I don't care if I die, but I want to get a chance at Wambe first.'

"'No, old boy,' thought I to myself, 'it isn't likely that I am going to leave you there while there is a chance of getting you out. I have played fox before now—there's still a double or two left in me. I must make a plan, that's all. And then there's that stockade of tusks. I am not going to leave that either.' Then I spoke to the woman.

"'You are called Maiwa?'

"'It is so.'

"'You are the daughter of Nala and the wife of Wambe?'

"'It is so.'

"'You fly from Wambe to Nala?'

"'I do.'

"'Why do you fly? Stay, I would give an order,'—and calling to Gobo, I ordered him to get the men ready for instant departure. The woman, who, as I have said, was quite young and very handsome, put her hand into a little pouch made of antelope hide which she wore fastened round the waist, and to my horror drew from it the withered hand of a child, which evidently had been carefully dried in the smoke.

"'I fly for this cause,' she answered, holding the poor little hand towards me. 'See now, I bore a child. Wambe was its father, and for eighteen months the child lived and I loved it. But Wambe loves not his children; he kills them all. He fears lest they should grow up to slay one so wicked, and he would have killed this child also, but I begged its life. One day, some soldiers passing the hut saw the child and saluted him, calling him the "chief who soon shall be." Wambe heard, and was mad. He smote the babe, and it wept. Then he said that it should weep for good cause. Among the things that he had stolen from the white men whom he slew is a trap that will hold lions. So strong is the trap that four men must stand on it, two on either side, before it can be opened.'"

Here old Quatermain broke off suddenly.

"Look here, you fellows," he said, "I can't bear to go on with this part of the story, because I never could stand either seeing or talking of the sufferings of children. You can guess what that devil did, and what the poor mother was forced to witness. Would you believe it, she told me the tale without a tremor, in the most matter-of-fact way. Only I noticed that her eyelid quivered all the time.

"'Well,' I said, as unconcernedly as though I had been talking of the death of a lamb, though inwardly I was sick with horror and boiling with rage, 'and what do you mean to do about the matter, Maiwa, wife of Wambe?'

"'I mean to do this, white man,' she answered, drawing herself up to her full height, and speaking in tones as hard as steel and cold as ice—'I mean to work, and work, and work, to bring this to pass, and to bring that to pass, until at length it comes to pass that with these living eyes I behold Wambe dying the death that he gave to his child and my child.'

"'Well said,' I answered.

"'Ay, well said, Macumazahn, well said, and not easily forgotten. Who could forget, oh, who could forget? See where this dead hand rests against my side; so once it rested when alive. And now, though it is dead, now every night it creeps from its nest and strokes my hair and clasps my fingers in its tiny palm. Every night it does this, fearing lest I should forget. Oh, my child! my child! ten days ago I held thee to my breast, and now this alone remains of thee,' and she kissed the dead hand and shivered, but never a tear did she weep.

"'See now,' she went on, 'the white man, the prisoner at Wambe's *kraal*, he was kind to me. He loved the child that is dead, yes, he wept when its father slew it, and at the risk of his life told Wambe, my husband—ah, yes, my husband!—that which he is! He too it was who made a plan. He said to me, "Go, Maiwa, after the custom of thy people, go purify thyself in the bush alone, having touched a dead one. Say to Wambe thou goest to purify thyself alone for fifteen days, according to the custom of thy people. Then fly to thy father, Nala, and stir him up to war against Wambe for the sake of the child that is dead." This then he said, and his words seemed good to me, and that same night ere I left to purify myself came news that a white man hunted in the country, and Wambe, being mad with drink, grew very wrath, and gave orders that an *impi* should be gathered to slay the white man and his people and seize his goods. Then did the "Smiter of Iron" (Every) write the message on the green leaves, and bid me seek thee out, and show forth the matter, that thou mightest save thyself by flight; and behold, this thing have I done, Macumazahn, the hunter, the Slayer of Elephants.'

"'Ah,' I said, 'I thank you. And how many men be there in the *impi* of Wambe?'

"'A hundred of men and half a hundred.'

"'And where is the *impi*?'

"'There to the north. It follows on thy spoor. I saw it pass yesterday, but myself I guessed that thou wouldst be nigher to the mountain, and came this way, and found thee. To-morrow at the daybreak the slayers will be here.'

"'Very possibly,' I thought to myself; 'but they won't find Macumazahn. I have half a mind to put some strychnine into the carcases of those elephants for their especial benefit though.' I knew that they would stop to eat the elephants, as indeed they did, to our great gain, but I abandoned the idea of poisoning them, because I was rather short of strychnine."

"Or because you did not like to play the trick, Quatermain?" I suggested with a laugh.

"I said because I had not enough strychnine. It would take a great deal of strychnine to poison three elephants effectually," answered the old gentleman testily.

I said nothing further, but I smiled, knowing that old Allan could never have resorted to such an artifice, however severe his strait. But that was his way; he always made himself out to be a most unmerciful person.

"Well," he went on, "at that moment Gobo came up and announced that we were ready to march. 'I am glad that you are ready,' I said, 'because if you don't march, and march quick, you will never march again, that is all. Wambe has an *impi* out to kill us, and it will be here presently.'

"Gobo turned positively green, and his knees knocked together. 'Ah, what did I say?' he exclaimed. 'Fate walks about loose in Wambe's country.'

"'Very good; now all you have to do is to walk a little quicker than he does. No, no, you don't leave those elephant tusks behind—I am not going to part with them I can tell you.'

"Gobo said no more, but hastily directed the men to take up their loads, and then asked which way we were to run.

"'Ah,' I said to Maiwa, 'which way?'

"'There,' she answered, pointing towards the great mountain spur which towered up into the sky some forty miles away, separating the territories of Nala and Wambe—'there, below that small peak, is one place where men may pass, and one only. Also it can easily be blocked from above. If men pass not there, then they must go round the great peak of the mountain, two days' journey and half a day.'

"'And how far is the peak from us?'

"'All to-night shall you walk and all to-morrow, and if you walk fast, at sunset you shall stand on the peak.'

"I whistled, for that meant a five-and-forty miles trudge without sleep. Then I called to the men to take each of them as much cooked elephant's meat as he could carry conveniently. I did the same myself, and forced the woman Maiwa to eat some as we went. This I did with difficulty, for at that time she seemed neither to sleep nor eat nor rest, so fiercely was she set on vengeance.

"Then we started, Maiwa guiding us. After going for a half-hour over gradually rising ground, we found ourselves on the further edge of a great bush-clad depression something like the bottom of a lake. This depression, through which we had been travelling, was covered with bush to a very great extent, indeed almost altogether so, except where it was pitted with glades such as that wherein I had shot the elephants.

"At the top of this slope Maiwa halted, and putting her hand over her eyes looked back. Presently she touched me on the arm and pointed across the sea of forest towards a comparatively vacant space of country some six or seven miles away. I looked, and suddenly I saw something flash in the red rays of the setting sun. A pause, and then another quick flash.

"'What is it?' I asked.

"'It is the spears of Wambe's *impi*, and they travel fast,' she answered coolly.

"I suppose that my face showed how little I liked the news, for she went on—

"'Fear not; they will stay to feast upon the elephants, and while they feast we shall journey. We may yet escape.'

"After that we turned and pushed on again, till at length it grew so dark that we had to wait for the rising of the moon, which lost us time, though it gave us rest. Fortunately none of the men had seen that ominous flashing of the spears; if they had, I doubt if even I could have kept control of them. As it was, they travelled faster than I had ever known loaded natives to go before, so thorough-paced was their desire to see the last of Wambe's country. I, however, took the precaution to march last of all, fearing lest they should throw away their loads to lighten themselves, or, worse still, the tusks; for these kind of fellows would be capable of throwing anything away if their own skins were at stake. If the pious Æneas, whose story you were reading to me the other night, had been a mongrel Delagoa Bay native, Anchises would have had a poor chance of getting out of Troy, that is, if he was known to have made a satisfactory will.

"At moonrise we set out again, and with short occasional halts travelled till dawn, when we were forced to rest and eat. Starting once more, about half-past five, we crossed the river at noon. Then began the long toilsome ascent through thick bush, the same in which I shot the bull buffalo, only some twenty miles to the west of that spot, and not more than twenty-five miles on the hither side of Wambe's *kraal*. There were six or seven miles of this dense bush, and hard work it was to get through it. Next came a belt of scattered forest which was easier to pass, though, in revenge, the ground was steeper. This was about two miles wide, and we passed it by about four in the afternoon. Above this scattered bush lay a long steep slope of boulder-strewn ground, which ran up to the foot of the little peak some three miles away. As we emerged, footsore and weary, on to this inhospitable plain, some of the men looking round caught sight of the spears of Wambe's *impi* advancing rapidly not more than a mile behind us.

"At first there was a panic, and the bearers tried to throw off their loads and run, but I harangued them, calling out to them that certainly I would shoot the first man who did so and that if they would but trust in me I would bring them through the mess. Now, ever since I had killed those three elephants single-handed, I had gained great influence over these men, and they listened to me. So off we went as hard as ever we could go—the members of the Alpine Club would not have been in it with us. We made the boulders burn, as a Frenchman would say.

"When we had done about a mile the spears began to emerge from the belt of scattered bush, and the whoop of their bearers as they viewed us broke upon our ears. Quick as our pace had been before, it grew much quicker now, for terror lent wings to my gallant crew. But they were sorely tired, and the loads were heavy, so that run, or rather climb, as we would, Wambe's soldiers, a scrubby-looking lot of men armed with big spears and small shields, but without plumes, climbed considerably faster. The last mile of that pleasing chase was like a fox hunt, we being the fox, and always in view. What astonished me was the extraordinary endurance and activity shown by Maiwa. She never even flagged. I think that girl's muscles must have been made of iron, or perhaps it was the strength of her will that supported her. At any rate she reached the foot of the peak second, poor Gobo, who was an excellent hand at running away, being first.

"Presently I came up panting, and glanced at the ascent. Before us was a wall of rock about one hundred and fifty feet in height, upon which the strata were laid so as to form a series of projections sufficiently resembling steps to make the ascent easy, comparatively speaking, except at one spot, where it was necessary to climb over a projecting angle of cliff and bear a little to the left. It was not a really difficult place, but what made it awkward was, that immediately beneath this projection gaped a deep fissure or donga, on the brink of which we now stood, originally dug out, no doubt, by the rush of water from the peak and cliff. This gulf beneath would be trying to the nerves of a weak-headed climber at the critical point, and so it proved in the result. The projecting angle once passed, the remainder of the ascent was very simple. At the summit, however, the brow of the cliff hung over and was pierced by a single narrow path cut through it by water, in such fashion that a single boulder rolled into it at the top would make the cliff quite impassable to men without ropes.

"At this moment Wambe's soldiers were about a thousand yards from us, so it was evident that we had no time to lose. I at once ordered the men to commence the ascent, the girl Maiwa, who was familiar with the pass, going first to show them the way. Accordingly they began to mount with alacrity, pushing and lifting their loads in front of them. When the first of them, led by Maiwa, reached the projecting angle, they put down their loads upon a ledge of rock and clambered over. Once there, by lying on their stomachs upon a boulder, they could reach the loads which were held to them by the men beneath, and in this way drag them over the awkward place, whence they were carried easily to the top.

"But all of this took time, and meanwhile the soldiers were coming up fast, screaming and brandishing their big spears. They were now within about four hundred yards, and several loads, together with all the tusks, had yet to be got over the rock. I was still standing at the bottom of the cliff, shouting directions to the men above, but it occurred to me that it would soon be time to move. Before doing so, however, I thought that it might be well to try and produce a moral effect upon the advancing enemy. In my hand I held a Winchester repeating carbine, but the distance was too great for me to use it with effect, so I turned to Gobo, who was shivering with terror at my side, and handing him the carbine, took my express from him.

"The enemy was now about three hundred and fifty yards away, and the express was only sighted to three hundred. Still I knew that it could be trusted for the extra fifty yards. Running in front of Wambe's soldiers were two men—captains, I suppose—one of them very tall. I put up the three hundred yard flap, and sitting down with my back against the rock, I drew a long breath to steady myself, and covered the tall man, giving him a full sight. Feeling that I was on him, I pulled, and before the sound of the striking bullet could reach my ears, I saw the man throw up his arms and pitch forward on to his head. His companion stopped dead, giving me a fair chance. I rapidly covered him, and fired the left barrel. He turned round once, and then sank down in a heap. This caused the enemy to hesitate—they had never seen men killed at such a distance before, and thought that there was something uncanny about the performance. Taking advantage of the lull, I gave the express back to Gobo, and slinging the Winchester repeater over my back I began to climb the cliff.

"When we reached the projecting angle all the loads were over, but the tusks still had to be passed up, and owing to their weight and the smoothness of their surface, this was a very difficult task. Of course I ought to have abandoned the tusks; often and often have I since reproached myself for not doing so. Indeed, I think that my obstinacy about them was downright sinful, but I was always obstinate about such things, and I could not bear the idea of leaving those splendid tusks which had cost me so much pains and danger to come by. Well, it nearly cost me my life also, and did cost poor Gobo his, as will be seen shortly, to say nothing of the loss inflicted by my rifle on the enemy.

170

When I reached the projection I found that the men, with their usual stupidity, were trying to hand up the tusks point first. Now the result of this was that those above had nothing to grip except the round polished surface of the ivory, and in the position in which they were, this did not give them sufficient hold to enable them to lift the weight. I told them to reverse the tusks and push them up, so that the rough and hollow ends came to the hands of the men above. This they did, and the first two were dragged up in safety.

"At this point, looking behind me, I saw the Matukus streaming up the slope in a rough extended order, and not more than a hundred yards away. Cocking the Winchester I turned and opened fire on them. I don't quite know how many I missed, but I do know that I never shot better in my life. I had to keep shifting myself from one enemy to the other, firing almost without getting a sight, that is, by the eye alone, after the fashion of the experts who break glass balls. But quick as the work was, men fell thick, and by the time that I had emptied the carbine of its twelve cartridges, for the moment the advance was checked. I rapidly pushed in some more cartridges, and hardly had I done so when the enemy, seeing that we were about to escape them altogether, came on once more with a tremendous yell. By this time the two halves of the single tusk of the great bull alone remained to be passed up. I fired and fired as effectively as before, but notwithstanding all that I could do, some men escaped my hail of bullets and began to ascend the cliff. Presently my rifle was again empty. I slung it over my back, and, drawing my revolver, turned to run for it, the attackers being now quite close. As I did so, a spear struck the cliff close to my head.

"The last half of the tusk was now vanishing over the rock, and I sung out to Gobo and the other man who had been pushing it up to vanish after it. Gobo, poor fellow, required no second invitation; indeed, his haste was his undoing. He went at the projecting rock with a bound. The end of the tusk was still hanging over, and instead of grasping the rock he caught at it. It twisted in his hand—he slipped— he fell; with one wild shriek he vanished into the abyss beneath, his falling body brushing me as it passed. For a moment we stood aghast, and presently the dull thud of his fall smote heavily upon our ears. Poor fellow, he had met the Fate which, as he declared, walked about loose in Wambe's country. Then with an oath the remaining man sprung at the rock and clambered over it in safety. Aghast at the awfulness of what had happened, I stood still, till I saw the great blade of a Matuku spear pass up between my feet. That brought me to my senses, and I began to clamber up the rock like a cat. I was half way round it. Already I had clasped the hand of that brave girl Maiwa, who came down to help me, the men having scrambled forward with the ivory, when I felt some one seize my ankle.

"'Pull, Maiwa, pull,' I gasped, and she certainly did pull. Maiwa was a very muscular woman, and never before did I appreciate the advantages of the physical development of females so keenly. She tugged at my left arm, the savage below tugged at my right leg, till I began to realize that something must give way ere long. Luckily I retained my presence of mind, like the man who threw his mother-in-law out of the window, and carried the mattress down-stairs, when a fire broke out in his house. My right hand was still free, and in it I held my revolver, which was secured to my wrist by a leather thong. The pistol was cocked, and I simply pointed it downwards and fired. The result was instantaneous—and so far as I am concerned, most satisfactory. The bullet hit the man beneath me somewhere, I am sure I don't know where; at any rate, he let go of my leg and plunged headlong into the gulf beneath to join Gobo. In another moment I was on the top of the rock, and going up the remaining steps like a lamplighter. A single other soldier appeared in pursuit, but one of my boys at the top fired my elephant gun at him. I don't know if he hit him or only frightened him; at any rate, he vanished whence he came. I do know, however, that he very nearly hit *me*, for I felt the wind of the bullet.

"Another thirty seconds, and I and the woman Maiwa were at the top of the cliff panting, but safe.

"My men, being directed thereto by Maiwa, had most fortunately rolled up some big boulders which lay about, and with these we soon managed to block the passage through the overhanging ridge of rock in such fashion that the soldiers below could not possibly climb over it. Indeed, so far as I could see, they did not even try to do so—their heart was turned to fat, as the Zulus say.

"Then having rested a few moments we took up the loads, including the tusks of ivory that had cost us so dear, and in silence marched on for a couple of miles or more, till we reached a patch of dense bush. And here, being utterly exhausted, we camped for the night, taking the precaution, however, of setting a guard to watch against any attempt at surprise."

CHAPTER 6

The Plan of Campaign

"Notwithstanding all that we had gone through, perhaps indeed on account of it, for I was thoroughly worn out, I slept that night as soundly as poor Gobo, round whose crushed body the hyenas would now be prowling. Rising refreshed at dawn we went on our way towards Nala's *kraal*, which we reached at nightfall. It is built on open ground after the Zulu fashion, in a ring fence and with beehive huts. The cattle *kraal* is behind and a little to the left. Indeed, both from their habits and their talk it was easy to see that these Butiana belong to that section of the Bantu people which, since T'Chaka's time, has been known as the Zulu race. We did not see the chief Nala that night. His daughter Maiwa went on to his private huts as soon as we arrived, and very shortly afterwards one of his head men came to us bringing a sheep and some *mealies* and milk with him. 'The chief sent us greeting,' he said, 'and would see us on the morrow.' Meanwhile he was ordered to bring us to a place of resting, where we and our goods should be safe and undisturbed. Accordingly he led the way to some very good huts just outside Nala's private enclosure, and here we slept comfortably.

"On the morrow about eight o'clock the head man came again, and said that Nala requested that I would visit him. I followed him into the private enclosure and was introduced to the chief, a fine-looking man of about fifty, with very delicately-shaped hands and feet, and a rather nervous mouth. The chief was seated on a tanned ox-hide outside his hut. By his side stood his daughter Maiwa, and squatted on their haunches round him were some twenty head men or *Indunas*, whose number was continually added to by fresh arrivals. These men saluted me as I entered, and the chief rose and took my hand, ordering a stool to be brought for me to sit on. When this was done, with much eloquence and native courtesy he thanked me for protecting his daughter in the painful and dangerous circumstances in which she found herself placed, and also complimented me very highly upon what he was pleased to call the bravery with which I had defended the pass in the rocks. I answered in appropriate terms, saying that it was to Maiwa herself that thanks were due, for had it not been for her warning and knowledge of the country we should not have been here to-day; while as to the defence of the pass, I was fighting for my life, and that put heart into me.

"These courtesies concluded, Nala called upon his daughter Maiwa to tell her tale to the head men, and this she did most simply and effectively. She reminded them that she had gone as an unwilling bride to Wambe—that no cattle had been paid for her, because Wambe had threatened war if she was not sent as a free gift. Since she had entered the *kraal* of Wambe her days had been days of heaviness and her nights of weeping. She had been beaten, she had been neglected and made to do the work of a low-born wife—she, a chief's daughter. She had borne a child, and this was the story of the child. Then amidst a dead silence she told them the awful tale which she had already narrated to me. When she had finished, her hearers gave a loud ejaculation. '*Ou!*' they said, '*Ou!* Maiwa, daughter of Nala!'

"'Ay,' she went on with flashing eyes, 'ay, it is true; my mouth is as full of truth as a flower of honey, and for tears my eyes are like the dew upon the grass at dawn. It is true I saw the child die—here is the proof of it, councillors,' and she drew forth the little dead hand and held it before them.

"'*Ou!*' they said again, '*Ou!* it is the dead hand!'

"'Yes,' she continued, 'it is the dead hand of my dead child, and I bear it with me that I may never forget, never for one short hour, that I live that I may see Wambe die, and be avenged. Will you bear it, my father, that your daughter and your daughter's child should be so treated by a Matuku? Will ye bear it, men of my own people?'

"'No,' said an old *Induna*, rising, 'it is not to be borne. Enough have we suffered at the hands of these Matuku dogs and their loud-tongued chief; let us put it to the issue.'

"'It is not to be borne indeed,' said Nala; 'but how can we make head against so great a people?'

"'Ask of him—ask of Macumazahn, the wise white man,' said Maiwa, pointing at me.

"'How can we overcome Wambe, Macumazahn the hunter?'

"'How does the jackal overreach the lion, Nala?'

"'By cleverness, Macumazahn.'

174

"'So shall you overcome Wambe, Nala.'

"At this moment an interruption occurred. A man entered and said that messengers had arrived from Wambe.

"'What is their message?' asked Nala.

"'They come to ask that thy daughter Maiwa be sent back, and with her the white hunter.'

"'How shall I make answer to this, Macumazahn?' said Nala, when the man had withdrawn.

"'Thus shalt thou answer,' I said after reflection; 'say that the woman shall be sent and I with her, and then bid the messengers be gone. Stay, I will hide myself here in the hut that the men may not see me,' and I did.

"Shortly afterwards, through a crack in the hut, I saw the messengers arrive, and they were great truculent-looking fellows. There were four of them, and evidently they had travelled night and day. They entered with a swagger and squatted down before Nala.

"'Your business?' said Nala, frowning.

"'We come from Wambe, bearing the orders of Wambe to Nala his servant,' answered the spokesman of the party.

"'Speak,' said Nala, with a curious twitch of his nervous-looking mouth.

"'These are the words of Wambe: "Send back the woman, my wife, who has run away from my *kraal*, and send with her the white man who has dared to hunt in my country without my leave, and to slay my soldiers." These are the words of Wambe.'

"'And if I say I will not send them?' asked Nala.

"'Then on behalf of Wambe we declare war upon you. Wambe will eat you up. He will wipe you out; your *kraals* shall be stamped flat—so,' and with an expressive gesture he drew his hand across his mouth to show how complete would be the annihilation of that chief who dared to defy Wambe.

"'These are heavy words,' said Nala. 'Let me take counsel before I answer.'

"Then followed a little piece of acting that was really very creditable to the untutored savage mind. The heralds withdrew, but not out of sight, and Nala went through the show of earnestly consulting his *Indunas*. The girl Maiwa too flung herself at his feet, and appeared to weep and implore his protection, while he wrung his hands as though in doubt and tribulation of mind. At length he summoned the messengers to draw near, and addressed them, while Maiwa sobbed very realistically at his side.

"'Wambe is a great chief,' said Nala, 'and this woman is his wife, whom he has a right to claim. She must return to him, but her feet are sore with walking, she cannot come now. In eight days from this day she shall be delivered at the *kraal* of Wambe; I will send her with a party of my men. As for the white hunter and his men, I have nought to do with them, and cannot answer for their misdeeds. They have wandered hither unbidden by me, and I will deliver them back whence they came, that Wambe may judge them according to his law; they shall be sent with the girl. For you, go your ways. Food shall be given you without the *kraal*, and a present for Wambe in atonement of the ill-doing of my daughter. I have spoken.'

"At first the heralds seemed inclined to insist upon Maiwa's accompanying them then and there, but on being shown the swollen condition of her feet, ultimately they gave up the point and departed.

"When they were well out of the way I emerged from the hut, and we went on to discuss the situation and make our plans. First of all, as I was careful to explain to Nala, I was not going to give him my experience and services for nothing. I heard that Wambe had a stockade round his *kraal* made of elephant tusks. These tusks, in the event of our succeeding in the enterprise, I should claim as my perquisite, with the proviso that Nala should furnish me with men to carry them down to the coast.

"To this modest request Nala and the head men gave an unqualified and hearty assent, the more hearty perhaps because they never expected to get the ivory.

"The next thing I stipulated was, that if we conquered, the white man John Every should be handed over to me, together with any goods which he might claim. His cruel captivity was, I need hardly say, the only reason that induced me to join in so hare-brained an expedition, but I was careful from motives of policy to keep this fact in the background. Nala accepted this condition. My third stipulation was that no women or children should be killed. This being also agreed to, we went on to consider ways and means. Wambe, it appeared, was a very powerful petty chief, that is, he could put at least six thousand fighting men into the field, and always had from three to four thousand collected about his *kraal*, which was supposed to be impregnable. Nala, on the contrary, at such short notice could not collect more than from twelve to thirteen hundred men, though, being of the Zulu stock, they were of much better stuff for fighting purposes than Wambe's Matukus.

"These odds, though large, under the circumstances were not

overwhelming. The real obstacle to our chance of success was the difficulty of delivering a crushing assault against Wambe's strong place. This was, it appeared, fortified all round with *schanses* or stone walls, and contained numerous caves and *koppies* in the hill-side and at the foot of the mountain which no force had ever been able to capture. It is said that in the time of the Zulu monarch Dingaan, a great *impi* of that king's having penetrated to this district, had delivered an assault upon the *kraal* then owned by a forefather of Wambe's, and been beaten back with the loss of more than a thousand men.

"Having thought the question over, I interrogated Maiwa closely as to the fortifications and the topographical peculiarities of the spot, and not without results. I discovered that the *kraal* was indeed impregnable to a front attack, but that it was very slightly defended to the rear, which ran up a slope of the mountain, indeed only by two lines of stone walls. The reason of this was that the mountain is quite impassable except by one secret path supposed to be known only to the chief and his councillors, and this being so, it had not been considered necessary to fortify it.

"'Well,' I said, when she had done, 'and now as to this secret path of thine—knowest thou aught of it?'

"'Ay,' she answered, 'I am no fool, Macumazahn. Knowledge learned is power earned. I won the secret of that path.'

"'And canst thou guide an *impi* thereon so that it shall fall upon the town from behind?'

"'Yes, I can do this, if only Wambe's people know not that the *impi* comes, for if they know, then they can block the way.'

"'So then here is my plan. Listen, Nala, and say if it be good, or if thou hast a better, show it forth. Let messengers go out and summon all thy *impi*, that it be gathered here on the third day from now. This being done, let the *impi*, led by Maiwa, march on the morrow of the fourth day, and crossing the mountains let it travel along on the other side of the mountains till it come to the place on the further side of which is the *kraal* of Wambe; that shall be some three days' journey in all.[1] Then on the night of the third day's journey, let Maiwa lead the *impi* in silence up the secret path, so that it comes to the crest of the mountain that is above the strong place, and here let it hide among the rocks.

"'Meanwhile on the sixth day from now let one of thy *Indunas*, Nala, bring with him two hundred men that have guns, and lead me

1. About one hundred and twenty miles.—Editor.

and my men as prisoners, and take also a girl from among the Butiana people, who by form and face is like unto Maiwa, and bind her hands, and pass by the road on which we came and through the cutting in the cliff on to the *kraal* of Wambe. But the men shall take no shields or plumes with them, only their guns and one short spear, and when they meet the people of Wambe they shall say that they come to give up the woman and the white man and his party to Wambe, and to make atonement to Wambe. So shall they pass in peace. And travelling thus, on the evening of the seventh day we shall come to the gates of the place of Wambe, and nigh the gates there is, so says Maiwa, a *koppie* very strong and full of rocks and caves, but having no soldiers on it except in time of war, or at the worst but a few such as can easily be overpowered.

"'This being done, at the dawn of day the *impi* on the mountain behind the town must light a fire and put wet grass on it, so that the smoke goes up. Then at the sight of the smoke we in the *koppie* will begin to shoot into the town of Wambe, and all the soldiers will run to kill us. But we will hold our own, and while we fight the *impi* shall charge down the mountain side and climb the *schanses*, and put those who defend them to the *assegai*, and then falling upon the town shall surprise it, and drive the soldiers of Wambe as a wind blows the dead husks of corn. This is my plan. I have spoken.'

"'*Ou!*' said Nala, 'it is good, it is very good. The white man is cleverer than a jackal. Yes, so shall it be; and may the snake of the Butiana people stand up upon its tail and prosper the war, for so shall we be rid of Wambe and the tyrannies of Wambe.'

"After that the girl Maiwa stood up, and once more producing the dreadful little dried hand, made her father and several of his head councillors swear by it and upon it that they would carry out the war of vengeance to the bitter end. It was a very curious sight to see. And by the way, the fight that ensued was thereafter known among the tribes of that district as the War of the Little Hand.

"The next two days were busy ones for us. Messengers were sent out, and every available man of the Butiana tribe was ordered up to 'a great dance.' The country was small, and by the evening of the second day, some twelve hundred and fifty men were assembled with their assegais and shields, and a fine hardy troop they were. At dawn of the following day, the fourth from the departure of the heralds, the main *impi*, having been doctored in the usual fashion, started under the command of Nala himself, who, knowing that his life and chieftainship hung upon the issue of the struggle, wisely determined to be present to direct it. With them went Maiwa, who was to guide them up the secret path. Of course we were obliged to give them two days' start, as they had more than a hundred miles of rough country to pass, including the crossing of the great mountain range which ran north and south, for it was necessary that the *impi* should make a wide detour in order to escape detection.

"At length, however, at dawn on the sixth day, I took the road, accompanied by my most unwilling bearers, who did not at all like the idea of thus putting their heads into the lion's mouth. Indeed, it was only the fear of Nala's spears, together with a vague confidence in myself, that induced them to accept the adventure. With me also were about two hundred Butianas, all armed with guns of various kinds, for many of these people had guns, though they were not very proficient in the use of them. But they carried no shields and wore no head-dress or armlets; indeed, every warlike appearance was carefully avoided. With our party went also a sister of Maiwa's, though by a different mother, who strongly resembled her in face and form, and whose mission it was to impersonate the runaway wife.

"That evening we camped upon the top of the cliff up which we had so barely escaped, and next morning at the first breaking of the light we rolled away the stones with which we had blocked the passage some days before, and descended to the hill-side beneath. Here the bodies, or rather the skeletons of the men who had fallen before my rifle, still lay about. The Matuku soldiers had left their comrades to be buried by the vultures. I descended the gully into which poor Gobo had fallen, and searched for his body, but in vain, although I found the spot where he and the other man had struck, together with the bones of the latter, which I recognized by the waist-cloth. Either some beast of prey had carried Gobo off, or the Matuku people had disposed of his remains, and also of my express rifle which he carried. At any rate, I never saw or heard any more of him.

"Once in Wambe's country, we adopted a very circumspect method of proceeding. About fifty men marched ahead in loose order to guard against surprise, while as many more followed behind. The remaining hundred were gathered in a bunch between, and in the centre of these men I marched, together with the girl who was personating Maiwa, and all my bearers. We were disarmed, and some of my men were tied together to show that we were prisoners, while the girl had a blanket thrown over her head, and moved along with an air of great dejection. We headed straight for Wambe's place, which was at a distance of about twenty-five miles from the mountain-pass.

"When we had gone some five miles we met a party of about fifty of Wambe's soldiers, who were evidently on the look-out for us. They stopped us, and their captain asked where we were going. The head man of our party answered that he was conveying Maiwa, Wambe's runaway wife, together with the white hunter and his men, to be given up to Wambe in accordance with his command. The captain then wanted to know why we were so many, to which our spokesman replied that I and my men were very desperate fellows, and that it was feared that if we were sent with a smaller escort we should escape, and bring disgrace and the wrath of Wambe upon their tribe. Thereon this gentleman, the Matuku captain, began to amuse himself at my expense, and mock me, saying that Wambe would make me pay for the soldiers whom I had killed. He would put me into the 'Thing that bites,' in other words, the lion trap, and leave me there to die like a jackal caught by the leg. I made no answer to this, though my wrath was great, but pretended to look frightened. Indeed there was not much pretence about it, I was frightened. I could not conceal from myself that ours was a most hazardous enterprise, and that it was very possible that I might make acquaintance with that lion trap before I was many days older. However, it seemed quite impossible to desert poor Every in his misfortune, so I had to go on, and trust to Providence, as I have so often been obliged to do before and since.

"And now a fresh difficulty arose. Wambe's soldiers insisted upon accompanying us, and what is more, did all they could to urge us forward, as they were naturally anxious to get to the chief's place before evening. But we, on the other hand, had excellent reasons for not arriving till night was closing in, since we relied upon the gloom to cover our advance upon the *koppie* which commanded the town. Finally, they became so importunate that we were obliged to refuse flatly to move faster, alleging as a reason that the girl was tired. They did not accept this excuse in good part, and at one time I thought that we should have come to blows, for there is no love lost between Butianas and Matukus. At last, however, either from motives of policy, or because they were so evidently outnumbered, they gave in and suffered us to go our own pace. I earnestly wished that they would have added to the obligation by going theirs, but this they declined absolutely to do. On the contrary, they accompanied us every foot of the way, keeping up a running fire of allusions to the 'Thing that bites' that jarred upon my nerves and discomposed my temper.

"About half-past four in the afternoon we came to a neck or ridge of stony ground, whence we could see Wambe's town plainly lying some six or seven miles away, and three thousand feet beneath us. The town is built in a valley, with the exception of Wambe's own *kraal*, that is situated at the mouth of some caves upon the slope of the opposing mountains, over which I hoped to see our *impi*'s spears flashing in the morrow's light. Even from where we stood, it was easy to see how strongly the place was fortified with *schanses* and stone walls, and how difficult of approach. Indeed, unless taken by surprise, it seemed to me quite impregnable to a force operating without cannon, and even cannon would not make much impression on rocks and stony *koppies* filled with caves.

"Then came the descent of the pass, and an arduous business it was, for the path—if it may be called a path—is almost entirely composed of huge water-worn boulders, from the one to the other of which we must jump like so many grasshoppers. It took us two hours to climb down, and, travelling through that burning sun, when at last we did reach the bottom, I for one was nearly played out. Shortly afterwards, just as it was growing dark, we came to the first line of fortifications, which consisted of a triple stone wall pierced by a gateway, so narrow that a man could hardly squeeze through it. We passed this without question, being accompanied by Wambe's soldiers. Then, came a belt of land three hundred paces or more in width, very rocky and broken, and having no huts upon it. Here in hollows in this belt the cattle were kraaled in case of danger. On the further side were more fortifications and another small gateway shaped like a V, and just beyond and through it I saw the *koppie* we had planned to seize looming up against the line of mountains behind.

"As we went I whispered my suggestions to our captain, with the result that at the second gateway he halted the cavalcade, and addressing the captain of Wambe's soldiers, said that we would wait here till we received Wambe's word to enter the town. The other man said that this was well, only he must hand over the prisoners to be taken up to the chief's *kraal*, for Wambe, was 'hungry to begin upon them,' and his 'heart desired to see the white man at rest before he closed his eyes in sleep,' and as for his wife, 'surely he would welcome her.' Our leader replied that he could not do this thing, because his orders were to deliver the prisoners to Wambe at Wambe's own *kraal*, and they might not be broken. How could he be responsible for the safety of the prisoners if he let them out of his hand? No, they would wait there till Wambe's word was brought.

"To this, after some demur, the other man consented, and went away, remarking that he would soon be back. As he passed me he called out with a sneer, pointing as he did so to the fading red in the western sky—'Look your last upon the light, White Man, for the Thing that Bites lives in the dark.'

"Next day it so happened that I shot this man, and, do you know, I think that he is about the only human being who has come to harm at my hands for whom I do not feel sincere sorrow and, in a degree, remorse."

CHAPTER 7

The Attack

"Just where we halted ran a little stream of water. I looked at it, and an idea struck me: probably there would be no water on the *koppie*. I suggested this to our captain, and, acting on the hint, he directed all the men to drink what they could, and also to fill the seven or eight cooking pots which we carried with us with water. Then came the crucial moment. How were we to get possession of the *koppie*? When the captain asked me, I said that I thought that we had better march up and take it, and this accordingly we went on to do. When we came to the narrow gateway we were, as I expected stopped by two soldiers who stood on guard there and asked our business. The captain answered that we had changed our minds, and would follow on to Wambe's *kraal*. The soldiers said no, we must now wait.

"To this we replied by pushing them to one side and marching in single file through the gateway, which was not distant more than a hundred yards from the *koppie*. While we were getting through, the men we had pushed away ran towards the town calling for assistance, a call that was promptly responded to, for in another minute we saw scores of armed men running hard in our direction. So we ran too, for the *koppie*. As soon as they understood what we were after, which they did not at first, owing to the dimness of the light, they did their best to get there before us. But we had the start of them, and with the exception of one unfortunate man who stumbled and fell, we were well on to the *koppie* before they arrived. This man they captured, and when fighting began on the following morning, and he refused to give any information, they killed him. Luckily they had no time to torture him, or they would certainly have done so, for these Matuku people are very fond of torturing their enemies.

"When we reached the *koppie*, the base of which covers about half an acre of ground, the soldiers who had been trying to cut us off halted, for they knew the strength of the position. This gave us a few minutes before the light had quite vanished to reconnoitre the place. We found that it was unoccupied, fortified with a regular labyrinth of stone walls, and contained three large caves and some smaller ones. The next business was to post the soldiers to such advantage as time would allow. My own men I was careful to place quite at the top. They were perfectly useless from terror, and I feared that they might try to escape and give information of our plans to Wambe. So I watched them like the apple of my eye, telling them that should they dare to stir they would be shot.

"Then it grew quite dark, and presently out of the darkness I heard a voice—it was that of the leader of the soldiers who had escorted us—calling us to come down. We replied that it was too dark to move, we should hit our feet against the stones. He insisted upon our descending, and we flatly refused, saying that if any attempt was made to dislodge us we would fire. After that, as they had no real intention of attacking us in the dark, the men withdrew, but we saw from the fires which were lit around that they were keeping a strict watch upon our position.

"That night was a wearing one, for we never quite knew how the situation was going to develop. Fortunately we had some cooked food with us, so we did not starve. It was lucky, however, that we drunk our fill before coming up, for, as I had anticipated, there was not a drop of water on the *koppie*.

"At length the night wore away, and with the first tinge of light I began to go my rounds, and stumbling along the stony paths, to make things as ready as I could for the attack, which I felt sure would be delivered before we were two hours older. The men were cramped and cold, and consequently low-spirited, but I exhorted them to the best of my ability, bidding them remember the race from which they sprang, and not to show the white feather before a crowd of Matuku dogs. At length it began to grow light, and presently I saw long columns of men advancing towards the *koppie*. They halted under cover at a distance of about a hundred and fifty yards, and just as the dawn broke a herald came forward and called to us. Our captain stood up upon a rock and answered him.

"'These are the words of Wambe,' the herald said. 'Come forth from the *koppie*, and give over the evil-doers, and go in peace, or stay in the *koppie* and be slain.'

"'It is too early to come out as yet,' answered our man in fine diplomatic style. 'When the sun sucks up the mist then we will come out. Our limbs are stiff with cold.'

"'Come forth even now,' said the herald.

"'Not if I know it, my boy,' said I to myself; but the captain replied that he would come out when he thought proper, and not before.

"'Then make ready to die,' said the herald, for all the world like the villain of a *transpontine* piece, and majestically stalked back to the soldiers.

"I made my final arrangements, and looked anxiously at the mountain crest a couple of miles or so away, from which the mist was now beginning to lift, but no column of smoke could I see. I whistled, for if the attacking force had been delayed or made any mistake, our position was likely to grow rather warm. We had barely enough water to wet the mouths of the men, and when once it was finished we could not hold the place for long in that burning heat.

"At length, just as the sun rose in glory over the heights behind us, the Matuku soldiers, of whom about fifteen hundred were now assembled, set up a queer whistling noise, which ended in a chant. Then some shots were fired, for the Matuku had a few guns, but without effect, though one bullet passed just by a man's head.

"'Now they are going to begin,' I thought to myself, and I was not far wrong, for in another minute the body of men divided into three companies, each about five hundred strong, and, heralded by a running fire, charged at us on three sides. Our men were now all well under cover, and the fire did us no harm. I mounted on a rock so as to command a view of as much of the *koppie* and plain as possible, and yelled to our men to reserve their fire till I gave the word, and then to shoot low and load as quickly as possible. I knew that, like all natives, they were sure to be execrable shots, and that they were armed with weapons made out of old gas-pipes, so the only chance of doing execution was to let the enemy get right on to us.

"On they came with a rush; they were within eighty yards now, and as they drew near the point of attack, I observed that they closed their ranks, which was so much the better for us.

"'Shall we not fire, my father?' sung out the captain.

"'No, confound you!' I answered.

"'Sixty yards—fifty—forty—thirty. Fire, you scoundrels!' I yelled, setting the example by letting off both barrels of my elephant gun into the thickest part of the company opposite to me.

"Instantly the place rang out with the discharge of two hundred and odd guns, while the air was torn by the passage of every sort of missile, from iron pot legs down to slugs and pebbles coated with lead. The result was very prompt. The Matukus were so near that we could not miss them, and at thirty yards a lead-coated stone out of a gas–pipe is as effective as a Martini rifle, or more so. Over rolled the attacking soldiers by the dozen, while the survivors, fairly frightened, took to their heels. We plied them with shot till they were out of range—I made it very warm for them with the elephant gun, by the way—and then we loaded up in quite a cheerful frame of mind, for we had not lost a man, whereas I could count more than fifty dead and wounded Matukus. The only thing that damped my ardour was that, stare as I would, I could see no column of smoke upon the mountain crest.

"Half an hour elapsed before any further steps were taken against us. Then the attacking force adopted different tactics. Seeing that it was very risky to try to rush us in dense masses, they opened out into skirmishing order and ran across the open space in lots of five and six. As it happened, right at the foot of the *koppie* the ground broke away a little in such fashion that it was almost impossible for us to search it effectually with our fire. On the hither side of this dip Wambe's soldiers were now congregating in considerable numbers. Of course we did them as much damage as we could while they were running across, but this sort of work requires good shots, and that was just what we had not got. Another thing was, that so many of our men would insist upon letting off the things they called guns at every little knot of the enemy that ran across. Thus, the first few lots were indeed practically swept away, but after that, as it took a long while to load the gas-pipes and old flint muskets, those who followed got across in comparative safety. For my own part, I fired away with the elephant gun and repeating carbine till they grew almost too hot to hold, but my individual efforts could do nothing to stop such a rush, or perceptibly to lessen the number of our enemies.

"At length there were at least a thousand men crowded into the dip of ground within a few yards of us, whence those of them who had guns kept up a continued fusillade upon the *koppie*. They killed two of my bearers in this way, and wounded a third, for being at the top of the *koppie* these men were most exposed to the fire from the dip at its base. Seeing that the situation was growing most serious, at length, by the dint of threats and entreaties, I persuaded the majority of our people to cease firing useless shots, to reload, and prepare for the rush. Scarcely had I done so when the enemy came for us with a roar. I am bound to say that I should never have believed that Matukus had it in them to make such a determined charge. A large party rushed round the base of the *koppie*, and attacked us in flank, while the others swarmed wherever they could get a foothold, so that we were taken on every side.

"'*Fire!*' I cried, and we did with terrible effect. Many of their men fell, but though we checked we could not stop them. They closed up and rushed the first fortification, killing a good number of its defenders. It was almost all cold steel work now, for we had no time to reload, and that suited the Butiana habits of fighting well enough, for the stabbing *assegai* is a weapon which they understand. Those of our people who escaped from the first line of walls took refuge in the second, where I stood myself, encouraging them, and there the fight raged fiercely. Occasionally parties of the enemy would force a passage, only to perish on the hither side beneath the Butiana spears. But still they kept it up, and I saw that, fight as we would, we were doomed. We were altogether outnumbered, and to make matters worse, fresh bodies of soldiers were pouring across the plain to the assistance of our assailants. So I made up my mind to direct a retreat into the caves, and there expire in a manner as heroic as circumstances would allow; and while mentally lamenting my hard fate and reflecting on my sins I fought away like a fiend. It was then, I remember, that I shot my friend the captain of our escort of the previous day. He had caught sight of me, and making a vicious dig at my stomach with a spear (which I successfully dodged), shouted out, or rather began to shout out, one of his unpleasant allusions to the 'Thing that——' He never got as far as 'bites,' because I shot him after 'that.'

"Well, the game was about up. Already I saw one man throw down his spear in token of surrender—which act of cowardice cost him his life, by the way—when suddenly a shout arose.

"'Look at the mountain,' they cried; 'there is an *impi* on the mountain side.'

"I glanced up, and there sure enough, about half-way down the mountain, nearing the first fortification, the long-plumed double line of Nala's warriors was rushing down to battle, the bright light of the morning glancing on their spears. Afterwards we discovered that the reason of their delay was that they had been stopped by a river in flood, and could not reach the mountain crest by dawn. When they did reach it, however, they saw instantly that the fight was already going on, was 'in flower,' as they put it, and so advanced at once without waiting to light signal-fires.

"Meanwhile they had been observed from the town, and parties of soldiers were charging up the steep side of the hill, to occupy the *schanses*, and the second line of fortifications behind them. The first line they did not now attempt to reach or defend; Nala pressed them too close. But they got to the *schanses* or pits protected with stone walls, and constructed to hold from a dozen to twenty men, and soon began to open fire from them, and from isolated rocks. I turned my eyes to the gates of the town, which were placed to the north and south. Already they were crowded with hundreds of fugitive women and children flying to the rocks and caves for shelter from the foe.

"As for ourselves, the appearance of Nala's *impi* produced a wonderful change for the better in our position. The soldiers attacking us turned, realizing that the town was being assailed from the rear, and clambering down the *koppie* streamed off to protect their homes against this new enemy. In five minutes there was not a man left except those who would move no more, or were too sorely wounded to escape. I felt inclined to ejaculate '*Saved!*' like the gentleman in the play, but did not because the occasion was too serious. What I did do was to muster all the men and reckon up our losses. They amounted to fifty-one killed and wounded, sixteen men having been killed outright. Then I sent men with the cooking-pots to the stream of water, and we drank. This done I set my bearers, being the most useless part of the community, from a fighting point of view, to the task of attending the injured, and turned to watch the fray.

"By this time Nala's *impi* had climbed the first line of fortifications without opposition, and was advancing in a long line upon the *schanses* or pits which were scattered about between it and the second line, singing a war chant as it came. Presently puffs of smoke began to start from the *schanses*, and with my glasses I could see several of our men falling over. Then as they came opposite a *schanse* that portion of the long line of warriors would thicken up and charge it with a wild rush. I could see them leap on to the walls and vanish into the depths beneath, some of their number falling backward on each occasion, shot or stabbed to death.

"Next would come another act in the tragedy. Out from the hither side of the *schanse* would pour such of its defenders as were left alive, perhaps three or four and perhaps a dozen, running for dear life, with the war dogs on their tracks. One by one they would be caught, then up flashed the great spear and down fell the pursued—dead. I saw ten of our men leap into one large *schanse*, but though I watched for some time nobody came out. Afterwards we inspected the place and found these men all dead, together with twenty-three Matukus. Neither side would give in, and they had fought it out to the bitter end.

"At last they neared the second line of fortifications, behind which the whole remaining Matuku force, numbering some two thousand men, was rapidly assembling. One little pause to get their breath, and

Nala's men came at it with a rush and a long wild shout of '*Bulala Matuku*' (kill the Matuku) that went right through me, thrilling every nerve. Then came an answering shout, and the sounds of heavy firing, and presently I saw our men retreating, somewhat fewer in numbers than they had advanced. Their welcome had been a warm one for the Matuku fight splendidly behind walls. This decided me that it was necessary to create a diversion; if we did not do so it seemed very probable that we should be worsted after all. I called to the captain of our little force, and rapidly put the position before him.

"Seeing the urgency of the occasion, he agreed with me that we must risk it, and in two minutes more, with the exception of my own men, whom I left to guard the wounded, we were trotting across the open space and through the deserted town towards the spot where the struggle was taking place, some seven hundred yards away. In six or eight minutes we reached a group of huts—it was a head man's *kraal*, that was situated about a hundred and twenty yards behind the fortified wall, and took possession of it unobserved. The enemy was too much engaged with the foe in front of him to notice us, and besides, the broken ground rose in a hog-back shape between. There we waited a minute or two and recovered our breath, while I gave my directions. So soon as we heard the Butiana *impi* begin to charge again, we were to run out in a line to the brow of the hogback and pour our fire into the mass of defenders behind the wall. Then the guns were to be thrown down and we must charge with the *assegai*. We had no shields, but that could not be helped; there would be no time to reload the guns, and it was absolutely necessary that the enemy should be disconcerted at the moment when the main attack was delivered.

"The men, who were as plucky a set of fellows as ever I saw, and whose blood was now thoroughly up, consented to this scheme, though I could see that they thought it rather a large order, as indeed I did myself. But I knew that if the *impi* was driven back a second time the game would be played, and for me at any rate it would be a case of the 'Thing that bites,' and this sure and certain knowledge filled my breast with valour.

"We had not long to wait. Presently we heard the Butiana war-song swelling loud and long; they had commenced their attack. I made a sign, and the hundred and fifty men, headed by myself, poured out of the *kraal*, and getting into a rough line ran up the fifty or sixty yards of slope that intervened between ourselves and the crest of the hog-backed ridge. In thirty seconds we were there, and immediately be-

189

yond us was the main body of the Matuku host waiting the onslaught of the enemy with guns and spears. Even now they did not see us, so intent were they upon the coming attack. I signed to my men to take careful aim, and suddenly called out to them to fire, which they did with a will, dropping thirty or forty Matukus.

"'*Charge!*' I shouted, again throwing down my smoking rifle and drawing my revolver, an example which they followed, snatching up their spears from the ground where they had placed them while they fired. The men set up a savage whoop, and we started. I saw the Matuku soldiers wheel around in hundreds, utterly taken aback at this new development of the situation. And looking over them, before we had gone twenty yards I saw something else. For of a sudden, as though they had risen from the earth, there appeared above the wall hundreds of great spears, followed by hundreds of savage faces shadowed with drooping plumes. With a yell they sprang upon the wall shaking their broad shields, and with a yell they bounded from it straight into our astonished foes.

"*Crash!* we were in them now, and fighting like demons. *Crash!* from the other side. Nala's *impi* was at its work, and still the spears and plumes appeared for a moment against the brown background of the mountain, and then sprang down and rushed like a storm upon the foe. The great mob of men turned this way and turned that way, astonished, bewildered, overborne by doubt and terror.

"Meanwhile the slayers stayed not their hands, and on every side spears flashed, and the fierce shout of triumph went up to heaven. There too on the wall stood Maiwa, a white garment streaming from her shoulders, an *assegai* in her hand, her breast heaving, her eyes flashing. Above all the din of battle I could catch the tones of her clear voice as she urged the soldiers on to victory. But victory was not yet. Wambe's soldiers gathered themselves together, and bore our men back by the sheer weight of numbers. They began to give, then once more they rallied, and the fight hung doubtfully.

"'Slay, you war-whelps,' cried Maiwa from the wall. 'Are you afraid, you women, you chicken-hearted women! Strike home, or die like dogs! What—you give way! Follow me, children of Nala.' And with one long cry she leapt from the wall as leaps a stricken antelope, and holding the spear poised rushed right into the thickest of the fray. The warriors saw her, and raised such a shout that it echoed like thunder against the mountains. They massed together, and following the flutter of her white robe crashed into the dense heart of the foe. Down went the Matuku before them like trees before a whirlwind. Nothing could stand in the face of such a rush as that. It was as the rush of a torrent bursting its banks. All along their line swept the wild desperate charge; and there, straight in the forefront of the battle, still waved the white robe of Maiwa.

"Then they broke, and, stricken with utter panic, Wambe's soldiers streamed away a scattered crowd of fugitives, while after them thundered the footfall of the victors.

"The fight was over, we had won the day; and for my part I sat down upon a stone and wiped my forehead, thanking Providence that I had lived to see the end of it. Twenty minutes later Nala's warriors began to return panting. 'Wambe's soldiers had taken to the bush and the caves,' they said, 'where they had not thought it safe to follow them,' adding significantly, that many had stopped on the way.

"I was utterly dazed, and now that the fight was over my energy seemed to have left me, and I did not pay much attention, till presently I was aroused by somebody calling me by my name. I looked up, and saw that it was the chief Nala himself, who was bleeding from a flesh wound in his arm. By his side stood Maiwa panting, but unhurt, and wearing on her face a proud and terrifying air.

"'They are gone, Macumazahn,' said the chief; 'there is little to fear from them, their heart is broken. But where is Wambe the chief?—and where is the white man thou camest to save?'

"'I know not,' I answered.

"Close to where we stood lay a Matuku, a young man who had been shot through the fleshy part of the calf. It was a trifling wound, but it prevented him from running away.

"'Say, thou dog,' said Nala, stalking up to him and shaking his red spear in his face, 'say, where is Wambe? Speak, or I slay thee. Was he with the soldiers?'

"'Nay, lord, I know not,' groaned the terrified man, 'he fought not with us; Wambe has no stomach for fighting. Perchance he is in his *kraal* yonder, or in the cave behind the *kraal*,' and he pointed to a small enclosure on the hillside, about four hundred yards to the right of where we were.

"'Let us go and see,' said Nala, summoning his soldiers."

Chapter 8

Maiwa is Avenged

"The *impi* formed up; alas, an hour before it had been stronger by a third than it was now. Then Nala detached two hundred men to collect and attend to the injured, and at my suggestion issued a stringent order that none of the enemy's wounded, and above all no women or children, were to be killed, as is the savage custom among African natives. On the contrary, they were to be allowed to send word to their women that they might come in to nurse them and fear nothing, for Nala made war upon Wambe the tyrant, and not on the Matuku tribe.

"Then we started with some four hundred men for the chief's *kraal*. Very soon we were there. It was, as I have said, placed against the mountain side, but within the fortified lines, and did not at all cover more than an acre and a half of ground. Outside was a tiny reed fence, within which, neatly arranged in a semi-circular line, stood the huts of the chief's principal wives. Maiwa of course knew every inch of the *kraal*, for she had lived in it, and led us straight to the entrance. We peeped through the gateway—not a soul was to be seen. There were the huts and there was the clear open space floored with a concrete of lime, on which the sun beat fiercely, but nobody could we see or hear.

"'The jackal has gone to earth,' said Maiwa; 'he will be in the cave behind his hut,' and she pointed with her spear towards another small and semi-circular enclosure, over which a large hut was visible, that had the cliff itself for a background. I stared at this fence; by George! it was true, it was entirely made of tusks of ivory planted in the ground with their points bending outwards. The smallest ones, though none were small, were placed nearest to the cliff on either side, but they gradually increased in size till they culminated in two enormous tusks, which, set up so that their points met, something in the shape of an inverted V, formed the gateway to the hut. I was dumbfounded with delight; and indeed, where is the elephant-hunter who would not be, if he suddenly saw five or six hundred picked tusks set up in a row, and only waiting for him to take them away? Of course the stuff was what is known as *black ivory*; that is, the exterior of the tusks had become black from years or perhaps centuries of exposure to wind and weather, but I was certain that it would be none the worse for that. Forgetting the danger of the deed, in my excitement I actually ran right across the open space, and drawing my knife scratched vigorously at one of the great tusks to see how deep the damage might be. As I thought, it was nothing; there beneath the black covering gleamed the pure white ivory. I could have capered for joy, for I fear that I am very mercenary at heart, when suddenly I heard the faint echo of a cry for assistance. 'Help!' screamed a voice in the Sisutu dialect from somewhere behind the hut; 'help! they are murdering me.'

"*I knew the voice*; it was John Every's. Oh, what a selfish brute was I! For the moment that miserable ivory had driven the recollection of him out of my head, and now—perhaps it was too late.

"Nala, Maiwa, and the soldiers had now come up. They too heard the voice and interpreted its tone, though they had not caught the words.

"'This way,' cried Maiwa, and we started at a run, passing round the hut of Wambe. Behind was the narrow entrance to a cave. We rushed through it heedless of the danger of the ambush, and this is what we saw, though very confusedly at first, owing to the gloom.

"In the centre of the cave, and with either end secured to the floor by strong stakes, stood a huge double-springed lion trap edged with sharp and grinning teeth. It was set, and beyond the trap, indeed almost over it, a terrible struggle was in progress. A naked or almost naked white man, with a great beard hanging down over his breast, in spite of his furious struggles, was being slowly forced and dragged towards the trap by six or eight women. Only one man was present, a fat, cruel-looking man with small eyes and a hanging lip. It was the chief Wambe, and he stood by the trap ready to force the victim down upon it so soon as the women had dragged him into the necessary position.

"At this instant they caught sight of us, and there came a moment's pause, and then, before I knew what she was going to do, Maiwa lifted the *assegai* she still held, and whirled it at Wambe's head. I saw the flash of light speed towards him, and so did he, for he stepped backward to avoid it—stepped backward right into the trap. He yelled with pain as the iron teeth of the 'Thing that bites' sprang up with a rattling sound like living fangs and fastened into him—such a yell I have not often heard. Now at last he tasted of the torture which he had inflicted upon so many, and though I trust I am a Christian, I cannot say that I felt sorry for him.

"The *assegai* sped on and struck one of the women who had hold of the unfortunate Every, piercing through her arm. This made her leave go, an example that the other women quickly followed, so that Every fell to the ground, where he lay gasping.

"'Kill the witches,' roared Nala, in a voice of thunder, pointing to the group of women.

"'Nay,' gasped Every, 'spare them. He made them do it,' and he pointed to the human fiend in the trap. Then Maiwa waved her hand to us to fall back, for the moment of her vengeance was come. We did so, and she strode up to her lord, and flinging the white robe from her stood before him, her fierce beautiful face fixed like stone.

"'Who am I?' she cried in so terrible a voice that he ceased his yells. 'Am I that woman who was given to thee for wife, and whose child thou slewest? Or am I an avenging spirit come to see thee die?

"'What is this?' she went on, drawing the withered baby-hand from the pouch at her side.

"'Is it the hand of a babe? and how came that hand to be thus alone? What cut it off from the babe? and where is the babe? Is it a hand? or is it the vision of a hand that shall presently tear thy throat?

"'Where are thy soldiers, Wambe? Do they sleep and eat and go forth to do thy bidding? or are they perchance dead and scattered like the winter leaves?'

"He groaned and rolled his eyes while the fierce-faced woman went on.

"'Art thou still a chief, Wambe? or does another take thy place and power, and say, Lord, what doest thou there? And what is that slave's leglet upon thy knee?

"'Is it a dream, Wambe, great lord and chief? or'—and she lifted her clenched hands and shook them in his face—'hath a woman's vengeance found thee out and a woman's wit o'ermatched thy tyrannous strength? and art thou about to slowly die in torments horrible to think on, oh, thou accursed murderer of little children?'

"And with one wild scream she dashed the dead hand of the child straight into his face, and then fell senseless on the floor. As for the demon in the trap, he shrank back so far as its iron bounds would allow, his yellow eyes starting out of his head with pain and terror, and then once more began to yell.

"The scene was more than I could bear.

"'Nala,' I said, 'this must stop. That man is a fiend, but he must not be left to die there. See thou to it.'

"'Nay,' answered Nala, 'let him taste of the food wherewith he hath fed so many; leave him till death shall find him.'

"'That I will not,' I answered. 'Let his end be swift; see thou to it.'

"'As thou wilt, Macumazahn,' answered the chief, with a shrug of the shoulders; 'first let the white man and Maiwa be brought forth.'

"So the soldiers came forward and carried Every and the woman into the open air. As the former was borne past his tormentor, the fallen chief, so cowardly was his wicked heart, actually prayed him to intercede for him, and save him from a fate which, but for our providential appearance, would have been Every's own.

"So we went away, and in another moment one of the biggest villains on the earth troubled it no more. Once in the fresh air Every recovered quickly. I looked at him, and horror and sorrow pierced me through to see such a sight. His face was the face of a man of sixty, though he was not yet forty, and his poor body was cut to pieces with stripes and scars, and other marks of the torments which Wambe had for years amused himself with inflicting on him.

"As soon as he recovered himself a little he struggled on to his knees, burst into a paroxysm of weeping, and clasping my legs with his emaciated arms, would have actually kissed my feet.

"'What are you about, old fellow?' I said, for I am not accustomed to that sort of thing, and it made me feel uncomfortable.

"'Oh, God bless you?' he moaned, 'God bless you! If only you knew what I have gone through; and to think that you should have come to help me, and at the risk of your own life! Well, you were always a true friend—yes, yes, a true friend.'

"'Bosh,' I answered testily; 'I'm a trader, and I came after that ivory,' and I pointed to the stockade of tusks. 'Did you ever hear of an elephant-hunter who would not have risked his immortal soul for them, and much more his carcase?'

"But he took no notice of my explanations, and went on God blessing me as hard as ever, till at last I bethought me that a nip of brandy, of which I had a flask full, might steady his nerves a bit. I gave it him, and was not disappointed in the result, for he brisked up wonderfully. Then I hunted about in Wambe's hut, and found a *kaross* to put over his poor bruised shoulders, and he was quite a man again.

"'Now,' I said, 'why did the late lamented Wambe want to put you in that trap?'

"'Because as soon as they heard that the fight was going against them, and that Maiwa was charging at the head of Nala's *impi*, one of the women told Wambe that she had seen me write something on some leaves and give them to Maiwa before she went away to purify herself. Then of course he guessed that I had to do with your seizing the *koppie* and holding it while the *impi* rushed the place from the mountain, so he determined to torture me to death before help could come. Oh, heavens! what a mercy it is to hear English again.'

"'How long have you been a prisoner here, Every?' I asked.

"'Six years and a bit, Quatermain; I have lost count of the odd months lately. I came up here with Major Aldey and three other gentlemen and forty bearers. That devil Wambe ambushed us, and murdered the lot to get their guns. They weren't much use to him when he got them, being breech-loaders, for the fools fired away all the ammunition in a month or two. However, they are all in good order, and hanging up in the hut there. They didn't kill me because one of them saw me mending a gun just before they attacked us, so they kept me as a kind of armourer. Twice I tried to make a bolt of it, but was caught each time. Last time Wambe had me flogged very nearly to death—you can see the scars upon my back. Indeed I should have died if it hadn't been for the girl Maiwa, who nursed me by stealth. He got that accursed lion trap among our things also, and I suppose he has tortured between one and two hundred people to death in it. It was his favourite amusement, and he would go every day and sit and watch his victim till he died. Sometimes he would give him food and water to keep him alive longer, telling him or her that he would let him go if he lived till a certain day. But he never did let them go. They all died there, and I could show you their bones behind that rock.'

"'The devil!' I said, grinding my teeth. 'I wish I hadn't interfered; I wish I had left him to the same fate.'

"'Well, he got a taste of it any way,' said Every; 'I'm glad he got a taste. There's justice in it, and now he's gone to hell, and I hope there is another one ready for him there. By Jove! I should like to have the setting of it.'

"And so he talked on, and I sat and listened to him, wondering how he had kept his reason for so many years. But he didn't talk as I have told it, in plain English. He spoke very slowly, and as though he had got something in his mouth, continually using native words because the English ones had slipped his memory.

"At last Nala came up and told us that food was made ready, and thankful enough we were to get it, I can tell you. After we had eaten we held a consultation. Quite a thousand of Wambe's soldiers were put *hors de combat*, but at least two thousand remained hidden in the bush and rocks, and these men, together with those in the outlying *kraals*, were a source of possible danger. The question arose, therefore, what was to be done—were they to be followed or left alone? I waited till everybody had spoken, some giving one opinion and some another, and then being appealed to I gave mine. It was to the effect that Nala should take a leaf out of the great Zulu T'Chaka's book, and incorporate the tribe, not destroy it. We had a good many women among the prisoners. Let them, I suggested, be sent to the hiding-places of the soldiers and make an offer. If the men would come and lay down their arms and declare allegiance to Nala, they and their town and cattle should be spared. Wambe's cattle alone would be seized as the prize of war. Moreover, Wambe having left no children, his wife Maiwa should be declared chieftainess of the tribe, under Nala. If they did not accept this offer by the morning of the second day it should be taken as a declaration that they wished to continue the war. Their town should be burned, their cattle, which our men were already collecting and driving in in great numbers, would be taken, and they should be hunted down.

"This advice was at once declared to be wise, and acted on. The women were despatched, and I saw from their faces that they never expected to get such terms, and did not think that their mission would be in vain. Nevertheless, we spent that afternoon in preparations against possible surprise, and also in collecting all the wounded of both parties into a hospital, which we extemporized out of some huts, and there attending to them as best we could.

"That evening Every had the first pipe of tobacco that he had tasted for six years. Poor fellow, he nearly cried with joy over it. The night passed without any sign of attack, and on the following morning we began to see the effect of our message, for women, children, and a few men came in in little knots, and took possession of their huts. It was of course rather difficult to prevent our men from looting, and generally going on as natives, and for the matter of that white men too, are in the habit of doing after a victory. But one man who after warning was caught maltreating a woman was brought out and killed by Nala's order, and though there was a little grumbling, that put a stop to further trouble.

"On the second morning the head men and numbers of their followers came in in groups, and about midday a deputation of the former presented themselves before us without their weapons. They were conquered, they said, and Wambe was dead, so they came to hear the words of the great lion who had eaten them up, and of the crafty white man, the jackal, who had dug a hole for them to fall in, and of Maiwa, Lady of War, who had led the charge and turned the fate of the battle.

"So we let them hear the words, and when we had done an old man rose and said, that in the name of the people he accepted the yoke that was laid upon their shoulders, and that the more gladly because even the rule of a woman could not be worse than the rule of Wambe. Moreover, they knew Maiwa, the Lady of War, and feared her not, though she was a witch and terrible to see in battle.

"Then Nala asked his daughter if she was willing to become chieftainess of the tribe under him.

"Maiwa, who had been very silent since her revenge was accomplished, answered yes, that she was, and that her rule should be good and gentle to those who were good and gentle to her, but the forward and rebellious she would smite with a rod of iron; which from my knowledge of her character I thought exceedingly probable.

"The head man replied that that was a good saying, and they did not complain at it, and so the meeting ended.

"Next day we spent in preparations for departure. Mine consisted chiefly in superintending the digging up of the stockade of ivory tusks, which I did with the greatest satisfaction. There were some five hundred of them altogether. I made inquiries about it from Every, who told me that the stockade had been there so long that nobody seemed to know exactly who had collected the tusks originally. There was, however, a kind of superstitious feeling about them which had always prevented the chiefs from trying to sell this great mass of ivory. Every and I examined it carefully, and found that although it was so old its quality was really as good as ever, and there was very little soft ivory in the lot. At first I was rather afraid lest, now that my services had been rendered, Nala should hesitate to part with so much valuable property, but this was not the case. When I spoke to him on the subject he merely said, 'Take it, Macumazahn, take it; you have earned it well,' and, to speak the truth, though I say it who shouldn't, I think I had. So we pressed several hundred Matuku bearers into our service, and next day marched off with the lot.

"Before we went I took a formal farewell of Maiwa, whom we left with a bodyguard of three hundred men to assist her in settling the country. She gave me her hand to kiss in a queenly sort of way, and then said:

"'Macumazahn, you are a brave man, and have been a friend to me in my need. If ever you want help or shelter, remember that Maiwa has a good memory for friend and foe. All I have is yours.'

"And so I thanked her and went. She was certainly a very remarkable woman. A year or two ago I heard that her father Nala was dead, and that she had succeeded to the chieftainship of both tribes, which she ruled with great justice and firmness.

"I can assure you that we ascended the pass leading to Wambe's town with feelings very different from those with which we had descended it a few days before. But if I was grateful for the issue of events, you can easily imagine what poor Every's feelings were. When we got to the top of the pass, before the whole *impi* he actually flopped down upon his knees and thanked Heaven for his escape, the tears running down his face. But then, as I have said, his nerves were shaken—though now that his beard was trimmed and he had some sort of clothes on his back, and hope in his heart, he looked a very different man from the poor wretch whom we had rescued from death by torture.

"Well, we separated from Nala at the little stairway or pass over the mountain—Every and I and the ivory going down the river which I had come up a few weeks before, and the chief returning to his own *kraal* on the further side of the mountain. He gave us an escort of a hundred and fifty men, however, with instructions to accompany us for six days' journey, and to keep the Matuku bearers in order and then return. I knew that in six days we should be able to reach a district where porters were plentiful, and whence we could easily get the ivory conveyed to Delagoa Bay.'

"And did you land it up safe?" I asked.

"Well no," said Quatermain, "we lost about a third of it in crossing a river. A flood came down suddenly just as the men were crossing and many of them had to throw down their tusks to save their lives. We had no means of dragging it up, and so we were obliged to leave it, which was very sad. However, we sold what remained for nearly seven thousand pounds, so we did not do so badly. I don't mean that I got seven thousand pounds out of it, because, you see, I insisted upon Every taking a half share. Poor fellow, he had earned it, if ever a man did. He set up a store in the old colony on the proceeds and did uncommonly well."

"And what did you do with the lion trap?" asked Sir Henry.

"Oh, I brought that away with me also, and when I reached Durban I put it in my house. But really I could not bear to sit opposite to it at nights as I smoked. Visions of that poor woman and the hand of her dead child would rise up in my mind, and also of all the horrors of which it had been the instrument. I began to dream at last that it held me by the leg. This was too much for my nerves, so I just packed it up and shipped it to its maker in England, whose name was stamped upon the steel, sending him a letter at the same time to tell him to what purpose the infernal machine had been put. I believe that he gave it to some museum or other."

"And what became of the tusks of the three bulls which you shot! You must have left them at Nala's *kraal*, I suppose."

The old gentleman's face fell at this question.

"Ah," he said, "that is a very sad story. Nala promised to send them with my goods to my agent at Delagoa, and so he did. But the men who brought them were unarmed, and, as it happened, they fell in with a slave caravan under the command of a half-bred Portuguese, who seized the tusks, and what is worse, swore that he had shot them. I paid him out afterwards, however," he added with a smile of satisfaction, "but it did not give me back my tusks, which no doubt have been turned into hair brushes long ago;" and he sighed.

"Well," said Good, "that is a capital yarn of yours, Quatermain, but———"

"But what?" he asked sharply, foreseeing a draw.

"But I don't think that it was so good as mine about the ibex—it hasn't the same *finish*."

Mr. Quatermain made no reply. Good was beneath it.

"Do you know, gentlemen," he said, "it is half-past two in the morning, and if we are going to shoot the big wood to-morrow we ought to leave here at nine-thirty sharp."

"Oh, if you shoot for a hundred years you will never beat the record of those three woodcocks," I said.

"Or of those three elephants," added Sir Henry.

And then we all went to bed, and I dreamed that I had married Maiwa, and was much afraid of that attractive but determined lady.

Marie

Dedication

Ditchingham
1912

My dear Sir Henry—

Nearly thirty-seven years have gone by, more than a generation, since first we saw the shores of Southern Africa rising from the sea. Since then how much has happened: the Annexation of the Transvaal, the Zulu War, the first Boer War, the discovery of the Rand, the taking of Rhodesia, the second Boer War, and many other matters which in these quick-moving times are now reckoned as ancient history.

Alas! I fear that were we to re-visit that country we should find but few faces which we knew. Yet of one thing we may be glad. Those historical events, in some of which you, as the ruler of Natal, played a great part, and I, as it chanced, a smaller one, so far as we can foresee, have at length brought a period of peace to Southern Africa. To-day the flag of England flies from the Zambezi to the Cape. Beneath its shadow may all ancient feuds and blood jealousies be forgotten. May the natives prosper also and be justly ruled, for after all in the beginning the land was theirs. Such, I know, are your hopes, as they are mine.

It is, however, with an earlier Africa that this story deals. In 1836, hate and suspicion ran high between the Home Government and its Dutch subjects. Owing to the freeing of the slaves and mutual misunderstandings, the Cape Colony was then in tumult, almost in rebellion, and the Boers, by thousands, sought new homes in the unknown, savage-peopled North. Of this blood-stained time I have tried to tell; of the Great Trek and its tragedies, such as the massacre of the true-hearted Retief and his companions at the hands of the Zulu king, Dingaan.

But you have read the tale and know its substance. What, then, re-

203

mains for me to say? Only that in memory of long-past days I dedicate it to you whose image ever springs to mind when I strive to picture an English gentleman as he should be. Your kindness I never shall forget; in memory of it, I offer you this book.

Ever sincerely yours,

H. Rider Haggard

To Sir Henry Bulwer, G.C.M.G.

Preface

The Author hopes that the reader may find some historical interest in the tale set out in these pages of the massacre of the Boer general, Retief, and his companions at the hands of the Zulu king, Dingaan. Save for some added circumstances, he believes it to be accurate in its details.

The same may be said of the account given of the hideous sufferings of the trek-Boers who wandered into the fever *veld*, there to perish in the neighbourhood of Delagoa Bay. Of these sufferings, especially those that were endured by Triechard and his companions, a few brief contemporary records still exist, buried in scarce works of reference. It may be mentioned, also, that it was a common belief among the Boers of that generation that the cruel death of Retief and his companions, and other misfortunes which befell them, were due to the treacherous plottings of an Englishman, or of Englishmen, with the despot, Dingaan.

Editor's Note

The following extract explains how the manuscript of *Marie*, and with it some others, one of which is named *Child of Storm*, came into the hands of the editor.

It is from a letter, dated January 17th, 1909, and written by Mr. George Curtis, the brother of Sir Henry Curtis, Bart., who, it will be remembered, was one of the late Mr. Allan Quatermain's friends and companions in adventure when he discovered King Solomon's Mines, and who afterwards disappeared with him in Central Africa. This extract runs as follows:

You may recall that our mutual and dear friend, old Allan Quatermain, left me the sole executor of his will, which he signed before he set out with my brother Henry for Zuvendis, where he was killed. The Court, however, not being satisfied that there was any legal proof of his death, invested the capital funds in trustee securities, and by my advice let his place in Yorkshire to a tenant who has remained in occupation of it during the last two decades. Now that tenant is dead, and at the earnest prayer of the Charities which benefit under Quatermain's will, and of myself—for in my uncertain state of health I have for long been most anxious to wind up this executorship—about eight months ago the Court at last consented to the distribution of this large fund in accordance with the terms of the will.

This, of course, involved the sale of the real property, and before it was put up to auction I went over the house in company of the solicitor appointed by the Court. On the top landing, in the room Quatermain used to occupy, we found a sealed cupboard that I opened. It proved to be full of various articles which evidently he had prized because of their associations with his earthy life. These I need not enumerate here, especially as I have reserved them as his residuary legatee and, in the event of my death, they will pass to you under my will.

Among these relics, however, I found a stout box, made of some red foreign wood, that contained various documents and letters and a bundle of manuscripts. Under the tape which fastened these manuscripts together, as you will see, is a scrap of paper on which is written, in blue pencil, a direction signed 'Allan Quatermain,' that in the event of anything happening to him, these MSS. are to be sent to you (for whom, as you know, he had a high regard), and that at your sole discretion you are to burn or publish them as you may see fit.

So, after all these years, as we both remain alive, I carry out our old friend's instructions and send you his bequest, which I trust may prove of interest and value. I have read the MS. called 'Marie,' and certainly am of the opinion that it ought to be published, for I think it a strange and moving tale of a great love—full, moreover, of forgotten history.

That named *Child of Storm* also seems very interesting as a study of savage life, and the others may be the same; but my eyes are troubling me so much that I have not been able to decipher them. I hope, however, that I may be spared long enough to see them in print.

Poor old Allan Quatermain. It is as though he had suddenly reappeared from the dead! So at least I thought as I perused these stories of a period of his life of which I do not remember his speaking to me.

And now my responsibility in this matter is finished and yours begins. Do what you like about the manuscripts.

George Curtis

As may be imagined, I, the editor, was considerably astonished when I received this letter and the accompanying bundle of closely-written MSS. To me also it was as though my old friend had risen from the grave and once more stood before me, telling some history of his stormy and tragic past in that quiet, measured voice that I have never been able to forget.

The first manuscript I read was that entitled *Marie*. It deals with Mr. Quatermain's strange experiences when as a very young man he accompanied the ill-fated Pieter Retief and the Boer Commission on an embassy to the Zulu despot, Dingaan. This, it will be remembered, ended in their massacre, Quatermain himself and his Hottentot servant Hans being the sole survivors of the slaughter. Also it deals with another matter more personal to himself, namely, his courtship of and marriage to his first wife, Marie Marais.

Of this Marie I never heard him speak, save once. I remember that on a certain occasion—it was that of a garden fete for a local charity—I was standing by Quatermain when someone introduced to him a young girl who was staying in the neighbourhood and had distinguished herself by singing very prettily at the fete. Her surname I forget, but her Christian name was Marie. He started when he heard it, and asked if she were French. The young lady answered No, but only of French extraction through her grandmother, who also was called Marie.

"Indeed?" he said. "Once I knew a maiden not unlike you who was also of French extraction and called Marie. May you prove more fortunate in life than she was, though better or nobler you can never be," and he bowed to her in his simple, courtly fashion, then turned away. Afterwards, when we were alone, I asked him who was this Marie of whom he had spoken to the young lady. He paused a little, then answered:

"She was my first wife, but I beg you not to speak of her to me or to anyone else, for I cannot bear to hear her name. Perhaps you will learn all about her one day." Then, to my grief and astonishment, he broke into something like a sob and abruptly left the room.

After reading the record of this Marie I can well understand why he was so moved. I print it practically as it left his hands.

There are other MSS. also, one of which, headed *Child of Storm*, relates the moving history of a beautiful and, I fear I must add, wicked Zulu girl named Mameena who did much evil in her day and went unrepentant from the world.

Another, amongst other things, tells the secret story of the causes of the defeat of Cetewayo and his armies by the English in 1879, which happened not long before Quatermain met Sir Henry Curtis and Captain Good.

These three narratives are, indeed, more or less connected with each other. At least, a certain aged dwarf, called Zikali, a witch-doctor and an terrible man, has to do with all of them, although in the first, *Marie*, he is only vaguely mentioned in connection with the massacre of Retief, whereof he was doubtless the primary instigator. As *Marie* comes first in chronological order, and was placed on the top of the pile by its author, I publish it first. With the others I hope to deal later on, as I may find time and opportunity.

But the future must take care of itself. We cannot control it, and its events are not in our hand. Meanwhile, I hope that those who in their youth have read of King Solomon's Mines and Zuvendis, and perhaps some others who are younger, may find as much of interest in these new chapters of the autobiography of Allan Quatermain as I have done myself.

CHAPTER 1

Allan Learns French

Although in my old age I, Allan Quatermain, have taken to writing—after a fashion—never yet have I set down a single word of the tale of my first love and of the adventures that are grouped around her beautiful and tragic history. I suppose this is because it has always seemed to me too holy and far-off a matter—as holy and far-off as is that heaven which holds the splendid spirit of Marie Marais. But now, in my age, that which was far-off draws near again; and at night, in the depths between the stars, sometimes I seem to see the opening doors through which I must pass, and leaning earthwards across their threshold, with outstretched arms and dark and dewy eyes, a shadow long forgotten by all save me—the shadow of Marie Marais.

An old man's dream, doubtless, no more. Still, I will try to set down that history which ended in so great a sacrifice, and one so worthy of record, though I hope that no human eye will read it until I also am forgotten, or, at any rate, have grown dim in the gathering mists of oblivion. And I am glad that I have waited to make this attempt, for it seems to me that only of late have I come to understand and appreciate at its true value the character of her of whom I tell, and the passionate affection which was her bounteous offering to one so utterly unworthy as myself. What have I done, I wonder, that to me should have been decreed the love of two such women as Marie and that of Stella, also now long dead, to whom alone in the world I told all her tale? I remember I feared lest she should take it ill, but this was not so. Indeed, during our brief married days, she thought and talked much of Marie, and some of her last words to me were that she was going to seek her, and that they would wait for me together in the land of love, pure and immortal.

So with Stella's death all that side of life came to an end for me, since during the long years which stretch between then and now I have never said another tender word to woman. I admit, however, that once, long afterwards, a certain little witch of a Zulu did say tender words to me, and for an hour or so almost turned my head, an art in which she had great skill. This I say because I wish to be quite honest, although it—I mean my head, for there was no heart involved in the matter—came straight again at once. Her name was Mameena, and I have set down her remarkable story elsewhere.

To return. As I have already written in another book, I passed my youth with my old father, a Church of England clergyman, in what is now the Cradock district of the Cape Colony.

Then it was a wild place enough, with a very small white population. Among our few neighbours was a Boer farmer of the name of Henri Marais, who lived about fifteen miles from our station, on a fine farm called Maraisfontein. I say he was a Boer, but, as may be guessed from both his Christian and surname, his origin was Huguenot, his forefather, who was also named Henri Marais—though I think the Marais was spelt rather differently then—having been one of the first of that faith who emigrated to South Africa to escape the cruelties of Louis XIV. at the time of the revocation of the Edict of Nantes.

Unlike most Boers of similar descent, these particular Marais— for, of course, there are many other families so called—never forgot their origin. Indeed, from father to son, they kept up some knowledge of the French tongue, and among themselves often spoke it after a fashion. At any rate, it was the habit of Henri Marais, who was excessively religious, to read his chapter of the Bible (which it is, or was, the custom of the Boers to spell out every morning, should their learning allow them to do so), not in the *taal* or patois Dutch, but in good old French. I have the very book from which he used to read now, for, curiously enough, in after years, when all these events had long been gathered to the past, I chanced to buy it among a parcel of other works at the weekly auction of odds and ends on the market square of Maritzburg. I remember that when I opened the great tome, bound over the original leather boards in buckskin, and discovered to whom it had belonged, I burst into tears. There was no doubt about it, for, as was customary in old days, this Bible had sundry fly-leaves sewn up with it for the purpose of the recording of events important to its owner.

The first entries were made by the original Henri Marais, and record how he and his compatriots were driven from France, his father having lost his life in the religious persecutions. After this comes a long list of births, marriages and deaths continued from generation to generation, and amongst them a few notes telling of such matters as the change of the dwelling-places of the family, always in French. Towards the end of the list appears the entry of the birth of the Henri Marais whom I knew, alas! too well, and of his only sister. Then is written his marriage to Marie Labuschagne, also, be it noted, of the Huguenot stock. In the next year follows the birth of Marie Marais, my Marie, and, after a long interval, for no other children were born, the death of her mother. Immediately below appears the following curious passage:

Le 3 Janvier, 1836. Je quitte ce pays voulant me sauver du maudit gouvernement Britannique comme mes ancêtres se sont sauves de ce diable—Louis XIV.
A bas les rois et les ministres tyrannique! Vive la liberté!

Which indicates very clearly the character and the opinions of Henri Marais, and the feeling among the trek-Boers at that time.

Thus the record closes and the story of the Marais ends—that is, so far as the writings in the Bible go, for that branch of the family is now extinct.

Their last chapter I will tell in due course.

There was nothing remarkable about my introduction to Marie Marais. I did not rescue her from any attack of a wild beast or pull her out of a raging river in a fashion suited to romance. Indeed, we interchanged our young ideas across a small and extremely massive table, which, in fact, had once done duty as a block for the chopping up of meat. To this hour I can see the hundreds of lines running criss-cross upon its surface, especially those opposite to where I used to sit.

One day, several years after my father had emigrated to the Cape, the Heer Marais arrived at our house in search, I think, of some lost oxen. He was a thin, bearded man with rather wild, dark eyes set close together, and a quick nervous manner, not in the least like that of a Dutch Boer—or so I recall him. My father received him courteously and asked him to stop to dine, which he did.

They talked together in French, a tongue that my father knew well, although he had not used it for years; Dutch he could not, or, rather, would not, speak if he could help it, and Mr. Marais preferred not to talk English. To meet someone who could converse in French delighted him, and although his version of the language was that of two centuries before and my father's was largely derived from reading, they got on very well together, if not too fast.

At length, after a pause, Mr. Marais, pointing to myself, a small and stubbly-haired youth with a sharp nose, asked my father whether he would like me to be instructed in the French tongue. The answer was that nothing would please him better.

"Although," he added severely, "to judge by my own experience where Latin and Greek are concerned, I doubt his capacity to learn anything."

So an arrangement was made that I should go over for two days in each week to Maraisfontein, sleeping there on the intervening night, and acquire a knowledge of the French tongue from a tutor whom Mr. Marais had hired to instruct his daughter in that language and other subjects. I remember that my father agreed to pay a certain proportion of this tutor's salary, a plan which suited the thrifty Boer very well indeed.

Thither, accordingly, I went in due course, nothing loth, for on the *veld* between our station and Maraisfontein many *pauw* and *koran*—that is, big and small bustards—were to be found, to say nothing of occasional buck, and I was allowed to carry a gun, which even in those days I could use fairly well. So to Maraisfontein I rode on the appointed day, attended by a Hottentot after-rider, a certain Hans, of whom I shall have a good deal to tell. I enjoyed very good sport on the road, arriving at the stead laden with one *pauw*, two *koran*, and a little klipspringer buck which I had been lucky enough to shoot as it bounded out of some rocks in front of me.

There was a peach orchard planted round Maraisfontein, which just then was a mass of lovely pink blossom, and as I rode through it slowly, not being sure of my way to the house, a lanky child appeared in front of me, clad in a frock which exactly matched the colour of the peach bloom. I can see her now, her dark hair hanging down her back, and her big, shy eyes staring at me from the shadow of the Dutch *kappie* which she wore. Indeed, she seemed to be all eyes, like a *dikkop* or thick-headed plover; at any rate, I noted little else about her.

I pulled up my pony and stared at her, feeling very shy and not knowing what to say. For a while she stared back at me, being afflicted, presumably, with the same complaint, then spoke with an effort, in a voice that was very soft and pleasant. "Are you the little Allan Quatermain who is coming to learn French with me?" she asked in Dutch.

"Of course," I answered in the same tongue, which I knew well; "but why do you call me little, missie? I am taller than you," I added indignantly, for when I was young my lack of height was always a sore point with me.

"I think not," she replied. "But get off that horse, and we will measure here against this wall."

So I dismounted, and, having assured herself that I had no heels to my boots (I was wearing the kind of raw-hide slippers that the Boers call *veld-shoon*), she took the writing slate which she was carrying—it had no frame, I remember, being, in fact, but a piece of the material used for roofing—and, pressing it down tight on my stubbly hair, which stuck up then as now, made a deep mark in the soft sandstone of the wall with the hard pointed pencil.

"There," she said, "that is justly done. Now, little Allan, it is your turn to measure me."

So I measured her, and, behold! she was the taller by a whole half-inch.

"You are standing on tiptoe," I said in my vexation.

"Little Allan," she replied, "to stand on tiptoe would be to lie before the good Lord, and when you come to know me better you will learn that, though I have a dreadful temper and many other sins, I do not lie."

I suppose that I looked snubbed and mortified, for she went on in her grave, grown-up way: "Why are you angry because God made me taller than you? especially as I am whole months older, for my father told me so. Come, let us write our names against these marks, so that in a year or two you may see how you outgrow me." Then with the slate pencil she scratched "Marie" against her mark very deeply, so that it might last, she said; after which I wrote "Allan" against mine.

Alas! Within the last dozen years chance took me past Maraisfontein once more. The house had long been rebuilt, but this particular wall yet stood. I rode to it and looked, and there faintly could still be seen the name Marie, against the little line, and by it the mark that I had made. My own name and with it subsequent measurements were gone, for in the intervening forty years or so the sandstone had flaked away in places. Only her autograph remained, and when I saw it I think that I felt even worse than I did on finding whose was the old Bible that I had bought upon the market square at Maritzburg.

I know that I rode away hurriedly without even stopping to inquire into whose hands the farm had passed. Through the peach orchard I rode, where the trees—perhaps the same, perhaps others—were once more in bloom, for the season of the year was that when Marie and I first met, nor did I draw rein for half a score of miles.

But here I may state that Marie always stayed just half an inch the taller in body, and how much taller in mind and spirit I cannot tell.

When we had finished our measuring match Marie turned to lead me to the house, and, pretending to observe for the first time the beautiful bustard and the two *koran* hanging from my saddle, also the klipspringer buck that Hans the Hottentot carried behind him on his horse, asked:

"Did you shoot all these, Allan Quatermain?"

"Yes," I answered proudly; "I killed them in four shots, and the *pauw* and *koran* were flying, not sitting, which is more than you could have done, although you are taller, Miss Marie."

"I do not know," she answered reflectively. "I can shoot very well with a rifle, for my father has taught me, but I never would shoot at living things unless I must because I was hungry, for I think that to kill is cruel. But, of course, it is different with men," she added hastily, "and no doubt you will be a great hunter one day, Allan Quatermain, since you can already aim so well."

"I hope so," I answered, blushing at the compliment, "for I love hunting, and when there are so many wild things it does not matter if we kill a few. I shot these for you and your father to eat."

"Come, then, and give them to him. He will thank you," and she led the way through the gate in the sandstone wall into the yard, where the outbuildings stood in which the riding horses and the best of the breeding cattle were kept at night, and so past the end of the long, one-storied house, that was stone-built and whitewashed, to the *stoep* or veranda in front of it.

On the broad *stoep*, which commanded a pleasant view over rolling, park-like country, where mimosa and other trees grew in clumps, two men were seated, drinking strong coffee, although it was not yet ten o'clock in the morning.

Hearing the sound of the horses, one of these, Mynheer Marais, whom I already knew, rose from his hide-strung chair. He was, as I think I have said, not in the least like one of the phlegmatic Boers, either in person or in temperament, but, rather, a typical Frenchman, although no member of his race had set foot in France for a hundred and fifty years. At least so I discovered afterwards, for, of course, in those days I knew nothing of Frenchmen.

His companion was also French, Leblanc by name, but of a very different stamp. In person he was short and stout. His large head was bald except for a fringe of curling, iron-grey hair which grew round it just above the ears and fell upon his shoulders, giving him the appearance of a tonsured but dishevelled priest. His eyes were blue and watery, his mouth was rather weak, and his cheeks were pale, full and flabby. When the Heer Marais rose, I, being an observant youth, noted that Monsieur Leblanc took the opportunity to stretch out a rather shaky hand and fill up his coffee cup out of a black bottle, which from the smell I judged to contain peach brandy.

In fact, it may as well be said at once that the poor man was a drunkard, which explains how he, with all his high education and great ability, came to hold the humble post of tutor on a remote Boer farm. Years before, when under the influence of drink, he had committed some crime in France—I don't know what it was, and never inquired—and fled to the Cape to avoid prosecution. Here he obtained a professorship at one of the colleges, but after a while appeared in the lecture-room quite drunk and lost his employment. The same thing happened in other towns, till at last he drifted to distant Maraisfontein, where his employer tolerated his weakness for the sake of the intellectual companionship for which something in his own nature seemed to crave. Also, he looked upon him as a compatriot in distress, and a great bond of union between them was their mutual and virulent hatred of England and the English, which in the case of Monsieur Leblanc, who in his youth had fought at Waterloo and been acquainted with the great Emperor, was not altogether unnatural.

Henri Marais's case was different, but of that I shall have more to say later.

"Ah, Marie," said her father, speaking in Dutch, "so you have found him at last," and he nodded towards me, adding: "You should be flattered, little man. Look you, this missie has been sitting for two hours in the sun waiting for you, although I told her you would not arrive much before ten o'clock, as your father the predicant said you would breakfast before you started. Well, it is natural, for she is lonely here, and you are of an age, although of a different race"; and his face darkened as he spoke the words.

"Father," answered Marie, whose blushes I could see even in the shadow of her cap, "I was not sitting in the sun, but under the shade of a peach tree. Also, I was working out the sums that Monsieur Leblanc set me on my slate. See, here they are," and she held up the slate, which was covered with figures, somewhat smudged, it is true, by the rubbing of my stiff hair and of her cap.

Then Monsieur Leblanc broke in, speaking in French, of which, as it chanced I understood the sense, for my father had grounded me in that tongue, and I am naturally quick at modern languages. At any rate, I made out that he was asking if I was the little *cochon d'anglais*, or English pig, whom for his sins he had to teach. He added that he judged I must be, as my hair stuck up on my head—I had taken off my hat out of politeness—as it naturally would do on a pig's back.

This was too much for me, so, before either of the others could speak, I answered in Dutch, for rage made me eloquent and bold:

"Yes, I am he; but, *mynheer*, if you are to be my master, I hope you will not call the English pigs any more to me."

"Indeed, gamin" (that is, little scamp), "and pray, what will happen if I am so bold as to repeat that truth?"

"I think, *mynheer*," I replied, growing white with rage at this new insult, "the same that has happened to yonder buck," and I pointed to the klipspringer behind Hans's saddle. "I mean that I shall shoot you."

"Peste! Au moins il a du courage, cet enfant" (At least the child is plucky), exclaimed Monsieur Leblanc, astonished. From that moment, I may add, he respected me, and never again insulted my country to my face.

Then Marais broke out, speaking in Dutch that I might understand:

"It is you who should be called pig, Leblanc, not this boy, for, early as it is, you have been drinking. Look! the brandy bottle is half empty. Is that the example you set to the young? Speak so again and I turn you out to starve on the *veld*. Allan Quatermain, although, as you may have heard, I do not like the English, I beg your pardon. I hope you will forgive the words this sot spoke, thinking that you did not understand," and he took off his hat and bowed to me quite in a grand manner, as his ancestors might have done to a king of France.

Leblanc's face fell. Then he rose and walked away rather unsteadily; as I learned afterwards, to plunge his head in a tub of cold water and swallow a pint of new milk, which were his favourite antidotes after too much strong drink. At any rate, when he appeared again, half an hour later, to begin our lesson, he was quite sober, and extremely polite.

When he had gone, my childish anger being appeased, I presented the Heer Marais with my father's compliments, also with the buck and the birds, whereof the latter seemed to please him more than the former. Then my saddle-bags were taken to my room, a little cupboard of a place next to that occupied by Monsieur Leblanc, and Hans was sent to turn the horses out with the others belonging to the farm, having first knee-haltered them tightly, so that they should not run away home.

This done, the Heer Marais showed me the room in which we were to have our lessons, one of the *sitkammer*, or sitting chambers, whereof, unlike most Boer stead, this house boasted two. I remember that the floor was made of *daga*, that is, ant-heap earth mixed with cow-dung, into which thousands of peach-stones had been thrown while it was still soft, in order to resist footwear—a rude but fairly efficient expedient, and one not unpleasing to the eye. For the rest, there was one window opening on to the veranda, which, in that bright climate, admitted a shaded but sufficient light, especially as it always stood open; the ceiling was of unplastered reeds; a large bookcase stood in the corner containing many French works, most of them the property of Monsieur Leblanc, and in the centre of the room was the strong, rough table made of native yellow-wood, that once had served as a butcher's block. I recollect also a coloured print of the great Napoleon commanding at some battle in which he was victorious, seated upon a white horse and waving a field-marshal's baton over piles of dead and wounded; and near the window, hanging to the reeds of the ceiling, the nest of a pair of red-tailed swallows, pretty creatures that, notwithstanding the mess they made, afforded to Marie and me endless amusement in the intervals of our work.

When, on that day, I shuffled shyly into this homely place, and, thinking myself alone there, fell to examining it, suddenly I was brought to a standstill by a curious choking sound which seemed to proceed from the shadows behind the bookcase. Wondering as to its cause, I advanced cautiously to discover a pink-clad shape standing in the corner like a naughty child, with her head resting against the wall, and sobbing slowly.

"Marie Marais, why do you cry?" I asked.

She turned, tossing back the locks of long, black hair which hung about her face, and answered:

"Allan Quatermain, I cry because of the shame which has been put upon you and upon our house by that drunken Frenchman."

"What of that?" I asked. "He only called me a pig, but I think I have shown him that even a pig has tusks."

"Yes," she replied, "but it was not you he meant; it was all the English, whom he hates; and the worst of it is that my father is of his mind. He, too, hates the English, and, oh! I am sure that trouble will come of his hatred, trouble and death to many."

"Well, if so, we have nothing to do with it, have we?" I replied with the cheerfulness of extreme youth.

"What makes you so sure?" she said solemnly. "Hush! here comes Monsieur Leblanc."

CHAPTER 2

The Attack on Maraisfontein

I do not propose to set out the history of the years which I spent in acquiring a knowledge of French and various other subjects, under the tuition of the learned but prejudiced Monsieur Leblanc. Indeed, there is "none to tell, sir." When Monsieur Leblanc was sober, he was a most excellent and well-informed tutor, although one apt to digress into many side issues, which in themselves were not uninstructive. When tipsy, he grew excited and harangued us, generally upon politics and religion, or rather its reverse, for he was an advanced freethinker, although this was a side to his character which, however intoxicated he might be, he always managed to conceal from the Heer Marais. I may add that a certain childish code of honour prevented us from betraying his views on this and sundry other matters. When absolutely drunk, which, on an average, was not more than once a month, he simply slept, and we did what we pleased—a fact which our childish code of honour also prevented us from betraying.

But, on the whole, we got on very well together, for, after the incident of our first meeting, Monsieur Leblanc was always polite to me. Marie he adored, as did every one about the place, from her father down to the meanest slave. Need I add that I adored her more than all of them put together, first with the love that some children have for each other, and afterwards, as we became adult, with that wider love by which it is at once transcended and made complete. Strange would it have been if this were not so, seeing that we spent nearly half of every week practically alone together, and that, from the first, Marie, whose nature was as open as the clear noon, never concealed her affection for me. True, it was a very discreet affection, almost sisterly, or even motherly, in its outward and visible aspects, as though she could never forget that extra half-inch of height or month or two of age.

Moreover, from a child she was a woman, as an Irishman might say, for circumstances and character had shaped her thus. Not much more than a year before we met, her mother, whose only child she was, and whom she loved with all her strong and passionate heart, died after a lingering illness, leaving her in charge of her father and his house. I think it was this heavy bereavement in early youth which coloured her nature with a grey tinge of sadness and made her seem so much older than her years.

So the time went on, I worshipping Marie in my secret thought, but saying nothing about it, and Marie talking of and acting towards me as though I were her dear younger brother. Nobody, not even her father or mine, or Monsieur Leblanc, took the slightest notice of this queer relationship, or seemed to dream that it might lead to ultimate complications which, in fact, would have been very distasteful to them all for reasons that I will explain.

Needless to say, in due course, as they were bound to do, those complications arose, and under pressure of great physical and moral excitement the truth came out. It happened thus.

Every reader of the history of the Cape Colony has heard of the great Kaffir War of 1835. That war took place for the most part in the districts of Albany and Somerset, so that we inhabitants of Cradock, on the whole, suffered little. Therefore, with the natural optimism and carelessness of danger of dwellers in wild places, we began to think ourselves fairly safe from attack. Indeed, so we should have been, had it not been for a foolish action on the part of Monsieur Leblanc.

It seems that on a certain Sunday, a day that I always spent at home with my father, Monsieur Leblanc rode out alone to some hills about five miles distant from Maraisfontein. He had often been cautioned that this was an unsafe thing to do, but the truth is that the foolish man thought he had found a rich copper mine in these hills, and was anxious that no one should share his secret. Therefore, on Sundays, when there were no lessons, and the Heer Marais was in the habit of celebrating family prayers, which Leblanc disliked, it was customary for him to ride to these hills and there collect geological specimens and locate the strike of his copper vein. On this particular Sabbath, which was very hot, after he had done whatever he intended to do, he dismounted from his horse, a tame old beast. Leaving it loose, he partook of the meal he had brought with him, which seems to have included a bottle of peach brandy that induced slumber.

Waking up towards evening, he found that his horse had gone, and at once jumped to the conclusion that it had been stolen by Kaffirs, although in truth the animal had but strolled over a ridge in search of grass. Running hither and thither to seek it, he presently crossed this ridge and met the horse, apparently being led away by two of the Red Kaffirs, who, as was usual, were armed with assegais. As a matter of fact these men had found the beast, and, knowing well to whom it belonged, were seeking its owner, whom, earlier in the day, they had seen upon the hills, in order to restore it to him. This, however, never occurred to the mind of Monsieur Leblanc, excited as it was by the fumes of the peach brandy.

Lifting the double-barrelled gun he carried, he fired at the first Kaffir, a young man who chanced to be the eldest son and heir of the chief of the tribe, and, as the range was very close, shot him dead. Thereon his companion, leaving go of the horse, ran for his life. At him Leblanc fired also, wounding him slightly in the thigh, but no more, so that he escaped to tell the tale of what he and every other native for miles round considered a wanton and premeditated murder. The deed done, the fiery old Frenchman mounted his nag and rode quietly home. On the road, however, as the peach brandy evaporated from his brain, doubts entered it, with the result that he determined to say nothing of his adventure to Henri Marais, who he knew was particularly anxious to avoid any cause of quarrel with the Kaffirs.

So he kept his own counsel and went to bed. Before he was up next morning the Heer Marais, suspecting neither trouble nor danger, had ridden off to a farm thirty miles or more away to pay its owner for some cattle which he had recently bought, leaving his home and his daughter quite unprotected, except by Leblanc and the few native servants, who were really slaves, that lived about the place.

Now on the Monday night I went to bed as usual, and slept, as I have always done through life, like a top, till about four in the morning, when I was awakened by someone tapping at the glass of my window. Slipping from the bed, I felt for my pistol, as it was quite dark, crept to the window, opened it, and keeping my head below the level of the sill, fearing lest its appearance should be greeted with an *assegai*, asked who was there.

"Me, *baas*," said the voice of Hans, our Hottentot servant, who, it will be remembered, had accompanied me as after-rider when first I went to Maraisfontein. "I have bad news. Listen. The *baas* knows that I have been out searching for the red cow which was lost. Well, I found her, and was sleeping by her side under a tree on the *veld* when, about two hours ago, a woman whom I know came up to my camp fire and woke me. I asked her what she was doing at that hour of the night, and she answered that she had come to tell me something. She said that some young men of the tribe of the chief Quabie, who lives in the hills yonder, had been visiting at their *kraal*, and that a few hours before a messenger had arrived from the chief saying that they must return at once, as this morning at dawn he and all his men were going to attack Maraisfontein and kill everyone in it and take the cattle!"

"Good God!" I ejaculated. "Why?"

"Because, young *baas*," drawled the Hottentot from the other side of the window, "because someone from Maraisfontein—I think it was the Vulture" (the natives gave this name to Leblanc on account of his bald head and hooked nose)—"shot Quabie's son on Sunday when he was holding his horse."

"Good God!" I said again, "the old fool must have been drunk. When did you say the attack was to be—at dawn?" and I glanced at the stars, adding, "Why, that will be within less than an hour, and the Baas Marais is away."

"Yes," croaked Hans; "and Missie Marie—think of what the Red Kaffirs will do with Missie Marie when their blood is up."

I thrust my fist through the window and struck the Hottentot's toad-like face on which the starlight gleamed faintly.

"Dog!" I said, "saddle my mare and the roan horse and get your gun. In two minutes I come. Be swift or I kill you."

"I go," he answered, and shot out into the night like a frightened snake.

Then I began to dress, shouting as I dressed, till my father and the Kaffirs ran into the room. As I threw on my things I told them all.

"Send out messengers," I said, "to Marais—he is at Botha's farm—and to all the neighbours. Send, for your lives; gather up the friendly Kaffirs and ride like hell for Maraisfontein. Don't talk to me, father; don't talk! Go and do what I tell you. Stay! Give me two guns, fill the saddle-bags with powder tins and *loopers*, and tie them to my mare. Oh! be quick, be quick!"

Now at length they understood, and flew this way and that with candles and lanterns. Two minutes later—it could scarcely have been more—I was in front of the stables just as Hans led out the bay mare, a famous beast that for two years I had saved all my money to buy. Someone strapped on the saddle-bags while I tested the girths; someone else appeared with the stout roan stallion that I knew would follow the mare to the death. There was not time to saddle him, so Hans clambered on to his back like a monkey, holding two guns under his arm, for I carried but one and my double-barrelled pistol.

"Send off the messengers," I shouted to my father. "If you would see me again send them swiftly, and follow with every man you can raise."

Then we were away with fifteen miles to do and five-and-thirty minutes before the dawn.

"Softly up the slope," I said to Hans, "till the beasts get their wind, and then ride as you never rode before."

Those first two miles of rising ground! I thought we should never come to the end of them, and yet I dared not let the mare out lest she should bucket herself. Happily she and her companion, the stallion—a most enduring horse, though not so very swift—had stood idle for the last thirty hours, and, of course, had not eaten or drunk since sunset. Therefore being in fine fettle, they were keen for the business; also we were light weights.

I held in the mare as she spurted up the rise, and the horse kept his pace to hers. We reached its crest, and before us lay the great level plain, eleven miles of it, and then two miles down hill to Maraisfontein.

"Now," I said to Hans, shaking loose the reins, "keep up if you can!"

Away sped the mare till the keen air of the night sung past my ears, and behind her strained the good roan horse with the Hottentot monkey on its back. Oh! what a ride was that!

Further I have gone for a like cause, but never at such speed, for I knew the strength of the beasts and how long it would last them. Half an hour of it they might endure; more, and at this pace they must founder or die. And yet such was the agony of my fear, that it seemed to me as though I only crept along the ground like a tortoise.

The roan was left behind, the sound of his foot-beats died away, and I was alone with the night and my fear. Mile added itself to mile, for now and again the starlight showed me a stone or the skeleton of some dead beast that I knew. Once I dashed into a herd of trekking game so suddenly, that a springbok, unable to stop itself, leapt right over me. Once the mare put her foot in an ant-bear hole and near-ly fell, but recovered herself—thanks be to God, unharmed—and I worked myself back into the saddle whence I had been almost shaken. If I had fallen; oh! if I had fallen!

We were near the end of the flat, and she began to fail. I had over-pressed her; the pace was too tremendous. Her speed lessened to an ordinary fast gallop as she faced the gentle rise that led to the brow. And now, behind me, once more I heard the sound of the hoofs of the roan. The tireless beast was coming up. By the time we reached the edge of the plateau he was quite near, not fifty yards behind, for I heard him whinny faintly.

Then began the descent. The morning star was setting, the east grew grey with light. Oh! could we get there before the dawn? Could we get there before the dawn? That is what my horse's hoofs beat out to me.

Now I could see the mass of the trees about the stead. And now I dashed into something, though until I was through it, I did not know that it was a line of men, for the faint light gleamed upon the spear of one of them who had been overthrown!

So it was no lie! The Kaffirs were there! As I thought it, a fresh horror filled my heart; perhaps their murdering work was already done and they were departing.

The minute of suspense—or was it but seconds?—seemed an eternity. But it ended at last. Now I was at the door in the high wall that enclosed the outbuildings at the back of the house, and there, by an inspiration, pulled up the mare—glad enough she was to stop, poor thing—for it occurred to me that if I rode to the front I should very probably be *assegaied* and of no further use. I tried the door, which was made of stout stinkwood planks. By design, or accident, it had been left unbolted. As I thrust it open Hans arrived with a rush, clinging to the roan with his face hidden in its mane. The beast pulled up by the side of the mare which it had been pursuing, and in the faint light I saw that an *assegai* was fixed in its flank.

Five seconds later we were in the yard and locking and barring the door behind us. Then, snatching the saddle-bags of ammunition from the horses, we left them standing there, and I ran for the back entrance of the house, bidding Hans rouse the natives, who slept in the outbuildings, and follow with them. If any one of them showed signs of treachery he was to shoot him at once. I remember that as I went I tore the spear out of the stallion's flank and brought it away with me.

Now I was hammering upon the back door of the house, which I could not open. After a pause that seemed long, a window was thrown wide, and a voice—it was Marie's—asked in frightened tones who was there.

"I, Allan Quatermain," I answered. "Open at once, Marie. You are in great danger; the Red Kaffirs are going to attack the house."

She flew to the door in her nightdress, and at length I was in the place.

"Thank God! you are still safe," I gasped. "Put on your clothes while I call Leblanc. No, stay, do you call him; I must wait here for Hans and your slaves."

Away she sped without a word, and presently Hans arrived, bringing with him eight frightened men, who as yet scarcely knew whether they slept or woke.

"Is that all?" I asked. "Then bar the door and follow me to the *sitkammer*, where the *baas* keeps his guns."

Just as we reached it, Leblanc entered, clad in his shirt and trousers, and was followed presently by Marie with a candle.

"What is it?" he asked.

I took the candle from Marie's hand, and set it on the floor close to the wall, lest it should prove a target for an *assegai* or a bullet. Even in those days the Kaffirs had a few firearms, for the most part captured or stolen from white men. Then in a few words I told them all.

"And when did you learn all this?" asked Leblanc in French.

"At the Mission Station a little more than half an hour ago," I answered, looking at my watch.

"At the station a little more than half an hour ago! *Peste!* it is not possible. You dream or are drunken," he cried excitedly.

"All right, *monsieur*, we will argue afterwards," I answered. "Meanwhile the Kaffirs are here, for I rode through them; and if you want to save your life, stop talking and act. Marie, how many guns are there?"

"Four," she answered, "of my father's; two *roers* and two smaller ones."

"And how many of these men"—and I pointed to the Kaffirs— "can shoot?"

"Three well and one badly, Allan."

"Good," I said. "Let them load the guns with *loopers*"—that is, slugs, not bullets—"and let the rest stand in the passage with their assegais, in case the Quabies should try to force the back door."

Now, in this house there were in all but six windows, one to each sitting-room, one to each of the larger bedrooms, these four opening on to the veranda, and one at either end of the house, to give light and air to the two small bedrooms, which were approached through the larger bedrooms. At the back, fortunately, there were no windows, for the stead was but one room deep with passage running from the front to the back door, a distance of little over fifteen feet.

As soon as the guns were loaded I divided up the men, a man with a gun at each window. The right-hand sitting-room window I took myself with two guns, Marie coming with me to load, which, like all girls in that wild country, she could do well enough. So we arranged ourselves in a rough-and-ready fashion, and while we were doing it felt quite cheerful—that is, all except Monsieur Leblanc, who, I noticed, seemed very much disturbed.

I do not for one moment mean to suggest that he was afraid, as he might well have been, for he was an extremely brave and even rash man; but I think the knowledge that his drunken act had brought this terrible danger upon us all weighed on his mind. Also there may have been more; some subtle fore-knowledge of the approaching end to a life that, when all allowances were made, could scarcely be called well spent. At any rate he fidgeted at his window-place cursing beneath his breath, and soon, as I saw out of the corner of my eye, began to have recourse to his favourite bottle of peach brandy, which he fetched out of a cupboard.

The slaves, too, were gloomy, as all natives are when suddenly awakened in the night; but as the light grew they became more cheerful. It is a poor Kaffir that does not love fighting, especially when he has a gun and a white man or two to lead him.

Now that we had made such little preparations as we could, which, by the way, I supplemented by causing some furniture to be piled up against the front and back doors, there came a pause, which, speaking for my own part—being, after all, only a lad at the time—I found very trying to the nerves. There I stood at my window with the two guns, one a double-barrel and one a single *roer*, or elephant gun, that took a tremendous charge, but both, be it remembered, flint locks; for, although percussion caps had been introduced, we were a little behind the times in Cradock. There, too, crouched on the ground beside me, holding the ammunition ready for re-loading, her long, black hair flowing about her shoulders, was Marie Marais, now a well-grown young woman. In the intense silence she whispered to me:

"Why did you come here, Allan? You were safe yonder, and now you will probably be killed."

"To try to save you," I answered simply. "What would you have had me do?"

"To try to save me? Oh! that is good of you, but you should have thought of yourself."

"Then I should still have thought of you, Marie."

"Why, Allan?"

"Because you are myself and more than myself. If anything happened to you, what would my life be to me?"

"I don't quite understand, Allan," she replied, staring down at the floor. "Tell me, what do you mean?"

"Mean, you silly girl," I said; "what can I mean, except that I love you, which I thought you knew long ago."

"Oh!" she said; "*now* I understand." Then she raised herself upon

227

her knees, and held up her face to me to kiss, adding, "There, that's my answer, the first and perhaps the last. Thank you, Allan dear; I am glad to have heard that, for you see one or both of us may die soon."

As she spoke the words, an *assegai* flashed through the window-place, passing just between our heads. So we gave over love-making and turned our attention to war.

Now the light was beginning to grow, flowing out of the pearly eastern sky; but no attack had yet been delivered, although that one was imminent that spear fixed in the plaster of the wall behind us showed clearly. Perhaps the Kaffirs had been frightened by the galloping of horses through their line in the dark, not knowing how many of them there might have been. Or perhaps they were waiting to see better where to deliver their onset. These were the ideas that occurred to me, but both were wrong.

They were staying their hands until the mist lifted a little from the hollow below the stead where the cattle *kraals* were situated, for while the fog remained they could not see to get the beasts out. These they wished to make sure of and drive away before the fight began, lest during its progress something should happen to rob them of their booty.

Presently, from these *kraals*, where the Heer Marais's horned beasts and sheep were penned at night, about one hundred and fifty of the former and some two thousand of the latter, to say nothing of the horses, for he was a large and prosperous farmer, there arose a sound of bellowing, neighing, and baaing, and with it that of the shouting of men.

"They are driving off the stock," said Marie. "Oh! my poor father, he is ruined; it will break his heart."

"Bad enough," I answered, "but there are things that might be worse. Hark!"

As I spoke there came a sound of stamping feet and of a wild war chant. Then in the edge of the mist that hung above the hollow where the cattle *kraals* were, figures appeared, moving swiftly to and fro, looking ghostly and unreal. The Kaffirs were marshalling their men for the attack. A minute more and it had begun. On up the slope they came in long, wavering lines, several hundreds of them, whistling and screaming, shaking their spears, their war-plumes and hair trappings blown back by the breeze, the lust of slaughter in their rolling eyes. Two or three of them had guns, which they fired as they ran, but where the bullets went I do not know, over the house probably.

I called out to Leblanc and the Kaffirs not to shoot till I did, for I knew that they were poor marksmen and that much depended upon our first volley being effective. Then as the captain of this attack came within thirty yards of the *stoep*—for now the light, growing swiftly, was strong enough to enable me to distinguish him by his apparel and the rifle which he held—I loosed at him with the *roer* and shot him dead. Indeed the heavy bullet passing through his body mortally wounded another of the Quabies behind. These were the first men that I ever killed in war.

As they fell, Leblanc and the rest of our people fired also, the slugs from their guns doing great execution at that range, which was just long enough to allow them to scatter. When the smoke cleared a little I saw that nearly a dozen men were down, and that the rest, dismayed by this reception, had halted. If they had come on then, while we were loading, doubtless they might have rushed the place; but, being un- used to the terrible effects of firearms, they paused, amazed. A number of them, twenty or thirty perhaps, clustered about the bodies of the fallen Kaffirs, and, seizing my second gun, I fired both barrels at these with such fearful effect that the whole regiment took to their heels and fled, leaving their dead and wounded on the ground. As they ran our servants cheered, but I called to them to be silent and load swiftly, knowing well that the enemy would soon return.

For a time, however, nothing happened, although we could hear them talking somewhere near the cattle *kraal*, about a hundred and fifty yards away. Marie took advantage of this pause, I remember, to fetch food and distribute it among us. I, for one, was glad enough to get it.

Now the sun was up, a sight for which I thanked Heaven, for, at any rate, we could no longer be surprised. Also, with the daylight, some of my fear passed away, since darkness always makes danger twice as terrible to man and beast. Whilst we were still eating and fortifying the window-places as best we could, so as to make them difficult to enter, a single Kaffir appeared, waving above his head a stick to which was tied a white ox-tail as a sign of truce. I ordered that no one should fire, and when the man, who was a bold fellow, had reached the spot where the dead captain lay, called to him, asking his business, for I could speak his language well.

He answered that he had come with a message from Quabie. This was the message: that Quabie's eldest son had been cruelly murdered by the fat white man called "Vulture" who lived with the Heer Marais, and that he, Quabie, would have blood for blood. Still, he did not wish to kill the young white chieftainess (that was Marie) or the others in the house, with whom he had no quarrel. Therefore if we would give up the fat white man that he might make him "die slowly," Quabie would be content with his life and with the cattle that he had already taken by way of a fine, and leave us and the house unmolested.

Now, when Leblanc understood the nature of this offer he went perfectly mad with mingled fear and rage, and began to shout and swear in French.

"Be silent," I said; "we do not mean to surrender you, although you have brought all this trouble on us. Your chance of life is as good as ours. Are you not ashamed to act so before these black people?"

When at last he grew more or less quiet I called to the messenger that we white folk were not in the habit of abandoning each other, and that we would live or die together. Still, I bade him tell Quabie that if we did die, the vengeance taken on him and all his people would be to wipe them out till not one of them was left, and therefore that he would do well not to cause any of our blood to flow. Also, I added, that we had thirty men in the house (which, of course, was a lie) and plenty of ammunition and food, so that if he chose to continue the attack it would be the worse for him and his tribe.

On hearing this the herald shouted back that we should every one of us be dead before noon if he had his way. Still, he would report my words faithfully to Quabie and bring his answer.

Then he turned and began to walk off. Just as he did so a shot was fired from the house, and the man pitched forward to the ground, then rose again and staggered back towards his people, with his right shoulder shattered and his arm swinging.

"Who did that?" I asked through the smoke, which prevented me from seeing.

"I, *parbleu!*" shouted Leblanc. "*Sapristi!* that black devil wanted to torture me, Leblanc, the friend of the great Napoleon. Well, at least I have tortured him whom I meant to kill."

"Yes, you fool," I answered; "and we, too, shall be tortured because of your wickedness. You have shot a messenger carrying a flag of truce, and that the Quabies will never forgive. Oh! I tell you that you have hit us as well as him, who had it not been for you might have been spared."

These words I said quite quietly and in Dutch, so that our Kaffirs might understand them, though really I was boiling with wrath.

But Leblanc did not answer quietly.

"Who are you," he shouted, "you wretched little Englishman, who dare to lecture me, Leblanc, the friend of the great Napoleon?"

Now I drew my pistol and walked up to the man.

"Be quiet, you drunken sot," I said, for I guessed that he had drunk more of the brandy in the darkness. "If you are not quiet and do not obey me, who am in command here, either I will blow your brains out, or I will give you to these men," and I pointed to Hans and the Kaffirs, who had gathered round him, muttering ominously. "Do you know what they will do with you? They will throw you out of the house, and leave you to settle your quarrel with Quabie alone." Leblanc looked first at the pistol, and next at the faces of the natives, and saw something in one or other of them, or in both, that caused him to change his note.

"Pardon, *monsieur*," he said; "I was excited. I knew not what I said. If you are young you are brave and clever, and I will obey you," and he went to his station and began to re-load his gun. As he did so a great shout of fury rose from the cattle *kraal*. The wounded herald had reached the Quabies and was telling them of the treachery of the white people.

The Rescue

The second Quabie advance did not begin till about half-past seven. Even savages love their lives and appreciate the fact that wounds hurt very much, and these were no exception to the rule. Their first rush had taught them a bitter lesson, of which the fruit was evident in the crippled or dying men who rolled to and fro baked in the hot sun within a few yards of the *stoep*, not to speak of those who would never stir again. Now, the space around the house being quite open and bare of cover, it was obvious that it could not be stormed without further heavy losses. In order to avoid such losses a civilised people would have advanced by means of trenches, but of these the Quabies knew nothing; moreover, digging tools were lacking to them.

So it came about that they hit upon another, and in the circumstances a not inefficient expedient. The cattle *kraal* was built of rough, unmortared stones. Those stones they took, each man carrying two or three, which, rushing forward, they piled up into scattered rough defences of about eighteen inches or two feet high. These defences were instantly occupied by as many warriors as could take shelter behind them, lying one on top of the other. Of course, those savages who carried the first stones were exposed to our fire, with the result that many of them fell, but there were always plenty more behind. As they were being built at a dozen different points, and we had but seven guns, before we could reload, a particular *schanz*, of which perhaps the first builders had fallen, would be raised so high that our slugs could no longer hurt those who lay behind it. Also, our supply of ammunition was limited, and the constant expenditure wasted it so much that at length only about six charges per man remained. At last, indeed, I was obliged to order the firing to cease, so that we might reserve ourselves for the great rush which could not now be much delayed.

Finding that they were no longer harassed by our bullets, the Quabies advanced more rapidly, directing their attack upon the south end of the house, where there was but one window, and thus avoiding the fire that might be poured upon them from the various openings under the veranda. At first I wondered why they selected this end, till Marie reminded me that this part of the dwelling was thatched with reeds, whereas the rest of the building, which had been erected more recently, was slated.

Their object was to fire the roof. So soon as their last wall was near enough (that is, about half-past ten of the clock) they began to throw into the thatch assegais to which were attached bunches of burning grass. Many of these went out, but at length, as we gathered from their shouts, one caught. Within ten minutes this part of the house was burning.

Now our state became desperate. We retreated across the central passage, fearing lest the blazing rafters should fall upon our natives, who were losing heart and would no longer stay beneath them. But the Quabies, more bold, clambered in through the south window, and attacked us in the doorway of the larger sitting-room.

Here the final fight began. As they rushed at us we shot, till they went down in heaps. Almost at our last charge they gave back, and just then the roof fell upon them.

Oh, what a terrible scene was that! The dense clouds of smoke, the screams of the trapped and burning men, the turmoil, the agony!

The front door was burst in by a flank onslaught.

Leblanc and a slave who was near him were seized by black, claw-like hands and dragged out. What became of the Frenchman I do not know, for the natives hauled him away, but I fear his end must have been dreadful, as he was taken alive. The servant I saw them *assegai*, so at least he died at once. I fired my last shot, killing a fellow who was flourishing a battle-axe, then dashed the butt of the gun into the face of the man behind him, felling him, and, seizing Marie by the hand, dragged her back into the northernmost room—that in which I was accustomed to sleep—and shut and barred the door.

"Allan," she gasped, "Allan dear, it is finished. I cannot fall into the hands of those men. Kill me, Allan."

"All right," I answered, "I will. I have my pistol. One barrel for you and one for me."

"No, no! Perhaps you might escape after all; but, you see, I am a woman, and dare not risk it. Come now, I am ready," and she knelt down, opening her arms to receive the embrace of death, and looked up at me with her lovely, pitiful eyes.

"It doesn't do to kill one's love and live on oneself," I answered hoarsely. "We have got to go together," and I cocked both barrels of the pistol.

The Hottentot, Hans, who was in the place with us, saw and understood.

"It is right, it is best!" he said; and turning, he hid his eyes with his hand.

"Wait a little, Allan," she exclaimed; "it will be time when the door is down, and perhaps God may still help us."

"He may," I answered doubtfully; "but I would not count on it. Nothing can save us now unless the others come to rescue us, and that's too much to hope for."

Then a thought struck me, and I added with a dreadful laugh: "I wonder where we shall be in five minutes."

"Oh! together, dear; together for always in some new and beautiful world, for you do love me, don't you, as I love you? Maybe that's better than living on here where we should be sure to have troubles and perhaps be separated at last."

I nodded my head, for though I loved life, I loved Marie more, and I felt that we were making a good end after a brave fight. They were battering at the door now, but, thank Heaven, Marais had made strong doors, and it held a while.

The wood began to give at last, an *assegai* appeared through a shattered plank, but Hans stabbed along the line of it with the spear he held, that which I had snatched from the flank of the horse, and it was dropped with a scream. Black hands were thrust through the hole, and the Hottentot hacked and cut at them with the spear. But others came, more than he could pierce, and the whole door-frame began to be dragged outwards.

"Now, Marie, be ready," I gasped, lifting the pistol.

"Oh, Christ receive me!" she answered faintly. "It won't hurt much, will it, Allan?"

"You will never feel anything," I whispered; as with the cold sweat pouring from me I placed the muzzle within an inch of her forehead and began to press the trigger. My God! yes, I actually began to press the trigger softly and steadily, for I wished to make no mistake.

It was at this very moment, above the dreadful turmoil of the roaring flames, the yells of the savages and the shrieks and groans of wounded and dying men, that I heard the sweetest sound which ever fell upon my ears—the sound of shots being fired, many shots, and quite close by.

"Great Heaven!" I screamed; "the Boers are here to save us. Marie, I will hold the door while I can. If I fall, scramble through the window—you can do it from the chest beneath—drop to the ground, and run towards the firing. There's a chance for you yet, a good chance."

"And you, you," she moaned. "I would rather die with you."

"Do what I bid you," I answered savagely, and bounded forward towards the rocking door.

It was falling outward, it fell, and on the top of it appeared two great savages waving broad spears. I lifted the pistol, and the bullet that had been meant for Marie's brain scattered that of the first of them, and the bullet which had been meant for my heart pierced that of the second. They both went down dead, there in the doorway.

I snatched up one of their spears and glanced behind me. Marie was climbing on to the chest; I could just see her through the thickening smoke. Another Quabie rushed on. Hans and I received him on the points of our assegais, but so fierce was his charge that they went through him as though he were nothing, and being but light, both of us were thrown backwards to the ground. I scrambled to my feet again, defenceless now, for the spear was broken in the Kaffir, and awaited the end. Looking back once more I saw that Marie had either failed to get through the window or abandoned the attempt. At any rate she was standing near the chest supporting herself by her right hand. In my despair I seized the blade end of the broken *assegai* and dragged it from the body of the Kaffir, thinking that it would serve to kill her, then turned to do the deed.

But even as I turned I heard a voice that I knew well shout: "Do you live, Marie?" and in the doorway appeared no savage, but Henri Marais.

Slowly I backed before him, for I could not speak, and the last dreadful effort of my will seemed to thrust me towards Marie. I reached her and threw my hand that still held the gory blade round her neck. Then as darkness came over me I heard her cry:

"Don't shoot, father. It is Allan, Allan who has saved my life!"

After that I remember no more. Nor did she for a while, for we both fell to the ground senseless.

When my senses returned to me I found myself lying on the floor of the wagon-house in the back yard. Glancing from my half-opened eyes, for I was still speechless, I saw Marie, white as a sheet, her hair all falling about her dishevelled dress. She was seated on one of those boxes that we put on the front of wagons to drive from, *voorkissies* they are called, and as her eyes were watching me I knew that she lived. By her stood a tall and dark young man whom I had never seen before. He was holding her hand and looking at her anxiously, and even then I felt angry with him. Also I saw other things; for instance, my old father leaning down and looking at *me* anxiously, and outside in the yard, for there were no doors to the wagon-house, a number of men with guns in their hands, some of whom I knew and others who were strangers. In the shadow, too, against the wall, stood my blood mare with her head hanging down and trembling all over. Not far from her the roan lay upon the ground, its flank quite red.

I tried to rise and could not, then feeling pain in my left thigh, looked and saw that it was red also. As a matter of fact an *assegai* had gone half through it and hit upon the bone. Although I never felt it at the time, this wound was dealt to me by that great Quabie whom Hans and I had received upon our spears, doubtless as he fell. Hans, by the way, was there also, an awful and yet a ludicrous spectacle, for the Quabie had fallen right on the top of him and lain so with results that may, be imagined. There he sat upon the ground, looking upwards, gasping with his fish-like mouth. Each gasp, I remember, fashioned itself into the word "*Allemachte!*" that is "Almighty," a favourite Dutch expression.

Marie was the first to perceive that I had come to life again. Shaking herself free from the clasp of the young man, she staggered towards me and fell upon her knees at my side, muttering words that I could not catch, for they choked in her throat. Then Hans took in the situation, and wriggling his unpleasant self to my other side, lifted my hand and kissed it. Next my father spoke, saying:

"Praise be to God, he lives! Allan, my son, I am proud of you; you have done your duty as an Englishman should."

"Had to save my own skin if I could, thank you, father," I muttered.

"Why as an Englishman more than any other sort of man, Mynheer Predicant?" asked the tall stranger, speaking in Dutch, although he evidently understood our language.

"The point is one that I will not argue now, sir," answered my father, drawing himself up. "But if what I hear is true, there was a Frenchman in that house who did not do his duty; and if you belong to the same nation, I apologise to you."

"Thank you, sir; as it happens, I do, half. The rest of me is Portuguese, not English, thank God."

"God is thanked for many things that must surprise Him," replied my father in a suave voice.

At that moment this rather disagreeable conversation, which even then both angered and amused me faintly, came to an end, for the Heer Marais entered the place.

As might have been expected in so excitable a man, he was in a terrible state of agitation. Thankfulness at the escape of his only, beloved child, rage with the Kaffirs who had tried to kill her, and extreme distress at the loss of most of his property—all these conflicting emotions boiled together in his breast like antagonistic elements in a crucible.

The resulting fumes were parti-coloured and overpowering. He rushed up to me, blessed and thanked me (for he had learnt something of the story of the defence), called me a young hero and so forth, hoping that God would reward me. Here I may remark that *he* never did, poor man. Then he began to rave at Leblanc, who had brought all this dreadful disaster upon his house, saying that it was a judgment on himself for having sheltered an atheist and a drunkard for so many years, just because he was French and a man of intellect. Someone, my father as a matter of fact, who with all his prejudices possessed a great sense of justice, reminded him that the poor Frenchman had expiated, or perchance was now expiating any crimes that he might have committed.

This turned the stream of his invective on to the Quabie Kaffirs, who had burned part of his house and stolen nearly all his stock, making him from a rich man into a poor one in a single hour. He shouted for vengeance on the "black devils," and called on all there to help him to recover his beasts and kill the thieves. Most of those present—they were about thirty in all, not counting the Kaffir and Hottentot afterriders—answered that they were willing to attack the Quabies. Being residents in the district, they felt, and, indeed, said, that his case to-day might and probably would be their case to-morrow. Therefore they were prepared to ride at once.

Then it was that my father intervened.

"*Heeren*," he said, "it seems to me that before you seek vengeance, which, as the Book tells us, is the Lord's, it would be well, especially for the Heer Marais, to return thanks for what has been saved to him. I mean his daughter, who might now very easily have been dead or worse."

He added that goods came or went according to the chances of fortune, but a beloved human life, once lost, could not be restored. This precious life had been preserved to him, he would not say by man—here he glanced at me—but by the Ruler of the world acting

237

through man. Perhaps those present did not quite understand what he (my father) had learned from Hans the Hottentot, that I, his son, had been about to blow out the brains of Marie Marais and my own when the sound of the shots of those who had been gathered through the warning which I left before I rode from the Mission Station, had stayed my hand. He called upon the said Hans and Marie herself to tell them the story, since I was too weak to do so.

Thus adjured, the little Hottentot, smothered as he was in blood, stood up. In the simple, dramatic style characteristic of his race, he narrated all that had happened since he met the woman on the *veld* but little over twelve hours before, till the arrival of the rescue party. Never have I seen a tale followed with deeper interest, and when at last Hans pointed to me lying on the ground and said, "There is he who did these things which it might be thought no man could do—he, but a boy," even from those phlegmatic Dutchmen there came a general cheer. But, lifting myself upon my hands, I called out:

"Whatever I did, this poor Hottentot did also, and had it not been for him I could not have done anything—for him and the two good horses."

Then they cheered again, and Marie, rising, said:

"Yes, father; to these two I owe my life."

After this, my father offered his prayer of thanksgiving in very bad Dutch—for, having begun to learn it late in life, he never could really master that language—and the stalwart Boers, kneeling round him, said "Amen." As the reader may imagine, the scene, with all its details, which I will not repeat, was both remarkable and impressive.

What followed this prayer I do not very well remember, for I became faint from exhaustion and the loss of blood. I believe, however, that the fire having been extinguished, they removed the dead and wounded from the unburnt portion of the house and carried me into the little room where Marie and I had gone through that dreadful scene when I went within an ace of killing her. After this the Boers and Marais's Kaffirs, or rather slaves, whom he had collected from where they lived away from the house, to the number of thirty or forty, started to follow the defeated Quabie, leaving about ten of their number as a guard. Here I may mention that of the seven or eight men who slept in the outbuildings and had fought with us, two were killed in the fight and two wounded. The remainder, one way or another, managed to escape unhurt, so that in all this fearful struggle, in which we inflicted so terrible a punishment upon the Kaffirs, we lost only three slain, including the Frenchman, Leblanc.

As to the events of the next three days I know only what I have been told, for practically during all that time I was off my head from loss of blood, complicated with fever brought on by the fearful excitement and exertion I had undergone. All I can recall is a vision of Marie bending over me and making me take food of some sort—milk or soup, I suppose—for it seems I would touch it from no other hand. Also I had visions of the tall shape of my white-haired father, who, like most missionaries, understood something of surgery and medicine, attending to the bandages on my thigh. Afterwards he told me that the spear had actually cut the walls of the big artery, but, by good fortune, without going through them. Another fortieth of an inch and I should have bled to death in ten minutes!

On this third day my mind was brought back from its wanderings by the sound of a great noise about the house, above which I heard the voice of Marais storming and shouting, and that of my father trying to calm him. Presently Marie entered the room, drawing-to behind her a Kaffir *karoos*, which served as a curtain, for the door, it will be remembered, had been torn out. Seeing that I was awake and reasonable, she flew to my side with a little cry of joy, and, kneeling down, kissed me on the forehead.

"You have been very ill, Allan, but I know you will recover now. While we are alone, which," she added slowly and with meaning, "I dare say we shall not be much in future, I want to thank you from my heart for all that you did to save me. Had it not been for you, oh! had it not been for you"—and she glanced at the blood stains on the earthen floor, put her hands before her eyes and shuddered.

"Nonsense, Marie," I answered, taking her hand feebly enough, for I was very weak. "Anyone else would have done as much, even if they did not love you as I do. Let us thank God that it was not in vain. But what is all that noise? Have the Quabies come back?"

She shook her head.

"No; the Boers have come back from hunting them."

"And did they catch them and recover the cattle?"

"Not so. They only found some wounded men, whom they shot, and the body of Monsieur Leblanc with his head cut off, taken away with other bits of him for medicine, they say to make the warriors brave. Quabie has burnt his *kraal* and fled with all his people to join the other Kaffirs in the Big Mountains. Not a cow or a sheep did they find, except a few that had fallen exhausted, and those had their throats cut. My father wanted to follow them and attack the Red Kaffirs in the mountains, but the others would not go. They said there are

239

thousands of them, and that it would be a mad war, from which not one of them would return alive. He is wild with grief and rage, for, Allan dear, we are almost ruined, especially as the British Government are freeing the slaves and only going to give us a very small price, not a third of their value. But, hark! he is calling me, and you must not talk much or excite yourself, lest you should be ill again. Now you have to sleep and eat and get strong. Afterwards, dear, you may talk"; and, bending down once more, she blessed and kissed me, then rose and glided away.

CHAPTER 4

Hernando Pereira

Several more days passed before I was allowed out of that little war-stained room of which I grew to hate the very sight. I entreated my father to take me into the air, but he would not, saying that he feared lest any movement should cause the bleeding to begin again or even the cut artery to burst. Moreover, the wound was not healing very well, the spear that caused it having been dirty or perhaps used to skin dead animals, which caused some dread of gangrene, that in those days generally meant death. As it chanced, although I was treated only with cold water, for antiseptics were then unknown, my young and healthy blood triumphed and no gangrene appeared.

What made those days even duller was that during them I saw very little of Marie, who now only entered the place in the company of her father. Once I managed to ask her why she did not come oftener and alone. Her face grew troubled as she whispered back, "Because it is not allowed, Allan," and then without another word left the place.

Why, I wondered to myself, was it not allowed, and an answer sprang up in my mind. Doubtless it was because of that tall young man who had argued with my father in the wagon-house. Marie had never spoken to me of him, but from the Hottentot Hans and my father I managed to collect a good deal of information concerning him and his business.

It appeared that he was the only child of Henri Marais's sister, who married a Portuguese from Delagoa Bay of the name of Pereira, who had come to the Cape Colony to trade many years before and settled there. Both he and his wife were dead, and their son, Hernando, Marie's cousin, had inherited all their very considerable wealth.

Indeed, now I remembered having heard this Hernando, or Hernan, as the Boers called him for short, spoken of in past years by the Heer Marais as the heir to great riches, since his father had made a

241

large fortune by trading in wine and spirits under some Government monopoly which he held. Often he had been invited to visit Maraisfontein, but his parents, who doted on him and lived in one of the settled districts not far from Cape Town, would never allow him to travel so far from them into these wild regions.

Since their death, however, things had changed. It appeared that on the decease of old Pereira the Governor of the Colony had withdrawn the wine and spirit monopoly, which he said was a job and a scandal, an act that made Hernando Pereira very angry, although he needed no more money, and had caused him to throw himself heart and soul into the schemes of the disaffected Boers. Indeed, he was now engaged as one of the organisers of the Great Trek which was in contemplation. In fact, it had already begun, into the partially explored land beyond the borders of the Colony, where the Dutch farmers proposed to set up dominions of their own.

That was the story of Hernando Pereira, who was to be—nay, who had already become—my rival for the hand of the sweet and beautiful Marie Marais.

One night when my father and I were alone in the little room where he slept with me, and he had finished reading his evening portion of Scripture aloud, I plucked up my courage to tell him that I loved Marie and wished to marry her, and that we had plighted our troth during the attack of the Kaffirs on the stead.

"Love and war indeed!" he said, looking at me gravely, but showing no sign of surprise, for it appeared that he was already acquainted with our secret. This was not wonderful, for he informed me afterwards that during my delirium I had done nothing except rave of Marie in the most endearing terms. Also Marie herself, when I was at my worst, had burst into tears before him and told him straight out that she loved me.

"Love and war indeed!" he repeated, adding kindly, "My poor boy, I fear that you have fallen into great trouble."

"Why, father?" I asked. "Is it wrong that we should love each other?"

"Not wrong, but, in the circumstances, quite natural—I should have foreseen that it was sure to happen. No, not wrong, but most unfortunate. To begin with, I do not wish to see you marry a foreigner and become mixed up with these disloyal Boers. I hoped that one day, a good many years hence, for you are only a boy, Allan, you would find an English wife, and I still hope it."

"Never!" I ejaculated.

"Never is a long word, Allan, and I dare say that what you are so

242

sure is impossible will happen after all," words that made me angry enough at the time, though in after years I often thought of them.

"But," he went on, "putting my own wishes, perhaps prejudices, aside, I think your suit hopeless. Although Henri Marais likes you well enough and is grateful to you just now because you have saved the daughter whom he loves, you must remember that he hates us English bitterly. I believe that he would almost as soon see his girl marry a half-caste as an Englishman, and especially a poor Englishman, as you are, and unless you can make money, must remain. I have little to leave you, Allan."

"I might make money, father, out of ivory, for instance. You know I am a good shot."

"Allan, I do not think you will ever make much money, it is not in your blood; or, if you do, you will not keep it. We are an old race, and I know our record, up to the time of Henry VIII. at any rate. Not one of us was ever commercially successful. Let us suppose, however, that you should prove yourself the exception to the rule, it can't be done at once, can it? Fortunes don't grow in a night, like mushrooms."

"No, I suppose not, father. Still, one might have some luck."

"Possibly. But meanwhile you have to fight against a man who has the luck, or rather the money in his pocket."

"What do you mean?" I asked, sitting up.

"I mean Hernando Pereira, Allan, Marais's nephew, who they say is one of the richest men in the Colony. I know that he wishes to marry Marie."

"How do you know it, father?"

"Because Marais told me so this afternoon, probably with a purpose. He was struck with her beauty when he first saw her after your escape, which he had not done since she was a child, and as he stopped to guard the house while the rest went after the Quabies—well, you can guess. Such things go quickly with these Southern men."

I hid my face in the pillow, biting my lips to keep back the groan that was ready to burst from them, for I felt the hopelessness of the situation. How could I compete with this rich and fortunate man, who naturally would be favoured of my betrothed's father? Then on the blackness of my despair rose a star of hope. I could not, but perchance Marie might. She was very strong-natured and very faithful. She was not to be bought, and I doubted whether she could be frightened.

"Father," I said, "I may never marry Marie, but I don't think that Hernando Pereira ever will either."

"Why not, my boy?"

243

"Because she loves me, father, and she is not one to change. I believe that she would rather die."

"Then she must be a very unusual sort of woman. Still, it may be so; the future will tell to those who live to see it. I can only pray and trust that whatever happens will be for the best for both of you. She is a sweet girl and I like her well, although she may be Boer—or French. And now, Allan, we have talked enough, and you had better go to sleep. You must not excite yourself, you know, or it may set up new inflammation in the wound."

"Go to sleep. Must not excite yourself." I kept muttering those words for hours, serving them up in my mind with a spice of bitter thought. At last torpor, or weakness, overcame me, and I fell into a kind of net of bad dreams which, thank Heaven! I have now forgotten. Yet when certain events happened subsequently I always thought, and indeed still think, that these or something like them, had been a part of those evil dreams.

On the morning following this conversation I was at length allowed to be carried to the *stoep*, where they laid me down, wrapped in a very dirty blanket, upon a *rimpi*-strung bench or primitive sofa. When I had satisfied my first delight at seeing the sun and breathing the fresh air, I began to study my surroundings. In front of the house, or what remained of it, so arranged that the last of them at either end we made fast to the extremities of the *stoep*, was arranged an arc of wagons, placed as they are in a laager and protected underneath by earth thrown up in a mound and by boughs of the mimosa thorn. Evidently these wagons, in which the guard of Boers and armed natives who still remained on the place slept at night, were set thus as a defence against a possible attack by the Quabies or other Kaffirs.

During the daytime, however, the centre wagon was drawn a little on one side to leave a kind of gate. Through this opening I saw that a long wall, also semicircular, had been built outside of them, enclosing a space large enough to contain at night all the cattle and horses that were left to the Heer Marais, together with those of his friends, who evidently did not wish to see their oxen vanish into the depths of the mountains. In the middle of this extemporised *kraal* was a long, low mound, which, as I learned afterwards, contained the dead who fell in the attack on the house. The two slaves who had been killed in the defence were buried in the little garden that Marie had made, and the headless body of Leblanc in a small walled place to the right of the stead, where lay some of its former owners and one or two relatives of the Heer Marais, including his wife.

244

Whilst I was noting these things Marie appeared at the end of the veranda, having come round the burnt part of the house, followed by Hernan Pereira. Catching sight of me, she ran to the side of my couch with outstretched arms as though she intended to embrace me. Then seeming to remember, stopped suddenly at my side, coloured to her hair, and said in an embarrassed voice:

"Oh, Heer Allan"—she had never called me *heer* in her life before—"I am so glad to find you out! How have you been getting on?"

"Pretty well, I thank you," I answered, biting my lips, "as you would have learnt, Marie, had you come to see me."

Next moment I was sorry for the words, for I saw her eyes fill with tears and her breast shake with something like a sob. However, it was Pereira and not Marie who answered, for at the moment I believe she could not speak.

"My good boy," he said in a pompous, patronising way and in English, which he knew perfectly, "I think that my cousin has had plenty to do caring for all these people during the last few days without running to look at the cut in your leg. However, I am glad to hear from your worthy father that it is almost well and that you will soon be able to play games again, like others of your age."

Now it was my turn to be unable to speak and to feel my eyes fill with tears, tears of rage, for remember that I was still very feeble. But Marie spoke for me.

"Yes, Cousin Hernan," she said in a cold voice, "thank God the Heer Allan Quatermain will soon be able to play games again, such bloody games as the defence of Maraisfontein with eight men against all the Quabie horde. Then Heaven help those who stand in front of his rifle," and she glanced at the mound that covered the dead Kaffirs, many of whom, as a matter of fact, I had killed.

"Oh! no offence, no offence, Marie," said Pereira in his smooth, rich voice. "I did not want to laugh at your young friend, who doubtless is as brave as they say all Englishmen are, and who fought well when he was lucky enough to have the chance of protecting you, my dear cousin. But after all, you know, he is not the only one who can hold a gun straight, as you seem to think, which I shall be happy to prove to him in a friendly fashion when he is stronger."

Here he stepped forward a pace and looked down at me, then added with a laugh, "*Allemachte!* I fear that won't be just at present. Why, the lad looks as though one might blow him away like a feather."

Still I said nothing, only glanced up at this tall and splendid man standing above me in his fine clothes, for he was richly dressed as the fashion of the time went, with his high colouring, broad shoulders, and face full of health and vigour. Mentally I compared him with myself, as I was after my fever and loss of blood, a poor, white-faced rat of a lad, with stubbly brown hair on my head and only a little down on my chin, with arms like sticks, and a dirty blanket for raiment. How could I compare with him in any way? What chance had I against this opulent bully who hated me and all my race, and in whose hands, even if I were well, I should be nothing but a child?

And yet, and yet as I lay there humiliated and a mock, an answer came into my mind, and I felt that whatever might be the case with my outward form; in spirit, in courage, in determination and in ability, in all, in short, that really makes a man, I was more than Pereira's equal. Yes, and that by the help of these qualities, poor as I was and frail as I seemed to be, I would beat him at the last and keep for myself what I had won, the prize of Marie's love.

Such were the thoughts which passed through me, and I think that something of the tenor of them communicated itself to Marie, who often could read my heart before my lips spoke. At any rate, her demeanour changed. She drew herself up. Her fine nostrils expanded and a proud look came into her dark eyes, as she nodded her head and murmured in a voice so low that I think I alone caught her words:

"Yes, yes, have no fear."

Pereira was speaking again (he had turned aside to strike the steel of his tinder-box, and was now blowing the spark to a glow before lighting his big pipe).

"By the way, Heer Allan," he said, "that is a very good mare of yours. She seems to have done the distance between the Mission Station and Maraisfontein in wonderful time, as, for the matter of that, the roan did too. I have taken a fancy to her, after a gallop on her back yesterday just to give her some exercise, and although I don't know that she is quite up to my weight, I'll buy her."

"The mare is not for sale, Heer Pereira," I said, speaking for the first time, "and I do not remember giving anyone leave to exercise her."

"No, your father did, or was it that ugly little beast of a Hottentot? I forget which. As for her not being for sale—why, in this world everything is for sale, at a price. I'll give you—let me see—oh, what does the money matter when one has plenty? I'll give you a hundred English pounds for that mare; and don't you think me a fool. I tell you I mean to get it back, and more, at the great races down in the south. Now what do you say?"

"I say that the mare is not for sale, Heer Pereira." Then a thought struck me, or an inspiration, and, as has always been my fashion, I acted on it at once. "But," I added slowly, "if you like, when I am a bit stronger I'll shoot you a match for her, you staking your hundred pounds and I staking the mare."

Pereira burst out laughing.

"Here, friends," he called to some of the Boers who were strolling up to the house for their morning coffee. "This little Englishman wants to shoot a match with me, staking that fine mare of his against a hundred pounds British; against me, Hernando Pereira, who have won every prize at shooting that ever I entered for. No, no, friend Allan, I am not a thief, I will not rob you of your mare."

Now among those Boers chanced to be the celebrated Heer Pieter Retief, a very fine man of high character, then in the prime of life, and of Huguenot descent like Heer Marais. He had been appointed by the Government one of the frontier commandants, but owing to some quarrel with the Lieutenant-Governor, Sir Andries Stockenstrom, had recently resigned that office, and at this date was engaged in organizing the trek from the Colony. I now saw Retief for the first time, and ah! then little did I think how and where I should see him for the last. But all that is a matter of history, of which I shall have to tell later.

Now, while Pereira was mocking and bragging of his prowess, Pieter Retief looked at me, and our eyes met.

"*Allemachte!*" he exclaimed, "is that the young man who, with half a dozen miserable Hottentots and slaves, held this stead for five hours against all the Quabie tribe and kept them out?"

Somebody said that it was, remarking that I had been about to shoot Marie Marais and myself when help came.

"Then, *Heer* Allan Quatermain," said Retief, "give me your hand," and he took my poor wasted fingers in his big palm, adding, "Your father must be proud of you to-day, as I should be if I had such a son. God in Heaven! where will you stop if you can go so far while you are yet a boy? Friends, since I came here yesterday I have got the whole story for myself from the Kaffirs and from this *mooi meisje* (pretty young lady)," and he nodded towards Marie. "Also I have gone over the ground and the house, and have seen where each man fell—it is easy by the blood marks—most of them shot by yonder Englishman, except one of the last three, whom he killed with a spear. Well, I tell you that never in all my experience have I known a better arranged or a more finely carried out defence against huge odds. Perhaps the best part of it, too, was the way in which this young lion acted on the information he received and the splendid ride he made from the Mission Station. Again I say that his father should be proud of him."

"Well, if it comes to that, I am, *mynheer*," said my father, who just then joined us after his morning walk, "although I beg you to say no more lest the lad should grow vain."

"Bah!" replied Retief, "fellows of his stamp are not vain; it is your big talkers who are vain," and he glanced out of the corner of his shrewd eye at Pereira, "your turkey cocks with all their tails spread. I think this little chap must be such another as that great sailor of yours—what do you call him, Nelson?—who beat the French into frothed eggs and died to live for ever. He was small, too, they say, and weak in the stomach."

I must confess I do not think that praise ever sounded sweeter in my ears than did these words of the Commandant Retief, uttered as they were just when I felt crushed to the dirt. Moreover, as I saw by Marie's and, I may add, by my father's face, there were other ears to which they were not ungrateful. The Boers also, brave and honest men enough, evidently appreciated them, for they said:

"*Ja! ja! das ist recht*" (That is right).

Only Pereira turned his broad back and busied himself with re-lighting his pipe, which had gone out.

Then Retief began again.

"What is it you were calling us to listen to, Mynheer Pereira? That this Heer Allan Quatermain had offered to shoot you a match? Well, why not? If he can hit Kaffirs running at him with spears, as he has done, he may be able to hit other things also. You say that you won‘t rob him of his money—no, it was his beautiful horse—because you have taken so many prizes shooting at targets. But did *you* ever hit a Kaffir running at *you* with an *assegai*, *mynheer*, you who live down there where everything is safe? If so, I never heard of it."

Pereira answered that he did not understand me to propose a shooting match at Kaffirs charging with assegais, but at something else—he knew not what.

"Quite so," said Retief. "Well, Mynheer Allan, what is it that you do propose?"

"That we should stand in the great *kloof* between the two *vleis* yonder—the Heer Marais knows the place—when the wild geese flight over an hour before sunset, and that he who brings down six of them in the fewest shots shall win the match."

"If our guns are loaded with *loopers* that will not be difficult," said Pereira.

"With *loopers* you would seldom kill a bird, *mynheer*," I replied, "for they come over from seventy to a hundred yards up. No, I mean with rifles."

"*Allemachte!*" broke in a Boer; "you will want plenty of ammunition to hit a goose at that height with a bullet."

"That is my offer," I said, "to which I add this, that when twenty shots have been fired by each man, he who has killed the most birds wins, even if he has not brought down the full six. Does the Heer Pereira accept? If so, I will venture to match myself against him, although he has won so many prizes."

The Heer Pereira seemed extremely doubtful; so doubtful, indeed, that the Boers began to laugh at him. In the end he grew rather angry, and said that he was willing to shoot me at bucks or swallows, or fireflies, or anything else I liked.

"Then let it be at geese," I answered, "since it is likely to be sometime before I am strong enough to ride after buck or other wild things.'"

So the terms of the match were formally written down by Marie, as my father, although he took a keen sporting interest in the result, would have nothing to do with what he called a "wager for money," and, except myself, there was no one else present with sufficient scholarship to pen a long document. Then we both signed them, Hernan Pereira not very willingly, I thought; and if my recovery was sufficiently rapid, the date was fixed for that day week. In case of any disagreement, the Heer Retief, who was staying at Maraisfontein, or in its neighbourhood, for a while, was appointed referee and stakeholder. It was also arranged that neither of us should visit the appointed place, or shoot at the geese before the match. Still we were at liberty to practise as much as we liked at anything else in the interval and to make use of any kind of rifle that suited us best.

By the time that these arrangements were finished, feeling quite tired with all the emotions of the morning, I was carried back to my room. Here my midday meal, cooked by Marie, was brought to me. As I finished eating it, for the fresh air had given me an appetite, my father came in, accompanied by the Heer Marais, and began to talk to me. Presently the latter asked me kindly enough if I thought I should be sufficiently strong to trek back to the station that afternoon in an ox-cart with springs to it and lying at full length upon a hide-strung "cartel" or mattress.

I answered, "Certainly," as I should have done had I been at the point of death, for I saw that he wished to be rid of me.

"The fact is, Allan," he said awkwardly, "I am not inhospitable as

249

you may think, especially towards one to whom I owe so much. But you and my nephew, Hernan, do not seem to get on very well together, and, as you may guess, having just been almost beggared, I desire no unpleasantness with the only rich member of my family."

I replied I was sure I did not wish to be the cause of any. It seemed to me, however, that the Heer Pereira wished to make a mock of me and to bring it home to me what a poor creature I was compared to himself—I a mere sick boy who was worth nothing.

"I know," said Marais uneasily, "my nephew has been too fortunate in life, and is somewhat overbearing in his manner. He does not remember that the battle is not always to the strong or the race to the swift, he who is young and rich and handsome, a spoiled child from the first. I am sorry, but what I cannot help I must put up with. If I cannot have my *mealies* cooked, I must eat them green. Also, Allan, have you never heard that jealousy sometimes makes people rude and unjust?" and he looked at me meaningly.

I made no answer, for when one does not quite know what to say it is often best to remain silent, and he went on:

"I am vexed to hear of this foolish shooting match which has been entered into without my knowledge or consent. If he wins he will only laugh at you the more, and if you win he will be angry."

"It was not my fault, *mynheer*," I answered. "He wanted to force me to sell the mare, which he had been riding without my leave, and kept bragging about his marksmanship. So at last I grew cross and challenged him."

"No wonder, Allan; I do not blame you. Still, you are silly, for it will not matter to him if he loses his money; but that beautiful mare is your ewe-lamb, and I should be sorry to see you parted from a beast which has done us so good a turn. Well, there it is; perhaps circumstances may yet put an end to this trial; I hope so."

"I hope they won't," I answered stubbornly.

"I dare say you do, being sore as a galled horse just now. But listen, Allan, and you, too, Predicant Quatermain; there are other and more important reasons than this petty squabble why I should be glad if you could go away for a while. I must take counsel with my countrymen about certain secret matters which have to do with our welfare and future, and, of course they would not like it if all the while there were two Englishmen on the place, whom they might think were spies."

"Say no more, Heer Marais," broke in my father hotly; "still less should we like to be where we are not wanted or are looked upon with suspicion for the crime of being English. By God's blessing, my son has been able to do some service to you and yours, but now that is all finished and forgotten. Let the cart you are so kind as to lend us be inspanned. We will go at once."

Then Henri Marais, who was a gentleman at bottom, although, even in those early days, violent and foolish when excited or under the influence of his race prejudices, began to apologise quite humbly, assuring my father that he forgot nothing and meant no offence. So they patched the matter up, and an hour later we started.

All the Boers came to see us off, giving me many kind words and saying how much they looked forward to meeting me again on the following Thursday. Pereira, who was among them, was also very genial, begging me to be sure and get well, since he did not wish to beat one who was still crippled, even at a game of goose shooting. I answered that I would do my best; as for my part, I did not like being beaten it any game which I had set my heart on winning, whether it were little or big. Then I turned my head, for I was lying on my back all this time, to bid good-bye to Marie, who had slipped out of the house into the yard where the cart was.

"Good-bye, Allan," she said, giving me her hand and a look from her eyes that I trusted was not seen. Then, under pretence of arranging the *kaross* which was over me, she bent down and whispered swiftly:

"Win that match if you love me. I shall pray God that you may every night, for it will be an omen."

I think the whisper was heard, though not the words, for I saw Pereira bite his lip and make a movement as though to interrupt her. But Pieter Retief thrust his big form in front of him rather rudely, and said with one of his hearty laughs:

"*Allemachte*! friend, let the missie wish a good journey to the young fellow who saved her life."

Next moment Hans, the Hottentot, screamed at the oxen in the usual fashion, and we rolled away through the gate.

But oh! if I had liked the Heer Retief before, now I loved him.

CHAPTER 5

The Shooting Match

My journey back to the Mission Station was a strange contrast to that which I had made thence a few days before. Then, the darkness, the swift mare beneath me rushing through it like a bird, the awful terror in my heart lest I should be too late, as with wild eyes I watched the paling stars and the first gathering grey of dawn. Now, the creaking of the ox-cart, the familiar *veld*, the bright glow of the peaceful sunlight, and in my heart a great thankfulness, and yet a new terror lest the pure and holy love which I had won should be stolen away from me by force or fraud.

Well, as the one matter had been in the hand of God, so was the other, and with that knowledge I must be content. The first trial had ended in death and victory. How would the second end? I wondered, and those words seemed to jumble themselves up in my mind and shape a sentence that it did not conceive. It was: "In the victory that is death," which, when I came to think of it, of course, meant nothing. How victory could be death I did not understand—at any rate, at that time, I who was but a lad of small experience.

As we trekked along comfortably enough, for the road was good and the cart, being on springs, gave my leg no pain, I asked my father what he thought that the Heer Marais had meant when he told us that the Boers had business at Maraisfontein, during which our presence as Englishmen would not be agreeable to them.

"Meant, Allan? He meant that these traitorous Dutchmen are plotting against their sovereign, and are afraid lest we should report their treason. Either they intend to rebel because of that most righteous act, the freeing of the slaves, and because we will not kill out all the Kaffirs with whom they chance to quarrel, or to trek from the Colony. For my part I think it will be the latter, for, as you have heard, some parties have already gone; and, unless I am mistaken, many more mean to follow, Marais and Retief and that plotter, Pereira, among them. Let them go; I say, the sooner the better, for I have no doubt that the English flag will follow them in due course."

"I hope that they won't," I answered with a nervous laugh; "at any rate, until I have won back my mare." (I had left her in Retief's care as stakeholder, until the match should be shot off.)

For the rest of that two and a half hours' trek my father, looking very dignified and patriotic, declaimed to me loudly about the bad behaviour of the Boers, who hated and traduced missionaries, loathed and abominated British rule and permanent officials, loved slavery and killed Kaffirs whenever they got the chance. I listened to him politely, for it was not wise to cross my parent when he was in that humour. Also, having mixed a great deal with the Dutch, I knew that there was another side to the question, namely, that the missionaries sometimes traduced them (as, in fact, they did), and that British rule, or rather, party government, played strange tricks with the interests of distant dependencies. That permanent officials and im-permanent ones too—such as governors full of a little brief authority—often misrepresented and oppressed them. That Kaffirs, encouraged by the variegated policy of these party governments and their servants, frequently stole their stock; and if they found a chance, murdered them with their women and children, as they had tried to do at Maraisfontein; though there, it is true, they had some provocation. That British virtue had liberated the slaves without paying their owners a fair price for them, and so forth.

But, to tell the truth, it was not of these matters of high policy, which were far enough away from a humble youth like myself, that I was thinking. What appealed to me and made my heart sick was the reflection that if Henri Marais and his friends trekked, Marie Marais must perforce trek with them; and that whereas I, an Englishman, could not be of that adventurous company, Hernando Pereira both could and would.

On the day following our arrival home, what between the fresh air, plenty of good food, for which I found I had an appetite, and liberal doses of Pontac—a generous Cape wine that is a kind of cross between port and Burgundy—I found myself so much better that I was able to hop about the place upon a pair of crutches which Hans improvised for me out of Kaffir sticks. Next morning, my improvement continuing at a rapid rate, I turned my attention seriously to the shooting match, for which I had but five days to prepare.

Now it chanced that some months before a young Englishman of good family—he was named the Honourable Vavasseur Smyth—who had accompanied an official relative to the Cape Colony, came our way in search of sport, of which I was able to show him a good deal of a humble kind. He had brought with him, amongst other weapons, what in those days was considered a very beautiful hair-triggered small-bore rifle fitted with a nipple for percussion caps, then quite a new invention. It was by a maker of the name of J. Purdey, of London, and had cost quite a large sum because of the perfection of its workmanship. When the Honourable V. Smyth—of whom I have never heard since—took his leave of us on his departure for England, being a generous-hearted young fellow, as a souvenir of himself, he kindly presented me with this rifle,[1] which I still have.

That was about six months earlier than the time of which I write, and during those months I had often used this rifle for the shooting of game, such as blesbuck and also of bustards. I found it to be a weapon of the most extraordinary accuracy up to a range of about two hundred yards, though when I rode off in that desperate hurry for Maraisfontein I did not take it with me because it was a single barrel

---

1. This single-barrelled percussion-cap rifle described by Allan Quatermain, which figures so prominently in the history of this epoch of his life, has been sent to me by Mr. Curtis, and is before me as I write. It was made in the year 1835 by J. Purdey, of 314½, Oxford Street, London, and is a beautiful piece of workmanship of its kind. Without the ramrod, which is now missing, it weighs only 5 lbs. 3¾ oz. The barrel is octagonal, and the rifled bore, designed to take a spherical bullet, is ½ in. in diameter. The hammer can be set to safety on the half-cock by means of a catch behind it. Another peculiarity of the weapon, one that I have never seen before, is that by pressing on the back of the trigger the ordinary light pull of the piece is so reduced that the merest touch suffices to fire it, thus rendering it hair-triggered in the fullest sense of the word. It has two flap-sights marked for 150 and 200 yards, in addition to the fixed sight designed for firing at 100 yards. On the lock are engraved a stag and a doe, the first lying down and the second standing. Of its sort and period, it is an extraordinarily well-made and handy gun, finished with horn at the end of what is now called the tongue, and with the stock cut away so as to leave a raised cushion against which the cheek of the shooter rests. What charge it took I do not know, but I should imagine from 2½ to 3 drachms of powder. It is easy to understand that in the hands of Allan Quatermain this weapon, obsolete as it is to-day, was capable of great things within the limits of its range, and that the faith he put in it at the trial of skill at the Groote Kloof, and afterwards in the fearful ordeal of the shooting of the vultures on the wing, upon the Mount of Slaughter, when the lives of many hung upon his marksmanship, was well justified. This, indeed, is shown by the results in both cases. In writing of this rifle, Messrs. Purdey informed me that copper percussion caps were experimented with by Colonel Forsyth in 1820, and that their firm sold them in 1824, at a cost of £1 15s. per 1,000, although their use did not become general until some years later.—*The Editor.*

and too small in the bore to load with *loopers* at a pinch. Still, in challenging Pereira, it was this gun and no other that I determined to use; indeed, had I not owned it I do not think that I should have ventured on the match.

As it happened, Mr. Smyth had left me with the rifle a large supply of specially cast bullets and of the new percussion caps, to say nothing of some very fine imported powder. Therefore, having ammunition in plenty, I set to work to practise. Seating myself upon a chair in a deep *kloof* near the station, across which rock pigeons and turtle doves were wont to fly in numbers at a considerable height, I began to fire at them as they flashed over me.

Now, in my age, I may say without fear of being set down a boaster, that I have one gift, that of marksmanship, which, I suppose, I owe to some curious combination of judgment, quickness of eye, and steadiness of hand. I can declare honestly that in my best days I never knew a man who could beat me in shooting at a living object; I say nothing of target work, of which I have little experience. Oddly enough, also, I believe that at this art, although then I lacked the practice which since has come to me in such plenty, I was as good as a youth as I have ever been in later days, and, of course, far better than I am now. This I soon proved upon the present occasion, for seated there in that *kloof*, after a few trials, I found that I could bring down quite a number of even the swift, straight-flying rock pigeons as they sped over me, and this, be it remembered, not with shot, but with a single bullet, a feat that many would hold to be incredible.

So the days passed, and I practised, every evening finding me a little better at this terribly difficult sport. For always I learned more as to the exact capacities of my rifle and the allowance that must be made according to the speed of the bird, its distance, and the complications of the wind and of the light. During those days, also, I recovered so rapidly that at the end of them I was almost in my normal condition, and could walk well with the aid of a single stick.

At length the eventful Thursday came, and about midday—for I lay in bed late that morning and did not shoot—I drove, or, rather, was driven, in a Cape cart with two horses to the place known as Groote Kloof or Great Gully. Over this gorge the wild geese flighted from their "pans" or feeding grounds on the high lands above, to other pans that lay some miles below, and thence, I suppose, straight out to the sea coast, whence they returned at dawn.

On arriving at the mouth of Groote Kloof about four o'clock in the afternoon, my father and I were astonished to see a great number of Boers assembled there, and among them a certain sprinkling of their younger womankind, who had come on horseback or in carts.

"Good gracious!" I said to my father; "if I had known there was to be such a fuss as this about a shooting match, I don't think I could have faced it."

"Hum," he answered; "I think there is more in the wind than your match. Unless I am much mistaken, it has been made the excuse of a public meeting in a secluded spot, so as to throw the Authorities off the scent."

As a matter of fact, my father was quite right. Before we arrived there that day the majority of those Boers, after full and long discussion, had arranged to shake the dust of the Colony off their feet, and find a home in new lands to the north.

Presently we were among them, and I noticed that, one and all, their faces were anxious and preoccupied. Pieter Retief caught sight of me being helped out of the cart by my father and Hans, whom I had brought to load, and for a moment looked puzzled. Evidently his thoughts were far away. Then he remembered and exclaimed in his jolly voice:

"Why! here is our little Englishman come to shoot off his match like a man of his word. Friend Marais, stop talking about your losses"—this in a warning voice—"and give him good day."

So Marais came, and with him Marie, who blushed and smiled, but to my mind looked more of a grown woman than ever before; one who had left girlhood behind her and found herself face to face with real life and all its troubles. Following her close, very close, as I was quick to notice, was Hernan Pereira. He was even more finely dressed than usual and carried in his hand a beautiful new, single-barrelled rifle, also fitted to take percussion caps, but, as I thought, of a very large bore for the purpose of goose shooting.

"So you have got well again," he said in a genial voice that yet did not ring true. Indeed, it suggested to me that he wished I had done nothing of the sort. "Well, Mynheer Allan, here you find me quite ready to shoot your head off." (He didn't mean that, though I dare say he was.) "I tell you that the mare is as good as mine, for I have been practising, haven't I, Marie? as the *aasvogels*" (that is, vultures) "round the stead know to their cost."

"Yes, Cousin Hernan," said Marie, "you have been practising, but so, perhaps, has Allan."

By this time all the company of Boers had collected round us, and began to evince a great interest in the pending contest, as was natural

256

among people who rarely had a gun out of their hands, and thought that fine shooting was the divinest of the arts. However, they were not allowed to stay long, as the Kaffirs said that the geese would begin their afternoon flight within about half an hour. So the spectators were all requested to arrange themselves under the sheer cliff of the *kloof*, where they could not be seen by the birds coming over them from behind, and there to keep silence. Then Pereira and I—I attended by my loader, but he alone, as he said a man at his elbow would bother him—and with us Retief, the referee, took our stations about a hundred and fifty yards from this face of cliff. Here we screened ourselves as well as we could from the keen sight of the birds behind some tall bushes which grew at this spot.

I seated myself on a camp-stool, which I had brought with me, for my leg was still too weak to allow me to stand long, and waited. Presently Pereira said through Retief that he had a favour to ask, namely, that I would allow him to take the first six shots, as the strain of waiting made him nervous. I answered, "Certainly," although I knew well that the object of the request was that he believed that the outpost geese—"spy-geese" we called them—which would be the first to arrive, would probably come over low down and slow, whereas those that followed, scenting danger, might fly high and fast. This, in fact, proved to be the case, for there is no bird more clever than the misnamed goose.

When we had waited about a quarter of an hour Hans said:

"*Hist!* Goose comes."

As he spoke, though as yet I could not see the bird, I heard its cry of "Honk, honk" and the swish of its strong wings.

Then it appeared, an old spur-winged gander, probably the king of the flock, flying so low that it only cleared the cliff edge by about twenty feet, and passed over not more than thirty yards up, an easy shot. Pereira fired, and down it came rather slowly, falling a hundred yards or so behind him, while Retief said:

"One for our side."

Pereira loaded again, and just as he had capped his rifle three more geese, also flying low, came over, preceded by a number of ducks, passing straight above us, as they must do owing to the shape of the gap between the land waves of the *veld* above through which they flighted. Pereira shot, and to my surprise, the second, not the first, bird fell, also a good way behind him.

"Did you shoot at that goose, or the other, nephew?" asked Retief.

"At that one for sure," he answered with a laugh.

257

"He lies," muttered the Hottentot; "he shot at the first and killed the second."

"Be silent," I answered. "Who would lie about such a thing?"

Again Pereira loaded. By the time that he was ready more geese were approaching, this time in a triangle of seven birds, their leader being at the point of the triangle, which was flying higher than those that had gone before. He fired, and down came not one bird, but two, namely, the captain and the goose to the right of and a little behind it.

"Ah! uncle," exclaimed Pereira, "did you see those birds cross each other as I pulled? That was a lucky one for me, but I won't count the second if the Heer Allan objects."

"No, I did not, nephew," answered Retief, "but doubtless they must have done so, or the same bullet could not have pierced both."

Both Hans and I only looked at each other and laughed. Still we said nothing.

From the spectators under the cliff there came a murmur of congratulation not unmixed with astonishment. Again Pereira loaded, aimed, and loosed at a rather high goose—it may have been about seventy yards in the air. He struck it right enough, for the feathers flew from its breast; but to my astonishment the bird, after swooping down as though it were going to fall, recovered itself and flew away straight out of sight.

"Tough birds, these geese!" exclaimed Pereira. "They can carry as much lead as a sea-cow."

"Very tough indeed," answered Retief doubtfully. "Never before did I see a bird fly away with an ounce ball through its middle."

"Oh! he will drop dead somewhere," replied Pereira as he rammed his powder down.

Within four minutes more Pereira had fired his two remaining shots, selecting, as he was entitled to do, low and easy young geese that came over him slowly. He killed them both, although the last of them, after falling, waddled along the ground into a tuft of high grass.

Now murmurs of stifled applause broke from the audience, to which Pereira bowed in acknowledgment.

"You will have to shoot very well, Mynheer Allan," said Retief to me, "if you want to beat that. Even if I rule out one of the two birds that fell to a single shot, as I think I shall, Hernan has killed five out of six, which can scarcely be bettered."

"Yes," I answered; "but, *mynheer*, be so good as to have those geese collected and put upon one side. I don't want them mixed up with mine, if I am lucky enough to bring any down."

He nodded, and some Kaffirs were sent to bring in the geese. Several of these, I noted, were still flapping and had to have their necks twisted, but at the time I did not go to look at them. While this was being done I called to Retief, and begged him to examine the powder and bullets I was about to use.

"What's the good?" he asked, looking at me curiously. "Powder is powder, and a bullet is a bullet."

"None, I dare say. Still, oblige me by looking at them, my uncle."

Then at my bidding Hans took six bullets and placed them in his hand, begging him to return them to us as they were wanted.

"They must be a great deal smaller than Hernan's," said Retief, "who, being stronger, uses a heavier gun."

"Yes," I answered briefly, as Hans put the charge of powder into the rifle, and drove home the wad. Then, taking a bullet from Retief's hand, he rammed that down on to the top of it, capped the gun, and handed it to me.

By now the geese were coming thick, for the flight was at its full. Only, either because some of those that had already passed had sighted the Kaffirs collecting the fallen birds and risen—an example which the others noted from afar and followed—or because in an unknown way warning of their danger had been conveyed to them, they were flying higher and faster than the first arrivals.

"You will have the worst of it, Allan," said Retief. "It should have been shot and shot about."

"Perhaps," I answered, "but that can't be helped now."

Then I rose from my stool, the rifle in my hand. I had not long to wait, for presently over came a wedge of geese nearly a hundred yards up. I aimed at the first fellow, holding about eight yards ahead of him to allow for his pace, and pressed. Next second I heard the clap of the bullet, but alas! it had only struck the outstretched beak, of which a small portion fell to the ground. The bird itself, after wavering a second, resumed its place as leader of the squad and passed away apparently unharmed.

"Baas, *baas*," whispered Hans as he seized the rifle and began to reload, "you were too far in front. These big water-birds do not travel as fast as the rock pigeons."

I nodded, wishing to save my breath. Then, quivering with excitement, for if I missed the next shot the match appeared to be lost, presently I took the rifle from his hand.

Scarcely had I done so when a single goose came over quite as high as the others and travelling "as though the black devil had kicked it," as Retief said. This time I allowed the same space to compensate for the object's increased speed and pressed.

Down it came like a stone, falling but a little way behind me with its head knocked off.

"*Baas, baas,*" whispered Hans, "still too far in front. Why aim at the eye when you have the whole body?"

Again I nodded, and at the same time heaved a sigh of relief. At least the match was still alive. Soon a large flight came over, mixed up with mallard and widgeon. I took the right-hand angle bird, so that it could not be supposed I had "browned the lot," as here in England they say of one who fires at a covey and not at a particular partridge. Down he came, shot straight through the breast. Then I knew that I had got my nerve, and felt no more fear.

To cut a long story short, although two of them were extremely difficult and high, one being, I should say, quite a hundred and twenty yards above me, and the other by no means easy, I killed the next three birds one after the other, and I verily believe could have killed a dozen more without a miss, for now I was shooting as I had never shot before.

"Say, nephew Allan," asked Retief curiously in the pause between the fifth and sixth shots, "why do your geese fall so differently to Hernan's?"

"Ask him! don't talk to me," I answered, and next instant brought down number five, the finest shot of the lot.

A sound of wonder and applause came from all the audience, and I saw Marie wave a white handkerchief.

"That's the end," said the referee.

"One minute before you stir," I answered. "I want to shoot at something else that is not in the match, just to see if I can kill two birds with one bullet like the Heer Pereira."

He granted my request with a nod, holding up his hand to prevent the audience from moving, and bidding Pereira, who tried to interrupt, to be silent.

Now, while the match was in progress I had noticed two falcons about the size of the British peregrine wheeling round and round high over the *kloof,* in which doubtless they bred, apparently quite undisturbed by the shooting. Or, perhaps, they had their eyes upon some of the fallen geese. I took the rifle and waited for a long while, till at last my opportunity came. I saw that the larger hen falcon was about to cross directly over the circle of its mate, there being perhaps a distance of ten yards between them. I aimed; I judged—for a second my mind was a kind of calculating machine—the different arcs and speeds of the birds must be allowed for, and the lowest was ninety yards away. Then, with something like a prayer upon my lips, I pressed while every eye stared upwards.

Down came the lower falcon; a pause of half a second, and down came the higher one also, falling dead upon its dead mate!

Now, even from those Boers, who did not love to see an Englishman excel, there broke a shout of acclamation. Never had they beheld such a shot as this; nor in truth had I.

"Mynheer Retief," I said, "I gave you notice that I intended to try to kill both of them, did I not?"

"You did. *Allemachte*! you did! But tell me, Allan Quatermain, are your eye and hand quite human?"

"You must ask my father," I answered with a shrug as I sat myself down upon my stool and mopped my brow.

The Boers came up with a rush, Marie flying ahead of them like a swallow, and their stout womenfolk waddling behind, and formed a circle round us, all talking at once. I did not listen to their conversation, till I heard Pereira, who was engaged in some eye-play with Marie, say in a loud voice:

"Yes, it was pretty, very pretty, but all the same, Uncle Retief, I claim the match, as I shot six geese against five."

"Hans," I said, "bring my geese," and they were brought, each with a neat hole through it, and laid down near those that Pereira had shot. "Now," I said to Retief, "examine the wounds in these birds, and then that on the second bird which the Heer Pereira killed when he brought down two at once. I think it will be found that his bullet must have splintered."

Retief went and studied all the birds, taking them up one by one. Then he threw down the last with a curse and cried in a great voice:

"Mynheer Pereira, why do you bring shame on us before these two Englishmen? I say that you have been using *loopers*, or else bullets that were sawn in quarters and glued or tied with thread. Look, look!" and he pointed to the wounds, of which in one case there were as many as three on a single bird.

"Why not?" answered Pereira coolly. "The bargain was that we were to use bullets, but it was never said that they should not be cut. Doubtless the Heer Allan's were treated in the same way."

"No," I answered, "when I said that I would shoot with a bullet I meant a whole bullet, not one that had been sawn in pieces and fixed together again, so that after it left the muzzle it might spread out like

261

shot. But I do not wish to talk about the matter. It is in the hands of the Heer Pieter Retief, who will give judgment as it pleases him."

Now, much excited argument ensued among the Boers, in the midst of which Marie managed to whisper to me unheard:

"Oh! I am glad, Allan, for whatever they may decide, you won, and the omen is good."

"I don't see what geese have to do with omens, sweetheart," I answered—"that is, since the time of the ancient Romans. Anyhow, I should say that the omens are bad, for there is going to be a row presently."

Just then Retief put up his hand, calling out:

"Silence! I have decided. The writing of the match did not say that the bullets were not to be cut, and therefore Hernan Pereira's birds must count. But that writing does say that any bird accidentally killed should not count, and therefore one goose must be subtracted from Pereira's total, which leaves the two shooters equal. So either the match is dead or, since the geese have ceased to come, it must be shot off another day."

"Oh! if there is any question," said Pereira, who felt that public opinion was much against him, "let the Englishman take the money. I dare say that he needs it, as the sons of missionaries are not rich."

"There is no question," I said, "since, rich or poor, not for a thousand pounds would I shoot again against one who plays such tricks. Keep your money, Mynheer Pereira, and I will keep my mare. The umpire has said that the match is dead, so everything is finished."

"Not quite," interrupted Retief, "for I have a word to say. Friend Allan, you have played fair, and I believe that there is no one who can shoot like you in Africa."

"That is so," said the audience of Boers.

"Mynheer Pereira," went on Retief, "although you, too, are a fine shot, as is well known, I believe that had you played fair also you would have been beaten, but as it is you have saved your hundred pounds. Mynheer Pereira," he added in a great voice, "you are a cheat, who have brought disgrace upon us Boers, and for my part I never want to shake your hand again."

Now, at these outspoken words, for when his indignation was aroused Retief was no measurer of language, Pereira's high-coloured face went white as a sheet.

"Mein Gott, mynheer," he said, "I am minded to make you answer for such talk," and his hand went to the knife at his girdle.

"What!" shouted Retief, "do you want another shooting match?

Well, if so I am ready with whole bullets or with split ones. None shall say that Pieter Retief was afraid of any man, and, least of all, of one who is not ashamed to try to steal a prize as a hyena steals a bone from a lion. Come on, Hernan Pereira, come on!"

Now, I am sure I cannot say what would have happened, although I am quite certain that Pereira had no stomach for a duel with the redoubtable Retief, a man whose courage was as proverbial throughout the land as was his perfect uprightness of character. At any rate, seeing that things looked very black, Henri Marais, who had been listening to this altercation with evident annoyance, stepped forward and said:

"Mynheer Retief and nephew Hernan, you are both my guests, and I will not permit quarrelling over this foolishness, especially as I am sure that Hernan never intended to cheat, but only to do what he thought was allowed. Why should he, who is one of the finest shots in the Colony, though it may be that young Allan Quatermain here is even better? Will you not say so, too, friend Retief, especially just now when it is necessary that we should all be as brothers?" he added pleadingly.

"No," thundered Retief, "I will not tell a lie to please you or anyone."

Then, seeing that the commandant was utterly uncompromising, Marais went up to his nephew and whispered to him for a while. What he said I do not know. The result of it was, however, that after favouring both Retief and myself with an angry scowl, Pereira turned and walked to where his horse stood, mounted it, and rode off, followed by two Hottentot after-riders.

That was the last I saw of Hernan Pereira for a long while to come, and heartily do I wish that it had been the last I ever saw of him. But this was not to be.

CHAPTER 6

The Parting

The Boers, who ostensibly had come to the *kloof* to see the shooting match, although, in fact, for a very different purpose, now began to disperse. Some of them rode straight away, while some went to wagons which they had outspanned at a distance, and trekked off to their separate homes. I am glad to say that before they left quite a number of the best of them came up and congratulated me both on the defence of Maraisfontein and on my shooting. Also not a few expressed their views concerning Pereira in very straightforward language.

Now, the arrangement was that my father and I were to sleep that night at Marais's stead, returning home on the following morning. But my father, who had been a silent but not unobservant witness of all this scene, coming to the conclusion that after what had happened we should scarcely be welcome there, and that the company of Pereira was to be avoided just now, went up to Marais and bade him farewell, saying that we would send for my mare.

"Not so, not so," he answered, "you are my guests to-night. Also, fear not, Hernan will be away. He has gone a journey upon some business."

As my father hesitated, Marais added: "Friend, I pray you to come, for I have some important words to say to you, which cannot be said here."

Then my father gave way, to my delight and relief. For if he had not, what chance would there have been of my getting some still more important words with Marie? So having collected the geese and the two falcons, which I proposed to skin for Marie, I was helped into the cart, and we drove off, reaching Maraisfontein just as night set in.

That evening, after we had eaten, Heer Marais asked my father and myself to speak with him in the sitting-room. By an afterthought also, or so it seemed to me, he told his daughter, who had been clearing away the dishes and with whom as yet I had found no opportunity to talk, to come in with us and close the door behind her.

When all were seated and we men had lit our pipes, though apprehension of what was to follow quite took away my taste for smoking, Marais spoke in English, which he knew to a certain extent. This was for the benefit of my father, who made it a point of honour not to understand Dutch, although he would answer Marais in that language when *he* pretended not to understand English. To me he spoke in Dutch, and occasionally in French to Marie. It was a most curious and polyglot conversation.

"Young Allan," he said, "and you, daughter Marie, I have heard stories concerning you that, although I never gave you leave to *opsit*" (that is, to sit up alone at night with candles, according to the Boer fashion between those who are courting), "you have been making love to each other."

"That is true, *mynheer*," I said. "I only waited an opportunity to tell you that we plighted our troth during the attack of the Quabies on this house."

"*Allemachte*! Allan, a strange time to choose," answered Marais, pulling at his beard; "the troth that is plighted in blood is apt to end in blood."

"A vain superstition to which I cannot consent," interrupted my father.

"Perhaps so," I answered. "I know not; God alone knows. I only know that we plighted our troth when we thought ourselves about to die, and that we shall keep that troth till death ends it."

"Yes, my father," added Marie, leaning forward across the scored yellow-wood table, her chin resting on her hand and her dark, buck-like eyes looking him in the face. "Yes, my father, that is so, as I have told you already."

"And I tell you, Marie, what I have told you already, and you too, Allan, that this thing may not be," answered Marais, hitting the table with his fist. "I have nothing to say against you, Allan; indeed, I honour you, and you have done me a mighty service, but it may not be."

"Why not, *mynheer*?" I asked.

"For three reasons, Allan, each of which is final. You are English, and I do not wish my daughter to marry an Englishman; that is the first. You are poor, which is no discredit to you, and since I am now ruined my daughter cannot marry a poor man; that is the second. You live here, and my daughter and I are leaving this country, therefore you cannot marry her; that is the third," and he paused.

"Is there not a fourth," I asked, "which is the real reason? Namely, that you wish your daughter to marry someone else."

"Yes, Allan; since you force me to it, there is a fourth. I have affianced my daughter to her cousin, Hernando Pereira, a man of substance and full age; no lad, but one who knows his own mind and can support a wife."

"I understand," I answered calmly, although within my heart a very hell was raging. "But tell me, *mynheer*, has Marie affianced herself—or perhaps she will answer with her own lips?"

"Yes, Allan," replied Marie in her quiet fashion, "I have affianced myself—to you and no other man."

"You hear, *mynheer*," I said to Marais.

Then he broke out in his usual excitable manner. He stormed, he argued, he rated us both. He said that he would never allow it; that first he would see his daughter in her grave. That I had abused his confidence and violated his hospitality; that he would shoot me if I came near his girl. That she was a minor, and according to the law he could dispose of her in marriage. That she must accompany him whither he was going; that certainly I should not do so, and much more of the same sort.

When at last he had tired himself out and smashed his favourite pipe upon the table, Marie spoke, saying:

"My father, you know that I love you dearly, for since my mother's death we have been everything to each other, have we not?"

"Surely, Marie, you are my life, and more than my life."

"Very well, my father. That being so, I acknowledge your authority over me, whatever the law may say. I acknowledge that you have the right to forbid me to marry Allan, and if you do forbid me—while I am under age, at any rate—I shall not marry him because of my duty to you. But"—here she rose and looked him full in the eyes, and oh! how stately she seemed at that moment in her simple strength and youthful grace!—"there is one thing, my father, that I do not acknowledge—your right to force me to marry any other man. As a woman with power over herself, I deny that right; and much as it pains me, my father, to refuse you anything, I say that first I will die. To Allan here I have given myself for good or for evil, and if I may not marry Allan, I will go to the grave unwed. If my words hurt you, I pray you to pardon me, but at the same time to remember that they are my words, which cannot be altered."

Marais looked at his daughter, and his daughter looked at Marais. At first I thought that he was about to curse her; but if this were so, something in her eyes seemed to change his mind, for all he said was:

"Intractable, like the rest of your race! Well, Fate may lead those who cannot be driven, and this matter I leave in the hands of Fate. While you are under age—that is, for two years or more—you may not marry without my consent, and have just promised not to do so. Presently we trek from this country into far-off lands. Who knows what may happen there?"

"Yes," said my father in a solemn voice, speaking for the first time, "who knows except God, Who governs all things, and will settle these matters according to His will, Henri Marais? Listen," he went on after a pause, for Marais made no answer, but sat himself down and stared gloomily at the table. "You do not wish my son to marry your daughter for various reasons, of which one is that you think him poor and a richer suitor has offered himself after a reverse of fortune has made *you* poor. Another and a greater, the true reason, is his English blood, which you hate so much that, although by God's mercy he saved her life, you do not desire that he should share her life. Is it not true?"

"Yes, it is true, Mynheer Quatermain. You English are bullies and cheats," he answered excitedly.

"And so you would give your daughter to one who has shown himself humble and upright, to that good hater of the English and plotter against his King, Hernando Pereira, whom you love because he alone is left of your ancient race."

Remembering the incident of the afternoon, this sarcasm reduced Marais to silence.

"Well," went on my father, "although I am fond of Marie, and know her to be a sweet and noble-hearted girl, neither do I wish that she should marry my son. I would see him wed to some English woman, and not dragged into the net of the Boers and their plottings. Still, it is plain that these two love each other with heart and soul, as doubtless it has been decreed that they should love. This being so, I tell you that to separate them and force another marriage upon one of them is a crime before God, of which, I am sure, He will take note and pay it back to you. Strange things may happen in those lands whither you go, Henri Marais. Will you not, then, be content to leave your child in safe keeping?"

"Never!" shouted Marais. "She shall accompany me to a new home, which is not under the shadow of your accursed British flag."

"Then I have no more to say. On your head be it here and hereafter," replied my father solemnly.

Now unable to control myself any longer I broke in:

"But I have, *mynheer*. To separate Marie and myself is a sin, and one

267

that will break her heart. As for my poverty, I have something, more perhaps than you think, and in this rich country wealth can be earned by those who work, as I would do for her sake. The man to whom you would give her showed his true nature this day, for he who can play so low a trick to win a wager, will play worse tricks to win greater things. Moreover, the scheme must fail since Marie will not marry him."

"I say she shall," replied Marais; "and that whether she does or not, she shall accompany me and not stay here to be the wife of an English boy."

"Accompany you I will, father, and share your fortunes to the last. But marry Hernando Pereira I will not," said Marie quietly.

"Perhaps, *mynheer*," I added, "days may come when once again you will be glad of the help of an 'English boy.'"

The words were spoken at random, a kind of ejaculation from the heart, caused by the sting of Marais's cruelty and insults, like the cry of a beast beneath a blow. Little did I know how true they would prove, but at times it is thus that truth is mysteriously drawn from some well of secret knowledge hidden in our souls.

"When I want your help I will ask for it," raved Marais, who, knowing himself to be in the wrong, strove to cover up that wrong with violence.

"Asked or unasked, if I live it shall be given in the future as in the past, Mynheer Marais. God pardon you for the woe you are bringing on Marie and on me."

Now Marie began to weep a little, and, unable to bear that sight, I covered my eyes with my hand. Marais, who, when he was not under the influence of his prejudices or passion, had a kind heart, was moved also, but tried to hide his feelings in roughness. He swore at Marie, and told her to go to bed, and she obeyed, still weeping. Then my father rose and said:

"Henri Marais, we cannot leave here to-night because the horses are kraaled, and it would be difficult to find them in this darkness, so we must ask your hospitality till dawn."

"*I* do not ask it," I exclaimed. "I go to sleep in the cart," and I limped from the room and the house, leaving the two men together.

What passed afterwards between them I do not quite know. I gathered that my father, who, when roused, also had a temper and was mentally and intellectually the stronger man, told Marais his opinion of his wickedness and folly in language that he was not likely to forget. I believe he even drove him to confess that his acts seemed cruel, excusing them, however, by announcing that he had sworn before God that his daughter should never marry an Englishman. Also he said that he had promised her solemnly to Pereira, his own nephew, whom he loved, and could not break his word.

"No," answered my father, "because, being mad with the madness that runs before destruction, you prefer to break Marie's heart and perhaps become guilty of her blood."

Then he left him.

The darkness was intense. Through it I groped my way to the cart, which stood where it had been outspanned on the *veld* at a little distance from the house, wishing heartily, so miserable was I, that the Kaffirs might choose that black night for another attack and make an end of me.

When I reached it and lit the lantern which we always carried, I was astonished to find that, in a rough fashion, it had been made ready to sleep in. The seats had been cleared out, the hind curtain fastened, and so forth. Also the pole was propped up with an ox-yoke so as to make the vehicle level to lie in. While I was wondering vaguely who could have done this, Hans climbed on to the step, carrying two *karosses* which he had borrowed or stolen, and asked if I was comfortable.

"Oh, yes!" I answered; "but why were you going to sleep in the cart?"

"Baas," he replied, "I was not; I prepared it for you. How did I know that you were coming? Oh, very simply. I sat on the *stoep* and listened to all the talk in the *sitkammer*. The window has never been mended, *baas*, since the Quabies broke it. God in Heaven! what a talk that was. I never knew that white people could have so much to say about a simple matter. You want to marry the Baas Marais's daughter; the *baas* wants her to marry another man who can pay more cattle. Well, among us it would soon have been settled, for the father would have taken a stick and beaten you out of the hut with the thick end. Then he would have beaten the girl with the thin end until she promised to take the other man, and all would have been settled nicely. But you Whites, you talk and talk, and nothing is settled. You still mean to marry the daughter, and the daughter still means not to marry the man of many cows. Moreover, the father has really gained nothing except a sick heart and much bad luck to come."

"Why much bad luck to come, Hans?" I asked idly, for his naive summing up of the case interested me in a vague way.

"Oh! Baas Allan, for two reasons. First, your reverend father, who made me true Christian, told him so, and a predicant so good as he, is one down whom the curse of God runs from Heaven like lightning runs down a tree. Well, the Heer Marais was sitting under that tree, and we all know what happens to him who is under a tree when the lightning strikes it. That my first Christian reason. My second black-man reason, about which there can be no mistake, for it has always been true since there was a black man, is that the girl is yours by blood. You saved her life with your blood," and he pointed to my leg, "and therefore bought her for ever, for blood is more than cattle. Therefore, too, he who would divide her from you brings blood on her and on the other man who tries to steal her, blood, blood! and on himself I know not what." And he waved his yellow arms, staring up at me with his little black eyes in a way that was most uncanny.

"Nonsense!" I said. "Why do you talk such bad words?"

"Because they are true words, Baas Allan. Oh, you laugh at the poor Totty; but I had it from my father, and he from his father from generation to generation, amen, and you will see. You will see, as I have seen before now, and as the Heer Marais will see, who, if the great God had not made him mad—for mad he is, *baas*, as we know, if you Whites don't—might have lived in his home till he was old, and have had a good son-in-law to bury him in his blanket."

Now I seemed to have had enough of this eerie conversation. Of course it is easy to laugh at natives and their superstitions, but, after a long life of experience, I am bound to admit that they are not always devoid of truth. The native has some kind of sixth sense which the civilised man has lost, or so it seems to me.

"Talking of blankets," I said in order to change the subject, "from whom did you get these *karosses*?"

"From whom? Why, from the Missie, of course, *baas*. When I heard that you were to sleep in the cart I went to her and borrowed them to cover you. Also, I had forgotten, she gave me a writing for you," and he felt about, first in his dirty shirt, then under his arm, and finally in his fuzzy hair, from which last hiding place he produced a little bit of paper folded into a pellet. I undid it and read these words, written with a pencil and in French:

I shall be in the peach orchard half an hour before sunrise. Be there if you would bid me farewell.—*M.*

"Is there any answer, *baas*?" asked Hans when I had thrust the note into my pocket. "If so I can take it without being found out." Then an inspiration seemed to strike him, and he added: "Why do you not take it yourself? The missie's window is easy to open, also I am sure she would be pleased to see you."

"Be silent," I said. "I am going to sleep. Wake me an hour before the cock-crow—and, stay—see that the horses have got out of the *kraal* so that you cannot find them too easily in case the Reverend wishes to start very early. But do not let them wander far, for here we are no welcome guests."

"Yes, *baas*. By the way, *baas*, the Heer Pereira, who tried to cheat you over those geese, is sleeping in an empty house not more than two miles away. He drinks coffee when he wakes up in the morning, and his servant, who makes it, is my good friend. Now would you like me to put a little something into it? Not to kill him, for that is against the law in the Book, but just to make him quite mad, for the Book says nothing about that. If so, I have a very good medicine, one that you white people do not know, which improves the taste of the coffee, and it might save much trouble. You see, if he came dancing about the place without any clothes on, like a common Kaffir, the Heer Marais, although *he* is really mad also, might not wish for him as a son-in-law."

"Oh! go to the devil if you are not there already," I replied, and turned over as though to sleep.

There was no need for me to have instructed that faithful creature, the astute but immoral Hans, to call me early, as the lady did her mother in the poem, for I do not think that I closed an eye that night. I spare my reflections, for they can easily be imagined in the case of an earnest-natured lad who was about to be bereft of his first love.

Long before the dawn I stood in the peach orchard, that orchard where we had first met, and waited. At length Marie came stealing between the tree trunks like a grey ghost, for she was wrapped in some light-coloured garment. Oh! once more we were alone together. Alone in the utter solitude and silence which precede the African dawn, when all creatures that love the night have withdrawn to their lairs and hiding places, and those that love the day still sleep their soundest.

She saw me and stood still, then opened her arms and clasped me to her breast, uttering no word. A while later she spoke almost in a whisper, saying:

"Allan, I must not stay long, for I think that if my father found us together, he would shoot you in his madness."

Now as always it was of me she thought, not of herself.

"And you, my sweet?" I asked.

"Oh!" she answered, "that matters nothing. Except for the sin of it I wish he would shoot me, for then I should have done with all this pain. I told you, Allan, when the Kaffirs were on us yonder, that it might be better to die; and see, my heart spoke truly."

"Is there no hope?" I gasped. "Will he really separate us and take you away into the wilderness?"

"Certainly, nothing can turn him. Yet, Allan, there is this hope. In two years, if I live, I shall be of full age, and can marry whom I will; and this I swear, that I will marry none but you, no, not even if you were to die to-morrow."

"I bless you for those words," I said.

"Why?" she asked simply. "What others could I speak? Would you have me do outrage to my own heart and go through life faithless and ashamed?"

"And I, I swear also," I broke in.

"Nay, swear nothing. While I live I know that you will love me, and if I should be taken, it is my wish that you should marry some other good woman, since it is not well or right that man should live alone. With us maids it is different. Listen, Allan, for the cocks are beginning to crow, and soon there will be light. You must bide here with your father. If possible, I will write to you from time to time, telling you where we are and how we fare. But if I do not write, know that it is because I cannot, or because I can find no messenger, or because the letters have miscarried, for we go into wild countries, amongst savages."

"Whither do you go?" I asked.

"I believe up towards the great harbour called Delagoa Bay, where the Portuguese rule. My cousin Hernan, who accompanies us"—and she shivered a little in my arms—"is half Portuguese. He tells the Boers that he has relations there who have written him many fine promises, saying they will give us good country to dwell in where we cannot be followed by the English, whom he and my father hate so much."

"I have heard that is all fever *veld*, and that the country between is full of fierce Kaffirs," I said with a groan.

"Perhaps. I do not know, and I do not care. At least, that is the notion in my father's head, though, of course, circumstances may change it. I will try to let you know, Allan, or if I do not, perhaps you will be able to find out for yourself. Then, then, if we both live and you still care for me, who will always care for you, when I am of age, you will join us and, say and do what they may, I will marry no other man. And if I die, as may well happen, oh! then my spirit shall watch over you and wait for you till you join me beneath the wings of God. Look, it grows light. I must go. Farewell, my love, my first and only love, till in life or death we meet again, as meet we shall."

Once more we clung together and kissed, muttering broken words, and then she tore herself from my embrace and was gone. But oh! as I heard her feet steal through the dew-laden grass, I felt as though my heart were being rent from my breast. I have suffered much in life, but I do not think that ever I underwent a bitterer anguish than in this hour of my parting from Marie. For when all is said and done, what joy is there like the joy of pure, first love, and what bitterness like the bitterness of its loss?

Half an hour later the flowering trees of Maraisfontein were behind us, while in front rolled the fire-swept *veld*, black as life had become for me.

Chapter 7

Allan's Call

A fortnight later Marais, Pereira and their companions, a little band in all of about twenty men, thirty women and children, and say fifty half-breeds and Hottentot after-riders, trekked from their homes into the wilderness. I rode to the crest of a table-topped hill and watched the long line of wagons, one of them containing Marie, crawl away northward across the *veld* a mile or more beneath.

Sorely was I tempted to gallop after them and seek a last interview with her and her father. But my pride forbade me. Henri Marais had given out that if I came near his daughter he would have me beaten back with *sjambocks* or hide whips. Perhaps he had gained some inkling of our last farewell in the peach orchard. I do not know. But I do know that if anyone had lifted a *sjambock* on me I should have answered with a bullet. Then there would have been blood between us, which is worse to cross than whole rivers of wrath and jealousy. So I just watched the wagons until they vanished, and galloped home down the rock-strewn slope, wishing that the horse would stumble and break my neck.

When I reached the station, however, I was glad that it had not done so, as I found my father sitting on the *stoep* reading a letter that had been brought by a mounted Hottentot. It was from Henri Marais, and ran thus:

"'*Reverend heer and friend Quatermain*,—I send this to bid you farewell, for although you are English and we have quarrelled at times, I honour you in my heart. Friend, now that we are starting, your warning words lie on me like lead, I know not why. But what is done cannot be undone, and I trust that all will come right. If not, it is because the Good Lord wills it otherwise.

Here my father looked up and said: "When men suffer from their own passion and folly, they always lay the blame on the back of Providence."

Then he went on, spelling out the letter:

"'I fear your boy Allan, who is a brave lad, as I have reason to know, and honest, must think that I have treated him harshly and without gratitude. But I have only done what I must do. True, Marie, who, like her mother, is very strong and stubborn in mind, swears that she will marry no one else; but soon Nature will make her forget all that, especially as such a fine husband waits for her hand. So bid Allan forget all about her also, and when he is old enough choose some English girl. I have sworn a great oath before my God that he shall never marry my daughter with my consent.

"'Friend, I write to ask you something because I trust you more than these slim agents. Half the price, a very poor one, that I have for my farm is still unpaid to me by Jacobus van der Merve, who remains behind and buys up all our lands. It is #100 English, due this day year, and I enclose you power of attorney to receive and give receipt for the same. Also there is due to me from your British Government #253 on account of slaves liberated which were worth quite #1,000. This also the paper gives you authority to receive. As regards my claims against the said cursed Government because of the loss brought on me by the Quabie Kaffirs, it will not acknowledge them, saying that the attack was caused by the Frenchman Leblanc, one of my household.'"

"And with good reason," commented my father.

"'When you have received these monies, if ever, I pray you take some safe opportunity of sending them to me, wherever I may be, which doubtless you will hear in due course, although by that time I hope to be rich again and not to need money. Farewell and God be with you, as I hope He will be with me and Marie and the rest of us trek-Boers. The bearer will overtake us with your answer at our first outspan.

"'Henri Marais.'"

"Well," said my father with a sigh, "I suppose I must accept his trust, though why he should choose an 'accursed Englishman' with whom he has quarrelled violently to collect his debts instead of one of his own beloved Boers, I am sure I do not know. I will go and write to him. Allan, see that the messenger and his horse get something to eat."

I nodded and went to the man, who was one of those that had defended Maraisfontein with me, a good fellow unless he got near liquor.

"Heer Allan," he said, looking round to see that we were not overheard, "I have a little writing for you also," and he produced from his pouch a note that was unaddressed.

I tore it open eagerly. Within was written in French, which no Boer would understand if the letter fell into his hands:

"Be brave and faithful, and remember, as I shall. Oh! love of my heart, adieu, adieu!"

This message was unsigned; but what need was there of signature?

I wrote an answer of a sort that may be imagined, though what the exact words were I cannot remember after the lapse of nearly half a century. Oddly enough, it is the things I said which I recall at such a distance of time rather than the things which I wrote, perhaps because, when once written, my mind being delivered, troubled itself with them no more. So in due course the Hottentot departed with my father's letter and my own, and that was the last direct communication which we had with Henri or Marie Marais for more than a year.

I think that those long months were on the whole the most wretched I have ever spent. The time of life which I was passing through is always trying; that period of emergence from youth into full and responsible manhood which in Africa generally takes place earlier than it does here in England, where young men often seem to me to remain boys up to five-and-twenty. The circumstances which I have detailed made it particularly so in my own case, for here was I, who should have been but a cheerful lad, oppressed with the sorrows and anxieties, and fettered by the affections of maturity.

I could not get Marie out of my mind; her image was with me by day and by night, especially by night, which caused me to sleep badly. I became morose, supersensitive, and excitable. I developed a cough, and thought, as did others, that I was going into a decline. I remember that Hans even asked me once if I would not come and peg out the exact place where I should like to be buried, so that I might be sure that there would be no mistake made when I could no longer speak for myself. On that occasion I kicked Hans, one of the few upon which I have ever touched a native. The truth was that I had not the slightest intention of being buried. I wanted to live and marry Marie, not to die and be put in a hole by Hans. Only I saw no prospect of marrying Marie, or even of seeing her again, and that was why I felt low-spirited.

Of course, from time to time news of the trek-Boers reached us, but it was extremely confused. There were so many parties of them; their adventures were so difficult to follow, and, I may add, often so terrible; so few of them could write; trustworthy messengers were so scanty; distances were so great. At any rate, we heard nothing of Marais's band except a rumour that they had trekked to a district in what is now the Transvaal, which is called Rustenberg, and thence on towards Delagoa Bay into an unknown *veld* where they had vanished. From Marie herself no letter came, which showed me clearly enough that she had not found an opportunity of sending one.

Observing my depressed condition, my father suggested as a remedy that I should go to the theological college at Cape Town and prepare myself for ordination. But the Church as a career did not appeal to me, perhaps because I felt that I could never be sufficiently good; perhaps because I knew that as a clergyman I should find no opportunity of travelling north when my call came. For I always believed that this call would come.

My father, who wished that I should hear another kind of call, was vexed with me over this matter. He desired earnestly that I should follow the profession which he adorned, and indeed saw no other open for me any more than I did myself. Of course he was right in a way, seeing that in the end I found none, unless big game hunting and Kaffir trading can be called a profession. I don't know, I am sure. Still, poor business as it may be, I say now when I am getting towards the end of life that I am glad I did not follow any other. It has suited me; that was the insignificant hole in the world's affairs which I was destined to fit, whose only gifts were a remarkable art of straight shooting and the more common one of observation mixed with a little untrained philosophy.

So hot did our arguments become about this subject of the Church, for, as may be imagined, in the course of them I revealed some unorthodoxy, especially as regards the matter of our methods of Christianising Kaffirs, that I was extremely thankful when a diversion occurred which took me away from home. The story of my defence of Maraisfontein had spread far, and that of my feats of shooting, especially in the Goose Kloof, still farther. So the end of it was that those in authority commandeered me to serve in one of the continual Kaffir frontier wars which was in progress, and instantly gave me a commission as a kind of lieutenant in a border corps.

Now the events of that particular war have nothing to do with the history that I am telling, so I do not propose even to touch on them. I served in it for a year, meeting with many adventures, one or two successes, and several failures. Once I was wounded slightly, twice I but just escaped with my life. Once I was reprimanded for taking a foolish risk and losing some men. Twice I was commended for what were called gallant actions, such as bringing a wounded comrade out of danger under a warm fire, mostly of assegais, and penetrating by night, almost alone, into the stronghold of a chieftain, and shooting him.

At length that war was patched up with an inconclusive peace and my corps was disbanded. I returned home, no longer a lad, but a man with experience of various kinds and a rather unique knowledge of Kaffirs, their languages, history, and modes of thought and action. Also I had associated a good deal with British officers, and from them acquired much that I had found no opportunity of studying before, especially, I hope, the ideas and standards of English gentlemen.

I had not been back at the Mission Station more than three weeks, quite long enough for me to begin to be bored with idleness and inactivity, when that call for which I had been waiting came at last.

One day a *smous*, that is a low kind of white man, often a Jew, who travels about trading with unsophisticated Boers and Kaffirs, and cheating them if he can, called at the station with his cartful of goods. I was about to send him away, having no liking for such gentry, when he asked me if I were named Allan Quatermain. I said "Yes," whereon he replied that he had a letter for me, and produced a packet wrapped up in sail-cloth. I asked him whence he had it, and he answered from a man whom he had met at Port Elizabeth, an east coast trader, who, hearing that he was coming into the Cradock district, entrusted him with the letter. The man told him that it was very important, and that I should reward the bearer well if it were delivered safely.

While the Jew talked (I think he was a Jew) I was opening the sail-cloth. Within was a piece of linen which had been oiled to keep out water, addressed in some red pigment to myself or my father. This, too, I opened, not without difficulty, for it was carefully sewn up, and found within it a letter-packet, also addressed to myself or my father, in the handwriting of Marie.

Great Heaven! How my heart jumped at that sight! Calling to Hans to make the *smous* comfortable and give him food, I went into my own room, and there read the letter, which ran thus:

My Dear Allan,—I do not know whether the other letters I have written to you have ever come to your hands, or indeed if this one will. Still, I send it on chance by a wandering Portuguese half-breed who is going to Delagoa Bay, about fifty miles, I believe, from the place where I now write, near the Crocodile River. My father has named it Maraisfontein, after our old home. If those letters reached you, you will have learned of the terrible things we went through on our journey; the attacks by the Kaffirs in the Zoutpansberg region, who destroyed one of our parties altogether, and so forth. If not, all that story must wait, for it is too long to tell now, and, indeed, I have but little paper, and not much pencil. It will be enough to say, therefore, that to the number of thirty-five white people, men, women and children, we trekked at the beginning of the summer season, when the grass was commencing to grow, from the Lydenburg district—an awful journey over mountains and through flooded rivers. After many delays, some of them months long, we reached this place, about eight weeks ago, for I write to you at the beginning of June, if we have kept correct account of the time, of which I am not certain.

It is a beautiful place to look at, a flat country of rich *veld*, with big trees growing on it, and about two miles from the great river that is called the Crocodile. Here, finding good water, my father and Hernan Pereira, who now rules him in all things, determined to settle, although some of the others wished to push on nearer to Delagoa Bay. There was a great quarrel about it, but in the end my father, or rather Hernan, had his will, as the oxen were worn out and many had already died from the bites of a poisonous fly which is called the tsetse. So we lotted out the land, of which there is enough for hundreds, and began to build rude houses.

Then trouble came upon us. The Kaffirs stole most of our horses, although they have not dared to attack us, and except two belonging to Hernan, the rest died of the sickness, the last of them but yesterday. The oxen, too, have all died of the tsetse bites or other illnesses. But the worst is that although this country looks so healthy, it is poisoned with fever, which comes up, I think, in the mists from the river. Already out of the thirty-five of us, ten are dead, two men, three women, and five children, while more are sick. As yet my father and I and my cousin Pereira have, by God's mercy, kept quite well; but although we are all very strong, how long this will continue I cannot tell. Fortunately we have plenty of ammunition and the place is thick with game, so that those of the men who remain strong can kill all the food we want, even shooting on foot, and we women have made a great quantity of biltong by salting flesh and drying it in the sun. So we shall not actually starve for a long while, even if the game goes away.

But, dear Allan, unless help comes to us I think that we shall die every one, for God alone knows the miseries that we suffer and the horrible sights of sickness and death that are around us. At this moment there lies by me a little girl who is dying of fever.

Oh, Allan, if you can help us, do so! Because of our sick it is impossible for us to get to Delagoa Bay, and if we did we have no money to buy anything there, for all that we had with us was lost in a wagon in a flooded river. It was a great sum, for it included Hernan's rich fortune which he brought from the Cape with him in gold. Nor can we move anywhere else, for we have no cattle or horses. We have sent to Delagoa Bay, where we hear these are to be had, to try to buy them on credit; but my cousin Hernan's relations, of whom he used to talk so much, are dead or gone away, and no one will trust us. With the neighbouring Kaffirs, too, who have plenty of cattle, we have quarrelled since, unfortunately, my cousin and some of the other Boers tried to take certain beasts of theirs without payment. So we are quite helpless, and can only wait for death.

Allan, my father says that he asked your father to collect some monies that were owing to him. If it were possible for you or other friends to come to Delagoa in a ship with that money, I think that it might serve to buy some oxen, enough for a few wagons. Then perhaps we might trek back and fall in with a party of Boers who, we believe, have crossed the Quathlamba Mountains into Natal. Or perhaps we might get to the Bay and find a ship to take us anywhere from this horrible place. If you could come, the natives would guide you to where we are.

But it is too much to hope that you will come, or that if you do come you will find us still alive.

Allan, my dearest, I have one more thing to say, though I must say it shortly, for the paper is nearly finished. I do not know, supposing that you are alive and well, whether you still care for me, who left you so long ago—it seems years and years—but *my* heart is where it was, and where I promised it should remain, in your keeping. Of course, Hernan has pressed me to marry him, and my father has wished it. But I have always said no, and now, in our wretchedness, there is no more talk of marriage at present, which is the one good thing that has happened to me. And, Allan, before so very long I shall be of age, if I live. Still I dare say you no longer think of marriage with me, who, perhaps, are already married to someone else, especially as now I and all of us are no better than wandering beggars. Yet I have thought it right to tell you these things, which you may like to know.

Oh, why did God ever put it into my father's heart to leave

the Cape Colony just because he hated the British Government and Hernan Pereira and others persuaded him? I know not, but, poor man, he is sorry enough now. It is pitiful to see him; at times I think that he is going mad.

The paper is done, and the messenger is going; also the sick child is dying and I must attend to her. Will this letter ever come to your hands, I wonder? I am sending with it the little money I have to pay for its delivery—about four pounds English. If not, there is an end. If it does, and you cannot come or send others, at least pray for us. I dream of you by night and think of you by day, for how much I love you I cannot tell.

In life or death I am

Your Marie

Such was this awful letter. I still have it; it lies before me, those ragged sheets of paper covered with faint pencil-writing that is blotted here and there with tear marks, some of them the tears of Marie who wrote, some of them the tears of me who read. I wonder if there exists a more piteous memorial of the terrible sufferings of the trek-Boers, and especially of such of them as forced their way into the poisonous *veld* around Delagoa, as did this Marais expedition and those under the command of Triechard. Better, like many of their people, to have perished at once by the spears of Umzilikazi and other savages than to endure these lingering tortures of fever and starvation.

As I finished reading this letter my father, who had been out visiting some of his Mission Kaffirs, entered the house, and I went into the sitting-room to meet him.

"Why, Allan, what is the matter with you?" he asked, noting my tear-stained face.

I gave him the letter, for I could not speak, and with difficulty he deciphered it.

"Merciful God, what dreadful news!" he said when he had finished. "Those poor people! those poor, misguided people! What can be done for them?"

"I know one thing that can be done, father, or at any rate can be attempted. I can try to reach them."

"Are you mad?" he asked. "How is it possible for you, one man, to get to Delagoa Bay, buy cattle, and rescue these folk, who probably are now all dead?"

"The first two things are possible enough, father. Some ship will take me to the Bay. You have Marais's money, and I have that five hundred pounds which my old aunt in England left me last year. Thank Heaven! owing to my absence on commando, it still lies untouched in the bank at Port Elizabeth. That is about eight hundred pounds in all, which would buy a great many cattle and other things. As for the third, it is not in our hands, is it? It may be that they cannot be rescued, it may be that they are dead. I can only go to see."

"But, Allan, Allan, you are my only son, and if you go it is probable that I shall never see you more."

"I have been through more dangers lately, father, and am still alive and well. Moreover, if Marie is dead"—I paused, then went on passionately—"Do not try to stop me, for I tell you, father, I will not be stopped. Think of the words in that letter and what a shameless hound I should be if I sat here quiet while Marie is dying yonder. Would you have done so if Marie had been my mother?"

"No," answered the old gentleman, "I should not. Go, and God be with you, Allan, and me also, for I never expect to see you again." And he turned his head aside for a while.

Then we went into matters. The *smous* was summoned and asked about the ship which brought the letter from Delagoa. It seemed that she was an English-owned brig known as the Seven Stars, and that her captain, one Richardson, proposed to sail back to the Bay on the morrow, that was the third of July, or in other words, within twenty-four hours.

Twenty-four hours! And Port Elizabeth was one hundred and eighteen miles away, and the Seven Stars might leave earlier if she had completed her cargo and wind and weather served. Moreover, if she did leave, it might be weeks or months before any other ship sailed for Delagoa Bay, for in those days, of course, there were no mail boats.

I looked at my watch. It was four o'clock in the afternoon, and from a calendar we had, which gave the tides at Port Elizabeth and other South African harbours, it did not seem probable that the Seven Stars would sail, if she kept to her date, before about eight on the morrow. One hundred and twenty miles to be covered in, say, fourteen hours over rough country with some hills! Well, on the other hand, the roads were fairly good and dry, with no flooded rivers to cross, although there might be one to swim, and there was a full moon. It could be done—barely, and now I was glad indeed that Hernan Pereira had not won my swift mare in that shooting match.

I called to Hans, who was loafing about outside, and said quietly:

"I ride to Port Elizabeth, and must be there by eight o'clock to-morrow morning."

"*Allemachte!*" exclaimed Hans, who had been that road several times.

"You will go with me, and from Port Elizabeth on to Delagoa Bay. Saddle the mare and the roan horse, and put a headstall on the chestnut to lead with you as a spare. Give them all a feed, but no water. We start in half an hour." Then I added certain directions as to the guns we would take, saddle-bags, clothes, blankets and other details, and bade him start about the business.

Hans never hesitated. He had been with me through my recent campaign, and was accustomed to sudden orders. Moreover, I think that if I had told him I was riding to the moon, beyond his customary exclamation of "*Allemachte!*" he would have made no objection to accompanying me thither.

The next half-hour was a busy time for me. Henri Marais's money had to be got out of the strong box and arranged in a belt of buck's hide that I had strapped about me. A letter had to be written by my father to the manager of the Port Elizabeth bank, identifying me as the owner of the sum lodged there in my name. A meal must be eaten and some food prepared for us to carry. The horses' shoes had to be seen to, and a few clothes packed in the saddle-bags. Also there were other things which I have forgotten. Yet within five-and-thirty minutes the long, lean mare stood before the door. Behind her, with a tall crane's feather in his hat, was Hans, mounted on the roan stallion, and leading the chestnut, a four-year-old which I had bought as a foal on the mare as part of the bargain. Having been corn fed from a colt it was a very sound and well-grown horse, though not the equal of its mother in speed.

In the passage my poor old father, who was quite bewildered by the rapidity and urgent nature of this business, embraced me.

"God bless you, my dear boy," he said. "I have had little time to think, but I pray that this may be all for the best, and that we may meet again in the world. But if not, remember what I have taught you, and if I survive you, for my part I shall remember that you died trying to do your duty. Oh, what trouble has the blind madness of Henri Marais brought upon us all! Well, I warned him that it would be so. Goodbye, my dear boy, good-bye: my prayers will follow you, and for the rest—Well, I am old, and what does it matter if my grey hairs come with sorrow to the grave?"

I kissed him back, and with an aching heart sprang to the saddle. In five more minutes the station was out of sight.

Thirteen and a half hours later I pulled rein upon the quay of Port Elizabeth just, only just, in time to catch Captain Richardson as he was entering his boat to row out to the Seven Stars, on which the canvas was already being hoisted. As well as I could in my exhausted state, I explained matters and persuaded him to wait till the next tide. Then, thanking God for the mare's speed—the roan had been left foundered thirty miles away, and Hans was following on the chestnut, but not yet up—I dragged the poor beast to an inn at hand. There she lay down and died. Well, she had done her work, and there was no other horse in the country that could have caught that boat.

An hour or so later Hans came in flogging the chestnut, and here I may add that both it and the roan recovered. Indeed I rode them for many years, until they were quite old. When I had eaten, or tried to eat something and rested awhile, I went to the bank, succeeded in explaining the state of the case to the manager, and after some difficulty, for gold was not very plentiful in Port Elizabeth, procured three hundred pounds in sovereigns. For the other two he gave me a bill upon some agent in Delagoa Bay, together with a letter of recommendation to him and the Portuguese governor, who, it appeared, was in debt to their establishment. By an afterthought, however, although I kept the letters, I returned him the bill and spent the #200 in purchasing a great variety of goods which I will not enumerate, that I knew would be useful for trading purposes among the east coast Kaffirs. Indeed, I practically cleared out the Port Elizabeth stores, and barely had time, with the help of Hans and the storekeepers, to pack and ship the goods before the Seven Stars put out to sea.

Within twenty-four hours from the time I had left the Mission Station, Hans and I saw behind us Port Elizabeth fading into the distance, and in front a waste of stormy waters.

CHAPTER 8

The Camp of Death

Everything went well upon that voyage, except with me personally. Not having been on the ocean since I was a child, I, who am naturally no good sailor, was extremely ill as day by day we ploughed through seas that grew ever more rough. Also, strong as I was, that fearful ride had overdone me. Added to these physical discomforts was my agonising anxiety of mind, which I leave anyone with imagination to picture for himself. Really there were times when I wished that the Seven Stars would plunge headlong to the bottom of the deep and put an end to me and my miseries.

These, however, so far as the bodily side of them was concerned, were, I think, surpassed by those of my henchman Hans, who, as a matter of fact, had never before set foot in any kind of boat. Perhaps this was fortunate, since had he known the horrors of the ocean, much as he loved me, he would, I am sure, by one means or another, have left me to voyage in the Seven Stars alone. There he lay upon the floor of my little cabin, rolling to and fro with the violent motion of the brig, overcome with terror. He was convinced that we were going to be drowned, and in the intervals of furious sea-sickness uttered piteous lamentations in Dutch, English, and various native tongues, mingled with curses and prayers of the most primitive and realistic order.

After the first twenty-four hours or so he informed me with many moans that the last bit of his inside had just come out of him, and that he was now quite hollow "like a gourd." Also he declared that all these evils had fallen upon him because he had been fool enough to forsake the religion of his people (what was that, I wonder), and allow himself to be "washed white," that is, be baptised, by my father.

I answered that as he had become white instead of staying yellow, I advised him to remain so, since it was evident that the Hottentot gods would have nothing more to do with one who had deserted them. Thereon he made a dreadful face, which even in the midst of my own woes caused me to laugh at him, uttered a prolonged groan, and became so silent that I thought he must be dead. However, the sailor who brought me my food—such food!—assured me that this was not so, and lashed him tight to the legs of the bunk by his arm and ankle so as to prevent him from being rolled to bits.

Next morning Hans was dosed with brandy, which, in his empty condition, made him extremely drunk, and from that time forward began to take a more cheerful view of things. Especially was this so when the hours for the "brandy medicine" came round. Hans, like most other Hottentots, loved spirits, and would put up with much to get them, even with my father's fiery indignation.

I think it was on the fourth day that at length we pitched and rolled ourselves over the shallow bar of Port Natal and found ourselves at peace for a while under shelter of the Point in the beautiful bay upon the shores of which the town of Durban now stands. Then it was but a miserable place, consisting of a few shanties which were afterwards burnt by the Zulus, and a number of Kaffir huts. For such white men as dwelt there had for the most part native followings, and, I may add, native wives.

We spent two days at this settlement of Durban, where Captain Richardson had some cargo to land for the English settlers, one or two of whom had started a trade with the natives and with parties of the emigrant Boers who were beginning to enter the territory by the overland route. Those days I passed on shore, though I would not allow Hans to accompany me lest he should desert, employing my time in picking up all the information I could about the state of affairs, especially with reference to the Zulus, a people with whom I was destined ere long to make an intimate acquaintance. Needless to say, I inquired both from natives and from white men whether anything was known of the fate of Marais's party, but no one seemed even to have heard of them. One thing I did learn, however, that my old friend, Pieter Retief, with a large following, had crossed the Quathlamba Mountains, which we now know as the Drakensberg, and entered the territory of Natal. Here they proposed to settle if they could get the leave of the Zulu king, Dingaan, a savage potentate of whom and of whose armies everyone seemed to live in terror.

On the third morning, to my great relief, for I was terrified lest we should be delayed, the Seven Stars sailed with a favouring wind. Three days later we entered the harbour of Delagoa, a sheet of water many miles long and broad. Notwithstanding its shallow entrance, it is the best natural port in south-eastern Africa, but now, alas! lost to the English.

Six hours later we anchored opposite a sandbank on which stood a dilapidated fort and a dirty settlement known as Lorenzo Marquez, where the Portuguese kept a few soldiers, most of them coloured. I pass over my troubles with the Customs, if such they could be called. Suffice it to say that ultimately I succeeded in landing my goods, on which the duty chargeable was apparently enormous. This I did by distributing twenty-five English sovereigns among various officials, beginning with the acting-governor and ending with a drunken black sweep who sat in a kind of sentry box on the quay.

Early next morning the Seven Stars sailed again, because of some quarrel with the officials, who threatened to seize her—I forget why. Her destination was the East African ports and, I think, Madagascar, where a profitable trade was to be done in carrying cattle and slaves. Captain Richardson said he might be back at Lorenzo Marquez in two or three months' time, or he might not. As a matter of fact the latter supposition proved correct, for the Seven Stars was lost on a sandbank somewhere up the coast, her crew only escaping to Mombasa after enduring great hardships.

Well, she had served my turn, for I heard afterwards that no other ship put into the Bay for a whole year from the date she left it. So if I had not caught her at Port Elizabeth I could not have come at all, except, of course, overland. This at best must have taken many months, and was moreover a journey that no man could enter on alone.

Now I get back to my story again.

There was no inn at Lorenzo Marquez. Through the kindness of one of his native or half-breed wives, who could talk a little Dutch, I managed, however, to get a lodging in a tumble-down house belonging to a dissolute person who called himself Don Jose Ximenes, but who was really himself a half-breed. Here good fortune befriended me. Don Jose, when sober, was a trader with the natives, and a year before had acquired from them two good buck wagons. Probably they were stolen from some wandering Boers or found derelict after their murder or death by fever. These wagons he was only too glad to sell for a song. I think I gave him twenty pounds English for the two, and thirty more for twelve oxen that he had bought at the same time as the wagons. They were fine beasts of the Afrikander breed, that after a long rest had grown quite fat and strong.

Of course twelve oxen were not enough to draw two wagons, or even one. Therefore, hearing that there were natives on the mainland who possessed plenty of cattle, I at once gave out that I was ready to buy, and pay well in blankets, cloth, beads and so forth. The result was that within two days I had forty or fifty to choose from, small animals of the Zulu character and, I should add, unbroken. Still they were sturdy and used to that *veld* and its diseases. Here it was that my twelve trained beasts came in. By putting six of them to each wagon, two as fore- and two as after-oxen, and two in the middle, Hans and I were able to get the other ten necessary to make up a team of sixteen under some sort of control.

Heavens! how we worked during the week or so which went by before it was possible for me to leave Lorenzo Marquez. What with mending up and loading the wagons, buying and breaking in the wild oxen, purchasing provisions, hiring native servants—of whom I was lucky enough to secure eight who belonged to one of the Zulu tribes and desired to get back to their own country, whence they had wandered with some Boers, I do not think that we slept more than two or three hours out of the twenty-four.

But, it may be asked, what was my aim, whither went I, what inquiries had I made? To answer the last question first, I had made every possible inquiry, but with little or no result. Marie's letter had said that they were encamped on the bank of the Crocodile River, about fifty miles from Delagoa Bay. I asked everyone I met among the Portuguese—who, after all, were not many—if they had heard of such an encampment of emigrant Boers. But these Portuguese appeared to have heard nothing, except my host, Don Jose, who had a vague recollection of something—he could not remember what.

The fact was at this time the few people who lived at Lorenzo Marquez were too sodden with liquor and other vices to take any interest in outside news that did not immediately concern them. Moreover, the natives whom they flogged and oppressed if they were their servants, or fought with if they were not, told them little, and almost nothing that was true, for between the two races there was an hereditary hate stretching back for generations. So from the Portuguese I gained no information.

Then I turned to the Kaffirs, especially to those from whom I had bought the cattle. *They* had heard that some Boers reached the banks of the Crocodile moons ago—how many they could not tell. But that country, they said, was under the rule of a chief who was hostile to them, and killed any of their people who ventured thither. Therefore they knew nothing for certain. Still, one of them stated that a woman whom he had bought as a slave, and who had passed through the district in question a few weeks before, told him that someone had told her that these Boers were all dead of sickness. She added that she had seen their wagon caps from a distance, so, if they were dead, "their wagons were still alive."

I asked to see this woman, but the native refused to produce her. After a great deal of talk, however, he offered to sell her to me, saying that he was tired of her. So I bargained with the man and finally agreed for her purchase for three pounds of copper wire and eight yards of blue cloth. Next morning she was produced, an extremely ugly person with a large, flat nose, who came from somewhere in the interior of Africa, having, I gathered, been taken captive by Arabs and sold from hand to hand. Her name, as near as I can pronounce it, was Jeel.

I had great difficulty in establishing communication with her, but ultimately found that one of my newly hired Kaffirs could understand something of her language. Even then it was hard to make her talk, for she had never seen a white man, and thought I had bought her for some dreadful purpose or other. However, when she found that she was kindly treated, she opened her lips and told me the same story that her late master had repeated, neither more nor less. Finally I asked her whether she could guide me to the place where she had seen the "live wagons."

She answered: "Oh, yes," as she had travelled many roads and never forgot any of them.

This, of course, was all I wanted from the woman, who, I may add, ultimately gave me a good deal of trouble. The poor creature seemed never to have experienced kindness, and her gratitude for the little I showed her was so intense that it became a nuisance. She followed me about everywhere, trying to do me service in her savage way, and even attempted to seize my food and chew it before I put it into my own mouth—to save me the trouble, I suppose. Ultimately I married her, somewhat against her will, I fear, to one of the hired Kaffirs, who made her a very good husband, although when he was dismissed from my service she wanted to leave him and follow me.

At length, under the guidance of this woman, Jeel, we made a start. There were but fifty miles to go, a distance that on a fair road any good horse would cover in eight hours, or less. But we had no horses, and there was no road—nothing but swamps and bush and rocky hills. With our untrained cattle it took us three days to travel the first twelve miles, though after that things went somewhat better.

It may be asked, why did I not send on? But whom could I send when no one knew the way, except the woman, Jeel, whom I feared to part with lest I should see her no more? Moreover, what was the use of sending, since the messengers could take no help? If everyone at the camp was dead, as rumour told us—well, they were dead. And if they lived, the hope was that they might live a little longer. Meanwhile, I dared not part with my guide, nor dared I leave the relief wagons to go on with her alone. If I did so, I knew that I should never see them again, since only the prestige of their being owned by a white man who was not a Portuguese prevented the natives from looting them.

It was a truly awful journey. My first idea had been to follow the banks of the Crocodile River, which is what I should have attempted had I not chanced on the woman, Jeel. Lucky was it that I did not do so, since I found afterwards that this river wound about a great deal and was joined by impassable tributaries. Also it was bordered by forests. Jeel's track, on the contrary, followed an old slave road that, bad as it was, avoided the swampy places of the surrounding country, and those native tribes which the experience of generations of the traders in this iniquitous traffic showed to be most dangerous.

Nine days of fearful struggle had gone by. We had camped one night below the crest of a long slope strewn with great rocks, many of which we were obliged to roll out of the path by main force in order to make a way for the wagons. The oxen had to lie in their yokes all night, since we dared not let them loose fearing lest they should stray; also lions were roaring in the distance, although, game being plentiful, these did not come near to us. As soon as there was any light we let out the teams to fill themselves on the tussocky grass that grew about, and meanwhile cooked and ate some food.

Presently the sun rose, and I saw that beneath us was a great stretch of plain covered with mist, and to the north, on our right, several denser billows of mist that marked the course of the Crocodile River.

By degrees this mist lifted, tall tops of trees appearing above it, till at length it thinned into vapour that vanished away as the sun rose. As I watched it idly, the woman, Jeel, crept up to me in her furtive fashion, touched me on the shoulder and pointed to a distant group of trees.

Looking closely at these trees, I saw between them what at first I took for some white rocks. Further examination, as the mist cleared, suggested to my mind, however, that they might be wagon tilts. Just then the Zulu who understood Jeel's talk came up. I asked him as well as I could, for at that time my knowledge of his tongue was very imperfect, what she wished to say. He questioned her, and answered that she desired to tell me that those were the moving houses of the Amaboona (the Boer people), just where she had seen them nearly two moons ago.

At this tidings my heart seemed to stand still, so that for more than a minute I could not speak. There were the wagons at last, but—oh! who and what should I find in them? I called Hans and bade him inspan as quickly as possible, explaining to him that yonder was Marais's camp.

"Why not let the oxen fill themselves first, *baas*?" he answered. "There is no hurry, for though the wagons are there, no doubt all the people are dead long ago."

"Do what I bid you, you ill-omened beast," I said, "instead of croaking of death like a crow. And listen: I am going to walk forward to that camp; you must follow with the wagons as fast as they can travel."

"No, *baas*, it is not safe that you should go alone. Kaffirs or wild beasts might take you."

"Safe or not, I am going; but if you think it wise, tell two of those Zulus to come with me."

A few minutes later I was on the road, followed by the two Kaffirs armed with spears. In my youth I was a good runner, being strong of leg and light in body, but I do not think that I ever covered seven miles, for that was about the distance to the camp, in quicker time than I did that morning. Indeed, I left those active Kaffirs so far behind that when I approached the trees they were not in sight. Here I dropped to a walk, as I said to myself—to get my breath. Really it was because I felt so terrified at what I might find that I delayed the discovery just for one minute more. While I approached, hope, however faint, still remained; when I arrived, hope might be replaced by everlasting despair.

Now I could see that there were some shanties built behind the wagons, doubtless those "rude houses" of which Marie had written. But I could not see anyone moving about them, or any cattle or any smoke, or other sign of life. Nor could I hear a single sound.

Doubtless, thought I to myself, Hans is right. They are all long dead.

My agony of suspense was replaced by an icy calm. At length I knew the worst. It was finished—I had striven in vain. I walked through the outlying trees and between two of the wagons. One of these I noticed, as we do notice things at such times, was the same in which Marais had trekked with his daughter, his favourite wagon that once I had helped to fit with a new *disselboom*.

Before me were the rough houses built of the branches of trees, daubed over with mud, or rather the backs of them, for they faced west. I stood still for a moment, and as I stood thought that I heard a faint sound as of someone reciting slowly. I crept along the end of the outermost house and, rubbing the cold sweat from my eyes, peeped round the corner, for it occurred to me that savages might be in possession. Then I saw what caused the sound. A tattered, blackened, bearded man stood at the head of a long and shallow hole saying a prayer.

It was Henri Marais, although at the time I did not recognise him, so changed was he. A number of little mounds to the right and left of him told me, however, that the hole was a grave. As I watched two more men appeared, dragging between them the body of a woman, which evidently they had not strength to carry, as its legs trailed upon the ground. From the shape of the corpse it seemed to be that of a tall young woman, but the features I could not see, because it was being dragged face downwards. Also the long hair hanging from the head hid them. It was dark hair, like Marie's. They reached the grave, and tumbled their sad burden into it; but I—I could not stir!

At length my limbs obeyed my will. I went forward to the men and said in a hollow voice in Dutch:

"Whom do you bury?"

"Johanna Meyer," answered someone mechanically, for they did not seem to have taken the trouble to look at me. As I listened to those words my heart, which had stood still waiting for the answer, beat again with a sudden bound that I could hear in the silence.

I looked up. There, advancing from the doorway of one of the houses, very slowly, as though overpowered by weakness, and leading by the hand a mere skeleton of a child, who was chewing some leaves, I saw—I saw *Marie Marais!* She was wasted to nothing, but I could not mistake her eyes, those great soft eyes that had grown so unnaturally large in the white, thin face.

She too saw me and stared for one moment. Then, loosing the child, she cast up her hands, through which the sunlight shone as through parchment, and slowly sank to the ground.

"She has gone, too," said one of the men in an indifferent voice. "I thought she would not last another day."

Now for the first time the man at the head of the grave turned. Lifting his hand, he pointed to me, whereon the other two men turned also.

"God above us!" he said in a choked voice, "at last I am quite mad. Look! there stands the spook of young Allan, the son of the English predicant who lived near Cradock."

As soon as I heard the voice I knew the speaker.

"Oh, Mynheer Marais!" I cried, "I am no ghost, I am Allan himself come to save you."

Marais made no answer; he seemed bewildered. But one of the men cried out crazily:

"How can you save us, youngster, unless you are ready to be eaten? Don't you see, we starve, we starve!"

"I have wagons and food," I answered.

"*Allemachte*! Henri," exclaimed the man, with a wild laugh, "do you hear what your English spook says? He says that he has wagons and *food, food, food!*"

Then Marais burst into tears and flung himself upon my breast, nearly knocking me down. I wrenched myself free of him and ran to Marie, who was lying face upwards on the ground. She seemed to hear my step, for her eyes opened and she struggled to a sitting posture.

"Is it really you, Allan, or do I dream?" she murmured.

"It is I, it is I," I answered, lifting her to her feet, for she seemed to weigh no more than a child. Her head fell upon my shoulder, and she too began to weep.

Still holding her, I turned to the men and said:

"Why do you starve when there is game all about?" and I pointed to two fat elands strolling among the trees not more than a hundred and fifty yards away.

"Can we kill game with stones?" asked one of them, "we whose powder was all burnt a month ago. Those buck," he added, with a wild laugh, "come here to mock us every morning; but they will not walk into our pitfalls. They know them too well, and we have no strength to dig others."

Now when I left my wagons I had brought with me that same Purdey rifle with which I had shot the geese in the match against Pereira, choosing it because it was so light to carry. I held up my hand for silence, set Marie gently on the ground, and began to steal towards the elands. Taking what shelter I could, I got within a hundred yards of them, when suddenly they took alarm, being frightened, in fact, by my two Zulu servants, who were now arriving.

Off they galloped, the big bull leading, and vanished behind some trees. I saw their line, and that they would appear again between two clumps of bush about two hundred and fifty yards away. Hastily I raised the full sight on the rifle, which was marked for two hundred yards, lifted it, and waited, praying to God as I did so that my skill might not fail me.

The bull appeared, its head held forward, its long horns lying flat upon the back. The shot was very long, and the beast very large to bring down with so small a bullet. I aimed right forward—clear of it, indeed—high too, in a line with its backbone, and pressed the trigger.

The rifle exploded, the bullet clapped, and the buck sprang forward faster than ever. I had failed! But what was this? Suddenly the great bull swung round and began to gallop towards us. When it was not more than fifty yards away, it fell in a heap, rolled twice over like a shot rabbit, and lay still. That bullet was in its heart.

The two Kaffirs appeared breathless and streaming with perspiration.

"Cut meat from the eland's flank; don't stop to skin it," I said in my broken Zulu, helping the words out with signs.

They understood, and a minute later were at work with their assegais. Then I looked about me. Near by lay a store of dead branches placed there for fuel.

"Have you fire?" I asked of the skeleton Boers, for they were nothing more.

"*Nein, nein,*" they answered; "our fire is dead."

I produced the tinder-box which I carried with me, and struck the flint. Ten minutes later we had a cheerful blaze, and within three-quarters of an hour good soup, for iron pots were not wanting—only food to put into them. I think that for the rest of that day those poor creatures did little else but eat, sleeping between their meals. Oh! the joy I had in feeding them, especially after the wagons arrived, bringing with them salt—how they longed for that salt!—sugar and coffee.

CHAPTER 9

The Promise

Of the original thirty-five souls, not reckoning natives, who had accompanied Henri Marais upon his ill-fated expedition, there now remained but nine alive at the new Maraisfontein. These were himself, his daughter, four Prinsloos—a family of extraordinary constitution—and three Meyers, being the husband of the poor woman I had seen committed to the grave and two of her six children. The rest, Hernan Pereira excepted, had died of fever and actual starvation, for when the fever lessened with the change of the seasons, the starvation set in. It appeared that, with the exception of a very little, they had stored their powder in a kind of outbuilding which they constructed, placing it at a distance for safety's sake. When most of the surviving men were away, however, a grass fire set light to this outbuilding and all the powder blew up.

After this, for a while they supplied the camp with food by the help of such ammunition as remained to them. When that failed they dug pits in which to catch game. In time the buck came to know of these pits, so that they snared no more.

Then, as the "biltong" or sun-dried meat they had made was all consumed, they were driven to every desperate expedient that is known to the starving, such as the digging up of bulbs, the boiling of grass, twigs and leaves, the catching of lizards, and so forth. I believe that they actually ate caterpillars and earthworms. But after their last fire went out through the neglect of the wretched Kaffir who was left to watch it, and having no tinder, they failed to relight it by friction, of course even this food failed them. When I arrived they had practically been three days without anything to eat except green leaves and grass, such as I saw the child chewing. In another seventy hours doubtless every one of them would have been dead.

Well, they recovered rapidly enough, for those who had survived its ravages were evidently now impervious to fever. Who can tell the joy that I experienced as I watched Marie returning from the very brink of the grave to a state of full and lovely womanhood? After all, we were not so far away from the primitive conditions of humanity, when the first duty of man was to feed his women and his children, and I think that something of that instinct remains with us. At least, I know I never experienced a greater pleasure than I did, when the woman I loved, the poor, starving woman, ate and ate of the food which *I* was able to give her—she who for weeks had existed upon locusts and herbs.

For the first few days we did not talk much except of the immediate necessities of the hour, which occupied all our thoughts. Afterwards, when Marais and his daughter were strong enough to bear it, we had some conversation. He began by asking how I came to find them.

I replied, through Marie's letter, which, it appeared, he knew nothing of, for he had forbidden her to write to me.

"It seems fortunate that you were disobeyed, *mynheer*," I said, to which he answered nothing.

Then I told the tale of the arrival of that letter at the Mission Station in the Cape Colony by the hand of a wandering *smous*, and of my desperate ride upon the swift mare to Port Elizabeth, where I just succeeded in catching the brig Seven Stars before she sailed. Also I told them of the lucky chances that enabled me to buy the wagons and find a guide to their camp, reaching it but a few hours before it was too late.

"It was a great deed," said Henri Marais, taking the pipe from his mouth, for I had brought tobacco among my stores. "But tell me, Allan, why did you do it for the sake of one who has not treated you kindly?"

"I did it," I answered, "for the sake of one who has always treated me kindly," and I nodded towards Marie, who was engaged in washing up the cooking pots at a distance.

"I suppose so, Allan; but you know she is affianced to another."

"I know that she is affianced to me, and to no other," I answered warmly, adding, "And pray where is this other? If he lives I do not see him here."

"No," replied Marais in a curious voice. "The truth is, Allan, that Hernan Pereira left us about a fortnight before you came. One horse remained, which was his, and with two Hottentots, who were also his servants, he rode back upon the track by which we came, to try to find help. Since then we have heard nothing of him."

"Indeed; and how did he propose to get food on the way?"

"He had a rifle, or rather they all three had rifles, and about a hundred charges between them, which escaped the fire."

"With a hundred charges of powder carefully used your camp would have been fed for a month, or perhaps two months," I remarked. "Yet he went away with all of them—to find help?"

"That is so, Allan. We begged him to stay, but he would not; and, after all, the charges were his own property. No doubt he thought he acted for the best, especially as Marie would have none of him," Marais added with emphasis.

"Well," I replied, "it seems that it is I who have brought you the help, and not Pereira. Also, by the way, *mynheer*, I have brought you the money my father collected on your account, and some #500 of my own, or what is left of it, in goods and gold. Moreover, Marie does not refuse me. Say, therefore, to which of us does she belong?"

"It would seem that it should be to you," he answered slowly, "since you have shown yourself so faithful, and were it not for you she would now be lying yonder," and he pointed to the little heaps that covered the bones of most of the expedition. "Yes, yes, it would seem that it should be to you, who twice have saved her life and once have saved mine also."

Now I suppose that he saw on my face the joy which I could not conceal, for he added hastily: "Yet, Allan, years ago I swore on the Book before God that never with my will should my daughter marry an Englishman, even if he were a good Englishman. Also, just before we left the Colony, I swore again, in her presence and that of Hernan Pereira, that I would not give her to you, so I cannot break my oath, can I? If I did, the good God would be avenged upon me."

"Some might think that when I came here the good God was in the way of being avenged upon you for the keeping of that evil oath," I answered bitterly, glancing, in my turn, at the graves.

"Yes, they might, Allan," he replied without anger, for all his troubles had induced a reasonable frame of mind in him—for a while. "Yet, His ways are past finding out, are they not?"

Now my anger broke out, and, rising, I said:

"Do you mean, Mynheer Marais, that notwithstanding the love between us, which you know is true and deep, and notwithstanding that I alone have been able to drag both of you and the others out of the claws of death, I am never to marry Marie? Do you mean that she is to be given to a braggart who deserted her in her need?"

"And what if I do mean that, Allan?"

"This: although I am still young, as you know well I am a man who can think and act for himself. Also, I am your master here—I have cattle and guns and servants. Well, I will take Marie, and if any should try to stop me, I know how to protect myself and her."

This bold speech did not seem to surprise him in the least or to make him think the worse of me. He looked at me for a while, pulling his long beard in a meditative fashion, then answered:

"I dare say that at your age I should have played the same game, and it is true that you have things in your fist. But, much as she may love you, Marie would not go away with you and leave her father to starve."

"Then you can come with us as my father-in-law, Mynheer Marais. At any rate, it is certain that I will not go away and leave her here to starve."

Now I think that something which he saw in my eye showed him that I was in earnest. At least, he changed his tone and began to argue, almost to plead.

"Be reasonable, Allan," he said. "How can you marry Marie when there is no predicant to marry you? Surely, if you love her so much, you would not pour mud upon her name, even in this wilderness?"

"She might not think it mud," I replied. "Men and women have been married without the help of priests before now, by open declaration and public report, for instance, and their children held to be born in wedlock. I know that, for I have read of the law of marriage."

"It may be, Allan, though I hold no marriage good unless the holy words are said. But why do you not let me come to the end of my story?"

"Because I thought it was ended, Mynheer Marais."

"Not so, Allan. I told you that I had sworn that she should never marry you with my will. But when she is of age, which will be in some six months' time, my will counts no longer, seeing that then she is a free woman who can dispose of herself. Also I shall be clear of my oath, for no harm will come to my soul if that happens which I cannot help. Now are you satisfied?"

"I don't know," I answered doubtfully, for somehow all Marais's casuistry, which I thought contemptible, did not convince me that he was sincere. "I don't know," I repeated. "Much may chance in six months."

"Of course, Allan. For instance, Marie might change her mind and marry someone else."

"Or I might not be there to marry, *mynheer*. Accidents sometimes happen to men who are not wanted, especially in wild countries or, for the matter of that, to those who are."

"*Allemachte*! Allan, you do not mean that I—"

"No, *mynheer*," I interrupted; "but there are other people in the world besides yourself—Hernan Pereira, for example, if he lives. Still, I am not the only one concerned in this matter. There is Marie yonder. Shall I call her?"

He nodded, preferring probably that I should speak to her in his presence rather than alone.

So I called Marie, who was watching our talk somewhat anxiously while she went about her tasks. She came at once, a very different Marie to the starving girl of a while before, for although she was still thin and drawn, her youth and beauty were returning to her fast under the influences of good food and happiness.

"What is it, Allan?" she asked gently. I told her all, repeating our conversation and the arguments which had been used on either side word for word, as nearly as I could remember them.

"Is that right?" I asked of Marais when I had finished.

"It is right; you have a good memory," he answered.

"Very well. And now what have you to say, Marie?"

"I, dear Allan? Why, this: My life belongs to you, who have twice saved this body of mine from death, as my love and spirit belong to you. Therefore, I should have thought it no shame if I had been given to you here and now before the people, and afterwards married by a clergyman when we found one. But my father has sworn an oath which weighs upon his mind, and he has shown you that within six months—a short six months—that oath dies of itself, since, by the law, he can no longer control me. So, Allan, as I would not grieve him, or perhaps lead him to say and do what is foolish, I think it would be well that we should wait for those six months, if, on his part, he promises that he will then do nothing to prevent our marriage."

"*Ja, ja*, I promise that then I will do nothing to prevent your marriage," answered Marais eagerly, like one who has suddenly seen some loophole of escape from an impossible position, adding, as though to himself, "But God may do something to prevent it, for all that."

"We are every one of us in the hand of God," she replied in her sweet voice. "Allan, you hear, my father has promised?"

"Yes, Marie, he has promised—after a fashion," I replied gloomily, for somehow his words struck a chill through me.

"I have promised, Allan, and I will keep my promise to you, as I have kept my oath to God, attempting to work you no harm, and leaving all in His hands. But you, on your part, must promise also that, till she is of age, you will not take Marie as a wife—no, not if you were left alone together in the *veld*. You must be as people who are affianced to each other, no more."

So, having no choice, I promised, though with a heavy heart. Then, I suppose in order to make this solemn contract public, Marais called the surviving Boers, who were loitering near, and repeated to them the terms of the contract that we had made.

The men laughed and shrugged their shoulders. But Vrouw Prinsloo, I remember, said outright that she thought the business foolish, since if anyone had a right to Marie, I had, wherever I chose to take her. She added that, as for Hernan Pereira, he was a "sneak and a stinkcat," who had gone off to save his own life, and left them all to die. If *she* were Marie, should they meet again, she would greet him with a pailful of dirty water in the face, as she herself meant to do if she got the chance.

Vrouw Prinsloo, it will be observed, was a very outspoken woman and, I may add, an honest one.

So this contract was settled. I have set it out at length because of its importance in our story. But now I wish—ah! how I wish that I had insisted upon being married to Marie then and there. If I had done so, I think I should have carried my point, for I was the "master of many legions" in the shape of cattle, food and ammunition, and rather than risk a quarrel with me, the other Boers would have forced Marais to give way. But we were young and inexperienced; also it was fated otherwise. Who can question the decrees of Fate written immutably, perhaps long before we were born, in the everlasting book of human destinies?

Yet, when I had shaken off my first fears and doubts, my lot and Marie's were very happy, a perfect paradise, indeed, compared with what we had gone through during that bitter time of silence and separation. At any rate, we were acknowledged to be affianced by the little society in which we lived, including her father, and allowed to be as much alone together as we liked. This meant that we met at dawn only to separate at nightfall, for, having little or no artificial light, we went to rest with the sun, or shortly after it. Sweet, indeed, was that companionship of perfect trust and love; so sweet, that even after all these years I do not care to dwell upon the holy memory of those blessed months.

So soon as the surviving Boers began to recover by the help of my stores and medicines and the meat which I shot in plenty, of course great discussions arose as to our future plans. First it was suggested that we should trek to Lorenzo Marquez, and wait for a ship there to take us down to Natal, for none of them would hear of returning beggared to the Cape to tell the story of their failure and dreadful bereavements. I pointed out, however, that no ship might come for a long while, perhaps for one or two years, and that Lorenzo Marquez and its neighbourhood seemed to be a poisonous place to live in!

The next idea was that we should stop where we were, one which I rather welcomed, as I should have been glad to abide in peace with Marie until the six months of probation had gone by.

However, in the end this was rejected for many good reasons. Thus half a score of white people, of whom four were members of a single family, were certainly not strong enough to form a settlement, especially as the surrounding natives might become actively hostile at any moment. Again, the worst fever season was approaching, in which we should very possibly all be carried off. Further, we had no breeding cattle or horses, which would not live in this *veld*, and only the ammunition and goods that I had brought with me.

So it was clear that but one thing remained to be done, namely, to trek back to what is now the Transvaal territory, or, better still, to Natal, for this route would enable us to avoid the worst of the mountains. There we might join some other party of the emigrant Boers—for choice, that of Retief, of whose arrival over the Drakensberg I was able to tell them.

That point settled, we made our preparations. To begin with, I had only enough oxen for two wagons, whereas, even if we abandoned the rest of them, we must take at least four. Therefore, through my Kaffirs, I opened negotiations with the surrounding natives, who, when they heard that I was not a Boer and was prepared to pay for what I bought, soon expressed a willingness to trade. Indeed, very shortly we had quite a market established, to which cattle were brought that I bargained for and purchased, giving cloth, knives, hoes, and the usual Kaffir goods in payment for the same.

Also, they brought *mealies* and other corn; and oh! the delight with which those poor people, who for months and months had existed upon nothing but flesh-meat, ate of this farinaceous food. Never shall I forget seeing Marie and the surviving children partake of their first meal of porridge, and washing the sticky stuff down with draughts of fresh, sugared milk, for with the oxen I had succeeded in obtaining two good cows. It is enough to say that this change of diet soon completely re-established their health, and made Marie more beautiful than she had ever been before.

Having got the oxen, the next thing was to break them to the yoke; for, although docile creatures enough, they had never even seen a wagon. This proved a long and difficult process, involving many trial trips; moreover, the selected wagons, one of which had belonged to Pereira, must be mended with very insufficient tools and without the help of a forge. Indeed, had it not chanced that Hans, the Hottentot, had worked for a wagon-maker at some indefinite period of his career, I do not think that we could have managed the job at all.

It was while we were busy with these tasks that some news arrived which was unpleasing enough to everyone, except perhaps to Henri Marais. I was engaged on a certain evening in trying to make sixteen of the Kaffir cattle pull together in the yoke, instead of tying themselves into a double knot and over-setting the wagon, when Hans, who was helping me, suddenly called out:

"Look! *baas*, here comes one of my brothers," or, in other words, a Hottentot.

Following the line of his hand, I saw a thin and wretched creature, clad only in some rags and the remains of a big hat with the crown out, staggering towards us between the trees.

"Why!" exclaimed Marie in a startled voice, for, as usual, she was at my side, "it is Klaus, one of my cousin Hernan's after-riders."

"So long as it is not your cousin Hernan himself, I do not care," I said.

Presently the poor, starved "Totty" arrived, and throwing himself down, begged for food. A cold shoulder of buck was given to him, which he devoured, holding it in both hands and tearing off great lumps of flesh with his teeth like a wild beast.

When at last he was satisfied, Marais, who had come up with the other Boers, asked him whence he came and what was his news of his master.

"Out of the bush," he answered, "and my news of the *baas* is that he is dead. At least, I left him so ill that I suppose he must be dead by now."

"Why did you leave him if he was ill?" asked Marais.

"Because he told me to, *baas*, that I might find help, for we were starving, having fired our last bullet."

"Is he alone, then?"

"Yes, yes, except for the wild beasts and the vultures. A lion ate the other man, his servant, a long while ago."

"How far is he off?" asked Marais again.

"Oh, *baas*, about five hours' journey on horseback on a good road." (This would be some thirty-five miles.)

Then he told this story: Pereira with his two Hottentot servants, he mounted and they on foot, had traversed about a hundred miles of rough country in safety, when at night a lion killed and carried off one of the Hottentots, and frightened away the horse, which was never seen again. Pereira and Klaus proceeded on foot till they came to a great river, on the banks of which they met some Kaffirs, who appear to have been Zulus on outpost duty. These men demanded their guns and ammunition to take to their king, and, on Pereira refusing to give them up, said that they would kill them both in the morning after they had made him instruct them in the use of the guns by beating him with sticks.

In the night a storm came on, under cover of which Pereira and Klaus escaped. As they dared not go forward for fear lest they should fall into the hands of the Zulus, they fled back northwards, running all night, only to find in the morning that they had lost their way in the bush. This had happened nearly a month before—or, at any rate, Klaus thought so, for no doubt the days went very slowly—during which time they had wandered about, trying to shape some sort of course by the sun with the object of returning to the camp. They met no man, black or white, and supported themselves upon game, which they shot and ate raw or sun-dried, till at length all their powder was done and they threw away their heavy *roers*, which they could no longer carry.

It was at this juncture that from the top of a tall tree Klaus saw a certain *koppie* a long way off, which he recognised as being within fifteen miles or so of Marais's camp. By now they were starving, only Klaus was the stronger of the two, for he found and devoured some carrion, a dead hyena I think it was. Pereira also tried to eat this horrible food, but, not having the stomach of a Hottentot, the first mouthful of it made him dreadfully ill. They sought shelter in a cave on the bank of a stream, where grew water-cresses and other herbs, such as wild asparagus. Here it was that Pereira told Klaus to try to make his way back to the camp, and, should he find anyone alive there, to bring him succour.

So Klaus went, taking the remaining leg of the hyena with him, and on the afternoon of the second day arrived as has been told.

CHAPTER 10

Vrouw Prinsloo Speaks Her Mind

Now, when the Hottentot's story was finished a discussion arose. Marais said that someone must go to see whether his nephew still lived, to which the other Boers replied "*Ja*" in an indifferent voice. Then the Vrouw Prinsloo took up her parable.

She remarked, as she had done before, that in her judgment Hernan Pereira was "a stinkcat and a sneak," who had tried to desert them in their trouble, and by the judgment of a just God had got into trouble himself. Personally, she wished that the lion had taken him instead of the worthy Hottentot, although it gave her a higher opinion of lions to conclude that it had not done so, because if it did it thought it would have been poisoned. Well, her view was that it would be just as well to let that traitor lie upon the bed which he had made. Moreover, doubtless by now he was dead, so what was the good of bothering about him?

These sentiments appeared to appeal to the Boers, for they remarked: "*Ja*, what is the good?"

"Is it right," asked Marais, "to abandon a comrade in misfortune, one of our own blood?"

"*Mein Gott!*" replied Vrouw Prinsloo; "he is no blood of mine, the evil-odoured Portuguese. But I admit he is of yours, Heer Marais, being your sister's son, so it is evident that you should be the one to go to seek after him."

"That seems to be so, Vrouw Prinsloo," said Marais in his meditative manner; "yet I must remember that I have Marie to look after."

"Ach! and so had he, too, until he remembered his own skin, and went off with the only horse and all the powder, leaving her and the rest of us to starve. Well, you won't go, and Prinsloo won't go, nor my boy either, for I'll see to that; so Meyer must go."

"*Nein, nein,* good *vrouw,*" answered Meyer, "I have those children that are left to me to consider."

"Then," exclaimed Vrouw Prinsloo triumphantly, "nobody will go, so let us forget this stinkcat, as he forgot us."

"Does it seem right," asked Marais again, "that a Christian man should be left to starve in the wilderness?" and he looked at me.

"Tell me, Heer Marais," I remarked, answering the look, "why should I of all people go to look for the Heer Pereira, one who has not dealt too well with me?"

"I do not know, Allan. Yet the Book tells us to turn the other cheek and to forget injuries. Still, it is for you to judge, remembering that we must answer for all things at the last day, and not for me. I only know that were I your age and not burdened with a daughter to watch over, *I* should go."

"Why should you talk to me thus?" I asked with indignation. "Why do you not go yourself, seeing that I am quite ready to look after Marie?" (Here the Vrouw Prinsloo and the other Boers tittered.) "And why do you not address your remarks to these other *heeren* instead of to me, seeing that they are the friends and trek-companions of your nephew?"

At this point the male Prinsloos and Meyer found that they had business elsewhere.

"It is for you to judge, yet remember, Allan, that it is an awful thing to appear before our Maker with the blood of a fellow creature upon our hands. But if you and these other hard-hearted men will not go, I at my age, and weak as I am with all that I have suffered, will go myself."

"Good," said Vrouw Prinsloo; "that is the best way out of it. You will soon get sick of the journey, Heer Marais, and we shall see no more of the stinkcat."

Marais rose in a resigned fashion, for he never deigned to argue with Vrouw Prinsloo, who was too many for him, and said:

"Farewell, Marie. If I do not return, you will remember my wishes, and my will may be found between the first leaves of our Holy Book. Get up, Klaus, and guide me to your master," and he administered a somewhat vicious kick to the gorged and prostrate Hottentot.

Now Marie, who all this while had stood silent, touched me on the shoulder and said:

"Allan, is it well that my father should go alone? Will you not accompany him?"

"Of course," I answered cheerfully; "on such a business there should be two, and some Kaffirs also to carry the man, if he still lives."

Now for the end of the story. As the Hottentot Klaus was too exhausted to move that night, it was arranged that we should start at dawn. Accordingly, I rose before the light, and was just finishing my breakfast when Marie appeared at the wagon in which I slept. I got up to greet her, and, there being no one in sight, we kissed each other several times.

"Have done, my heart," she said, pushing me away. "I come to you from my father, who is sick in his stomach and would see you."

"Which means that I shall have to go after your cousin alone," I replied with indignant emphasis.

She shook her head, and led me to the little shanty in which she slept. Here by the growing light, that entered through the doorway for it had no window, I perceived Marais seated upon a wooden stool with his hands pressed on his middle and groaning.

"Good morning, Allan," he said in a melancholy voice; "I am ill, very ill, something that I have eaten perhaps, or a chill in the stomach, such as often precedes fever or dysentery."

"Perhaps you will get better as you walk, *mynheer*," I suggested, for, to tell the truth, I misdoubted me of this chill, and knew that he had eaten nothing but what was quite wholesome.

"Walk! God alone knows how I can walk with something gripping my inside like a wagon-maker's vice. Yet I will try, for it is impossible to leave that poor Hernan to die alone; and if I do not go to seek him, it seems that no one else will."

"Why should not some of my Kaffirs go with Klaus?" I asked.

"Allan," he replied solemnly, "if you were dying in a cave far from help, would you think well of those who sent raw Kaffirs to succour you when they might have come themselves, Kaffirs who certainly would let you die and return with some false story?"

"I don't know what I should think, Heer Marais. But I do know that if *I* were in that cave and Pereira were in this camp, neither would he come himself, nor so much as send a savage to save *me*."

"It may be so, Allan. But even if another's heart is black, should yours be black also? Oh! I will come, though it be to my death," and, rising from the stool with the most dreadful groan, he began to divest himself of the tattered blanket in which he was wrapped up.

"Oh! Allan, my father must not go; it will kill him," exclaimed Marie, who took a more serious view of his case than I did.

"Very well, if you think so," I answered. "And now, as it is time for me to be starting, good-bye."

"You have a good heart, Allan," said Marais, sinking back upon his stool and resuming his blanket, while Marie looked despairingly first at one and then at the other of us.

Half an hour later I was on the road in the very worst of tempers. "Mind what you are about," called Vrouw Prinsloo after me. "It is not lucky to save an enemy, and if I know anything of that stinkcat, he will bite your finger badly by way of gratitude. Bah! lad, if I were you I should just camp for a few days in the bush, and then come back and say that I could find nothing of Pereira except the dead hyenas that had been poisoned by eating him. Good luck to you all the same, Allan; may I find such a friend in need. It seems to me that you were born to help others."

Beside the Hottentot Klaus, my companions on this unwelcome journey were three of the Zulu Kaffirs, for Hans I was obliged to leave in charge of my cattle and goods with the other men. Also, I took a pack-ox, an active beast that I had been training to carry loads and, if necessary a man, although as yet it was not very well broken.

All that day we marched over extremely rough country, till at last darkness found us in a mountainous *kloof*, where we slept, surrounded by watch-fires because of the lions. Next morning at the first light we moved on again, and about ten o'clock waded through a stream to a little natural cave, where Klaus said he had left his master. This cave seemed extremely silent, and, as I hesitated for a moment at its mouth, the thought crossed my mind that if Pereira were still there, he must be dead. Indeed, do what I would to suppress it, with that reflection came a certain feeling of relief and even of pleasure. For well I knew that Pereira alive was more dangerous to me than all the wild men and beasts in Africa put together. Thrusting back this unworthy sentiment as best I could, I entered the cave alone, for the natives, who dread the defilement of the touch of a corpse, lingered outside.

It was but a shallow cavity washed out of the overhanging rock by the action of water; and as soon as my eyes grew accustomed to its gloom, I saw that at the end of it lay a man. So still did he lie, that now I was almost certain that his troubles were over. I went up to him and touched his face, which was cold and clammy, and then, quite convinced, turned to leave the place, which, I thought, if a few rocks were piled in the mouth of it, would make an excellent sepulchre.

Just as I stepped out into the sunlight, and was about to call to the men to collect the rocks, however, I thought that I heard a very faint groan behind me, which at the moment I set down to imagination. Still, I returned, though I did not much like the job, knelt down by the figure, and waited with my hand over its heart. For five minutes or more I stayed here, and then, quite convinced, was about to leave again when, for the second time, I heard that faint groan. Pereira was not dead, but only on the extreme brink of death!

I ran to the entrance of the cave, calling the Kaffirs, and together we carried him out into the sunlight. He was an awful spectacle, mere bone with yellow skin stretched over it, and covered with filth and clotted blood from some hurt. I had brandy with me, of which I poured a little down his throat, whereon his heart began to beat feebly. Then we made some soup, and poured that down his throat with more brandy, and the end of it was he came to life again.

For three days did I doctor that man, and really I believe that if at any time during those days I had relaxed my attentions even for a couple of hours, he would have slipped through my fingers, for at this business Klaus and the Kaffirs were no good at all. But I pulled him round, and on the third morning he came to his senses. For a long while he stared at me, for I had laid him in the mouth of the cave, where the light was good, although the overhanging rocks protected him from the sun. Then he said:

"*Allemachte!* you remind me of someone, young man. I know. It is of that damned English boy who beat me at the goose shooting, and made me quarrel with Oom (uncle) Retief, the jackanapes that Marie was so fond of. Well, whoever you are, you can't be he, thank God."

"You are mistaken, Heer Pereira," I answered. "I am that same damned young English jackanapes, Allan Quatermain by name, who beat you at shooting. But if you take my advice, you will thank God for something else, namely, that your life has been saved."

"Who saved it?" he asked.

"If you want to know, I did; I have been nursing you these three days."

"You, Allan Quatermain! Now, that is strange, for certainly I would not have saved yours," and he laughed a little, then turned over and went to sleep.

From that time forward his recovery was rapid, and two days later we began our journey back to Marais's camp, the convalescent Pereira being carried in a litter by the four natives. It was a task at which they grumbled a good deal, for the load was heavy over rough ground, and whenever they stumbled or shook him he cursed at them. So much did he curse, indeed, that at length one of the Zulus, a man with a rough temper, said that if it were not for the *Inkoos*, meaning myself, he would put his *assegai* through him, and let the vultures carry him. After this Pereira grew much more polite. When the bearers became exhausted we set him on the pack-ox, which two of us led, while the other two supported him on either side. It was in this fashion that at last we arrived at the camp one evening.

Here the Vrouw Prinsloo was the first to greet us. We found her standing in the game path which we were following, quite a quarter of a mile from the wagons, with her hands set upon her broad hips and her feet apart. Her attitude was so defiant, and had about it such an air of premeditation, that I cannot help thinking she had got wind of our return, perhaps from having seen the smoke of our last fires, and was watching for us. Also, her greeting was warm.

"Ah! here you come, Hernan Pereira," she cried, "riding on an ox, while better men walk. Well, now, I want a chat with you. How came it that you went off in the night, taking the only horse and all the powder?"

"I went to get help for you," he replied sulkily.

"Did you, did you, indeed! Well, it seems that it was you who wanted the help, after all. What do you mean to pay the Heer Allan Quatermain for saving your life, for I am sure he has done so? You have got no goods left, although you were always boasting about your riches; they are now at the bottom of a river, so it will have to be in love and service."

He muttered something about my wanting no payment for a Christian act.

"No, he wants no payment, Hernan Pereira, he is one of the true sort, but you'll pay him all the same and in bad coin if you get the chance. Oh! I have come out to tell you what I think of you. You are a stinkcat; do you hear that? A thing that no dog would bite if he could help it! You are a traitor also. You brought us to this cursed country, where you said your relatives would give us wealth and land, and then, after famine and fever attacked us, you rode away, and left us to die to save your own dirty skin. And now you come back here for help, saved by him whom you cheated in the Goose Kloof, by him whose true love you have tried to steal. Oh, *mein Gott!* why does the Almighty leave such fellows alive, while so many that are good and honest and innocent lie beneath the soil because of stinkcats like you?"

So she went on, striding at the side of the pack-ox, and reviling Pereira in a ceaseless stream of language, until at length he thrust his thumbs into his ears and glared at her in speechless wrath.

Thus it was that at last we arrived in the camp, where, having seen us coming, all the Boers were gathered. They are not a particularly humorous people, but this spectacle of the advance of Pereira seated on the pack-ox, a steed that is becoming to few riders, with the furious and portly Vrouw Prinsloo striding at his side and shrieking abuse at him, caused them to burst into laughter. Then Pereira's temper gave out, and he became even more abusive than Vrouw Prinsloo.

"Is this the way you receive me, you *veld*-hogs, you common Boers, who are not fit to mix with a man of position and learning like myself?" he began.

"Then in God's name why do you mix with us, Hernan Pereira?" asked the saturnine Meyer, thrusting his face forward till the Newgate fringe he wore by way of a beard literally seemed to curl with wrath. "When we were hungry you did not wish it, for you slunk away and left us, taking all the powder. But now that we are full again, thanks to the little Englishman, and you are hungry, you come back. Well, if I had my way I would give you a gun and six days' rations, and turn you out to shift for yourself."

"Don't be afraid, Jan Meyer," shouted Pereira from the back of the pack-ox. "As soon as I am strong enough I will leave you in charge of your English captain here"—and he pointed to me—"and go to tell our people what sort of folk you are."

"That is good news," interrupted Prinsloo, a stolid old Boer, who stood by puffing at his pipe. "Get well, get well as soon as you can, Hernan Pereira."

It was at this juncture that Marais arrived, accompanied by Marie. Where he came from I do not know, but I think he must have been keeping in the background on purpose to see what kind of a reception Pereira would meet with.

"Silence, brothers," he said. "Is this the way you greet my nephew, who has returned from the gate of death, when you should be on your knees thanking God for his deliverance?"

"Then go on your knees and thank Him yourself, Henri Marais," screamed the irrepressible Vrouw Prinsloo. "I give thanks for the safe return of Allan here, though it is true they would be warmer if he had left this stinkcat behind him. *Allemachte!* Henri Marais, why do you make so much of this Portuguese fellow? Has he bewitched you? Or is it because he is your sister's son, or because you want to force Marie there to marry him? Or is it, perhaps, that he knows of something bad in your past life, and you have to bribe him to keep his mouth shut?"

Now, whether this last unpleasant suggestion was a mere random arrow drawn from Vrouw Prinsloo's well-stored quiver, or whether the *vrouw* had got hold of the tail-end of some long-buried truth, I do not know. Of course, however, the latter explanation is possible. Many men have done things in their youth which they do not wish to see dug up in their age; and Pereira may have learned a family secret of the kind from his mother.

At any rate, the effect of the old lady's words upon Marais was quite remarkable. Suddenly he went into one of his violent and constitutional rages. He cursed Vrouw Prinsloo. He cursed everybody else, assuring them severally and collectively that Heaven would come even with them. He said there was a plot against him and his nephew, and that I was at the bottom of it, I who had made his daughter fond of my ugly little face. So furious were his words, whereof there were many more which I have forgotten, that at length Marie began to cry and ran away. Presently, too, the Boers strolled off, shrugging their shoulders, one of them saying audibly that Marais had gone quite mad at last, as he always thought he would.

Then Marais followed them, throwing up his arms and still cursing as he went, and, slipping over the tail of the pack-ox, Pereira followed him. So the Vrouw Prinsloo and I were left alone, for the coloured men had departed, as they always do when white people begin to quarrel.

"There, Allan, my boy," said the *vrouw* in triumph, "I have found the sore place on the mule's back, and didn't I make him squeal and kick, although on most days of the week he seems to be such a good and quiet mule—at any rate, of late."

"I dare say you did, *vrouw*," I said wrathfully, "but I wish you would leave Mynheer Marais's sore places alone, seeing that if the squeals are for you, the kicks are for me."

"What does that matter, Allan?" she asked. "He always was your enemy, so that it is just as well you should see his heels when you are out of reach of them. My poor boy, I think you will have a bad time of it between the stinkcat and the mule, although you have done so much for both of them. Well, there is one thing—Marie has a true heart. She will never marry any man except yourself, Allan—even if you are not here to marry," she added by an afterthought.

The old lady paused a little, staring at the ground. Then she looked up and said:

"Allan, my dear" (for she was really fond of me, and called me thus at times), "you didn't take the advice I gave you, namely, to look for Pereira and not to find him. Well, I will give you some more, which you *will* take if you are wise."

"What is it?" I asked doubtfully; for, although she was upright enough in her own way, the Vrouw Prinsloo could bring herself to look at things in strange lights. Like many other women, she judged of moral codes by the impulses of her heart, and was quite prepared to stretch them to suit circumstances or to gain an end which she considered good in itself.

"Just this, lad. Do you make a two days' march with Marie into the bush. I want a little change, so I will come, too, and marry you there; for I have got a prayer-book, and can spell out the service if we go through it once or twice first."

Now, the vision of Marie and myself being married by the Vrouw Prinsloo in the vast and untrodden *veld*, although attractive, was so absurd that I laughed.

"Why do you laugh, Allan? Anyone can marry people if there is no one else there; indeed, I believe that they can marry themselves."

"I dare say," I answered, not wishing to enter into a legal argument with the *vrouw*. "But you see, *tante*, I solemnly promised her father that I would not marry her until she was of age, and if I broke my word I should not be an honest man."

"An honest man!" she exclaimed with the utmost contempt; "an honest man! Well, are Marais and Hernan Pereira honest men? Why do you not cut your stick the same length as theirs, Allan Quatermain? I tell you that your *verdomde* honesty will be your ruin. You remember my words later on," and she marched off in high dudgeon.

When she had gone I went to my wagons, where Hans was waiting for me with a detailed and interminable report of everything that had happened in my absence. Glad was I to find that, except for the death of one sickly ox, nothing had gone wrong. When at length he had ended his long story, I ate some food which Marie sent over for me ready cooked, for I was too tired to join any of the Boers that night. Just as I had finished my meal and was thinking of turning in, Marie herself appeared within the circle of the camp-fire's light. I sprang up and ran to her, saying that I had not expected to see her that evening, and did not like to come to the house.

"No," she answered, drawing me back into the shadows, "I understand. My father seems very much upset, almost mad, indeed. If the Vrouw Prinsloo's tongue had been a snake's fang, it could not have stung him worse."

"And where is Pereira?" I asked.

"Oh! my cousin sleeps in the other room. He is weak and worn out. All the same, Allan, he wanted to kiss me. So I told him at once how matters stood between you and me, and that we were to be married in six months."

"What did he say to that?" I asked.

"He turned to my father and said: 'Is this true, my uncle?' And my father answered: 'Yes, that is the best bargain I could make with the Englishman, seeing that you were not here to make a better.'"

"And what happened then, Marie?"

"Oh, then Hernan thought a while. At last he looked up and said: 'I understand. Things have gone badly. I acted for the best, who went away to try to find help for all of you. I failed. Meanwhile the Englishman came and saved you. Afterwards he saved me also. Uncle, in all this I see God's hand; had it not been for this Allan none of us would be alive. Yes, God used him that we might be kept alive. Well, he has promised that he will not marry Marie for six months. And you know, my uncle, that some of these English are great fools; they keep their promises even to their own loss. Now, in six months much may happen; who knows what will happen?'"

"Were you present when you heard all this, Marie?" I asked.

"No, Allan; I was the other side of the reed partition. But at those words I entered and said: 'My father and Cousin Hernan, please understand that there is one thing which will never happen.'

"'What is that?' asked my cousin.

"'It will never happen that I shall marry you, Hernan,' I replied.

"'Who knows, Marie, who knows?' he said.

"'I do, Hernan,' I answered. 'Even if Allan were to die to-morrow, I would not marry you, either then or twenty years hence. I am glad that he has saved your life, but henceforth we are cousins, nothing more.'

"'You hear what the girl tells us,' said my father; 'why do you not give up the business? What is the use of kicking against the pricks?'

"'If one wears stout boots and kicks hard enough, the pricks give way,' said Hernan. 'Six months is a long time, my uncle.'

"'It may be so, cousin,' I said; 'but remember that neither six months nor six years, nor six thousand years, are long enough to make me marry any man except Allan Quatermain, who has just rescued you from death. Do you understand?'

"'Yes,' he replied, 'I understand that you will not marry me. Only then I promise that you shall not marry either Allan Quatermain or any other man.'

"'God will decide that,' I answered, and came away, leaving him and my father together. And now, Allan, tell me all that has happened since we parted."

So I told her everything, including the Vrouw Prinsloo's advice.

"Of course, Allan, you were quite right," she remarked when I had finished; "but I am not sure that the Vrouw Prinsloo was not also right in her own fashion. I am afraid of my cousin Hernan, who holds my father in his hand—fast, fast. Still, we have promised, and must keep our word."

CHAPTER 11

The Shot in the Kloof

I think it was about three weeks after these events that we began our southward trek. On the morning subsequent to our arrival at Marais's camp, Pereira came up to me when several people were present, and, taking my hand, thanked me in a loud voice for having saved his life. Thenceforward, he declared, I should be dearer to him than a brother, for was there not a blood bond between us?

I answered I did not think any such bond existed; indeed, I was not sure what it meant. I had done my duty by him, neither less nor more, and there was nothing further to be said.

It turned out, however, that there was a great deal further to be said, since Pereira desired to borrow money, or, rather, goods, from me. He explained that owing to the prejudices of the vulgar Boers who remained alive in that camp, and especially of the scandalous-tongued Vrouw Prinsloo, both he and his uncle had come to the conclusion that it would be wise for him to remove himself as soon as possible. Therefore he proposed to trek away alone.

I answered that I should have thought he had done enough solitary travelling in this *veld*, seeing how his last expedition had ended. He replied that he had, indeed, but everyone here was so bitter against him that no choice was left. Then he added with an outburst of truth:

"*Allemachte!* Mynheer Quatermain, do you suppose that it is pleasant for me to see you making love all day to the maid who was my betrothed, and to see her paying back the love with her eyes? Yes, and doubtless with her lips, too, from all I hear."

"You could leave her whom you called your betrothed, but who never was betrothed to anyone but me with her own will, to starve in the *veld*, *mynheer*. Why, then, should you be angry because I picked up that which you threw away, that, too, which was always my own and not yours? Had it not been for me, there would now be no maid left for us to quarrel over, as, had it not been for me, there would be no man left for me to quarrel with about the maid."

"Are you God, then, Englishman, that you dispose of the lives of men and women at your will? It was He Who saved us, not you."

"He may have saved you, but it was through me. I carried out the rescue of these poor people whom you deserted, and I nursed you back to life."

"I did not desert them; I went to get help for them."

"Taking all the powder and the only horse with you! Well, that is done with, and now you want to borrow goods to pay for cattle—from me, whom you hate. You are not proud, Mynheer Pereira, when you have an end to serve, whatever that end may be," and I looked at him. My instinct warned me against this false and treacherous man, who, I felt, was even then plotting in his heart to bring some evil upon me.

"No, I am not proud. Why should I be, seeing that I mean to repay you twice over for anything which you may lend me now?"

I reflected a while. Certainly our journey to Natal would be pleasanter if Pereira were not of the company. Also, if he went with us, I was sure that before we came to the end of that trek, one or other of us would leave his bones on the road. In short, not to put too fine a point on it, I feared lest in this way or in that he would bring me to my death in order that he might possess himself of Marie. We were in a wild country, with few witnesses and no law courts, where such deeds might be done again and again and the doer never called to account for lack of evidence and judges.

So I made up my mind to fall in with his wishes, and we began to bargain. The end of it was that I advanced him enough of my remaining goods to buy the cattle he required from the surrounding natives. It was no great quantity, after all, seeing that in this uncivilised place an ox could be purchased for a few strings of beads or a cheap knife. Further, I sold him a few of the beasts that I had broken, a gun, some ammunition and certain other necessaries, for all of which things he gave me a note of hand written in my pocket-book. Indeed, I did more; for as none of the Boers would help him I assisted Pereira to break in the cattle he bought, and even consented when he asked me to give him the services of two of the Zulus whom I had hired.

All these preparations took a long while. If I remember right, twelve more days had gone by before Pereira finally trekked off from Marais's camp, by which time he was quite well and strong again.

We all assembled to see the start, and Marais offered up a prayer for his nephew's safe journey and our happy meeting again in Natal at the laager of Retief, which was to be our rendezvous, if that leader were still in Natal. No one else joined in the prayer. Only Vrouw Prinsloo audibly added another of her own. It was to the effect that he might not come back a second time, and that she might never see his face again, either at Retief's laager or anywhere else, if it would please the good Lord so to arrange matters.

The Boers tittered; even the Meyer children tittered, for by this time the hatred of the Vrouw Prinsloo for Hernan Pereira was the joke of the place. But Pereira himself pretended not to hear, said good-bye to us all affectionately, adding a special petition for the Vrouw Prinsloo, and off we went.

I say "we went" because with my usual luck, to help him with the half-broken oxen, I was commandeered to accompany this man to his first outspan, a place with good water about twelve miles from the camp, where he proposed to remain for the night.

Now, as we started about ten o'clock in the morning and the *veld* was fairly level, I expected that we should reach this outspan by three or four in the afternoon, which would give me time to walk back before sunset. In fact, however, so many accidents happened of one sort or another, both to the wagon itself, of which the woodwork had shrunk with long standing in the sun, and to the cattle, which, being unused to the yoke, tied themselves in a double knot upon every opportunity, that we only arrived there at the approach of night.

The last mile of that trek was through a narrow gorge cut out by water in the native rock. Here trees grew sparsely, also great ferns, but the bottom of the gorge, along which game were accustomed to travel, was smooth enough for wagons, save for a few fallen boulders, which it was necessary to avoid.

When at length we reached the outspan I asked the Hottentot, Klaus, who was assisting me to drive the team, where his master was, for I could not see him anywhere. He answered that he had gone back down the *kloof* to look for something that had fallen from the wagon, a bolt I think he said.

"Very good," I replied. "Then tell him, if we do not meet, that I have returned to the camp."

As I set out the sun was sinking below the horizon, but this did not trouble me overmuch, as I had a rifle with me, that same light rifle with which I had shot the geese in the great match. Also I knew that the moon, being full, would be up presently.

The sun sank, and the *kloof* was plunged in gloom. The place seemed

317

eerie and lonesome, and suddenly I grew afraid. I began to wonder where Pereira was, and what he might be doing. I even thought of turning back and finding some way round, only having explored all this district pretty thoroughly in my various shooting expeditions from the camp, I knew there was no practicable path across those hills. So I went on with my rifle at full cock, whistling to keep up my courage, which, of course, in the circumstances was a foolish thing to do. It occurred to me at the time that it was foolish, but, in truth, I would not give way to the dark suspicions which crossed my mind. Doubtless by now Pereira had passed me and reached the outspan.

The moon began to shine—that wonderful African moon, which turns night to day—throwing a network of long, black shadows of trees and rocks across the game track I was following. Right ahead of me was a particularly dark patch of this shadow, caused by a projecting wall of cliff, and beyond it an equally bright patch of moonlight. Somehow I misdoubted me of that stretch of gloom, for although, of course, I could see nothing there, my quick ear caught the sound of movements.

I halted for a moment. Then, reflecting that these were doubtless caused by some night-walking creature, which, even should it chance to be dangerous, would flee at the approach of man, I plunged into it boldly. As I emerged at the other end—the shadow was eighteen or twenty paces long—it occurred to me that if any enemy were lurking there, I should be an easy target as I entered the line of clear light. So, almost instinctively, for I do not remember that I reasoned the thing out, after my first two steps forward in the light I gave a little spring to the left, where there was still shadow, although it was not deep. Well was it for me that I did so, for at that moment I felt something touch my cheek and heard the loud report of a gun immediately behind me.

Now, the wisest course would have been for me to run before whoever had fired found time to reload. But a kind of fury seized me, and run I would not. On the contrary, I turned with a shout, and charged back into the shadow. Something heard me coming, something fled in front of me. In a few seconds we were out into the moonlight beyond, and, as I expected, I saw that this something was a man—Pereira!

He halted and wheeled round, lifting the stock of his gun, club fashion.

"Thank God! it is you, Heer Allan," he said; "I thought you were a tiger."

"Then it is your last thought, murderer," I answered, raising my rifle.

"Don't shoot," he said. "Would you have my blood upon you? Why do you want to kill me?"

"Why did you try to kill me?" I answered, covering him.

"I try to kill you! Are you mad? Listen, for your own sake. I sat down on the bank yonder waiting for the moon, and, being tired, fell asleep. Then I woke up with a start, and, thinking from the sounds that a tiger was after me, fired to scare it. *Allemachte!* man, if I had aimed at you, could I have missed at that distance?"

"You did not quite miss, and had I not stepped to the left, you would have blown my head off. Say your prayers, you dog!"

"Allan Quatermain," he exclaimed with desperate energy, "you think I lie, who speak the truth. Kill me if you will, only then remember that you will hang for it. We court one woman, that is known, and who will believe this story of yours that I tried to shoot you? Soon the Kaffirs will come to look for me, probably they are starting already, and will find my body with your bullet in my heart. Then they will take it back to Marais's camp, and I say—who will believe your story?"

"Some, I think, murderer," but as I spoke the words a chill of fear struck me. It was true, I could prove nothing, having no witnesses, and henceforward I should be a Cain among the Boers, one who had slain a man for jealousy. His gun was empty; yes, but it might be said that I had fired it after his death. And as for the graze upon my cheek—why, a twig might have caused it. What should I do, then? Drive him before me to the camp, and tell this tale? Even then it would be but my word against his. No, he had me in a forked stick. I must let him go, and trust that Heaven would avenge his crime, since I could not. Moreover, by now my first rage was cooling, and to execute a man thus—

"Hernan Pereira," I said, "you are a liar and a coward. You tried to butcher me because Marie loves me and hates you, and you want to force her to marry you. Yet I cannot shoot you down in cold blood as you deserve. I leave it to God to punish you, as, soon or late, He will, here or hereafter; you who thought to slaughter me and trust to the hyenas to hide your crime, as they would have done before morning. Get you gone before I change my mind, and be swift."

Without another word he turned and ran swiftly as a buck, leaping from side to side as he ran, to disturb my aim in case I should shoot.

When he was a hundred yards away or more I, too, turned and ran, never feeling safe till I knew there was a mile of ground between us.

It was past ten o'clock that night when I got back to the camp, where I found Hans the Hottentot about to start to look for me, with two of the Zulus, and told him that I had been detained by accidents to the wagon. The Vrouw Prinsloo was still up also, waiting to hear of my arrival.

"What was the accident, Allan?" she asked. "It looks as though there had been a bullet in it," and she pointed to the bloody smear upon my cheek.

I nodded.

"Pereira's?" she asked again.

I nodded a second time.

"Did you kill him?"

"No; I let him go. It would have been said that I murdered him," and I told her what had happened.

"*Ja*, Allan," she remarked when I had finished. "I think you were wise, for you could have proved nothing. But oh! for what fate, I wonder, is God Almighty saving up that stinkcat. Well, I will go and tell Marie that you are back safe, for her father won't let her out of the hut so late; but nothing more unless you wish it."

"No, *tante*; I think nothing more, at any rate at present."

Here I may state, however, that within a few days Marie and everyone else in the camp knew the story in detail, except perhaps Marais, to whom no one spoke of his nephew. Evidently Vrouw Prinsloo had found herself unable to keep secret such an example of the villainy of her aversion, Pereira. So she told her daughter, who told the others quickly enough, though I gathered that some of them set down what had happened to accident. Bad as they knew Pereira to be, they could not believe that he was guilty of so black a crime.

About a week later the rest of us started from Marais's camp, a place that, notwithstanding the sadness of many of its associations, I confess I left with some regret. The trek before us, although not so very long, was of an extremely perilous nature. We had to pass through about two hundred miles of country of which all we knew was that its inhabitants were the Amatonga and other savage tribes. Here I should explain that after much discussion we had abandoned the idea of retracing the route followed by Marais on his ill-fated journey towards Delagoa.

Had we taken this it would have involved our crossing the terrible Lobombo Mountains, over which it was doubtful whether our light cattle could drag the wagons. Moreover, the country beyond the mountains was said to be very bare of game and also of Kaffirs, so that food might be lacking. On the other hand, if we kept to the east of the mountains the *veld* through which we must pass was thickly populated, which meant that in all probability we could buy grain.

What finally decided us to adopt this route, however, was that here in these warm, low-lying lands there would be grass for the oxen. Indeed, now, at the beginning of spring, in this part of Africa it was already pushing. Even if it were not, the beasts could live upon what herbage remained over from last summer and on the leaves of trees, neither of which in this winter *veld* ever become quite lifeless, whereas on the sere and fire-swept plains beyond the mountains they might find nothing at all. So we determined to risk the savages and the lions which followed the game into these hot districts, especially as it was not yet the fever season or that of the heavy rains, so that the rivers would be fordable.

I do not propose to set out our adventures in detail, for these would be too long. Until the great one of which I shall have to tell presently, they were of an annoying rather than of a serious nature. Travelling as we did, between the mountains and the sea, we could not well lose our way, especially as my Zulus had passed through that country; and when their knowledge failed us, we generally managed to secure the services of local guides. The roads, however, or rather the game tracks and Kaffir paths which we followed, were terrible, for with the single exception of that of Pereira for part of the distance, no wagon had ever gone over them before. Indeed, a little later in the year they could not have been travelled at all. Sometimes we stuck in bogs out of which we had to dig the wheels, and sometimes in the rocky bottoms of streams, while once we were obliged literally to cut our way through a belt of dense bush from which it took us eight days to escape.

Our other chief trouble came from the lions, whereof there were great numbers in this *veld*. The prevalence of these hungry beasts forced us to watch our cattle very closely while they grazed, and at night, wherever it was possible, to protect them and ourselves in "bombast," or fences of thorns, within which we lit fires to scare away wild beasts. Notwithstanding these precautions, we lost several of the oxen, and ourselves had some narrow escapes.

Thus, one night, just as Marie was about to enter the wagon where the women slept, a great lion, desperate with hunger, sprang over the fence. She leapt away from the beast, and in so doing caught her foot and fell down, whereon the lion came for her. In another few seconds she would have been dead, or carried off living.

But as it chanced, Vrouw Prinsloo was close at hand. Seizing a flaming bough from the fire, that intrepid woman ran at the lion and, as it opened its huge mouth to roar or bite, thrust the burning end of the bough into its throat. The lion closed its jaws upon it, then finding the mouthful not to its taste, departed even more quickly than it had come, uttering the most dreadful noises, and leaving Marie quite unhurt. Needless to say, after this I really worshipped the Vrouw Prinsloo, though she, good soul, thought nothing of the business, which in those days was but a common incident of travel.

I think it was on the day after this lion episode that we came upon Pereira's wagon, or rather its remains. Evidently he had tried to trek along a steep, rocky bank which overhung a stream, with the result that the wagon had fallen into the stream-bed, then almost dry, and been smashed beyond repair.

The Tonga natives of the neighbourhood, who had burned most of the woodwork in order to secure the precious iron bolts and fittings, informed us that the white man and his servants who were with the wagon had gone forward on foot some ten days before, driving their cattle with them. Whether this story were true or not we had no means of finding out. It was quite possible that Pereira and his companions had been murdered, though as we found the Tongas very quiet folk if well treated and given the usual complimentary presents for wayleaves, this did not seem probable. Indeed, a week later our doubts upon this point were cleared up thus.

We had reached a big *kraal* called Fokoti, on the Umkusi River, which appeared to be almost deserted. We asked an old woman whom we met where its people had gone. She answered that they had fled towards the borders of Swaziland, fearing an attack from the Zulus, whose territories began beyond this Umkusi River. It seemed that a few days before a Zulu *impi* or regiment had appeared upon the banks of the river, and although there was no war at the time between the Zulus and the Tongas, the latter had thought it wise to put themselves out of reach of those terrible spears.

On hearing this news we debated whether it would not be well for us to follow their example and, trekking westwards, try to find a pass in the mountains. Upon this point there was a division of opinion among us. Marais, who was a fatalist, wished to go on, saying that the good Lord would protect us, as He had done in the past.

"*Allemachte!*" answered the Vrouw Prinsloo. "Did He protect all those who lie dead at Marais's camp, whither your folly led us, *mynheer*? The good Lord expects us to look after our own skins, and I know that these Zulus are of the same blood as Umsilikazi's Kaffirs, who have killed so many of our people. Let us try the mountains, say I."

Of course her husband and son agreed with her, for to them the *vrouw's* word was law; but Marais, being, as usual, obstinate, would not give way. All that afternoon they wrangled, while I held my tongue, declaring that I was willing to abide by the decision of the majority. In the end, as I foresaw they would, they appealed to me to act as umpire between them.

"Friends," I answered, "if you had asked me my opinion before, I should have voted for trying the mountains, beyond which, perhaps, we might find some Boers. I do not like this story of the Zulu *impi*. I think that someone has told them of our coming, and that it is us they mean to attack and not the Tongas, with whom they are at peace. My men say that it is not usual for *impis* to visit this part of the country."

"Who could have told them?" asked Marais.

"I don't know, *mynheer*. Perhaps the natives have sent on word, or perhaps—Hernan Pereira."

"I knew that you would suspect my nephew, Allan," he exclaimed angrily.

"I suspect no one; I only weigh what is probable. However, it is too late for us to move to-night either south or westwards, so I think I will sleep over the business and see what I can find out from my Zulus."

That night, or rather the following morning, the question was settled for us, for when I woke up at dawn, it was to see the faint light glimmering on what I knew must be spears. We were surrounded by a great company of Zulus, as I discovered afterwards, over two hundred strong. Thinking that after their fashion they were preparing to attack us at dawn, I called the news to the others, whereon Marais rushed forward, just as he had left his bed, cocking his *roer* as he came.

"For the love of God, do not shoot!" I said. "How can we resist so many? Soft words are our only chance."

Still he attempted to fire, and would have done so had I not thrown myself upon him and literally torn the gun from his hand. By this time the Vrouw Prinsloo had come up, a very weird spectacle, I recollect, in what she called her "sleep-garments," that included a night-cap made of a worn jackal skin and a kind of otter-pelt stomacher.

"Accursed fool!" she said to Marais, "would you cause all our throats to be cut? Go forward, you, Allan, and talk to those *swartzels*" (that is, black creatures), "gently, as you would to a savage dog. You have a tongue steeped in oil, and they may listen to you."

"Yes," I answered; "that seems the best thing to do. If I should not return, give my love to Marie."

So I beckoned to the headman of my Zulus whom I had hired at Delagoa, to accompany me, and marched forward boldly quite unarmed. We were encamped upon a rise of ground a quarter of a mile from the river, and the *impi*, or those of them whom we could see, were at the foot of this rise about a hundred and sixty yards away. The light was growing now, and when I was within fifty paces of them they saw me. At some word of command a number of men rushed toward me, their fighting shields held over their bodies and their spears up.

"We are dead!" exclaimed my Kaffir in a resigned voice. I shared his opinion, but thought I might as well die standing as running away.

Now I should explain that though as yet I had never mixed with these Zulus, I could talk several native dialects kindred to that which they used very well indeed. Moreover, ever since I had hired men of their race at Delagoa, I had spent all my spare time in conversing with them and acquiring a knowledge of their language, history and customs. So by this time I knew their tongue fairly, although occasionally I may have used terms which were unfamiliar to them.

Thus it came about that I was able to shout to them, asking what was their business with us. Hearing themselves addressed in words which they understood, the men halted, and seeing that I was unarmed, three of them approached me.

"We come to take you prisoners, white people, or to kill you if you resist," said their captain.

"By whose order?" I asked.

"By the order of Dingaan our king."

"Is it so? And who told Dingaan that we were here?"

"The Boer who came in front of you."

"Is it so?" I said again. "And now what do you need of us?"

"That you should accompany us to the *kraal* of Dingaan."

"I understand. We are quite willing, since it lies upon our road. But then why do you come against us, who are peaceful travellers, with your spears lifted?"

"For this reason. The Boer told us that there is among you a 'child of George'" (an Englishman), "a terrible man who would kill us unless we killed or bound him first. Show us this child of George that we may make him fast, or slay him, and we will not hurt the rest of you."

"I am the child of George," I answered, "and if you think it necessary to make me fast, do so."

Now the Zulus burst out laughing.

"You! Why, you are but a boy who weighs no more than a fat girl," exclaimed their captain, a great, bony fellow who was named Kambula.

"That may be so," I answered; "but sometimes the wisdom of their fathers dwells in the young. I am the son of George who saved these

Boers from death far away, and I am taking them back to their own people. We desire to see Dingaan, your king. Be pleased therefore to lead us to him as he has commanded you to do. If you do not believe what I tell you, ask this man who is with me, and his companions who are of your own race. They will tell you everything."

Then the captain Kambula called my servant apart and talked with him for a long while.

When the interview was finished he advanced to me and said:

"Now I have heard all about you. I have heard that although young you are very clever, so clever that you do not sleep, but watch by night as well as by day. Therefore, that I, Kambula, name you Macumazahn, Watcher-by-night, and by that name you shall henceforth be known among us. Now, Macumazahn, son of George, bring out these Boers whom you are guiding that I may lead them in their moving huts to the Great Place, Umgungundhlovu, where dwells Dingaan the king. See, we lay down our spears and will come to meet them unarmed, trusting to you to protect us, O Macumazahn, Son of George," and he cast his *assegai* to the ground.

"Come," I said, and led them to the wagons.

CHAPTER 12

Dingaan's Bet

As I advanced to the wagons accompanied by Kambula and his two companions, I saw that Marais, in a state of great excitement, was engaged in haranguing the two Prinsloo men and Meyer, while the Vrouw Prinsloo and Marie appeared to be attempting to calm him.

"They are unarmed," I heard him shout. "Let us seize the black devils and hold them as hostages."

Thereon, led by Marais, the three Boer men came towards us doubtfully, their guns in their hands.

"Be careful what you are doing," I called to them. "These are envoys," and they hung back a little while Marais went on with his haranguing.

The Zulus looked at them and at me, then Kambula said:

"Are you leading us into a trap, Son of George?"

"Not so," I answered; "but the Boers are afraid of you and think to take you prisoners."

"Tell them," said Kambula quietly, "that if they kill us or lay a hand on us, as no doubt they can do, very soon every one of them will be dead and their women with them."

I repeated this ultimatum energetically enough, but Marais shouted:

"The Englishman is betraying us to the Zulus! Do not trust him; seize them as I tell you."

What would have happened I am sure I do not know; but just then the Vrouw Prinsloo came up and caught her husband by the arm.

"You shall have no part in this fool's business. If Marais wishes to seize the Zulus, let him do so himself. Are you mad or drunk that you should think that Allan would wish to betray Marie to the Kaffirs, to say nothing of the rest of us?" and she began to wave an extremely dirty *vatdoek*, or dishcloth, which she always carried about with her and used for every purpose, towards Kambula as a sign of peace.

Now the Boers gave way, and Marais, seeing himself in a minority, glowered at me in silence.

"Ask these white people, O Macumazahn," said Kambula, "who is their captain, for to the captain I would speak."

I translated the question, and Marais answered:

"I am."

"No," broke in Vrouw Prinsloo, "*I* am. Tell them, Allan, that these men are all fools and have given the rule to me, a woman."

So I told them. Evidently this information surprised them a little, for they discussed together. Then Kambula said:

"So be it. We have heard that the people of George are now ruled by a woman, and as you, Macumazahn, are one of that people, doubtless it is the same among your party."

Here I may add that thenceforward the Zulus always accepted the Vrouw Prinsloo as the *Inkosikaas* or chieftainess of our little band, and with the single exception of myself, whom they looked upon as her "mouth," or *induna*, would only transact business with or give directions to her. The other Boers they ignored completely.

This point of etiquette settled, Kambula bade me repeat what he had already told me, that we were prisoners whom he was instructed by Dingaan to convey to his Great Place, and that if we made no attempt to escape we should not be hurt upon the journey.

I did so, whereon the *vrouw* asked as I had done, who had informed Dingaan that we were coming.

I repeated to her word for word what the Zulus had told me, that it was Pereira, whose object seems to have been to bring about my death or capture.

Then the *vrouw* exploded.

"Do you hear that, Henri Marais?" she screamed. "It is your stink-cat of a nephew again. Oh! I thought I smelt him! Your nephew has betrayed us to these Zulus that he may bring Allan to his death. Ask them, Allan, what this Dingaan has done with the stinkcat."

So I asked, and was informed they believed that the king had let Pereira go on to his own people in payment of the information that he had given him.

"My God!" said the *vrouw*, "I hoped that he had knocked him on the head. Well, what is to be done now?"

"I don't know," I answered. Then an idea occurred to me, and I said to Kambula:

"It seems to be me, the son of George, that your king wants. Take me, and let these people go on their road."

327

The three Zulus began to discuss this point, withdrawing themselves a little way so that I could not overhear them. But when the Boers understood the offer that I had made, Marie, who until now had been silent, grew more angry than ever I had seen her before.

"It shall not be!" she said, stamping her foot. "Father, I have been obedient to you for long, but if you consent to this I will be obedient no more. Allan saved my cousin Hernan's life, as he saved all our lives. In payment for that good deed Hernan tried to murder him in the *kloof*—oh! be quiet, Allan; I know all the story. Now he has betrayed him to the Zulus, telling them that he is a terrible and dangerous man who must be killed. Well, if he is to be killed, I will be killed with him, and if the Zulus take him and let us free, I go with him. Now make up your mind."

Marais tugged at his beard, staring first at his daughter and then at me. What he would have answered I do not know, for at that moment Kambula stepped forward and gave his decision.

It was to the effect that although it was the Son of George whom Dingaan wanted, his orders were that all with him were to be taken also. Those orders could not be disobeyed. The king would settle the matter as to whether some of us were to be killed and some let free, or if all were to be killed or let free, when we reached his House. Therefore he commanded that "we should tie the oxen to the moving huts and cross the river at once."

This was the end of that scene. Having no choice we inspanned and continued our journey, escorted by the company of two hundred savages. I am bound to say that during the four or five days that it took us to reach Dingaan's *kraal* they behaved very well to us. With Kambula and his officers, all of them good fellows in their way, I had many conversations, and from them learned much as to the state and customs of the Zulus. Also the peoples of the districts through which we passed flocked round us at every outspan, for most of them had never seen a white man before, and in return for a few beads brought us all the food that we required. Indeed, the beads, or their equivalents, were nothing but a present, since, by the king's command, they must satisfy our wants. This they did very thoroughly. For instance, when on the last day's trek, some of our oxen gave out, numbers of Zulus were inspanned in place of them, and by their help the wagons were dragged to the great *kraal*, Umgungundhlovu.

Here an outspan place was assigned to us near to the house, or rather the huts, of a certain missionary of the name of Owen, who with great courage had ventured into this country. We were received with the utmost kindness by him and his wife and household, and it is impossible for me to say what pleasure I found, after all my journeyings, in meeting an educated man of my own race.

Near to our camp was a stone-covered *koppie*, where, on the morning after our arrival, I saw six or eight men executed in a way that I will not describe. Their crime, according to Mr. Owen, was that they had bewitched some of the king's oxen.

While I was recovering from this dreadful spectacle, which, fortunately, Marie did not witness, the captain Kambula arrived, saying that Dingaan wished to see me. So taking with me the Hottentot Hans and two of the Zulus whom I had hired at Delagoa Bay—for the royal orders were that none of the other white people were to come, I was led through the fence of the vast town in which stood two thousand huts—the "multitude of houses" as the Zulus called it—and across a vast open space in the middle.

On the farther side of this space, where, before long, I was fated to witness a very tragic scene, I entered a kind of labyrinth. This was called *siklohlo*, and had high fences with numerous turns, so that it was impossible to see where one was going or to find the way in or out. Ultimately, however, I reached a great hut named *intunkulu*, a word that means the "house of houses," or the abode of the king, in front of which I saw a fat man seated on a stool, naked except for the *moocha* about his middle and necklaces and armlets of blue beads. Two warriors held their broad shields over his head to protect him from the sun. Otherwise he was alone, although I felt sure that the numerous passages around him were filled with guards, for I could hear them moving.

On entering this place Kambula and his companions flung themselves upon their faces and began to sing praises of which the king took no notice. Presently he looked up, and appearing to observe me for the first time asked:

"Who is that white boy?"

Then Kambula rose and said:

"O king, this is the Son of George, whom you commanded me to capture. I have taken him and the Amaboona" (that is, the Boers), "his companions, and brought them all to you, O king."

"I remember," said Dingaan. "The big Boer who was here, and whom Tambusa"—he was one of Dingaan's captains—"let go against my will, said that he was a terrible man who should be killed before he worked great harm to my people. Why did you not kill him, Kambula, although it is true he does not look very terrible?"

"Because the king's word was that I should bring him to the king living," answered Kambula. Then he added cheerfully: "Still, if the king wishes it, I can kill him at once."

"I don't know," said Dingaan doubtfully; "perhaps he can mend guns." Next, after reflecting a while, he bade a shield-holder to fetch someone, I could not hear whom.

"Doubtless," thought I to myself, "it is the executioner," and at that thought a kind of mad rage seized me. Why should my life be ended thus in youth to satisfy the whim of a savage? And if it must be so, why should I go alone?

In the inside pocket of my ragged coat I had a small loaded pistol with two barrels. One of those barrels would kill Dingaan—at five paces I could not miss that bulk—and the other would blow out my brains, for I was not minded to have my neck twisted or to be beaten to death with sticks. Well, if it was to be done, I had better do it at once. Already my hand was creeping towards the pocket when a new idea, or rather two ideas, struck me.

The first was that if I shot Dingaan the Zulus would probably massacre Marie and the others—Marie, whose sweet face I should never see again. The second was that while there is life there is hope. Perhaps, after all, he had not sent for an executioner, but for someone else. I would wait. A few minutes more of existence were worth the having.

The shield-bearer returned, emerging from one of the narrow, reed-hedged passages, and after him came no executioner, but a young white man, who, as I knew from the look of him, was English. He saluted the king by taking off his hat, which I remember was stuck round with black ostrich feathers, then stared at me.

"O Tho-maas" (that is how he pronounced "Thomas"), said Dingaan, "tell me if this boy is one of your brothers, or is he a Boer?"

"The king wants to know if you are Dutch or British," said the white lad, speaking in English.

"As British as you are," I answered. "I was born in England, and come from the Cape."

"That may be lucky for you," he said, "because the old witch-doctor, Zikali, has told him that he must not kill any English. What is your name? Mine is Thomas Halstead. I am interpreter here."

"Allan Quatermain. Tell Zikali, whoever he may be, that if he sticks to his advice I will give him a good present."

"What are you talking about?" asked Dingaan suspiciously.

"He says he is English, no Boer, O king; that he was born across the Black Water, and that he comes from the country out of which all the Boers have trekked."

At this intelligence Dingaan pricked up his ears.

"Then he can tell me about these Boers," he said, "and what they are after, or could if he were able to speak my tongue. I do not trust you to interpret, you Tho-maas, whom I know to be a liar," and he glowered at Halstead.

"I can speak your tongue, though not very well, O king," I interrupted, "and I can tell you all about the Boers, for I have lived among them."

"*Ow!*" said Dingaan, intensely interested. "But perhaps you are also a liar. Or are you a praying man, like that fool yonder, who is named Oweena?"—he meant the missionary Mr. Owen—"whom I spare because it is not lucky to kill one who is mad, although he tries to frighten my soldiers with tales of a fire into which they will go after they are dead. As though it matters what happens to them after they are dead!" he added reflectively, taking a pinch of snuff.

"I am no liar," I answered. "What have I to lie about?"

"You would lie to save your own life, for all white men are cowards; not like the Zulus, who love to die for their king. But how are you named?"

"Your people call me Macumazahn."

"Well, Macumazahn, if you are no liar, tell me, is it true that these Boers rebelled against their king who was named George, and fled from him as the traitor Umsilikazi did from me?"

"Yes," I answered, "that is true."

"Now I am sure that you are a liar," said Dingaan triumphantly. "You say that you are English and therefore serve your king, or the *Inkosikaas*" (that is the Great Lady), "who they tell me now sits in his place. How does it come about then that you are travelling with a party of these very Amaboona who must be your enemies, since they are the enemies of your king, or of her who follows after him?"

Now I knew that I was in a tight place, for on this matter of loyalty, Zulu, and indeed all native ideas, are very primitive. If I said that I had sympathy with the Boers, Dingaan would set me down as a traitor. If I said that I hated the Boers, then still I should be a traitor because I associated with them, and a traitor in his eyes would be one to be killed. I do not like to talk religion, and anyone who has read what I have written in various works will admit that I have done so rarely, if ever. Yet at that moment I put up a prayer for guidance, feeling that my young life hung upon the answer, and it came to me—whence I do not know. The essence of that guidance was that I should tell the simple truth to this fat savage. So I said to him:

"The answer is this, O king. Among those Boers is a maiden whom I love and who betrothed herself to me since we were 'so high.' Her father took her north. But she sent a message to me saying that her people died of fever and she starved. So I went up in a ship to save her, and have saved her, and those who remained alive of her people with her."

"*Ow!*" said Dingaan; "I understand that reason. It is a good reason. However many wives he may have, there is no folly that a man will not commit for the sake of some particular girl who is not yet his wife. I have done as much myself, especially for one who was called Nada the Lily, of whom a certain Umslopogaas robbed me, one of my own blood of whom I am much afraid."[1]

For a while he brooded heavily, then went on:

"Your reason is good, Macumazahn, and I accept it. More, I promise you this. Perhaps I shall kill these Boers, or perhaps I shall not kill them. But if I make up my mind to kill them, this girl of yours shall be spared. Point her out to Kambula here—not to Tho-maas, for he is a liar and would tell me the wrong one—and she shall be spared."

"I thank you, O king," I said; "but what is the use of that if I am to be killed?"

"I did not say that you were to be killed, Macumazahn, though perhaps I shall kill you, or perhaps I shall not kill you. It depends upon whether I find you to be a liar, or not a liar. Now the Boer whom Tambusa let go against my wish said that you are a mighty magician as well as a very dangerous man, one who can shoot birds flying on the wing with a bullet, which is impossible. Can you do so?"

"Sometimes," I answered.

"Very good, Macumazahn. Now we will see if you are a wizard or a liar. I will make a bet with you. Yonder by your camp is a hill called Hloma Amabutu, a hill of stones where evildoers are slain. This afternoon some wicked ones die there, and when they are dead the vultures will come to devour them. Now this is my bet with you. When those vultures come you shall shoot at them, and if you kill three out of the first five on the wing—not on the ground, Macumazahn—then I will spare these Boers. But if you miss them, then I shall know that you are a liar and no wizard, and I will kill them every one on the hill Hloma Amabutu. I will spare none of them except the girl, whom perhaps I will take as a wife. As to you, I will not yet say what I will do with you."

---

1. See the author's book *Nada the Lily*.

Now my first impulse was to refuse this monstrous wager, which meant that the lives of a number of people were to be set against my skill in shooting. But young Thomas Halstead, guessing the words that were about to break from me, said in English:

"Accept unless you are a fool. If you don't he will cut the throats of every one of them and stick your girl into the *emposeni*" (that is harem), "while you will become a prisoner as I am."

These were words that I could not resent or neglect, so although despair was in my heart, I said coolly:

"Be it so, O king. I take your wager. If I kill three vultures out of five as they hover over the hill, then I have your promise that all those who travel with me shall be allowed to go hence in safety."

"Yes, yes, Macumazahn; but if you fail to kill them, remember that the next vultures you shoot at shall be those that come to feed upon their flesh, for then I shall know that you are no magician, but a common liar. And now begone, Tho-maas. I will not have you spying on me; and you, Macumazahn, come hither. Although you talk my tongue so badly, I would speak with you about the Boers."

So Halstead went, shrugging his shoulders and muttering as he passed me:

"I hope you really *can* shoot."

After he had left I sat alone for a full hour with Dingaan while he cross-examined me about the Dutch, their movements and their aims in travelling to the confines of his country.

I answered his questions as best I could, trying to make out a good case for them.

At length, when he grew weary of talking, he clapped his hands, whereon a number of fine girls appeared, two of whom carried pots of beer, from which he offered me drink.

I replied that I would have none, since beer made the hand shake and that on the steadiness of my hand that afternoon depended the lives of many. To do him justice he quite understood the point. Indeed, he ordered me to be conducted back to the camp at once that I might rest, and even sent one of his own attendants with me to hold a shield over my head as I walked so that I should be protected from the sun.

"*Hamba gachle*" (that is "Go softly"), said the wicked old tyrant to me as I departed under the guidance of Kambula. "This afternoon, one hour before sundown, I will meet you at Hloma Amabutu, and there shall be settled the fate of these Amaboona, your companions."

When I reached the camp it was to find all the Boers clustered together waiting for me, and with them the Reverend Mr. Owen and his people, including a Welsh servant of his, a woman of middle age who, I remember, was called Jane.

"Well," said the Vrouw Prinsloo, "and what is your news, young man?"

"My news, aunt," I answered, "is that one hour before sundown to-day I have to shoot vultures on the wing against the lives of all of you. This you owe to that false-hearted hound Hernan Pereira, who told Dingaan that I am a magician. Now Dingaan would prove it. He thinks that only by magic can a man shoot soaring vultures with a bullet, and as he is determined to kill you all, except perhaps Marie, in the form of a bet he has set me a task which he believes to be impossible. If I fail, the bet is lost, and so are your lives. If I succeed I think your lives will be spared, since Kambula there tells me that the king always makes it a point of honour to pay his bets. Now you have the truth, and I hope you like it," and I laughed bitterly.

When I had finished a perfect storm of execration broke from the Boers. If curses could have killed Pereira, surely he would have died upon the spot, wherever he might be. Only two of them were silent, Marie, who turned very pale, poor girl, and her father. Presently one of them, I think it was Meyer, rounded on him viciously and asked him what he thought now of that devil, his nephew.

"I think there must be some mistake," answered Marais quietly, "since Hernan cannot have wished that we should all be put to death."

"No," shouted Meyer; "but he wished that Allan Quatermain should, which is just as bad; and now it has come about that once more our lives depend upon this English boy."

"At any rate," replied Marais, looking at me oddly, "it seems that he is not to be killed, whether he shoots the vultures or misses them."

"That remains to be proved, *mynheer*," I answered hotly, for the insinuation stung me. "But please understand that if all of you, my companions, are to be slaughtered, and Marie is to be put among this black brute's women, as he threatens, I have no wish to live on."

"My God! does he threaten that?" said Marais. "Surely you must have misunderstood him, Allan."

"Do you think that I should lie to you on such a matter—" I began.

But, before I could proceed, the Vrouw Prinsloo thrust herself between us, crying:

"Be silent, you, Marais, and you too, Allan. Is this a time that you should quarrel and upset yourself, Allan, so that when the trial comes you will shoot your worst and not your best? And is this a time, Henri

Marais, that you should throw insults at one on whom all our lives hang, instead of praying for God's vengeance upon your accursed nephew? Come, Allan, and take food. I have fried the liver of that heifer which the king sent us; it is ready and very good. After you have eaten it you must lie down and sleep a while."

Now among the household of the Reverend Mr. Owen was an English boy called William Wood, who was not more than twelve or fourteen years of age. This lad knew both Dutch and Zulu, and acted as interpreter to the Owen family during the absence on a journey of a certain Mr. Hulley, who really filled that office. While this conversation was taking place in Dutch he was engaged in rendering every word of it into English for the benefit of the clergyman and his family. When Mr. Owen understood the full terror of the situation, he broke in saying:

"This is not a time to eat or to sleep, but a time to pray that the heart of the savage Dingaan may be turned. Come, let us pray!"

"Yes," rejoined Vrouw Prinsloo, when William Wood had translated. "Do you pray, Predicant, and all the rest of you who have nothing else to do, and while you are about it pray also that the bullets of Allan Quatermain may not be turned. As for me and Allan, we have other things to see to, so you must pray a little harder to cover us as well as yourselves. Now you come along, nephew Allan, or that liver may be overdone and give you indigestion, which is worse for shooting than even bad temper. No, not another word. If you try to speak any more, Henri Marais, I will box your ears," and she lifted a hand like a leg of mutton, then, as Marais retreated before her, seized me by the collar as though I were a naughty boy and led me away to the wagons.

335

CHAPTER 13

The Rehearsal

By the women's wagon we found the liver cooked in its frying-pan, as the *vrouw* had said. Indeed, it was just done to a turn. Selecting a particularly massive slice, she proceeded to take it from the pan with her fingers in order to set it upon a piece of tin, from which she had first removed the more evident traces of the morning meal with her constant companion, the ancient and unwashen *vatdoek*. As it chanced the effort was not very successful, since the boiling liver fat burnt the *vrouw's* fingers, causing her to drop it on the grass, and, I am sorry to add, to swear as well. Not to be defeated, however, having first sucked her fingers to ease their smart, she seized the sizzling liver with the *vatdoek* and deposited it upon the dirty tin.

"There, nephew," she said triumphantly, "there are more ways of killing a cat than by drowning. What a fool I was not to think of the *vatdoek* at first. *Allemachte!* how the flesh has burnt me; I don't suppose that being killed would hurt much more. Also, if the worst comes to the worst, it will soon be over. Think of it, Allan, by to-night I may be an angel, dressed in a long white nightgown like those my mother gave me when I was married, which I cut up for baby-clothes because I found them chilly wear, having always been accustomed to sleep in my vest and petticoat. Yes, and I shall have wings, too, like those on a white gander, only bigger if they are to carry *my* weight."

"And a crown of Glory," I suggested.

"Yes, of course, a crown of Glory—very large, since I shall be a martyr; but I hope one will only have to wear it on Sundays, as I never could bear anything heavy on my hair; moreover, it would remind me of a Kaffir's head-ring done in gold, and I shall have had enough of Kaffirs. Then there will be the harp," she went on as her imagination took fire at the prospect of these celestial delights. "Have you ever seen a harp, Allan? I haven't except that which King David carries in the picture in the Book, which looks like a broken *rimpi* chair frame set up edgeways. As for playing the thing, they will have to teach me, that's all, which will be a difficult business, seeing that I would sooner listen to cats on the roof than to music, and as for making it—"

So she chattered on, as I believe with the object of diverting and amusing me, for she was a shrewd old soul who knew how important it was that I should be kept in an equable frame of mind at this crisis in our fates.

Meanwhile I was doing my best with the lump of liver, that tasted painfully of *vatdoek* and was gritty with sand. Indeed, when the *vrouw's* back was turned I managed to throw the most of it to Hans behind me, who swallowed it at a gulp as a dog does, since he did not wish to be caught chewing it.

"God in heaven! how fast you eat, nephew," said the *vrouw*, catching sight of my empty tin. Then, eyeing the voracious Hottentot suspiciously, she added: "That yellow dog of yours hasn't stolen it, has he? If so, I'll teach him."

"No, no, *vrouw*," answered Hans in alarm. "No meat has passed my lips this day, except what I licked out of the pan after breakfast."

"Then, Allan, you will certainly have indigestion, which is just what I wanted to avoid. Have I not often told you that you should chew your bit twenty times before you swallow, which I would do myself if I had any back teeth left? Here, drink this milk; it is only a little sour and will settle your stomach," and she produced a black bottle and subjected it to the attentions of the *vatdoek*, growing quite angry when I declined it and sent for water.

Next she insisted upon my getting into her own bed in the wagon to sleep, forbidding me to smoke, which she said made the hand shake. Thither, then, I went, after a brief conversation with Hans, whom I directed to clean my rifle thoroughly. For I wished to be alone and knew that I had little chance of solitude outside of that somewhat fusty couch.

To tell the truth, although I shut my eyes to deceive the *vrouw*, who looked in occasionally to see how I was getting on, no sleep came to me that afternoon—at least, not for a long while. How could I sleep in that hot place when my heart was torn with doubt and terror? Think of it, reader, think of it! An hour or two, and on my skill would hang the lives of eight white people—men, women, and children, and the safety or the utter shame of the woman whom I loved and who loved me. No, she should be spared the worst. I would give her my pistol, and if there were need she would know what to do.

337

The fearful responsibility was more than I could bear. I fell into a veritable agony; I trembled and even wept a little. Then I thought of my father and what he would do in such circumstances, and began to pray as I had never prayed before.

I implored the Power above me to give me strength and wisdom; not to let me fail in this hour of trouble, and thereby bring these poor people to a bloody death. I prayed till the perspiration streamed down my face; then suddenly I fell into sleep or swoon. I don't know how long I lay thus, but I think it must have been the best part of an hour. At last I woke up all in an instant, and as I woke I distinctly heard a tiny voice, unlike any other voice in the whole world, speak inside my head, or so it seemed to me, saying:

"Go to the hill Hloma Amabutu, and watch how the vultures fly. Do what comes into your mind, and even if you seem to fail, fear nothing."

I sat up on the old *vrouw*'s bed, and felt that some mysterious change had come over me. I was no longer the same man. My doubts and terrors had gone; my hand was like a rock; my heart was light. I knew that I should kill those three vultures. Of course the story seems absurd, and easy to be explained by the state of my nerves under the strain which was being put upon them, and for aught I know that may be its true meaning. Yet I am not ashamed to confess that I have always held, and still hold, otherwise. I believe that in my extremity some kindly Power did speak to me in answer to my earnest prayers and to those of others, giving me guidance and, what I needed still more, judgment and calmness. At any rate, that this was my conviction at the moment may be seen from the fact that I hastened to obey the teachings of that tiny, unnatural voice.

Climbing out of the wagon, I went to Hans, who was seated near by in the full glare of the hot sun, at which he seemed to stare with unblinking eyes.

"Where's the rifle, Hans?" I said.

"*Intombi* is here, *baas*, where I have put her to keep her cool, so that she may not go off before it is wanted," and he pointed to a little grave-like heap of gathered grass at his side.

The natives, I should explain, named this particular gun *Intombi*, which means a young girl, because it was so much slimmer and more graceful than other guns.

"Is it clean?" I asked.

"Never was she cleaner since she was born out of the fire, *baas*. Also, the powder has been sifted and set to dry in the sun with the caps, and the bullets have been trued to the barrel, so that there may be no accidents when it comes to the shooting. If you miss the *aasvogels*, *baas*, it will not be the fault of *Intombi* or of the powder and the bullets; it will be your own fault."

"That's comforting," I answered. "Well, come on, I want to go to the Death-hill yonder."

"Why, *baas*, before the time?" asked the Hottentot, shrinking back a little. "It is no place to visit till one is obliged. These Zulus say that ghosts sit there even in the daylight, haunting the rocks where they were made ghosts."

"Vultures sit or fly there also, Hans; and I would see how they fly, that I may know when and where to shoot at them."

"That is right, *baas*," said the clever Hottentot. "This is not like firing at geese in the Groote Kloof. The geese go straight, like an *assegai* to its mark. But the *aasvogels* wheel round and round, always on the turn; it is easy to miss a bird that is turning, *baas*."

"Very easy. Come on."

Just as we were starting Vrouw Prinsloo appeared from behind the other wagon, and with her Marie, who, I noticed, was very pale and whose beautiful eyes were red, as though with weeping.

The *vrouw* asked me where we were going. I told her. After considering a little, she said that was a good thought of mine, as it was always well to study the ground before a battle.

I nodded, and led Marie aside behind some thorn trees that grew near.

"Oh! Allan, what will be the end of this?" she asked piteously. High as was her courage it seemed to fail her now.

"A good end, dearest," I answered. "We shall come out of this hole safely, as we have of many others."

"How do you know that, Allan, which is known to God alone?"

"Because God told me, Marie," and I repeated to her the story of the voice I had heard in my dream, which seemed to comfort her.

"Yet, yet," she exclaimed doubtfully, "it was but a dream, Allan, and dreams are such uncertain things. You may fail, after all."

"Do I look like one who will fail, Marie?"

She studied me from head to foot, then answered:

"No, you do not, although you did when you came back from the king's huts. Now you are quite changed. Still, Allan, you may fail, and then—what? Some of those dreadful Zulus have been here while you were sleeping, bidding us all make ready to go to the Hill of Death. They say that Dingaan is in earnest. If you do not kill the vultures, he will kill us. It seems that they are sacred birds, and if they escape he will think he has nothing to fear from the white men and their magic, and so will make a beginning by butchering us. I mean the rest of us, for I am to be kept alive, and oh! what shall I do, Allan?"

I looked at her, and she looked at me. Then I took the double-barrelled pistol out of my pocket and gave it to her.

"It is loaded and on the half-cock," I said.

She nodded, and hid it in her dress beneath her apron. Then without more words we kissed and parted, for both of us feared to prolong that scene.

The hill Hloma Amabutu was quite close to our encampment and the huts of the Reverend Mr. Owen, scarcely a quarter of a mile off, I should say, rising from the flat *veld* on the further side of a little depression that hardly amounted to a valley. As we approached it I noticed its peculiar and blasted appearance, for whereas all around the grass was vivid with the green of spring, on this place none seemed to grow. An eminence strewn with tumbled heaps of blackish rock, and among them a few struggling, dark-leaved bushes; that was its appearance. Moreover, many of these boulders looked as though they had been splashed and lined with whitewash, showing that they were the resting-place of hundreds of gorged vultures.

I believe it is the Chinese who declare that particular localities have good or evil influences attached to them, some kind of spirit of their own, and really Hloma Amabutu and a few other spots that I am acquainted with in Africa give colour to the fancy. Certainly as I set foot upon that accursed ground, that Golgotha, that Place of Skulls, a shiver went through me. It may have been caused by the atmosphere, moral and actual, of the mount, or it may have been a prescience of a certain dreadful scene which within a few months I was doomed to witness there. Or perhaps the place itself and the knowledge of the trial before me sent a sudden chill through my healthy blood. I cannot say which it was, but the fact remains as I have stated, although a minute or two later, when I saw what kind of sleepers lay upon that mount, it would not have been necessary for me to seek any far-fetched explanation of my fear.

Across this hill, winding in and out between the rough rocks that lay here, there and everywhere like hailstones after a winter storm, ran sundry paths. It seems that the shortest road to various places in the neighbourhood of the Great *Kraal* ran over it, and although no Zulu ever dared to set foot there between sun-set and rise, in the daytime they used these paths freely enough. But I suppose that they also held that this evil-omened field of death had some spirit of its

340

own, some invisible but imminent fiend, who needed to be propitiated, lest soon he should claim them also.

This was their method of propitiation, a common one enough, I believe, in many lands, though what may be its meaning I cannot tell. As the traveller came to those spots where the paths cut across each other, he took a stone and threw it on to a heap that had been accumulated there by the hands of other travellers. There were many such heaps upon the hill, over a dozen, I think, and the size of them was great. I should say that the biggest contained quite fifty loads of stones, and the smallest not fewer than twenty or thirty.

Now, Hans, although he had never set foot there before, seemed to have learned all the traditions of the place, and what rites were necessary to avert its curse. At any rate, when we came to the first heap, he cast a stone upon it, and begged me to do the same. I laughed and refused, but when we reached the second heap the same thing happened. Again I refused, whereon, before we came to a third and larger pile, Hans sat down upon the ground and began to groan, swearing that he would not go one step farther unless I promised to make the accustomed offering.

"Why not, you fool?" I asked.

"Because if you neglect it, *baas*, I think that we shall stop here for ever. Oh! you may laugh, but I tell you that already you have brought ill-luck upon yourself. Remember my words, *baas*, when you miss two of the five *aasvogels*."

"Bosh!" I exclaimed, or, rather, its Dutch equivalent. Still, as this talk of missing vultures touched me nearly, and it is always as well to conform to native prejudices, at the next and two subsequent heaps I cast my stone as humbly as the most superstitious Zulu in the land.

By this time we had reached the summit, which may have been two hundred yards long. It was hog-backed in shape, with a kind of depression in the middle cleared of stones, either by the hand of man or nature, and not unlike a large circus in its general conformation.

Oh! the sight that met my eyes. All about lay the picked and scattered bones of men and women, many of them broken up by the jaws of hyenas. Some were quite fresh, for the hair still clung to the skulls, others blanched and old. But new or ancient there must have been hundreds of them. Moreover, on the sides of the hill it was the same story, though there, for the most part, the bones had been gathered into gleaming heaps. No wonder that the vultures loved Hloma Amabutu, the Place of Slaughter of the bloody Zulu king.

Of these horrible birds, however, at the moment not one was to be seen. As there had been no execution for a few hours they were seeking their food elsewhere. Now, for my own purposes, I wanted to see them, since otherwise my visit was in vain, and presently bethought myself of a method of securing their arrival.

"Hans," I said, "I am going to pretend to kill you, and then you must lie quite still out there like one dead. Even if the *aasvogels* settle on you, you must lie quite still, so that I may see whence they come and how they settle."

The Hottentot did not take at all kindly to this suggestion. Indeed, he flatly refused to obey me, giving sundry good reasons. He said that this kind of rehearsal was ill-omened; that coming events have a way of casting their shadow before, and he did not wish to furnish the event. He said that the Zulus declared that the sacred *aasvogels* of Hloma Amabutu were as savage as lions, and that when once they saw a man down they would tear him to pieces, dead or living. In short, Hans and I came to an acute difference of opinion. As for every reason it was necessary that my view should prevail, however, I did not hesitate to put matters to him very plainly.

"Hans," I said, "you have to be a bait for vultures; choose if you will be a live bait or a dead bait," and I cocked the rifle significantly, although, in truth, the last thing that I wished or intended to do was to shoot my faithful old Hottentot friend. But Hans, knowing all I had at stake, came to a different conclusion.

"*Allemachte! baas*," he said, "I understand, and I do not blame you. Well, if I obey alive, perhaps my guardian Snake" (or spirit) "will protect me from the evil omen, and perhaps the *aasvogels* will not pick out my eyes. But if once you send a bullet through my stomach—why, then everything is finished, and for Hans it is 'Good night, sleep well.' I will obey you, *baas*, and lie where you wish, only, I pray you, do not forget me and go away, leaving me with those devil birds."

I promised him faithfully that I would not. Then we went through a very grim little pantomime. Proceeding to the centre of the arena-like space, I lifted the gun, and appeared to dash out Hans' brains with its butt. He fell upon his back, kicked about a little, and lay still. This finished Act 1.

Act 2 was that, capering like a brute of a Zulu executioner, I retired from my victim and hid myself in a bush on the edge of the plateau at a distance of forty yards. After this there was a pause. The place was intensely bright with sunshine and intensely silent; as silent as the skeletons of the murdered men about me; as silent as Hans, who lay there looking so very small and dead in that big theatre where no grass grew. It was an eerie wait in such surroundings, but at length the curtain rang up for Act 3.

In the infinite arch of blue above me I perceived a speck, no larger than a mote of dust. The *aasvogel* on watch up there far out of the range of man's vision had seen the deed, and, by sinking downwards, signalled it to his companions that were quartering the sky for fifty miles round; for these birds prey by sight, not by smell. Down he came and down, and long before he had reached the neighbourhood of earth other specks appeared in the distant blue. Now he was not more than four or five hundred yards above me, and began to wheel, floating round the place upon his wide wings, and sinking as he wheeled. So he sank softly and slowly until he was about a hundred and fifty feet above Hans. Then suddenly he paused, hung quite steady for a few seconds, shut his wings and fell like a bolt, only opening them again just before he reached the earth.

Here he settled, tilting forward in that odd way which vultures have, and scrambling a few awkward paces until he gained his balance. Then he froze into immobility, gazing with in awful, stony glare at the prostrate Hans, who lay within about fifteen feet of him. Scarcely was this *aasvogel* down, when others, summoned from the depths of sky, did as he had done. They appeared, they sank, they wheeled, always from east to west, the way the sun travels. They hovered for a few seconds, then fell like stones, pitched on to their beaks, recovered themselves, waddled forward into line, and sat gazing at Hans. Soon there was a great ring of them about him, all immovable, all gazing, all waiting for something.

Presently that something appeared in the shape of an *aasvogel* which was nearly twice as big as any of the others. This was what the Boers and the natives call the "king vulture," one of which goes with every flock. He it is who rules the roost and also the carcase, which without his presence and permission none dare to attack. Whether this vile fowl is of a different species from the others, or whether he is a bird of more vigorous growth and constitution that has outgrown the rest and thus become their overlord, is more than I can tell. At least it is certain, as I can testify from long and constant observation, that almost every flock of vultures has its king.

When this particular royalty had arrived, the other *aasvogels*, of which perhaps there were now fifty or sixty gathered round Hans, began to show signs of interested animation. They looked at the king bird, they looked at Hans, stretching out their naked red necks and winking their brilliant eyes. I, however, did not pay particular attention to those upon the earth, being amply occupied in watching their fellows in the air.

With delight I observed that the vulture is a very conservative creature. They all did what doubtless they have done since the days of Adam
or earlier—wheeled, and then hung that little space of time before they
dropped to the ground like lead. This, then, would be the moment at
which to shoot them, when for four or five seconds they offered practically a sitting target. Now, at that distance, always under a hundred yards,
I knew well that I could hit a tea plate every shot, and a vulture is much
larger than a tea plate. So it seemed to me that, barring accidents, I had
little to fear from the terrible trial of skill which lay before me. Again
and again I covered the hovering birds with my rifle, feeling that if I had
pressed the trigger I should have pierced them through.

Thinking it well to practise, I continued this game for a long while,
till at last it came to an unexpected end. Suddenly I heard a scuffling
sound. Dropping my glance I saw that the whole mob of *aasvogels*
were rushing in upon Hans, helping themselves forward by flapping
their great wings, and that about three feet in front of them was their
king. Next instant Hans vanished, and from the centre of that fluffy,
stinking mass there arose a frightful yell.

As a matter of fact, as I found afterwards, the king vulture had
fastened on to his snub nose, whilst its dreadful companions, having
seized other portions of his frame, were beginning to hang back after
their fashion in order to secure some chosen morsel. Hans kicked and
screamed, and I rushed in shouting, causing them to rise in a great,
flapping cloud that presently vanished this way and that. Within a
minute they had all gone, and the Hottentot and I were left alone.

"That is good," I said. "You played well."

"Good! *baas*," he answered, "and I with two cuts in my nose in
which I can lay my finger, and bites all over me. Look how my trousers
are torn. Look at my head—where is the hair? Look at my nose. Good!
Played well! It is those *verdomde aasvogels* that played. Oh! *baas*, if you
had seen and smelt them, you would not say that it was good. See, one
more second and I, who have two nostrils, should have had four."

"Never mind, Hans," I said, "it is only a scratch, and I will make
you a present of some new trousers. Also, here is tobacco for you.
Come to the bush; let us talk."

So we went, and when Hans was a little composed I told him all
that I had observed about the habits of the *aasvogel* in the air, and he
told me all that he had observed about their habits on the ground,
which, as I might not shoot them sitting, did not interest me. Still, he
agreed with me that the right moment to fire would be just before
they pounced.

Whilst we were still talking we heard a sound of shouts, and, looking over the brow of the hill that faced towards Umgungundhlovu, we saw a melancholy sight. Being driven up the slope towards us by three executioners and a guard of seven or eight soldiers, their hands tied behind their backs, were three men, one very old, one of about fifty years of age, and one a lad, who did not look more than eighteen. As I soon heard, they were of a single family, the grandfather, the father, and the eldest son, who had been seized upon some ridiculous charge of witchcraft, but really in order that the king might take their cattle.

Having been tried and condemned by the *Nyangas*, or witch-doctors, these poor wretches were now doomed to die. Indeed, not content with thus destroying the heads of the tribe, present and to come, for three generations, all their descendants and collaterals had already been wiped out by Dingaan, so that he might pose as sole heir to the family cattle.

Such were the dreadful cruelties that happened in Zululand in those days.

CHAPTER 14

The Play

The doomed three were driven by their murderers into the centre of the depression, within a few yards of which Hans and I were standing.

After them came the head executioner, a great brute who wore a curiously shaped leopard-skin cap—I suppose as a badge of office—and held in his hand a heavy *kerry*, the shaft of which was scored with many notches, each of them representing a human life.

"See, White Man," he shouted, "here is the bait which the king sends to draw the holy birds to you. Had it not been that you needed such bait, perhaps these wizards would have escaped. But the Black One said the little Son of George, who is named Macumazahn, needs them that he may show his magic, and therefore they must die to-day."

Now, at this information I turned positively sick. Nor did it make me feel better when the youngest of the victims, hearing the executioner's words, flung himself upon his knees, and began to implore me to spare him. His grandfather also addressed me, saying:

"Chief, will it not be enough if I die? I am old, and my life does not matter. Or if one is not sufficient, take me and my son, and let the lad, my grandson, go free. We are all of us innocent of any witchcraft, and he is not even old enough to practise such things, being but an unmarried boy. Chief, you, also, are young. Would not your heart be heavy if you had to be slain when the sun of your life was still new in the sky? Think, White Chief, what your father would feel, if you have one, should he be forced to see you killed before his eyes, that some stranger might use your body to show his skill with a magic weapon by slaying the wild things that would eat it."

Now, almost with tears, I broke in, explaining to the venerable man as well as I could that their horrible fate had nothing to do with me. I told him that I was innocent of their blood, who was forced to be there to try to shoot vultures on the wing in order to save my white companions from a doom similar to their own. He listened attentively, asking a question now and again, and when he had mastered my meaning, said with a most dignified calmness:

"Now I understand, White Man, and am glad to learn that you are not cruel, as I thought. My children," he added, turning to the others, "let us trouble this *Inkoos* no more. He only does what he must do to save the lives of his brethren by his skill, if he can. If we continue to plead with him and stir his heart to pity, the sorrow swelling in it may cause his hand to shake, and then they will die also, and their blood be on his head and ours. My children, it is the king's will that we should be slain. Let us make ready to obey the king, as men of our House have always done. White lord, we thank you for your good words. May you live long, and may good fortune sleep in your hut to the end. May you shoot straight, also, with your magic tool, and thereby win the lives of your company out of the hand of the king. Farewell, *Inkoos*," and since he could not lift his bound hands in salutation, he bowed to me, as did the others.

Then they walked to a little distance, and, seating themselves on the ground, began to talk together, and after a while to drone some strange chant in unison. The executioners and the guards also sat down not far away, laughing, chatting, and passing a horn of snuff from hand to hand. Indeed, I observed that the captain of them even took some snuff to the victims, and held it in his palm beneath their noses while they drew it up their nostrils and politely thanked him between the sneezes.

As for myself, I lit a pipe and smoked it, for I seemed to require a stimulant, or, rather, a sedative. Before it was finished Hans, who was engaged in doctoring his scratches made by the vultures' beaks with a concoction of leaves which he had been chewing, exclaimed suddenly in his matter-of-fact voice:

"See, *baas*, here they come, the white people on one side and the black on the other, just like the goats and the sheep at Judgment Day in the *Book*."

I looked, and there to my right appeared the party of Boers, headed by the Vrouw Prinsloo, who held the remnants of an old umbrella over her head. To the left advanced a number of Zulu nobles and councillors, in front of whom waddled Dingaan arrayed in his bead dancing dress. He was supported by two stalwart body-servants, whilst a third held a shield over his head to protect him from the sun, and a fourth carried a large stool, upon which he was to sit. Behind each party, also, I perceived a number of Zulus in their war-dress, all of them armed with broad stabbing spears.

The two parties arrived at the stone upon which I was sitting almost simultaneously, as probably it had been arranged that they should do, and halted, staring at each other. As for me, I sat still upon my stone and smoked on.

"*Allemachte*! Allan," puffed the Vrouw Prinsloo, who was breathless with her walk up the hill, "so here you are! As you did not come back, I thought you had run away and left us, like that stinkcat Pereira."

"Yes, *tante* (aunt), here I am," I answered gloomily, "and I wish to heaven that I was somewhere else."

Just then Dingaan, having settled his great bulk upon the stool and recovered his breath, called to the lad Halstead, who was with him, and said:

"O Tho-maas, ask your brother, Macumazahn, if he is ready to try to shoot the vultures. If not, as I wish to be fair, I will give him a little more time to make his magic medicine."

I replied sulkily that I was as ready as I was ever likely to be.

Then the Vrouw Prinsloo, understanding that the king of the Zulus was before her, advanced upon him, waving her umbrella. Catching hold of Halstead, who understood Dutch, she forced him to translate an harangue, which she addressed to Dingaan.

Had he rendered it exactly as it came from her lips, we should all have been dead in five minutes, but, luckily, that unfortunate young man had learnt some of the guile of the serpent during his sojourn among the Zulus, and varied her vigorous phrases. The gist of her discourse was that he, Dingaan, was a black-hearted and bloody-minded villain, with whom the Almighty would come even sooner or later (as, indeed, He did), and that if he dared to touch one hair of her or of her companions' heads, the Boers, her countrymen, would prove themselves to be the ministers of the Almighty in that matter (as, indeed, they did). As translated by Halstead into Zulu, what she said was that Dingaan was the greatest king in the whole world; in fact, that there was not, and never had been, any such a king either in power, wisdom, or personal beauty, and that if she and her companions had to die, the sight of his glory consoled them for their deaths.

"Indeed," said Dingaan suspiciously, "if that is what this man-woman says, her eyes tell one story and her lips another. Oh! Tho-maas, lie no more. Speak the true words of the white chieftainess, lest I should find them out otherwise, and give you to the slayers."

Thus adjured, Halstead explained that he had not yet told all the words. The "man-woman," who was, as he, Dingaan, supposed, a great chieftainess among the Dutch, added that if he, the mighty and glorious king, the earth-shaker, the world-eater, killed her or any of her subjects, her people would avenge her by killing him and his people.

"Does she say that?" said Dingaan. "Then, as I thought, these Boers are dangerous, and not the peaceful folk they make themselves out to be," and he brooded for a while, staring at the ground. Presently he lifted his head and went on: "Well, a bet is a bet, and therefore I will not wipe out this handful, as otherwise I would have done at once. Tell the old cow of a chieftainess that, notwithstanding her threats, I stick to my promise. If the little Son of George, Macumazahn, can shoot three vultures out of five by help of his magic, then she and her servants shall go free. If not, the vultures which he has missed shall feed on them, and afterwards I will talk with her people when they come to avenge her. Now, enough of this indaba. Bring those evildoers here that they may thank and praise me, who give them so merciful an end."

So the grandfather, the father, and the son were hustled before Dingaan by the soldiers, and greeted him with the royal salute of *bayete*.

"O king," said the old man, "I and my children are innocent. Yet if it pleases you, O king, I am ready to die, and so is my son. Yet we pray you to spare the little one. He is but a boy, who may grow up to do you good service, as I have done to you and your House for many years."

"Be silent, you white-headed dog!" answered Dingaan fiercely. "This lad is a wizard, like the rest of you, and would grow up to bewitch me and to plot with my enemies. Know that I have stamped out all your family, and shall I then leave him to breed another that would hate me? Begone to the World of Spirits, and tell them how Dingaan deals with sorcerers."

The old man tried to speak again, for evidently he loved this grandchild of his, but a soldier struck him in the face, and Dingaan shouted:

"What! Are you not satisfied? I tell you that if you say more I will force you to kill the boy with your own hand. Take them away."

Then I turned and hid my face, as did all the white folk. Presently I heard the old man, whom they had saved to the last that he might witness the deaths of his descendants, cry in a loud voice:

"On the night of the thirtieth full moon from this day I, the farsighted, I, the prophet, summon thee, Dingaan, to meet me and mine in the Land of Ghosts, and there to pay—"

Then with a roar of horror the executioners fell on him and he died. When there was silence I looked up, and saw that the king, who had turned a dirty yellow hue with fright, for he was very superstitious, was trembling and wiping the sweat from his brow.

"You should have kept the wizard alive," he said in a shaky voice to the head slayer, who was engaged in cutting three more nicks on the handle of his dreadful *kerry*. "Fool, I would have heard the rest of his lying message."

The man answered humbly that he thought it best it should remain unspoken, and got himself out of sight as soon as possible. Here I may remark that by an odd coincidence Dingaan actually was killed about thirty moons from that time. Mopo, his general, who slew his brother Chaka, slew him also with the help of Umslopogaas, the son of Chaka. In after years Umslopogaas told me the story of the dreadful ghost-haunted death of this tyrant, but, of course, he could not tell me exactly upon what day it happened. Therefore I do not know whether the prophecy was strictly accurate.[1]

The three victims lay dead in the hollow of the Hill of Death. Presently the king, recovering himself, gave orders that the spectators should be moved back to places where they could see what happened without frightening the vultures. So the Boers, attended by their band of soldiers, who were commanded to slay them at once if they attempted to escape, went one way, and Dingaan and his Zulus went the other, leaving Hans and myself alone behind our bush. As the white people passed me, Vrouw Prinsloo wished me good luck in a cheerful voice, although I could see that her poor old hand was shaking, and she was wiping her eyes with the *vatdoek*. Henri Marais, also in broken tones, implored me to shoot straight for his daughter's sake. Then came Marie, pale but resolute, who said nothing, but only looked me in the eyes, and touched the pocket of her dress, in which I knew the pistol lay hid. Of the rest of them I took no notice.

The moment, that dreadful moment of trial, had come at last; and oh! the suspense and the waiting were hard to bear. It seemed an age before the first speck, that I knew to be a vulture, appeared thousands of feet above me and began to descend in wide circles.

"Oh, *baas*," said poor Hans, "this is worse than shooting at the geese in the Groote Kloof. Then you could only lose your horse, but now—"

"Be silent," I hissed, "and give me the rifle."

The vulture wheeled and sank, sank and wheeled. I glanced towards the Boers, and saw that they were all of them on their knees. I glanced towards the Zulus, and saw that they were watching as, I think, they had never watched anything before, for to them this was a new excitement. Then I fixed my eyes upon the bird.

---

1. For the history of the death of Dingaan, see the Author's *Nada the Lily*.

Its last circle was accomplished. Before it pounced it hung on wide, outstretched wings, as the others had done, its head towards me. I drew a deep breath, lifted the rifle, got the foresight dead upon its breast, and touched the hair-trigger. As the charge exploded I saw the *aasvogel* give a kind of backward twist. Next instant I heard a loud clap, and a surge of joy went through me, for I thought that the bullet had found its billet. But alas! it was not so.

The clap was that of the air disturbed by the passing of the ball and the striking of this air against the stiff feathers of the wings. Anyone who has shot at great birds on the wing with a bullet will be acquainted with the sound. Instead of falling the vulture recovered itself. Not knowing the meaning of this unaccustomed noise, it dropped quietly to earth and sat down near the bodies, pitching forward in the natural way and running a few paces, as the others had done that afternoon. Evidently it was quite unhurt.

"Missed!" gasped Hans as he grasped the rifle to load it. "Oh! why did you not throw a stone on to the first heap?"

I gave Hans a look that must have frightened him; at any rate, he spoke no more. From the Boers went up a low groan. Then they began to pray harder than ever, while the Zulus clustered round the king and whispered to him. I learned afterwards that he was giving heavy odds against me, ten to one in cattle, which they were obliged to take, unwillingly enough.

Hans finished loading, capped and cocked the rifle, and handed it to me. By now other vultures were appearing. Being desperately anxious to get the thing over one way or another, at the proper moment I took the first of them. Again I covered it dead and pressed. Again as the gun exploded I saw that backward lurch of the bird, and heard the clap of the air upon its wings. Then—oh horror!—this *aasvogel* turned quietly, and began to mount the ladder of the sky in the same fashion as it had descended. I had missed once more.

"The second heap of stones has done this, *baas*," said Hans faintly, and this time I did not even look him. I only sat down and buried my face in my hands. One more such miss, and then—

Hans began to whisper to me.

"Baas," he said, "those *aasvogels* see the flash of the gun, and shy at it like a horse. Baas, you are shooting into their faces, for they all hang with their beaks toward you before they drop. You must get behind them, and fire into their tails, for even an *aasvogel* cannot see with its tail."

I let fall my hands and stared at him. Surely the poor fellow had been inspired from on high! I understood it all now. While their beaks were towards me, I might fire at fifty vultures and never hit one, for each time they would swerve from the flash, causing the bullet to miss them, though but by a little.

"Come," I gasped, and began to walk quickly round the edge of the depression to a rock, which I saw opposite about a hundred yards away. My journey took me near the Zulus, who mocked me as I passed, asking where my magic was, and if I wished to see the white people killed presently. Dingaan was now offering odds of fifty cattle to one against me, but no one would take the bet even with the king.

I made no answer; no, not even when they asked me "if I had thrown down my spear and was running away." Grimly, despairingly, I marched on to the rock, and took shelter behind it with Hans. The Boers, I saw, were still upon their knees, but seemed to have ceased praying. The children were weeping; the men stared at each other; Vrouw Prinsloo had her arm about Marie's waist. Waiting there behind the rock, my courage returned to me, as it sometimes does in the last extremity. I remembered my dream and took comfort. Surely God would not be so cruel as to suffer me to fail and thereby bring all those poor people to their deaths.

Snatching the rifle from Hans, I loaded it myself; nothing must be trusted to another. As I put on the cap a vulture made its last circle. It hung in the air just as the others had done, and oh! its tail was towards me. I lifted, I aimed between the gathered-up legs, I pressed and shut my eyes, for I did not dare to look.

I heard the bullet strike, or seem to strike, and a few seconds later I heard something else—the noise of a heavy thud upon the ground. I looked, and there with outstretched wings lay the foul bird dead, stone dead, eight or ten paces from the bodies.

"*Allemachte*! that's better," said Hans. "You threw stones on to *all* the other heaps, didn't you, *baas*?"

The Zulus grew excited, and the odds went down a little. The Boers stretched out their white faces and stared at me; I saw them out of the corner of my eye as I loaded again. Another vulture came; seeing one of its companions on the ground, if in a somewhat unnatural attitude, perhaps it thought that there could be nothing to fear. I leaned against my rock, aimed, and fired, almost carelessly, so sure was I of the result. This time I did not shut my eyes, but watched to see what happened.

The bullet struck the bird between its thighs, raked it from end to end, and down it came like a stone almost upon the top of its fellow.

"Good, good!" said Hans with a guttural chuckle of delight. "Now, *baas*, make no mistake with the third, and *als sall recht kommen* (all shall be well)."

"Yes," I answered; "*if* I make no mistake with the third."

I loaded the rifle again myself, being very careful to ram down the powder well and to select a bullet that fitted perfectly true to the bore. Moreover, I cleared the nipple with a thorn, and shook a little fine powder into it, so as to obviate any chance of a miss-fire. Then I set on the cap and waited. What was going on among the Boers or the Zulus I do not know. In this last crisis of all our fates I never looked, being too intent upon my own part in the drama.

By now the vultures appeared to have realised that something unusual was in progress, which threatened danger to them. At any rate, although by this time they had collected in hundreds from east, west, north, and south, and were wheeling the heavens above in their vast, majestic circles, none of them seemed to care to descend to prey upon the bodies. I watched, and saw that among their number was that great king bird which had bitten Hans in the face; it was easy to distinguish him, because he was so much larger than the others. Also, he had some white at the tips of his wings. I observed that certain of his company drew near to him in the skies, where they hung together in a knot, as though in consultation.

They separated out again, and the king began to descend, deputed probably to spy out the land. Down he came in ever-narrowing turns, till he reached the appointed spot for the plunge, and, according to the immemorial custom of these birds, hung a while before he pounced with his head to the south and his great, spreading tail towards me.

This was my chance, and, rejoicing in having so large a mark, I got the sight upon him and pulled. The bullet thudded, some feathers floated from his belly, showing that it had gone home, and I looked to see him fall as the others had done. But alas! he did not fall. For a few seconds he rocked to and fro upon his great wings, then commenced to travel upwards in vast circles, which grew gradually more narrow, till he appeared to be flying almost straight into the empyrean. I stared and stared. Everybody stared, till that enormous bird became, first a mere blot upon the blue, and at length but a speck. Then it vanished altogether into regions far beyond the sight of man.

"Now there is an end," I said to Hans.

"*Ja, baas,*" answered the Hottentot between his chattering teeth, "there is an end. You did not put in enough powder. Presently we shall all be dead."

"Not quite," I said with a bitter laugh. "Hans, load the rifle, load it quick. Before they die there shall be another king in Zululand."

"Good, good!" he exclaimed as he loaded desperately. "Let us take that fat pig of a Dingaan with us. Shoot him in the stomach, *baas*; shoot him in the stomach, so that he too may learn what it is to die slowly. Then cut my throat, here is my big knife, and afterwards cut your own, if you have not time to load the gun again and shoot yourself, which is easier."

I nodded, for it was in my mind to do these things. Never could I stand still and see those poor Boers killed, and I knew that Marie would look after herself.

Meanwhile, the Zulus were coming towards me, and the soldiers who had charge of them were driving up Marais's people, making pretence to thrust them through with their assegais, and shouting at them as men do at cattle. Both parties arrived in the depression at about the same time, but remained separated by a little space. In this space lay the corpses of the murdered men and the two dead *aasvogels*, with Hans and myself standing opposite to them.

"Well, little Son of George," puffed Dingaan, "you have lost your bet, for you did but kill two vultures out of five with your magic, which was good as far as it went, but not good enough. Now you must pay, as I would have paid had you won."

Then he stretched out his hand, and issued the dreadful order of *bulala amalongu!* (Kill the white people). "Kill them one by one, that I may see whether they know how to die, all except Macumazahn and the tall girl, whom I keep."

Some of the soldiers made a dash and seized the Vrouw Prinsloo, who was standing in front of the party.

"Wait a little, King," she called out as the assegais were lifted over her. "How do you know that the bet is lost? He whom you call Macumazahn hit that last vulture. It should be searched for before you kill us."

"What does the old woman say?" asked Dingaan, and Halstead translated slowly.

"True," said Dingaan. "Well, now I will send her to search for the vulture in the sky. Come back thence, Fat One, and tell us if you find it."

The soldiers lifted their assegais, waiting the king's word. I pretended to look at the ground, and cocked my rifle, being determined that if he spoke it, it should be his last. Hans stared upwards—I suppose to avoid the sight of death—then suddenly uttered a wild yell, which caused everyone, even the doomed people, to turn their eyes to him. He was pointing to the heavens, and they looked to see at what he pointed.

This was what they saw. Far, far above in that infinite sea of blue there appeared a tiny speck, which his sharp sight had already discerned, a speck that grew larger and larger as it descended with terrific and ever-growing speed.

354

It was the king vulture falling from the heavens—dead!

Down it came between the Vrouw Prinsloo and the slayers, smashing the lifted *assegai* of one of them and hurling him to the earth. Down it came, and lay there a mere mass of pulp and feathers.

"O Dingaan," I said in the midst of the intense silence that followed, "it seems that it is I who have won the bet, not you. I killed this king of birds, but being a king it chose to die high up and alone, that is all."

Dingaan hesitated, for he did not wish to spare the Boers, and I, noting his hesitation, lifted my rifle a little. Perhaps he saw it, or perhaps his sense of honour, as he understood the word, overcame his wish for their blood. At any rate, he said to one of his councillors:

"Search the carcase of that vulture and see if there is a bullet hole in it."

The man obeyed, feeling at the mass of broken bones and flesh. By good fortune he found, not the hole, for that was lost in the general destruction of the tissues, but the ball itself, which, having pierced the thick body from below upwards, had remained fast in the tough skin just by the back-bone where the long, red neck emerges from between the wings. He picked it out, for it was only hanging in the skin, and held it up for all to see.

"Macumazahn has won his bet," said Dingaan. "His magic has conquered, though by but a very little. Macumazahn, take these Boers, they are yours, and begone with them out of my country."

CHAPTER 15

Retief Asks a Favour

Now and again during our troubled journey through life we reach little oases of almost perfect happiness, set jewel-like here and there in the thorny wilderness of time. Sometimes these are hours of mere animal content. In others they are made beautiful by waters blowing from our spiritual springs of being, as in those rare instances when the material veil of life seems to be rent by a mighty hand, and we feel the presence and the comfort of God within us and about us, guiding our footsteps to the ineffable end, which is Himself. Occasionally, however, all these, physical satisfaction and love divine and human, are blended to a whole, like soul and body, and we can say, "Now I know what is joy."

Such an hour came to me on the evening of that day of the winning of my bet with Dingaan, when a dozen lives or so were set against my nerve and skill. These had not failed me, although I knew that had it not been for the inspiration of the Hottentot Hans (who sent it, I wonder?) they would have been of no service at all. With all my thought and experience, it had never occurred to me that the wonderful eyes of the vultures would see the flash of the powder even through the pervading sunlight, and swerve before the deadly bullet could reach them.

On that night I was indeed a hero in a small way. Even Henri Marais thawed and spoke to me as a father might to his child, he who always disliked me in secret, partly because I was an Englishman, partly because I was everything to his daughter and he was jealous, and partly for the reason that I stood in the path of his nephew, Hernan Pereira, whom he either loved or feared, or both. As for the rest of them, men, women and children, they thanked and blessed me with tears in their eyes, vowing that, young as I was, thenceforth I and no other should be their leader. As may be imagined, although it is true that she set down my success to her meal of bullock's liver and the nap which she had insisted on my taking, the Vrouw Prinsloo was the most enthusiastic of them all.

"Look at him," she said, pointing with her fat finger at my insignificant self and addressing her family. "If only I had such a husband or a son, instead of you lumps that God has tied to me like clogs to the heels of a she-ass, I should be happy."

"God did that in order to prevent you from kicking, old *vrouw*," said her husband, a quiet man with a vein of sardonic humour. "If only He had tied another clog to your tongue, I should be happy also"; whereon the *vrouw* smacked his head and her children got out of the way sniggering.

But the most blessed thing of all was my interview with Marie. All that took place between us can best be left to the imagination, since the talk of lovers, even in such circumstances, is not interesting to others. Also, in a sense, it is too sacred to repeat. One sentence I will set down, however, because in the light of after events I feel that it was prophetic, and not spoken merely by chance. It was at the end of our talk, as she was handing me back the pistol that I had given her for a certain dreadful purpose.

"Three times you have saved my life, Allan—once at Maraisfontein, once from starvation, and now from Dingaan, whose touch would have meant my death. I wonder whether it will ever be my turn to save yours?"

She looked down for a little while, then lifted her head and laid her hand upon my shoulder, adding slowly: "Do you know, Allan, I think that it will at the—" and suddenly she turned and left me with her sentence unfinished.

So thus it came about that by the help of Providence I was enabled to rescue all these worthy folk from a miserable and a bloody death. And yet I have often reflected since that if things had gone differently; if, for instance, that king *aasvogel* had found strength to carry itself away to die at a distance instead of soaring straight upwards like a towering partridge, as birds injured in the lungs will often do—I suppose in search of air—it might have been better in the end. Then I should certainly have shot Dingaan dead and every one of us would as certainly have been killed on the spot. But if Dingaan had died that day, Retief and his companions would never have been massacred. Also as the peaceful Panda, his brother, would, I suppose, have succeeded to the throne, probably the subsequent slaughter at Weenen, and all the after fighting, would never have taken place.

But so it was fated, and who am I that I should quarrel with or even question the decrees of fate? Doubtless these things were doomed to happen, and they happened in due course. There is nothing more to be said.

Early on the following morning we collected our oxen, which, although still footsore, were now full fed and somewhat rested. An hour or two later began our trek, word having come to us from Dingaan that we must start at once. Also he sent us guides, under the command of the captain Kambula, to show us the road to Natal.

I breakfasted that day with the Reverend Mr. Owen and his people, my object being to persuade him to come away with us, as I did not consider that Zululand was a safe place for white women and children. My mission proved fruitless. Mrs. Hulley, the wife of the absent interpreter, who had three little ones, Miss Owen and the servant, Jane Williams, were all of them anxious enough to do as I suggested. But Mr. and Mrs. Owen, who were filled with the true fervour of missionaries, would not listen. They said that God would protect them; that they had only been a few weeks in the country, and that it would be the act of cowards and of traitors to fly at the very beginning of their work. Here I may add that after the massacre of Retief they changed their opinion, small blame to them, and fled as fast as anyone else.

I told Mr. Owen how very close I had gone to shooting Dingaan, in which event they might all have been killed with us. This news shocked him much. Indeed, he lectured me severely on the sins of bloodthirstiness and a desire for revenge. So, finding that we looked at things differently, and that it was of no use wasting breath in argument, I wished him and his people good-bye and good fortune and went upon my way, little guessing how we should meet again.

An hour later we trekked. Passing by the accursed hill, Hloma Amabutu, where I saw some gorged vultures sleeping on the rocks, we came to the gate of the Great *Kraal*. Here, to my surprise, I saw Dingaan with some of his councillors and an armed guard of over a hundred men, seated under the shade of two big milk trees. Fearing treachery, I halted the wagons and advised the Boers to load their rifles and be ready for the worst. A minute or so later young Thomas Halstead arrived and told me that Dingaan wished to speak with us. I asked him if that meant that we were to be killed. He answered, "No, you are quite safe." The king had received some news that had put him in a good humour with the white people, and he desired to bid us farewell, that was all.

So we trekked boldly to where Dingaan was, and, stopping the wagons, went up to him in a body. He greeted us kindly enough, and even gave me his fat hand to shake.

"Macumazahn," he said, "although it has cost me many oxen, I am glad that your magic prevailed yesterday. Had it not done so I should have killed all these your friends, which would have been a cause of war between me and the Amaboona. Now, this morning I have learned that these Amaboona are sending a friendly embassy to me under one of their great chiefs, and I think that you will meet them on the road. I charge you, therefore, to tell them to come on, having no fear, as I will receive them well and listen to all they have to say."

I answered that I would do so.

"Good," he replied. "I am sending twelve head of cattle with you, six of them for your food during your journey, and six as a present to the embassy of the Amaboona. Also Kambula, my captain, has charge to see you safely over the Tugela River."

I thanked him and turned to go, when suddenly his eye fell upon Marie, who, foolishly enough, took this opportunity to advance from among the others and speak to me about something—I forget what.

"Macumazahn, is that the maiden of whom you spoke to me?" asked Dingaan; "she whom you are going to marry?"

I answered, "Yes."

"By the head of the Black One," he exclaimed, "she is very fair. Will you not make a present of her to me, Macumazahn?"

I answered, "No; she is not mine to give away."

"Well, then, Macumazahn, I will pay you a hundred head of cattle for her, which is the price of a royal wife, and give you ten of the fairest girls in Zululand in exchange."

I answered that it could not be.

Now the king began to grow angry.

"I will keep her, whether you wish it or no," he said.

"Then you will keep her dead, O Dingaan," I replied, "for there is more of that magic which slew the vultures."

Of course, I meant that Marie would be dead. But as my knowledge of the Zulu tongue was imperfect, he understood the words to mean that *he* would be dead, and I think they frightened him. At any rate, he said:

"Well, I promised you all safe-conduct if you won your bet, so *hamba gachle* (go in peace). I wish to have no quarrel with the white folk, but, Macumazahn, you are the first of them who has refused a gift to Dingaan. Still, I bear you no grudge, and if you choose to come back again, you will be welcome, for I perceive that, although so small, you are very clever and have a will of your own; also that you mean what you say and speak the truth. Tell the People of George that my heart is soft towards them." Then he turned and walked away through the gates of the *kraal*.

Glad enough was I to see the last of him, for now I knew that we were safe, except from such accidents as may overtake any travellers through a wild country. For the present, at any rate until after he had seen this embassy, Dingaan wished to stand well with the Boers. Therefore it was obvious that he would never make an irreparable quarrel with them by treacherously putting us to death as we trekked through his country. Being sure of this, we went on our way with light hearts, thanking Heaven for the mercies which had been shown to us.

It was on the third day of our trek, when we were drawing near to the Tugela, that we met the Boer embassy, off-saddled by a little stream where we proposed to outspan to rest the oxen while we ate our midday meal. They were sleeping in the heat of the day and saw nothing of us till we were right on to them, when, catching sight of our Zulu advance guard, they sprang up and ran for their rifles. Then the wagons emerged from the bush, and they stared astonished, wondering who could be trekking in that country.

We called to them in Dutch not to be afraid and in another minute we were among them. While we were yet some way off my eye fell upon a burly, white-bearded man whose figure seemed to be familiar to me, and towards him I went, taking no heed of the others, of whom there may have been six or seven. Soon I was sure, and advancing with outstretched hand, said:

"Good-day, Mynheer Piet Retief. Who would have thought that we who parted so far away and so long ago would live to meet among the Zulus?"

He stared at me.

"Who is it? Who is it? *Allemachte*! I know now. The little Englishman, Allan Quatermain, who shot the geese down in the Old Colony. Well, I should not be surprised, for the man you beat in that match told me that you were travelling in these parts. Only I understood him to say that the Zulus had killed you."

"If you mean Hernan Pereira," I answered, "where did you meet him?"

"Why, down by the Tugela there, in a bad way. However, he can tell you all about that himself, for I have brought him with me to show us the path to Dingaan's *kraal*. Where is Pereira? Send Pereira here. I want to speak with him."

360

"Here I am," answered a sleepy voice, the hated voice of Pereira himself, from the other side of a thick bush, where he had been slumbering. "What is it, commandant? I come," and he emerged, stretching himself and yawning, just as the remainder of my party came up. He caught sight of Henri Marais first of all, and began to greet him, saying: "Thank God, my uncle, you are safe!"

Then his eyes fell on me, and I do not think I ever saw a man's face change more completely. His jaw dropped, the colour left his cheeks, leaving them of the yellow which is common to persons of Portuguese descent; his outstretched hand fell to his side.

"Allan Quatermain!" he ejaculated. "Why, I thought that you were dead."

"As I should have been, Mynheer Pereira, twice over if you could have had your way," I replied.

"What do you mean, Allan?" broke in Retief.

"I will tell you what he means," exclaimed the Vrouw Prinsloo, shaking her fat fist at Pereira. "That yellow dog means that twice he has tried to murder Allan—Allan, who saved his life and ours. Once he shot at him in a *kloof* and grazed his cheek; look, there is the scar of it. And once he plotted with the Zulus to slaughter him, telling Dingaan that he was an evildoer and a wizard, who would bring a curse upon his land."

Now Retief looked at Pereira.

"What do you say to this?" he asked.

"What do I say?" repeated Pereira, recovering himself. "Why, that it is a lie or a misunderstanding. I never shot at Heer Allan in any *kloof*. Is it likely that I should have done so when he had just nursed me back to life? I never plotted with the Zulus for his death, which would have meant the deaths of my uncle and my cousin and of all their companions. Am I mad that I should do such a thing?"

"Not mad, but bad," screamed the *vrouw*. "I tell you, Heer Retief, it is no lie. Ask those with me," she added, appealing to the others, who, with the exception of Marais, answered as with one voice:

"No; it is no lie."

"Silence!" said the commandant. "Now, nephew Allan, tell us your story."

So I told him everything, of course leaving out all details. Even then the tale was long, though it did not seem to be one that wearied my hearers.

"*Allemachte!*" said Retief when I had finished, "this is a strange story, the strangest that ever I heard. If it is true, Hernan Pereira, you deserve to have your back set against a tree and to be shot."

"God in heaven!" he answered, "am I to be condemned on such a tale—I, an innocent man? Where is the evidence? This Englishman tells all this against me for a simple reason—that he has robbed me of the love of my cousin, to whom I was affianced. Where are his witnesses?"

"As to the shooting at me in the *kloof*, I have none except God who saw you," I answered. "As to the plot that you laid against me among the Zulus, as it chances, however, there is one, Kambula, the captain who was sent to take me as you had arranged, and who now commands our escort."

"A savage!" exclaimed Pereira. "Is the tale of a savage to be taken against that of a white man? Also, who will translate his story? You, Mynheer Quatermain, are the only one here who knows his tongue, if you do know it, and you are my accuser."

"That is true," remarked Retief. "Such a witness should not be admitted without a sworn interpreter. Now listen; I pass judgment as commandant in the field. Hernan Pereira, I have known you to be a rogue in the past, for I remember that you cheated this very young man, Allan Quatermain, at a friendly trial of skill at which I was present; but since then till now I have heard nothing more of you, good or bad. To-day this Allan Quatermain and a number of my own countrymen bring grave charges against you, which, however, at present are not capable of proof or disproof. Well, I cannot decide those charges, whatever my own opinion may be. I think that you had better go back with your uncle, Henri Marais, to the trek-Boers, where they can be laid before a court and settled according to law."

"If so, he will go back alone," said the Vrouw Prinsloo. "He will not go back with us, for we will elect a field-cornet and shoot him— the stinkcat, who left us to starve and afterwards tried to kill little Allan Quatermain, who saved our lives"; and the chorus behind her echoed:

"*Ja, ja*, we will shoot him."

"Hernan Pereira," said Retief, rubbing his broad forehead, "I don't quite know why it is, but no one seems to want you as a companion. Indeed, to speak truth, I don't myself. Still, I think you would be safer with me than with these others whom you seem to have offended. Therefore, I suggest that you come on with us. But listen here, man," he added sternly, "if I find you plotting against us among the Zulus, that hour you are dead. Do you understand?"

"I understand that I am one slandered," replied Pereira. "Still, it is Christian to submit to injuries, and therefore I will do as you wish. As to these bearers of false witness, I leave them to God."

"And I leave you to the devil," shouted Vrouw Prinsloo, "who will certainly have you soon or late. Get out of my sight, stinkcat, or I will pull your hair off." And she rushed at him, flapping her dreadful *vatdoek*—which she produced from some recess in her raiment—in his face, driving him away as though he were a noxious insect.

Well, he went I know not where, and so strong was public opinion against him that I do not think that even his uncle, Henri Marais, sought him out to console him.

When Pereira was gone, our party and that of Retief fell into talk, and we had much to tell. Especially was the commandant interested in the story of my bet with Dingaan, whereby I saved the lives of all my companions by shooting the vultures.

"It was not for nothing, nephew, that God Almighty gave you the power of holding a gun so straight," said Retief to me when he understood the matter. "I remember that when you killed those wildfowl in the Groote Kloof with bullets, which no other man could have done, I wondered why you should have such a gift above all the rest of us, who have practised for so many more years. Well, now I understand. God Almighty is no fool; He knows His business. I wish you were coming back with me to Dingaan; but as that tainted man, Hernan Pereira, is of my company, perhaps it is better that you should stay away. Tell me, now, about this Dingaan; does he mean to kill us?"

"Not this time, I think, uncle," I answered; "because first he wishes to learn all about the Boers. Still, do not trust him too far just because he speaks you softly. Remember, that if I had missed the third vulture, we should all have been dead by now. And, if you are wise, keep an eye upon Hernan Pereira."

"These things I will do, nephew, especially the last of them; and now we must be getting on. Stay; come here, Henri Marais; I have a word to say to you. I understand that this little Englishman, Allan Quatermain, who is worth ten bigger men, loves your daughter, whose life he has saved again and again, and that she loves him. Why, then, do you not let them marry in a decent fashion?"

"Because before God I have sworn her to another man—to my nephew, Hernan Pereira, whom everyone slanders," answered Marais sulkily. "Until she is of age that oath holds."

"Oho!" said Retief, "you have sworn your lamb to that hyena, have you? Well, look out that he does not crack your bones as well as hers, and perhaps some others also. Why does God give some men a worm in their brains, as He does to the wildebeest, a worm that always makes them run the wrong way? I don't know, I am sure; but you who are very

363

religious, Henri Marais, might think the matter over and tell me the answer when next we meet. Well, this girl of yours will soon be of age, and then, as I am commandant down yonder where she is going, I'll see she marries the man she wants, whatever you say, Henri Marais. Heaven above us! I only wish it were my daughter he was in love with. A fellow who can shoot to such good purpose might have the lot of them"; and uttering one of his great, hearty laughs, he walked off to his horse.

On the morrow of this meeting we forded the Tugela and entered the territory that is now called Natal. Two days' short trekking through a beautiful country brought us to some hills that I think were called Pakadi, or else a chief named Pakadi lived there, I forget which. Crossing these hills, on the further side of them, as Retief had told us we should do, we found a large party of the trek-Boers, who were already occupying this land on the hither side of the Bushman's River, little knowing, poor people, that it was fated to become the grave of many of them. To-day, and for all future time, that district is and will be known by the name of Weenen, or the Place of Weeping, because of those pioneers who here were massacred by Dingaan within a few weeks of the time of which I write.

Nice as the land was, for some reason or other it did not quite suit my fancy, and therefore, in view of my approaching marriage with Marie, having purchased a horse from one of the trek-Boers, I began to explore the country round. My object was to find a stretch of fertile *veld* where we could settle when we were wedded, and such a spot I discovered after some trouble. It lay about thirty miles away to the east, in the loop of a beautiful stream that is now known as the Mooi River.

Enclosed in this loop were some thirty thousand acres of very rich, low-lying soil, almost treeless and clothed with luxuriant grasses where game was extraordinarily numerous. At the head of it rose a flat-topped hill, from the crest of which, oddly enough, flowed a plentiful stream of water fed by a strong spring. Half-way down this hill, facing to the east, and irrigable by the stream, was a plateau several acres in extent, which furnished about the best site for a house that I know in all South Africa. Here I determined we would build our dwelling-place and become rich by the breeding up of great herds of cattle. I should explain that this ground, which once, as the remains of their old *kraals* showed, had belonged to a Kaffir tribe killed out by Chaka, the Zulu king, was to be had for the taking.

Indeed, as there was more land than we could possibly occupy, I persuaded Henri Marais, the Prinsloos and the Meyers, with whom

I had trekked from Delagoa, to visit it with me. When they had seen it they agreed to make it their home in the future, but meanwhile elected to return to the other Boers for safety's sake. So with the help of some Kaffirs, of whom there were a few in the district, remnants of those tribes which Chaka had destroyed, I pegged out an estate of about twelve thousand acres for myself, and, selecting a site, set the natives to work to build a rough mud house upon it which would serve as a temporary dwelling. I should add that the Prinsloos and the Meyers also made arrangements for the building of similar shelters almost alongside of my own. This done, I returned to Marie and the trek-Boers.

On the morning after my return to the camp Piet Retief appeared there with his five or six companions. I asked him how he had got on with Dingaan.

"Well enough, nephew," he answered. "At first the king was somewhat angry, saying that we Boers had stolen six hundred head of his cattle. But I showed him that it was the chief, Sikonyela, who lives yonder on the Caledon River, who had dressed up his people in white men's clothes and put them upon horses, and afterwards drove the cattle through one of our camps to make it appear that we were the thieves. Then he asked me what was my object in visiting him. I answered that I sought a grant of the land south of the Tugela to the sea.

"'Bring me back the cattle that you say Sikonyela has stolen,' he said, 'and we will talk about this land.' To this I agreed and soon after left the *kraal*."

"What did you do with Hernan Pereira, uncle?" I asked.

"This, Allan. When I was at Umgungundhlovu I sought out the truth of that story you told me as to his having made a plot to get you killed by the Zulus on the ground that you were a wizard."

"And what did you discover, uncle?"

"I discovered that it was true, for Dingaan told me so himself. Then I sent for Pereira and ordered him out of my camp, telling him that if he came back among the Boers I would have him put on his trial for attempted murder. He said nothing, but went away."

"Whither did he go?"

"To a place that Dingaan gave him just outside his *kraal*. The king said that he would be useful to him, as he could mend guns and teach his soldiers to shoot with them. So there, I suppose, he remains, unless he has thought it wiser to make off. At any rate, I am sure that he will not come here to trouble you or anyone."

"No, uncle, but he may trouble you *there*," I said doubtfully.

"What do you mean, Allan?"

"I don't quite know, but he is black-hearted, a traitor by nature, and in one way or the other he will stir up sorrow. Do you think that he will love you, for instance, after you have hunted him out like a thief?"

Retief shrugged his shoulders and laughed as he answered:

"I will take my chance of that. What is the use of troubling one's head about such a snake of a man? And now, Allan, I have something to ask you. Are you married yet?"

"No, uncle, nor can be for another five weeks, when Marie comes of age. Her father still holds that his oath binds him, and I have promised that I will not take her till then."

"Does he indeed, Allan? I think that Henri Marais is *kransick* (that is, cracked), or else his cursed nephew, Hernan, has fascinated him, as a snake does a bird. Still, I suppose that he has the law on his side, and, as I am commandant, I cannot advise anyone to break the law. Now listen. It is no use your staying here looking at the ripe peach you may not pluck, for that only makes the stomach sick. Therefore the best thing that you can do is to come with me to get those cattle from Sikonyela, for I shall be very glad of your company. Afterwards, too, I want you to return with me to Zululand when I go for the grant of all this country."

"But how about my getting married?" I asked in dismay.

"Oh! I dare say you will be able to marry before we start. Or if not, it must be when we return. Listen now; do not disappoint me in this matter, Allan. None of us can speak Zulu except you, who takes to these savage languages like a duck to water, and I want you to be my interpreter with Dingaan. Also the king specially asked that you should come with me when I brought the cattle, as he seems to have taken a great fancy to you. He said that you would render his words honestly, but that he did not trust the lad whom he has there to translate into Dutch and English. So you see it will help me very much in this big business if you come with me."

Still I hesitated, for some fear of the future lay heavy on my heart, warning me against this expedition.

"*Allemachte!*" said Retief angrily, "if you will not grant me a favour, let it be. Or is it that you want reward? If so, all I can promise you is twenty thousand acres of the best land in the country when we get it."

"No, Mynheer Retief," I replied; "it is no question of reward; and as for the land, I have already pegged out my farm on a river about thirty miles to the east. It is that I do not like to leave Marie alone, fearing lest her father should play some trick on me as regards her and Hernan Pereira."

"Oh, if that is all you are afraid of, Allan, I can soon settle matters; for I will give orders to the Predicant Celliers that he is not to marry Marie Marais to anyone except yourself, even if she asks him. Also I will order that if Hernan Pereira should come to the camp, he is to be shut up until I return to try him. Lastly, as commandant, I will name Henri Marais as one of those who are to accompany us, so that he will be able to plot nothing against you. Now are you satisfied?"

I said "Yes" as cheerfully as I could, though I felt anything but cheerful, and we parted, for, of course, the Commandant Retief had much to occupy him.

Then I went and told Marie what I had promised. Somewhat to my surprise she said that she thought I had acted wisely.

"If you stayed here," she added, "perhaps some new quarrel would arise between you and my father which might make bitterness afterwards. Also, dear, it would be foolish for you to offend the Commandant Retief, who will be the great man in this country, and who is very fond of you. After all, Allan, we shall only be separated for a little while, and when that is done we have the rest of our lives to spend together. As for me, do not be afraid, for you know I will never marry anyone but you—no, not to save myself from death."

So I left her somewhat comforted, knowing how sound was her judgment, and went off to make my preparations for the expedition to Sikonyela's country.

All this conversation with Retief I have set down in full, as nearly as I can remember it, because of its fateful consequences. Ah! if I could have foreseen; if only I could have foreseen!

CHAPTER 16

The Council

Two days later we started to recover Dingaan's cattle, sixty or seventy of us, all well armed and mounted. With us went two of Dingaan's captains and a number of Zulus, perhaps a hundred, who were to drive the cattle if we recovered them. As I could speak their language I was more or less in command of this Zulu contingent, and managed to make myself very useful in that capacity. Also, during the month or so of our absence, by continually conversing with them, I perfected myself considerably in my knowledge of their beautiful but difficult tongue.

Now it is not my intention to write down the details of this expedition, during which there was no fighting and nothing serious happened. We arrived in due course at Sikonyela's and stated our errand. When he saw how numerous and well armed we were, and that behind us was all the might of the Zulu army, that wily old rascal thought it well to surrender the stolen cattle without further to-do, and with these some horses which he had lifted from the Boers. So, having received them, we delivered them over to the Zulu captains, with instructions to drive them carefully to Umgungundhlovu. The commandant sent a message by these men to the effect that, having fulfilled his part of the compact, he would wait upon Dingaan as soon as possible in order to conclude the treaty about the land.

This business finished, Retief took me and a number of the Boers to visit other bodies of the emigrant Dutch who were beyond the Drakensberg, in what is now the Transvaal territory. This occupied a long time, as these Boers were widely scattered, and at each camp we had to stop for several days while Retief explained everything to its leaders. Also he arranged with them to come down into Natal, so as to be ready to people it as soon as he received the formal cession of the country from Dingaan. Indeed, most of them began to trek at

368

once, although jealousies between the various commandants caused some of the bands, luckily for themselves, to remain on the farther side of the mountains.

At length, everything being settled, we rode away, and reached the Bushman's River camp on a certain Saturday afternoon. Here, to my joy, we found all well. Nothing had been heard of Hernan Pereira, while the Zulus, if we might judge from messengers who came to us, seemed to be friendly. Marie, also, had now quite recovered from the fears and hardships which she had undergone. Never had I seen her look so sweet and beautiful as she did when she greeted me, arrayed no longer in rags, but in a simple yet charming dress made of some stuff that she had managed to buy from a trader who came up to the camp from Durban. Moreover, I think that there was another reason for the change, since the light of dawning happiness shone in her deep eyes.

The day, as I have said, was Saturday, and on the Monday she would come of age and be free to dispose of herself in marriage, for on that day lapsed the promise which we had given to her father. But, alas! by a cursed perversity of fate, on this very Monday at noon the Commandant Retief had arranged to ride into Zululand on his second visit to Dingaan, and with Retief I was in honour bound to go.

"Marie," I said, "will not your father soften towards us and let us be married to-morrow, so that we may have a few hours together before we part?"

"I do not know, my dear," she answered, blushing, "since about this matter he is very strange and obstinate. Do you know that all the time you were absent he never mentioned your name, and if anyone else spoke it he would get up and go away!"

"That's bad," I said. "Still, if you are willing, we might try."

"Indeed and indeed, Allan, I am willing, who am sick of being so near to you and yet so far. But how shall we do so?"

"I think that we will ask the Commandant Retief and the Vrouw Prinsloo to plead for us, Marie. Let us go to seek them."

She nodded, and hand in hand we walked through the Boers, who nudged each other and laughed at us as we passed to where the old *vrouw* was seated on a stool by her wagon drinking coffee. I remember that her *vatdoek* was spread over her knees, for she also had a new dress, which she was afraid of staining.

"Well, my dears," she said in her loud voice, "are you married already that you hang so close together?"

"No, my aunt," I answered; "but we want to be, and have come to you to help us."

"That I will do with all my heart, though to speak truth, young people, at your age, as things are, I should have been inclined to help myself, as I have told you before. Heaven above us! what is it that makes marriage in the sight of God? It is that male and female should declare themselves man and wife before all folk, and live as such. The pastor and his mumblings are very well if you can get them, but it is the giving of the hand, not the setting of the ring upon it; it is the vowing of two true hearts, and not words read out of a book, that make marriage. Still, this is bold talk, for which any reverend predicant would reprove me, for if young folk acted on it, although the tie might hold good in law, what would become of his fee? Come, let us seek the commandant and hear what he has to say. Allan, pull me up off this stool, where, if I had my way, after so much travelling, I should like to sit while a house was built over my head and for the rest of my life."

I obeyed, not without difficulty, and we went to find Retief.

At the moment he was standing alone, watching two wagons that had just trekked away. These contained his wife with other members of his family, and some friends whom he was sending, under the charge of the Heer Smit, to a place called Doornkop, that lay at a distance of fifteen miles or more. At this Doornkop he had already caused a rough house, or rather shed, to be built for the Vrouw Retief's occupation, thinking that she would be more comfortable and perhaps safer there during his absence than at the crowded camp in a wagon.

"*Allemachte!* Allan," he said, catching sight of me, "my heart is sore; I do not know why. I tell you that when I kissed my old woman good-bye just now I felt as though I should never see her again, and the tears came into my eyes. I wish we were all safe back from Dingaan. But there, there, I will try to get over to see her to-morrow, as we don't start till Monday. What is it that you want, Allan, with that *mooi mesje* of yours?"—and he pointed to the tall Marie.

"What would any man want with such a one, save to marry her?" broke in the Vrouw Prinsloo. "Now, commandant, listen while I set out the tale."

"All right, aunt, only be brief, for I have no time to spare."

She obeyed, but I cannot say that she was brief.

When at last the old lady paused, breathless, Retief said:

"I understand everything; there is no need for you young people to talk. Now we will go and see Henri Marais, and, if he is not madder than usual, make him listen to reason."

370

So we walked to where Marais's wagon stood at the end of the line, and found him sitting on the *disselboom* cutting up tobacco with his pocket-knife.

"Good-day, Allan," he said, for we had not met since my return. "Have you had a nice journey?"

I was about to answer when the commandant broke in impatiently:

"See here, see here, Henri, we have not come to talk about Allan's journey, but about his marriage, which is more important. He rides with me to Zululand on Monday, as you do, and wants to wed your daughter to-morrow, which is Sunday, a good day for the deed."

"It is a day to pray, not to give and be given in marriage," commented Marais sulkily. "Moreover, Marie does not come of age before Monday, and until then the oath that I made to God holds."

"My *vatdoek* for your oath!" exclaimed the *vrouw*, flapping that awful rag in his face. "How much do you suppose that God cares what you in your folly swore to that stinkcat of a nephew of yours? Do you be careful, Henri Marais, that God does not make of your precious oath a stone to fall upon your head and break it like a peanut-shell."

"Hold your chattering tongue, old woman," said Marais furiously. "Am I to be taught my duty to my conscience and my daughter by you?"

"Certainly you are, if you cannot teach them to yourself," began the *vrouw*, setting her hands upon her hips.

But Retief pushed her aside, saying:

"No quarrelling here. Now, Henri Marais, your conduct about these two young people who love each other is a scandal. Will you let them be married to-morrow or not?"

"No, commandant, I will not. By the law I have power over my daughter till she is of age, and I refuse to allow her to marry a cursed Englishman. Moreover, the Predicant Celliers is away, so there is none to marry them."

"You speak strange words, Mynheer Marais," said Retief quietly, "especially when I remember all that this 'cursed Englishman' has done for you and yours, for I have heard every bit of that story, though not from him. Now hearken. You have appealed to the law, and, as commandant, I must allow your appeal. But after twelve o'clock to-morrow night, according to your own showing, the law ceases to bind your daughter. Therefore, on Monday morning, if there is no clergyman in the camp and these two wish it, I, as commandant, will marry them before all men, as I have the power to do."

Then Marais broke into one of those raving fits of temper which were constitutional in him, and to my mind showed that he was never quite sane. Oddly enough, it was on poor Marie that he concentrated his wrath. He cursed her horribly because she had withstood his will and refused to marry Hernan Pereira. He prayed that evil might fall on her; that she might never bear a child, and that if she did, it might die, and other things too unpleasant to mention.

We stared at him astonished, though I think that had he been any other man than the father of my betrothed, I should have struck him. Retief, I noticed, lifted his hand to do so, then let it fall again, muttering: "Let be; he is possessed with a devil."

At last Marais ceased, not, I think, from lack of words, but because he was exhausted, and stood before us, his tall form quivering, and his thin, nervous face working like that of a person in convulsions. Then Marie, who had dropped her head beneath this storm, lifted it, and I saw that her deep eyes were all ablaze and that she was very white.

"You are my father," she said in a low voice, "and therefore I must submit to whatever you choose to say to me. Moreover, I think it likely that the evil which you call down will fall upon me, since Satan is always at hand to fulfil his own wishes. But if so, my father, I am sure that this evil will recoil upon your own head, not only here, but hereafter. There justice will be done to both of us, perhaps before very long, and also to your nephew, Hernan Pereira."

Marais made no answer; his rage seemed to have spent itself. He only sat himself again upon the *disselboom* of the wagon and went on cutting up the tobacco viciously, as though he were slicing the heart of a foe. Even the Vrouw Prinsloo was silent and stared at him whilst she fanned herself with the *vatdoek*. But Retief spoke.

"I wonder if you are mad, or only wicked, Henri Marais," he said. "To curse your own sweet girl like this you must be one or the other—a single child who has always been good to you. Well, as you are to ride with me on Monday, I pray that you will keep your temper under control, lest it should bring us into trouble, and you also. As for you, Marie, my dear, do not fret because a wild beast has tried to toss you with his horns, although he happens to be your father. On Monday morning you pass out of his power into your own, and on that day I will marry you to Allan Quatermain here. Meanwhile, I think you are safest away from this father of yours, who might take to cutting your throat instead of that tobacco. Vrouw Prinsloo, be so good as to look after Marie Marais, and on Monday morning next bring her before me to be wed. Until then, Henri Marais, I, as commandant, shall set a guard over you, with orders to seize you if it should be necessary. Now I advise you to take a walk, and when you are calm again, to pray God to forgive you your wicked words, lest they should be fulfilled and drag you down to judgment."

Then we all went, leaving Henri Marais still cutting up his tobacco on the *disselboom*.

On the Sunday I met Marais walking about the camp, followed by the guard whom Retief had set over him. To my surprise he greeted me almost with affection.

"Allan," he said, "you must not misunderstand me. I do not really wish ill to Marie, whom I love more dearly than I do my life; God alone knows how much I love her. But I made a promise to her cousin, Hernan, my only sister's only child, and you will understand that I cannot break that promise, although Hernan has disappointed me in many ways—yes, in many ways. But if he is bad, as they say, it comes with that Portuguese blood, which is a misfortune that he cannot help, does it not? However bad he may be, as an honest man I am bound to keep my promise, am I not? Also, Allan, you must remember that you are English, and although you may be a good fellow in yourself, that is a fault which you cannot expect me to forgive. Still, if it is fated that you should marry my daughter and breed English children—Heaven above! to think of it, English children!—well, there is nothing more to be said. Don't remember the words I spoke to Marie. Indeed, I can't remember them myself. When I grow angry, a kind of rush of blood comes into my brain, and then I forget what I have said," and he stretched out his hand to me.

I shook it and answered that I understood he was not himself when he spoke those dreadful words, which both Marie and I wished to forget.

"I hope you will come to our wedding to-morrow," I added, "and wipe them out with a father's blessing."

"To-morrow! Are you really going to be married to-morrow?" he exclaimed, his sallow face twitching nervously. "O God, it was another man that I dreamed to see standing by Marie's side. But he is not here; he has disgraced and deserted me. Well, I will come, if my gaolers will suffer it. Good-bye, you happy bridegroom of to-morrow, good-bye."

Then he swung round and departed, followed by the guards, one of whom touched his brow and shook his head significantly as he passed me.

I think that Sunday seemed the longest day I ever spent. The Vrouw Prinsloo would scarcely allow me even a glimpse of Marie, because of some fad she had got into her mind that it was either not proper or not fortunate, I forget which, that a bride and bridegroom should associate on the eve of their marriage. So I occupied myself as best I could. First I wrote a long letter to my father, the third that I had sent, telling him everything that was going to happen, and saying how grieved I was that he could not be present to marry us and give us his blessing.

This letter I gave to a trader who was trekking to the bay on the following morning, begging him to forward it by the first opportunity.

That duty done, I saw about the horses which I was taking into Zululand, three of them, two for myself and one for Hans, who accompanied me as after-rider. Also the saddlery, saddle-bags, guns and ammunition must be overhauled, all of which took some time.

"You are going to spend a strange *wittebroodsweek* (white-bread-week, or, in other words, honeymoon), *baas*," said Hans, squinting at me with his little eyes, as he brayed away at a buckskin which was to serve as a saddle-cloth. "Now, if *I* was to be married to-morrow, I should stop with my pretty for a few days, and only ride off somewhere else when I was tired of her, especially if that somewhere else chanced to be Zululand, where they are so fond of killing people."

"I dare say you would, Hans; and so would I, if I could, you be sure. But, you see, the commandant wants me to interpret, and therefore it is my duty to go with him."

"Duty; what is duty, *baas*? Love I understand. It is for love of you that I go with you; also for fear lest you should cause me to be beaten if I refused. Otherwise I would certainly stop here in the camp, where there is plenty to eat and little work to do, as, were I you, I should do also for love of that white missie. But duty—*pah!* that is a fool-word, which makes bones of a man before his time and leaves his girl to others."

"Of course, you do not understand, Hans, any more than you coloured people understand what gratitude is. But what do you mean about this trek of ours? Are you afraid?"

He shrugged his shoulders. "A little, perhaps, *baas*. At least, I should be if I thought about the morrow, which I don't, since to-day is enough for me, and thinking about what one can't know makes the head ache. Dingaan is not a nice man, *baas*; we saw that, didn't we? He is a hunter who knows how to set a trap. Also he has the Baas Pereira up there to help him. So perhaps you might be more comfortable here kissing Missie Marie. Why do you not say that you have hurt your leg and cannot run? It would not be much trouble to walk about on a crutch for a day or two, and when the commandant was well gone, your leg might heal and you could throw the stick away."

"Get thee behind me, Satan," I muttered to myself, and was about to give Hans a piece of my mind when I recollected that the poor fellow had his own way of looking at things and could not be blamed. Also, as he said, he loved me, and only suggested what he thought would tend to my joy and safety. How could I suppose that he would be interested in the success of a diplomatic mission to Dingaan, or think anything about it except that it was a risky business? So I only said:

"Hans, if you are afraid, you had better stop behind. I can easily find another after-rider."

"Is the *baas* angry with me that he should speak so?" asked the Hottentot. "Have I not always been true to him; and if I should be killed, what does it matter? Have I not said that I do not think about to-morrow, and we must all go to sleep sometime? No; unless the *baas* beats me back, I shall come with him. But, *baas*"—this in a wheedling tone—"you might give me some brandy to drink your health in to-night. It is very good to get drunk when one has to be sober, and perhaps dead, for a long time afterwards. It would be nice to remember when one is a spook, or an angel with white wings, such as the old *baas*, your father, used to tell us about in school on the Sabbath."

At this point, finding Hans hopeless, I got up and walked away, leaving him to finish our preparations.

That evening there was a prayer-meeting in the camp, for although no pastor was present, one of the Boer elders took his place and offered up supplications which, if simple and even absurd in their wording, at least were hearty enough. Amongst other requests, I remember that he petitioned for the safety of those who were to go on the mission to Dingaan and of those who were to remain behind. Alas! those prayers were not heard, for it pleased the Power to Whom they were addressed to decree otherwise.

After this meeting, in which I took an earnest share, Retief who just before it began had ridden in from Doornkop, whither he had been to visit his wife, held a kind of council, whereat the names of those who had volunteered or been ordered to accompany him, were finally taken down. At this council there was a good deal of discussion, since many of the Boers did not think the expedition wise—at any rate, if it was to be carried out on so large a scale. One of them, I forget which, an old man, pointed out that it might look like a war party, and that it would be wiser if only five or six went, as they had done before, since then there could be no mistake as to the peaceful nature of their intentions.

Retief himself combated this view, and at last turned suddenly to me, who was listening near by, and said:

"Allan Quatermain, you are young, but you have a good judgment; also, you are one of the very few who know Dingaan and can speak his language. Tell us now, what do you think?"

Thus adjured, I answered, perhaps moved thereto more than I thought by Hans's talk, that I, too, considered the thing dangerous, and that someone whose life was less valuable than the commandant's should go in command.

"Why do you say so, nephew," he said irritably, "seeing that all white men's lives are of equal value, and I can smell no danger in the business?"

"Because, commandant, I do smell danger, though what danger I cannot say, any more than a dog or a buck can when it sniffs something in the air and barks or runs. Dingaan is a tamed tiger just now, but tigers are not house cats that one can play with them, as I know, who have felt his claws and just, only just, come out from between them."

"What do you mean, nephew?" asked Retief in his direct fashion. "Do you believe that this *swartzel*" (that is, black creature) "means to kill us?"

"I believe that it is quite possible," I answered.

"Then, nephew, being a reasonable man as you are, you must have some ground for your belief. Come now, out with it."

"I have none, commandant, except that one who can set the lives of a dozen folk against a man's skill in shooting at birds on the wing, and who can kill people to be a bait for those birds, is capable of anything. Moreover, he told me that he did not love you Boers, and why should he?"

Now, all those who were standing about seemed to be impressed with this argument. At any rate, they turned towards Retief, anxiously waiting for his reply.

"Doubtless," answered the commandant, who, as I have said, was irritable that night, "doubtless those English missionaries have poisoned the king's mind against us Boers. Also," he added suspiciously, "I think you told me, Allan, that the king said he liked you and meant to spare you, even if he killed your companions, just because you also are English. Are you sure that you do not know more than you choose to tell us? Has Dingaan perhaps confided something to you—just because you are English?"

Then noting that these words moved the assembled Boers, in whom race prejudice and recent events had created a deep distrust of any born of British blood, I grew very angry and answered:

"Commandant, Dingaan confided nothing to me, except that some

Kaffir witch-doctor, who is named Zikali, a man I never saw, had told him that he must not kill an Englishman, and therefore he wished to spare me, although one of your people, Hernan Pereira, had whispered to him that I ought to be killed. Yet I say outright that I think you are foolish to visit this king with so large a force. Still, I am ready to do so myself with one or two others. Let me go, then, and try to persuade him to sign this treaty as to the land. If I am killed or fail, you can follow after me and do better."

"*Allemachte!*" exclaimed Retief; "that is a fair offer. But how do I know, nephew, that when we came to read the treaty we should not find that it granted all the land to you English and not to us Boers? No, no, don't look angry. That was not a right thing to say, for you are honest whatever most of your blood may be. Nephew Allan, you who are a brave man, are afraid of this journey. Now, why is that, I wonder? Ah! I have it. I had forgotten. You are to be married to-morrow morning to a very pretty girl, and it is not natural that you should wish to spend the next fortnight in Zululand. Don't you see, brothers, he wants to get out of it because he is going to be married, as it is natural that he should, and therefore he tries to frighten us all? When we were going to be married, should we have wished to ride away at once to visit some stinking savage? Ach! I am glad I thought of that just as I was beginning to turn his gloomy colour, like a chameleon on a black hat, for it explains everything," and he struck his thigh with his big hand and burst into a roar of laughter.

All the company of Boers who stood around began to laugh also, uproariously, for this primitive joke appealed to them. Moreover, their nerves were strained; they also dreaded this expedition, and therefore they were glad to relieve themselves in bucolic merriment. Everything was clear to them now. Feeling myself in honour bound to go on the embassy, as I was their only interpreter, I, artful dog, was trying to play upon their fears in order to prevent it from starting, so that I might have a week or two of the company of my new-wed wife. They saw and appreciated the joke.

"He's slim, this little Englishman," shouted one.

"Don't be angry with him. We should have done as much ourselves," replied another.

"Leave him behind," said a third. "Even the Zulus do not send a new-married man on service." Then they smacked me on the back, and hustled me in their rude, kindly manner, till at length I fell into a rage and hit one of them on the nose, at which he only laughed the louder, although I made it bleed.

"See here, friends," I said, as soon as silence was restored; "married or no, whoever does not ride to Dingaan, I ride to him, although it is against my judgment. Let those laugh loudest who laugh last."

"Good!" cried one; "if you set the pace we shall soon be home again, Allan Quatermain. Who would not with Marie Marais at the end of the journey?"

Then, followed by their rough and mocking laughter, I broke away from them, and took refuge in my wagon, little guessing that all this talk would be brought up against me on a day to come.

In a certain class of uneducated mind foresight is often interpreted as guilty knowledge.

CHAPTER 17

The Marriage

I was awakened on my wedding morning by the crash and bellowing of a great thunderstorm. The lightning flashed fearfully all about us, killing two oxen quite near to my wagon, and the thunder rolled and echoed till the very earth seemed to shake. Then came a wail of cold wind, and after that the swish of torrential rain. Although I was well accustomed to such natural manifestations, especially at this season of the year, I confess that these sights and sounds did not tend to raise my spirits, which were already lower than they should have been on that eventful day. Hans, however, who arrived to help me put on my best clothes for the ceremony, was for once consoling.

"Don't look sick, *baas*," he said, "for if there is storm in the morning, there is shine at night."

"Yes," I answered, speaking more to myself than to him, "but what will happen between the storm of the morning and the peace of the night?"

It was arranged that the commission, which, counting the native after-riders, consisted of over a hundred people, among them several boys, who were little more than children, was to ride at one hour before noon. Nobody could get about to make the necessary preparations until the heavy rain had passed away, which it did a little after eight o'clock. Therefore when I left the wagon to eat, or try to eat some breakfast, I found the whole camp in a state of bustle.

Boers were shouting to their servants, horses were being examined, women were packing the saddle-bags of their husbands and fathers with spare clothes, the pack-beasts were being laden with biltong and other provisions, and so forth.

In the midst of all this tumult I began to wonder whether my private business would not be forgotten, since it seemed unlikely that time could be found for marriages. However, about ten o'clock when, having done everything that I had to do, I was sitting disconsolately upon my wagon box, being too shy to mix with that crowd of busy mockers or to go to the Prinsloos' camp to make inquiries, the *vrouw* herself appeared.

"Come on, Allan," she said, "the commandant is waiting and swearing because you are not there. Also, there is another waiting, and oh! she looks lovely. When they see her, every man in the camp will want her for himself, whether he has got a wife or not, for in that matter, although you mayn't think so just now, they are all the same as the Kaffirs. Oh! I know them, I know them, a white skin makes no difference."

While she held forth thus in her usual outspoken fashion, the *vrouw* was dragging me along by the hand, just as though I were a naughty little boy. Nor could I get free from that mighty grip, or, when once her great bulk was in motion, match my weight against it. Of course, some of the younger Boers, who, knowing her errand, had followed her, set up a shout of cheers and laughter, which attracted everybody to the procession.

"It is too late to hang back now, Englishman."

"You must make the best of a bad business."

"If you wanted to change your mind, you should have done it before," men and women roared and screamed with many other such bantering words, till at length I felt myself turn the colour of a red vlei lily.

So we came at last to where Marie stood, the centre of an admiring circle. She was clothed in a soft white gown made of some simple but becoming stuff, and she wore upon her dark hair a wreath woven by the other maidens in the camp, a bevy of whom stood behind her.

Now we were face to face. Our eyes met, and oh! hers were full of love and trust. They dazzled and bewildered me. Feeling that I ought to speak, and not knowing what to say, I merely stammered "Good morning," whereon everyone broke into a roar of laughter, except Vrouw Prinsloo, who exclaimed:

"Did any one ever see such a fool?" and even Marie smiled.

Then Piet Retief appeared from somewhere dressed in tall boots and rough riding clothes, such as the Boers wore in those days. Handing the *roer* he was carrying to one of his sons, after much fumbling he produced a book from his pocket, in which the place was marked with a piece of grass.

"Now then," he said, "be silent, all, and show respect, for remember I am not a man just now. I am a parson, which is quite a different thing, and, being a commandant and a *veld* cornet and other officers all rolled into one, by virtue of the law I am about to marry these young people, so help me God. Don't any of you witnesses ever say afterwards that they are not rightly and soundly married, because I tell you that they are, or will be." He paused for breath, and someone said, "Hear, hear," or its Dutch equivalent, whereon, having glared the offender into silence, Retief proceeded:

"Young man and young woman, what are your names?"

"Don't ask silly questions, commandant," broke in Vrouw Prinsloo; "you know their names well enough."

"Of course I do, aunt," he answered; "but for this purpose I must pretend not to know them. Are you better acquainted with the law than I am? But stay, where is the father, Henri Marais?"

Someone thrust Marais forward, and there he stood quite silent, staring at us with a queer look upon his face and his gun in his hand, for he, too, was ready to ride.

"Take away that gun," said Retief; "it might go off and cause disturbance or perhaps accidents," and somebody obeyed. "Now, Henri Marais, do you give your daughter to be married to this man?"

"No," said Marais softly.

"Very well, that is just like you, but it doesn't matter, for she is of age and can give herself. Is she not of age, Henri Marais? Don't stand there like a horse with the staggers, but tell me; is she not of age?"

"I believe so," he answered in the same soft voice.

"Then take notice, people all, that this woman is of age, and gives herself to be married to this man, don't you, my dear?"

"Yes," answered Marie.

"All right, now for it," and, opening the book, he held it up to the light, and began to read, or, rather, to stumble, through the marriage service.

Presently he stuck fast, being, like most Boers of his time, no great scholar, and exclaimed:

"Here, one of you help me with these hard words."

As nobody volunteered, Retief handed the book to me, for he knew that Marais would not assist him, saying:

"You are a scholar, Allan, being a clergyman's son. Read on till we come to the important bits, and I will say the words after you, which will do just as well and be quite according to law."

So I read, Heaven knows how, for the situation was trying enough, until I came to the crucial questions, when I gave the book back.

"Ah!" said Retief; "this is quite easy. Now then, Allan, do you take this woman to be your wife? Answer, putting in your name, which is left blank in the book."

I replied that I did, and the question was repeated to Marie, who did likewise.

"Well then, there you are," said Retief, "for I won't trouble you with all the prayers, which I don't feel myself parson enough to say. Oh! no, I forgot. Have you a ring?"

I drew one off my finger that had been my mother's—I believe it had served this same purpose at the wedding of her grandmother— and set the thin little hoop of gold upon the third finger of Marie's left hand. I still wear that ring to-day.

"It should have been a new one," muttered Vrouw Prinsloo.

"Be silent, aunt," said Retief; "are there any jewellers' shops here in the *veld*? A ring is a ring, even if it came off a horse's bit. There, I think that is all. No, wait a minute, I am going to say a prayer of my own over you, not one out of this book, which is so badly printed that I cannot read it. Kneel down, both of you; the rest may stand, as the grass is so wet."

Now, bethinking herself of Marie's new dress, the *vrouw* produced her *vatdoek* from a capacious pocket, and doubled up that dingy article for Marie to kneel on, which she did. Then Pieter Retief, flinging down the book, clasped his hands and uttered this simple, earnest prayer, whereof, strangely enough, every word remains fast in my mind. Coming as it did, not from a printed page, but from his honest and believing heart, it was very impressive and solemn.

"O God above us, Who sees all and is with us when we are born, when we are married, when we die, and if we do our duty for all time afterwards in Heaven, hear our prayer. I pray Thee bless this man and this woman who appear here before Thee to be wed. Make them love each other truly all their lives, be these long or short, be they sick or well, be they happy or in sorrow, be they rich or poor. Give them children to be reared up in Thy Word, give them an honest name and the respect of all who know them, and at last give them Thy Salvation through the Blood of Jesus the Saviour. If they are together, let them rejoice in each other. If they are apart, let them not forget each other. If one of them dies and the other lives, let that one who lives look forward to the day of reunion and bow the head to Thy Will, and keep that one who dies in Thy holy Hand. O Thou Who knowest all things, guide the lives of these two according to Thy eternal purpose, and teach them to be sure that whatever Thou doest, is done for the best. For Thou art a faithful Creator, Who wishes good to His children and not evil, and at the last Thou wilt give them that good if they do but trust in Thee through daylight and through darkness. Now let no man dare to put asunder those whom Thou hast joined together, O Lord God Almighty, Father of us all. Amen."

So he prayed, and all the company echoed that Amen from their hearts. That is all except one, for Henri Marais turned his back on us and walked away.

"So," said Retief, wiping his brow with the sleeve of his coat, "you are the last couple that ever I mean to marry. The work is too hard for a layman who has bad sight for print. Now kiss each other; it is the right thing to do."

So we kissed, and the congregation cheered.

"Allan," went on the commandant, pulling out a silver watch like a turnip, "you have just half an hour before we ride, and the Vrouw Prinsloo says that she has made you a wedding meal in that tent there, so you had best go eat it." To the tent we went accordingly, to find a simple but bounteous feast prepared, of which we partook, helping each other to food, as is, or was, the custom with new-wedded folk. Also, many Boers came in and drank our healths, although the Vrouw Prinsloo told them that it would have been more decent to leave us alone. But Henri Marais did not come or drink our healths.

Thus the half-hour went all too swiftly, and not a word did we get alone. At last in despair, seeing that Hans was already waiting with the horses, I drew Marie aside, motioning to everyone to stand back.

"Dearest wife," I said in broken words, "this is a strange beginning to our married life, but you see it can't be helped."

"No, Allan," she answered, "it can't be helped; but oh! I wish my heart were happier about your journey. I fear Dingaan, and if anything should chance to you I shall die of grief."

"Why should anything chance, Marie? We are a strong and well-armed party, and Dingaan looks on us peacefully."

"I don't know, husband, but they say Hernan Pereira is with the Zulus, and he hates you."

"Then he had better mind his manners, or he will not be here long to hate anybody," I answered grimly, for my gorge rose at the thought of this man and his treacheries.

"Vrouw Prinsloo," I called to the old lady, who was near, "be pleased to come hither and listen. And, Marie, do you listen also. If by chance I should hear anything affecting your safety, and send you a message by someone you can trust, such as that you should remove yourselves elsewhere or hide, promise me that you will obey it without question."

"Of course I will obey you, husband. Have I not just sworn to do so?" Marie said with a sad smile.

"And so will I, Allan," said the *vrouw*, "not because I have sworn anything, but because I know you have a good head on your shoulders, and so will my man and the others of our party. Though why you should think you will have any message to send, I can't guess, unless you know something that is hidden from us," she added shrewdly. "You say you don't; well, it is not likely you would tell us if you did. Look! They are calling, you must go. Come on, Marie, let us see them off."

So we went to where the commission was gathered on horseback, just in time to hear Retief addressing the people, or, rather, the last of his words.

"Friends," he said, "we go upon an important business, from which I hope we shall return happily within a very little time. Still, this is a rough country, and we have to deal with rough people. Therefore my advice to all you who stay behind is that you should not scatter, but keep together, so that in case of any trouble the men who are left may be at hand to defend this camp. For if they are here you have nothing to fear from all the savages in Africa. And now God be with you, and good-bye. Come, trek, brothers, trek!"

Then followed a few moments of confusion while men kissed their wives, children and sisters in farewell, or shook each other by the hand. I, too, kissed Marie, and, tumbling on to my horse somehow, rode away, my eyes blind with tears, for this parting was bitter. When I could see clearly again I pulled up and looked back at the camp, which was now at some distance. It seemed a peaceful place indeed, for although the storm of the morning was returning and a pall of dark cloud hung over it, the sun still shone upon the white wagon caps and the people who went to and fro among them.

Who could have thought that within a little time it would be but a field of blood, that those wagons would be riddled with assegais, and that the women and children who were moving there must most of them lie upon the *veld* mutilated corpses dreadful to behold? Alas! the Boers, always impatient of authority and confident that their own individual judgment was the best, did not obey their commandant's order to keep together. They went off this way and that, to shoot the game which was then so plentiful, leaving their families almost without protection. Thus the Zulus found and slew them.

Presently as I rode forward a little apart from the others someone overtook me, and I saw that it was Henri Marais.

"Well, Allan," he said, "so God has given you to me for a son-in-law. Who would have thought it? You do not look to me like a new-married man, for that marriage is not natural when the bridegroom rides off and leaves the bride of an hour. Perhaps you will never be really married after all, for God, Who gives sons-in-law, can also take them away, especially when He was not asked for them. Ah!" he went on, lapsing into French, as was his wont when moved, *"qui vivra verra! qui vivra verra!"* Then, shouting this excellent but obvious proverb at the top of his voice, he struck his horse with the butt of his gun, and galloped away before I could answer him.

At that moment I hated Henri Marais as I had never hated anyone before, not even his nephew Hernan. Almost did I ride to the commandant to complain of him, but reflecting to myself, first that he was undoubtedly half mad, and therefore not responsible for his actions, and secondly that he was better here with us than in the same camp with my wife, I gave up the idea. Yet alas! it is the half-mad who are the most dangerous of lunatics.

Hans, who had observed this scene and overheard all Marais's talk, and who also knew the state of the case well enough, sidled his horse alongside of me, and whispered in a wheedling voice:

"Baas, I think the old *baas* is *kransick* and not safe. He looks like one who is going to harm someone. Now, *baas*, suppose I let my gun off by accident; you know we coloured people are very careless with guns! The Heer Marais would never be troubled with any more fancies, and you and the Missie Marie and all of us would be safer. Also, *you* could not be blamed, nor could I, for who can help an accident? Guns will go off sometimes, *baas*, when you don't want them to."

"Get out," I answered. Yet if Hans's gun had chanced to "go off," I believe it might have saved a multitude of lives!

CHAPTER 18

The Treaty

Our journey to Umgungundhlovu was prosperous and without incident. When we were within half a day's march from the Great Kraal we overtook the herd of cattle that we had recaptured from Sikonyela, for these beasts had been driven very slowly and well rested that they might arrive in good condition. Also the commandant was anxious that we should present them ourselves to the king.

Driving this multitude of animals before us—there were over five thousand head of them—we reached the Great Place on Saturday the 3rd of February about midday, and forced them through its gates into the cattle *kraals*. Then we off-saddled and ate our dinner under those two milk trees near the gate of the *kraal* where I had bid good-bye to Dingaan.

After dinner messengers came to ask us to visit the king, and with them the youth, Thomas Halstead, who told the commandant that all weapons must be left behind, since it was the Zulu law that no man might appear before the king armed. To this Retief demurred, whereon the messengers appealed to me, whom they had recognised, asking if that were not the custom of their country.

I answered that I had not been in it long enough to know. Then there was a pause while they sent for someone to bear evidence; at the time I did not know whom, as I was not near enough to Thomas Halstead to make inquiries. Presently this someone appeared, and turned out to be none other than Hernan Pereira.

He advanced towards us attended by Zulus, as though he were a chief, looking fat and well and handsomer than ever. Seeing Retief, he lifted his hat with a flourish and held out his hand, which, I noted, the commandant did not take.

"So you are still here, Mynheer Pereira!" he said coldly. "Now be good enough to tell me, what is this matter about the abandoning of our arms?"

"The king charges me to say—" began Hernan.

"Charges you to say, Mynheer Pereira! Are you then this black man's servant? But continue."

"That none must come into his private enclosure armed."

"Well, then, *mynheer*, be pleased to go tell this king that we do not wish to come to his private enclosure. I have brought the cattle that he desired me to fetch, and I am willing to deliver them to him wherever he wishes, but we will not unarm in order to do so."

Now there was talk, and messengers were despatched, who returned at full speed presently to say that Dingaan would receive the Boers in the great dancing place in the midst of the *kraal*, and that they might bring their guns, as he wished to see how they fired them.

So we rode in, making as fine a show as we could, to find that the dancing place, which measured a good many acres in extent, was lined round with thousands of plumed but unarmed warriors arranged in regiments.

"You see," I heard Pereira say to Retief, "these have no spears."

"No," answered the commandant, "but they have sticks, which when they are a hundred to one would serve as well."

Meanwhile the vast mob of cattle were being driven in a double stream past a knot of men at the head of the space, and then away through gates behind. When the beasts had all gone we approached these men, among whom I recognised the fat form of Dingaan draped in a bead mantle. We ranged ourselves in a semicircle before him, and stood while he searched us with his sharp eyes. Presently he saw me, and sent a councillor to say that I must come and interpret for him.

So, dismounting, I went with Retief, Thomas Halstead, and a few of the leading Boers.

"*Sakubona* (Good day), Macumazahn," said Dingaan. "I am glad that you have come, as I know that you will speak my words truly, being one of the People of George whom I love, for Tho-maas here I do not trust, although he is also a Son of George."

I told Retief what he said.

"Oh!" he exclaimed with a grunt, "it seems that you English are a step in front of us Boers, even here."

Then he went forward and shook hands with the king, whom, it will be remembered, he had visited before.

After that the "indaba" or talk began, which I do not propose to set out at length, for it is a matter of history. It is enough to say that Dingaan, after thanking Retief for recovering the cattle, asked where was Sikonyela, the chief who had stolen them, as he wished to kill him. When he learned that Sikonyela remained in his own country, he became, or affected to become, angry. Then he asked where were the sixty horses which he heard we had captured from Sikonyela, as they must be given up to him.

Retief, by way of reply, touched his grey hairs, and inquired whether Dingaan thought that he was a child that he, Dingaan, should demand horses which did not belong to him. He added that these horses had been restored to the Boers, from whom Sikonyela had stolen them.

When Dingaan had expressed himself satisfied with this answer, Retief opened the question of the treaty. The king replied however, that the white men had but just arrived, and he wished to see them dance after their own fashion. As for the business, it might "sit still" till another day.

So in the end the Boers "danced" for his amusement. That is, they divided into two parties, and charged each other at full gallop, firing their guns into the air, an exhibition which seemed to fill all present with admiration and awe. When they paused, the king wished them to go on firing "a hundred shots apiece," but the commandant declined, saying he had no more powder to waste.

"What do you want powder for in a peaceful country?" asked Dingaan suspiciously.

Retief answered through me:

"To kill food for ourselves, or to protect ourselves if any evil-minded men should attack us."

"Then it will not be wanted here," said Dingaan, "since I will give you food, and as I, the king, am your friend, no man in Zululand dare be your enemy."

Retief said he was glad to hear it, and asked leave to retire with the Boers to his camp outside the gate, as they were all tired with riding. This Dingaan granted, and we said good-bye and went away. Before I reached the gate, however, a messenger, I remember it was my old friend Kambula, overtook me, and said that the king wished to speak with me alone. I answered him that I could not speak with the king alone without the permission of the commandant. Thereon Kambula said:

"Come with me, I pray you, O Macumazahn, since otherwise you will be taken by force."

Now, I told Hans to gallop on to Retief, and tell him of my predicament, for already I saw that at some sign from Kambula I was being surrounded by Zulus. He did so, and presently Retief came back himself accompanied only by one man, and asked me what was the matter now. I informed him, translating Kambula's words, which he repeated in his presence.

"Does the fellow mean that you will be seized if you do not go, or I refuse to allow you to do so?"

To this question Kambula's answer was:

"That is so, *Inkoos*, since the king has private words for the ear of Macumazahn. Therefore we must obey orders, and take him before the king, living or dead."

"*Allemachte!*" exclaimed Retief, "this is serious," and, as though to summon them to my help, he looked behind him towards the main body of the Boers, who by this time were nearly all of them through the gate, which was guarded by a great number of Zulus. "Allan," he went on, "if you are not afraid, I think that you must go. Perhaps it is only that Dingaan has some message about the treaty to send to me through you."

"I am not afraid," I answered. "What is the use of being afraid in a place like this?"

"Ask that Kaffir if the king gives you safe conduct," said Retief.

I did so, and Kambula answered:

"Yes, for this visit. Who am I that I can speak the king's unspoken words?" (which meant, guarantee his will in the future.)

"A dark saying," commented Retief. "But go, Allan, since you must, and God bring you back safe again. It is clear that Dingaan did not ask that you should come with me for nothing. Now I wish I had left you at home with that pretty wife of yours."

So we parted, I going to the king's private enclosure on foot and without my rifle, since I was not allowed to appear before him armed, and the commandant towards the gate of the *kraal* accompanied by Hans, who led my horse. Ten minutes later I stood before Dingaan, who greeted me kindly enough, and began to ask a number of questions about the Boers, especially if they were not people who had rebelled against their own king and run away from him.

I answered, Yes, they had run away, as they wanted more room to live; but I had told him all about that when I saw him before. He said he knew I had, but he wished to hear "whether the same words came out of the same mouth, or different words," so that he might know if I were a true man or not. Then, after pausing a while, he looked at me in his piercing fashion and asked:

"Have you brought me a present of that tall white girl with eyes like two stars, Macumazahn? I mean the girl whom you refused to me, and whom I could not take because you had won your bet, which gave all the white people to you; she for whose sake you make brothers of these Boers, who are traitors to their king?"

"No, O Dingaan," I answered; "there are no women among us. Moreover, this maid is now my wife."

"Your wife!" he exclaimed angrily. "By the Head of the Black One, have you dared to make a wife of her whom I desired? Now say, boy, you clever Watcher by Night; you little white ant, who work in the dark and only peep out at the end of your tunnel when it is finished; you wizard, who by your magic can snatch his prey out of the hand of the greatest king in all the world—for it was magic that killed those vultures on Hloma Amabutu, not your bullets, Macumazahn—say, why should I not make an end of you at once for this trick?"

I folded my arms and looked at him. A strange contrast we must have made, this huge, black tyrant with the royal air, for to do him justice he had that, at whose nod hundreds went the way of death, and I, a mere insignificant white boy, for in appearance, at any rate, I was nothing more.

"O Dingaan," I said coolly, knowing that coolness was my only chance, "I answer you in the words of the Commandant Retief, the great chief. Do you take me for a child that I should give up my own wife to you who already have so many? Moreover, you cannot kill me because I have the word of your captain, Kambula, that I am safe with you."

This reply seemed to amuse him. At any rate, with one of those almost infantile changes of mood which are common to savages of every degree, he passed from wrath to laughter.

"You are quick as a lizard," he said. "Why should I, who have so many wives, want one more, who would certainly hate me? Just because she is white, and would make the others, who are black, jealous, I suppose. Indeed, they would poison her, or pinch her to death in a month, and then come to tell me she had died of fretting. Also, you are right; you have my safe conduct, and must go hence unharmed this time. But look you, little lizard, although you escape me between the stones, I will pull off your tail. I have said that I want to pluck this tall white flower of yours, and I will pluck her. I know where she dwells. Yes, just where the wagon she sleeps in stands in the line, for my spies have told me, and I will give orders that whoever is killed, she is to be spared and brought to me living. So perhaps you will meet this wife of yours here, Macumazahn."

Now, at these ominous words, that might mean so much or so little, the sweat started to my brow, and a shiver went down my back.

"Perhaps I shall and perhaps I shall not, O king," I answered. "The world is as full of chances to-day as it was not long ago when I shot at the sacred vultures on Hloma Amabutu. Still, I think that my wife will never be yours, O king."

"*Ow!*" said Dingaan; "this little white ant is making another tunnel, thinking that he will come up at my back. But what if I put down my heel and crush you, little white ant? Do you know," he added confidentially, "that the Boer who mends my guns and whom here we call 'Two-faces,' because he looks towards you whites with one eye and towards us blacks with the other, is still very anxious that I should kill you? Indeed, when I told him that my spies said that you were to ride with the Boers, as I had requested that you should be their Tongue, he answered that unless I promised to give you to the vultures, he would warn them against coming. So, since I wanted them to come as I had arranged with him, I promised."

"Is it so, O king?" I asked. "And pray why does this Two-faces, whom we name Pereira, desire that I should be killed?"

"*Ow!*" chuckled the obese old ruffian; "cannot you with all your cleverness guess that, O Macumazahn? Perhaps it is he who needs the tall white maiden, and not I. Perhaps if he does certain things for me, I have promised her to him in payment. And perhaps," he added, laughing quite loud, "I shall trick him after all, keeping her for myself, and paying him in another way, for can a cheat grumble if he is out-cheated?"

I answered that I was an honest man, and knew nothing about cheats, or at what they could or could not grumble.

"Yes, Macumazahn," replied Dingaan quite genially. "That is where you and I are alike. We are both honest, quite honest, and therefore friends, which I can never be with these Amaboona, who, as you and others have told me, are traitors. We play our game in the light, like men, and who wins, wins, and who loses, loses. Now hear me, Macumazahn, and remember what I say. Whatever happens to others, whatever you may see, you are safe while I live. Dingaan has spoken. Whether I get the tall white girl, or do not get her, still *you* are safe; it is on my head," and he touched the gum-ring in his hair.

"And why should I be safe if others are unsafe, O king?" I asked.

"Oh! if you would know that, ask a certain ancient prophet named Zikali, who was in this land in the days of Senzangacona, my father, and before then—that is, if you can find him. Also, I like you, who are not a flat-faced fool like these Amaboona, but have a brain that turns in and out through difficulties, as a snake does through reeds; and it would be a pity to kill one who can shoot birds wheeling high above him in the air, which no one else can do. So whatever you see and whatever you hear, remember that you are safe, and shall go safely from this land, or stay safely in it if you will, to be my voice to speak with the Sons of George.

"Now return to the commandant, and say to him that my heart is his heart, and that I am very pleased to see him here. To-morrow, and perhaps the next day, I will show him some of the dances of my people, and after that I will sign the writing, giving him all the land he asks and everything else he may desire, more than he can wish, indeed. *Hamba gachle*, Macumazahn," and, rising with surprising quickness from his chair, which was cut out of a single block of wood, he turned and vanished through the little opening in the reed fence behind him that led to his private huts.

As I was being conducted back to the Boer camp by Kambula, who was waiting for me outside the gate of the labyrinth which is called *isiklohlo*, I met Thomas Halstead, who was lounging about, I think in order to speak with me. Halting, I asked him straight out what the king's intentions were towards the Boers.

"Don't know," he answered, shrugging his shoulders, "but he seems so sweet on them that I think he must be up to mischief. He is wonderfully fond of you, too, for I heard him give orders that the word was to be passed through all the regiments that if anyone so much as hurt you, he should be killed at once. Also, you were pointed out to the soldiers when you rode in with the rest, that they might all of them know you."

"That's good for me as far as it goes," I replied. "But I don't know why I should need special protection above others, unless there is someone who wants to harm me."

"There is that, Allan Quatermain. The indunas tell me that the good-looking Portuguese, whom they call 'Two-faces,' asks the king to kill you every time he sees him. Indeed, I've heard him myself."

"That's kind of him," I answered, "but, then, Hernan Pereira and I never got on. Tell me what is he talking about to the king when he isn't asking him to kill me."

"Don't know," he said again. "Something dirty, I'll be bound. One may be sure of that by the native name they have given him. I think, however," he added in a whisper, "that he has had a lot to do with the Boers being allowed to come here at all in order to get their treaty signed. At least, one day when I was interpreting and Dingaan swore that he would not give them more land than was enough to bury

392

them in, Pereira told him that it didn't matter what he signed, as 'what was written with the pen could be scratched out with the spear.'"

"Indeed! And what did the king say to that?"

"Oh! he laughed and said it was true, and that he would give the Boer commission all their people wanted and something over for themselves. But don't you repeat that, Quatermain, for if you do, and it gets to the ear of Dingaan, I shall certainly be killed. And, I say, you're a good fellow, and I won a big bet on you over that vulture shooting, so I will give you a bit of advice, which you will be wise to take. You get out of this country as soon as you can, and go to look after that pretty Miss Marais, whom you are sweet on. Dingaan wants her, and what Dingaan wants he gets in this part of the world."

Then, without waiting to be thanked, he turned and disappeared among a crowd of Zulus, who were following us from curiosity, leaving me wondering whether or no Dingaan was right when he called this young man a liar. His story seemed to tally so well with that told by the king himself, that on the whole I thought he was not.

Just after I had passed the main gateway of the great town, where, his office done, Kambula saluted and left me, I saw two white men engaged in earnest conversation beneath one of the milk trees which, as I think I have already mentioned, grow, or grew, there. They were Henri Marais and his nephew. Catching sight of me, Marais walked off, but Pereira advanced and spoke to me, although, warned perhaps by what had happened to him in the case of Retief, I am glad to say he did not offer me his hand.

"Good day to you, Allan," he said effusively. "I have just heard from my uncle that I have to congratulate you, about Marie I mean, and, believe me, I do so with all my heart."

Now, as he spoke these words, remembering what I had just heard, my blood boiled in me, but I thought it wise to control myself, and therefore only answered:

"Thank you."

"Of course," he went on, "we have both striven for this prize, but as it has pleased God that you should win it, why, I am not one to bear malice."

"I am glad to hear it," I replied. "I thought that perhaps you might be. Now tell me, to change the subject, how long will Dingaan keep us here?"

"Oh! two or three days at most. You see, Allan, luckily I have been able to persuade him to sign the treaty about the land without further trouble. So as soon as that is done, you can all go home."

"The commandant will be very grateful to you," I said. "But what are you going to do?"

"I do not know, Allan. You see, I am not a lucky fellow like yourself with a wife waiting for me. I think that perhaps I shall stop here a while. I see a way of making a great deal of money out of these Zulus; and having lost everything upon that Delagoa Bay trek, I want money."

"We all do," I answered, "especially if we are starting in life. So when it is convenient to you to settle your debts I shall be glad."

"Oh! have no fear," he exclaimed with a sudden lighting up of his dark face, "I will pay you what I owe you, every farthing, with good interest thrown in."

"The king has just told me that is your intention," I remarked quietly, looking him full in the eyes. Then I walked on, leaving him staring after me, apparently without a word to say.

I went straight to the hut that was allotted to Retief in the little outlying guard-*kraal*, which had been given to us for a camp. Here I found the commandant seated on a Kaffir stool engaged in painfully writing a letter, using a bit of board placed on his knees as a desk.

He looked up, and asked me how I had got on with Dingaan, not being sorry, as I think, of an excuse to pause in his clerical labours.

"Listen, commandant," I said, and, speaking in a low voice, so as not to be overheard, I told him every word that had passed in the interviews I had just had with Dingaan, with Thomas Halstead, and with Pereira.

He heard me out in silence, then said:

"This is a strange and ugly story, Allan, and if it is true, Pereira must be an even bigger scoundrel than I thought him. But I can't believe that it is true. I think that Dingaan has been lying to you for his own purposes; I mean about the plot to kill you."

"Perhaps, commandant. I don't know, and I don't much care. But I am sure that he was not lying when he said he meant to steal away my wife either for himself or for Pereira."

"What, then, do you intend to do, Allan?"

"I intend, commandant, with your permission to send Hans, my after-rider, back to the camp with a letter for Marie, telling her to re-move herself quietly to the farm I have chosen down on the river, of which I told you, and there to lie hid till I come back."

"I think it needless, Allan. Still, if it will ease your mind, do so, since I cannot spare you to go yourself. Only you must not send this Hottentot, who would talk and frighten the people. I am despatch-ing a messenger to the camp to tell them of our safe arrival and good

394

reception by Dingaan. He can take your letter, in which I order you to say to your wife that if she and the Prinsloos and the Meyers go to this farm of yours, they are to go without talking, just as though they wanted a change, that is all. Have the letter ready by dawn to-morrow morning, as I trust mine may be," he added with a groan.

"It shall be ready, commandant; but what about Hernan Pereira and his tricks?"

"This about the accursed Hernan Pereira," exclaimed Retief, striking the writing-board with his fist. "On the first opportunity I will myself take the evidence of Dingaan and of the English lad, Halstead. If I find they tell me the same story they have told you, I will put Pereira on his trial, as I threatened to do before; and should he be found guilty, by God! I will have him shot. But for the present it is best to do nothing, except keep an eye on him, lest we should cause fear and scandal in the camp, and, after all, not prove the case. Now go and write your letter, and leave me to write mine."

So I went and wrote, telling Marie something, but by no means all of that I have set down. I bade her, and the Prinsloos and the Meyers, if they would accompany her, as I was sure they would, move themselves off at once to the farm I had beaconed out thirty miles away from the Bushman's River, under pretence of seeing how the houses that were being built there were getting on. Or if they would not go, I bade her go alone with a few Hottentot servants, or any other companions she could find.

This letter I took to Retief, and read it to him. At my request, also, he scrawled at the foot of it:

I have seen the above and approve it, knowing all the story, which may be true or false. Do as your husband bids you, but do not talk of it in the camp except to those whom he mentions.
Pieter Retief

So the messenger departed at dawn, and in due course delivered my letter to Marie.

The next day was Sunday. In the morning I went to call upon the Reverend Mr. Owen, the missionary, who was very glad to see me. He informed me that Dingaan was in good mind towards us, and had been asking him if he would write the treaty ceding the land which the Boers wanted. I stopped for service at the huts of Mr. Owen, and then returned to the camp. In the afternoon Dingaan celebrated a great war dance for us to witness, in which about twelve thousand soldiers took part.

It was a wonderful and awe-inspiring spectacle, and I remember that each of the regiments employed had a number of trained oxen which manoeuvred with them, apparently at given words of command. We did not see Dingaan that day, except at a distance, and after the dance was over returned to our camp to eat the beef which he had provided for us in plenty.

On the third day—that was Monday, the 5th of February, there were more dancings and sham fights, so many more, indeed, that we began to weary of this savage show. Late in the afternoon, however, Dingaan sent for the commandant and his men to come to see him, saying that he wished to talk with him about the matter of the treaty. So we went; but only three or four, of whom I was one, were admitted to Dingaan's presence, the rest remaining at a little distance, where they could see us but were out of earshot.

Dingaan then produced a paper which had been written by the Reverend Mr. Owen. This document, which I believe still exists, for it was found afterwards, was drawn up in legal or semi-legal form, beginning like a proclamation, "Know all men."

It ceded "the place called Port Natal, together with all the land annexed—that is to say, from Tugela to the Umzimvubu River westward, and from the sea to the north"—to the Boers, "for their everlasting property." At the king's request, as the deed was written in English by Mr. Owen, I translated it to him, and afterwards the lad Halstead translated it also, being called in to do so when I had finished.

This was done that my rendering might be checked, and the fact impressed all the Boers very favourably. It showed them that the king desired to understand exactly what he was to sign, which would not have been the case had he intended any trick or proposed to cheat them afterwards. From that moment forward Retief and his people had no further doubts as to Dingaan's good faith in this matter, and foolishly relaxed all precautions against treachery.

When the translating was finished, the commandant asked the king if he would sign the paper then and there. He answered, "No; he would sign it on the following morning, before the commission returned to Natal." It was then that Retief inquired of Dingaan, through Thomas Halstead, whether it was a true story which he had heard, that the Boer called Pereira, who had been staying with him, and whom the Zulus knew by the name of "Two-faces," had again asked him, Dingaan, to have me, Allan Quatermain, whom they called Macumazahn, killed. Dingaan laughed and answered:

"Yes, that is true enough, for he hates this Macumazahn. But let the

396

little white Son of George have no fear, since my heart is soft towards him, and I swear by the head of the Black One that he shall come to no harm in Zululand. Is he not my guest, as you are?"

He then went on to say that if the commandant wished it, he would have "Two-faces" seized and killed because he had dared to ask for my life. Retief answered that he would look into that matter himself, and after Thomas Halstead had confirmed the king's story as to Pereira's conduct, he rose and said good-bye to Dingaan.

Of this matter of Hernan Pereira, Retief said little as we went back to the camp outside the *Kraal*, though the little that he did say showed his deep anger. When we arrived at the camp, however, he sent for Pereira and Marais and several of the older Boers. I remember that among these were Gerrit Bothma, Senior, Hendrik Labuschagne and Matthys Pretorius, Senior, all of them persons of standing and judgment. I also was ordered to be present. When Pereira arrived, Retief charged him openly with having plotted my murder, and asked him what he had to say. Of course, his answer was a flat denial, and an accusation against me of having invented the tale because we had been at enmity over a maiden whom I had since married.

"Then, Mynheer Pereira," said Retief, "as Allan Quatermain here has won the maiden who is now his wife, it would seem that his cause of enmity must have ceased, whereas yours may well have remained. However, I have no time to try cases of the sort now. But I warn you that this one will be looked into later on when we get back to Natal, whither I shall take you with me, and that meanwhile an eye is kept on you and what you do. Also I warn you that I have evidence for all that I say. Now be so good as to go, and to keep out of my sight as much as possible, for I do not like a man whom these Kaffirs name 'Two-faces.' As for you, friend Henri Marais, I tell you that you would do well to associate yourself less with one whose name is under so dark a cloud, although he may be your own nephew, whom all know you love blindly."

So far as I recollect neither of them made any answer to this direct speech. They simply turned and went away. But on the next morning, that of the fatal 6th of February, when I chanced to meet the Commandant Retief as he was riding through the camp making arrangements for our departure to Natal, he pulled up his horse and said:

"Allan, Hernan Pereira has gone, and Henri Marais with him, and for my part I am not sorry, for doubtless we shall meet again, in this world or the next, and find out all the truth. Here, read this, and give it back to me afterwards"; and he threw me a paper and rode on.

I opened the folded sheet and read as follows:

"To the Commandant Retief, Governor of the Emigrant Boers,

"Mynheer Commandant,

"I will not stay here, where such foul accusations are laid on me by black Kaffirs and the Englishman, Allan Quatermain, who, like all his race, is an enemy of us Boers, and, although you do not know it, a traitor who is plotting great harm against you with the Zulus. Therefore I leave you, but am ready to meet every charge at the right time before a proper Court. My uncle, Henri Marais, comes with me, as he feels that his honour is also touched. Moreover, he has heard that his daughter, Marie, is in danger from the Zulus, and returns to protect her, which he who is called her husband neglects to do. Allan Quatermain, the Englishman, who is the friend of Dingaan, can explain what I mean, for he knows more about the Zulu plans than I do, as you will find out before the end."

Then followed the signatures of Hernan Pereira and Henri Marais.

I put the letter in my pocket, wondering what might be its precise meaning, and in particular that of the absurd and undefined charge of treachery against myself. It seemed to me that Pereira had left us because he was afraid of something—either that he might be placed upon his trial or of some ultimate catastrophe in which he would be involved. Marais probably had gone with him for the same reason that a bit of iron follows a magnet, because he never could resist the attraction of this evil man, his relative by birth. Or perhaps he had learned from him the story of his daughter's danger, upon which I had already acted, and really was anxious about her safety. For it must always be remembered that Marais loved Marie passionately, however ill the reader of this history may think that he behaved to her. She was his darling, the apple of his eye, and her great offence in his sight was that she cared for me more than she did for him. That is one of the reasons why he hated me as much as he loved her.

Almost before I had finished reading this letter, the order came that we were to go in a body to bid farewell to Dingaan, leaving our arms piled beneath the two milk trees at the gate of the town. Most of our after-riders were commanded to accompany us—I think because Retief wished to make as big a show as possible to impress the Zulus. A few of these Hottentots, however, were told to stay behind that they might collect the horses, that were knee-haltered and grazing at a distance, and saddle them up. Among these was Hans, for, as it chanced, I saw and sent him with the others, so that I might be sure that my own horses would be found and made ready for the journey.

Just as we were starting, I met the lad William Wood, who had come down from the Mission huts, where he lived with Mr. Owen, and was wandering about with an anxious face.

"How are you, William?" I asked.

"Not very well, Mr. Quatermain," he answered. "The fact is," he added with a burst of confidence, "I feel queerly about you all. The Kaffirs have told me that something is going to happen to you, and I think you ought to know it. I daren't say any more," and he vanished into the crowd.

At that moment I caught sight of Retief riding to and fro and shouting out orders. Going to him, I caught him by the sleeve, saying:

"Commandant, listen to me."

"Well, what is it now, nephew?" he asked absently.

I told him what Wood had said, adding that I also was uneasy; I did not know why.

"Oh!" he answered with impatience, "this is all hailstones and burnt grass" (meaning that the one would melt and the other blow away, or in our English idiom, stuff and rubbish). "Why are you always trying to scare me with your fancies, Allan? Dingaan is our friend, not our enemy. So let us take the gifts that fortune gives us and be thankful. Come, march."

This he said about eight o'clock in the morning.

We strolled through the gates of the Great *Kraal*, most of the Boers, who, as usual, had piled their arms under the two milk trees, lounging along in knots of four or five, laughing and chatting as they went. I have often thought since, that although every one of them there, except myself, was doomed within an hour to have taken the dreadful step from time into eternity, it seems strange that advancing fate should have thrown no shadow on their hearts. On the contrary, they were quite gay, being extremely pleased at the successful issue of their mission and the prospect of an immediate return to their wives and children. Even Retief was gay, for I heard him joking with his companions about myself and my "white-bread-week," or honeymoon, which, he said, was drawing very near.

As we went, I noticed that most of the regiments who had performed the great military dances before us on the previous day were gone. Two, however, remained—the *Ischlangu Inhlope*, that is the "White Shields," who were a corps of veterans wearing the ring on their heads, and the *Ischlangu Umnyama*, that is the "Black Shields," who were all of them young men without rings. The "White Shields" were ranged along the fence of the great open place to our left, and the "Black Shields" were similarly placed to our right, each regiment numbering about fifteen hundred men. Except for their *kerries* and dancing-sticks they were unarmed.

Presently we reached the head of the dancing ground, and found Dingaan seated in his chair with two of his great indunas, Umhlela and Tambusa, squatting on either side of him. Behind him, standing in and about the entrance to the labyrinth through which the king had come, were other indunas and captains. On arriving in front of Dingaan we saluted him, and he acknowledged the salutation with pleasant words and smiles. Then Retief, two or three of the other Boers, Thomas Halstead and I went forward, whereon the treaty was produced again and identified as the same document that we had seen on the previous day.

At the foot of it someone—I forget who—wrote in Dutch, *"De merk van Koning Dingaan"* (that is, The mark of King Dingaan.) In the space left between the words *merk* and *van* Dingaan made a cross with a pen that was given to him, Thomas Halstead holding his hand and showing him what to do.

After this, three of his indunas, or great councillors, who were named Nwara, Yuliwana and Manondo, testified as witnesses for the Zulus, and M. Oosthuyzen, A. C. Greyling and B. J. Liebenberg, who were standing nearest to Retief, as witnesses for the Boers.

This done, Dingaan ordered one of his *isibongos*, or praisers, to run to and fro in front of the regiments and others there assembled, and proclaim that he had granted Natal to the Boers to be their property for ever, information which the Zulus received with shouts. Then Dingaan asked Retief if he would not eat, and large trenchers of boiled beef were brought out and handed round. This, however, the Boers refused, saying they had already breakfasted. Thereon the king said that at least they must drink, and pots of *twala*, or Kaffir beer, were handed round, of which all the Boers partook.

While they were drinking, Dingaan gave Retief a message to the Dutch farmers, to the effect that he hoped they would soon come and occupy Natal, which henceforth was their country. Also, black-hearted villain that he was, that they would have a pleasant journey home. Next he ordered the two regiments to dance and sing war songs, in order to amuse his guests. This they began to do, drawing nearer as they danced.

It was at this moment that a Zulu appeared, pushing his way through the captains who were gathered at the gate of the labyrinth, and delivered some message to one of the indunas, who in turn passed it on to the king.

"*Ow!* is it so?" said the king with a troubled look. Then his glance fell on me as though by accident, and he added: "Macumazahn, one of my wives is taken very ill suddenly, and says she must have some of the medicine of the white men before they go away. Now, you tell me that you are a new-married man, so I can trust you with my wives. I pray you to go and find out what medicine it is that she needs, for you can speak our tongue."

I hesitated, then translated what he had said to Retief.

"You had best go, nephew," said the commandant; "but come back quickly, for we ride at once."

Still I hesitated, not liking this business; whereon the king began to grow angry.

"What!" he said, "do you white men refuse me this little favour, when I have just given you so much—you who have wonderful medicines that can cure the sick?"

"Go, Allan, go," said Retief, when he understood his words, "or he will grow cross and everything may be undone."

So, having no choice, I went through the gateway into the labyrinth.

Next moment men pounced on me, and before I could utter a word a cloth was thrown over my mouth and tied tight behind my head.

I was a prisoner and gagged.

CHAPTER 19

Depart in Peace

A tall Kaffir, one of the king's household guards, who carried an *assegai*, came up to me and whispered:

"Hearken, little Son of George. The king would save you, if he can, because you are not Dutch, but English. Yet, know that if you try to cry out, if you even struggle, you die," and he lifted the *assegai* so as to be ready to plunge it through my heart.

Now I understood, and a cold sweat broke out all over me. My companions were to be murdered, every one! Oh! gladly would I have given my life to warn them. But alas! I could not, for the cloth upon my mouth was so thick that no sound could pass it.

One of the Zulus inserted a stick between the reeds of the fence. Working it to and fro sideways, he made an opening just in a line with my eyes—out of cruelty, I suppose, for now I must see everything.

For some time—ten minutes, I dare say—the dancing and beer-drinking went on. Then Dingaan rose from his chair and shook the hand of Retief warmly, bidding him *"Hamba gachle,"* that is, Depart gently, or in peace. He retreated towards the gate of the labyrinth, and as he went the Boers took off their hats, waving them in the air and cheering him. He was almost through it, and I began to breathe again.

Doubtless I was mistaken. After all, no treachery was intended.

In the very opening of the gate Dingaan turned, however, and said two words in Zulu which mean:

"Seize them!"

Instantly the warriors, who had now danced quite close and were waiting for these words, rushed upon the Boers. I heard Thomas Halstead call out in English:

"We are done for," and then add in Zulu, "Let me speak to the king!"

Dingaan heard also, and waved his hand to show that he refused to listen, and as he did so shouted thrice:

"*Bulala abatagati!*" that is, Slay the wizards!

I saw poor Halstead draw his knife and plunge it into a Zulu who was near him. The man fell, and again he struck at another soldier, cutting his throat. The Boers also drew their knives—those of them who had time—and tried to defend themselves against these black devils, who rushed on them in swarms. I heard afterwards that they succeeded in killing six or eight of them and wounding perhaps a score. But it was soon over, for what could men armed only with pocket-knives do against such a multitude?

Presently, amidst a hideous tumult of shouts, groans, curses, prayers for mercy, and Zulu battle cries, the Boers were all struck down—yes, even the two little lads and the Hottentot servants. Then they were dragged away, still living, by the soldiers, their heels trailing on the ground, just as wounded worms or insects are dragged by the black ants.

Dingaan was standing by me now, laughing, his fat face working nervously.

"Come, Son of George," he said, "and let us see the end of these traitors to your sovereign."

Then I was pulled along to an eminence within the labyrinth, whence there was a view of the surrounding country. Here we waited a little while, listening to the tumult that grew more distant, till presently the dreadful procession of death reappeared, coming round the fence of the Great *Kraal* and heading straight for the Hill of Slaughter, Hloma Amabutu. Soon its slopes were climbed, and there among the dark-leaved bushes and the rocks the black soldiers butchered them, every one.

I saw and swooned away.

I believe that I remained senseless for many hours, though towards the end of that time my swoon grew thin, as it were, and I heard a hollow voice speaking over me in Zulu.

"I am glad that the little Son of George has been saved," said the echoing voice, which I did not know, "for he has a great destiny and will be useful to the black people in time to come." Then the voice went on:

"O House of Senzangacona! now you have mixed your milk with blood, with white blood. Of that bowl you shall drink to the dregs, and afterwards must the bowl be shattered"; and the speaker laughed—a deep, dreadful laugh that I was not to hear again for years.

I heard him go away, shuffling along like some great reptile, and then, with an effort, opened my eyes. I was in a large hut, and the only light in the hut came from a fire that burned in its centre, for it was night time. A Zulu woman, young and good-looking, was bending over a gourd near the fire, doing something to its contents. I spoke to her light-headedly.

"O woman," I said, "is that a man who laughed over me?"

"Not altogether, Macumazahn," she answered in a pleasant voice. "That was Zikali, the Mighty Magician, the Counsellor of Kings, the Opener of Roads; he whose birth our grandfathers do not remember; he whose breath causes the trees to be torn out by the roots; he whom Dingaan fears and obeys."

"Did he cause the Boers to be killed?" I asked.

"Mayhap," she answered. "Who am I that I should know of such matters?"

"Are you the woman who was sick whom I was sent to visit?" I asked again.

"Yes, Macumazahn, I was sick, but now I am well and you are sick, for so things go round. Drink this," and she handed me a gourd of milk.

"How are you named?" I inquired as I took it.

"Naya is my name," she replied, "and I am your jailer. Don't think that you can escape me, though, Macumazahn, for there are other jailers without who carry spears. Drink."

So I drank and bethought me that the draught might be poisoned. Yet so thirsty was I that I finished it, every drop.

"Now am I a dead man?" I asked, as I put down the gourd.

"No, no, Macumazahn," she who called herself Naya replied in a soft voice; "not a dead man, only one who will sleep and forget."

Then I lost count of everything and slept—for how long I know not.

When I awoke again it was broad daylight; in fact, the sun stood high in the heavens. Perhaps Naya had put some drug into my milk, or perhaps I had simply slept. I do not know. At any rate, I was grateful for that sleep, for without it I think that I should have gone mad. As it was, when I remembered, which it took me some time to do, for a while I went near to insanity.

I recollect lying there in that hut and wondering how the Almighty could have permitted such a deed as I had seen done. How could it be reconciled with any theory of a loving and merciful Father? Those poor Boers, whatever their faults, and they had many, like the rest of us, were in the main good and honest men according to their lights.

Yet they had been doomed to be thus brutally butchered at the nod of a savage despot, their wives widowed, their children left fatherless, or, as it proved in the end, in most cases murdered or orphaned!

The mystery was too great—great enough to throw off its balance the mind of a young man who had witnessed such a fearsome scene as I have described.

For some days really I think that my reason hung just upon the edge of that mental precipice. In the end, however, reflection and education, of which I had a certain amount, thanks to my father, came to my aid. I recalled that such massacres, often on an infinitely larger scale, had happened a thousand times in history, and that still through them, often, indeed, by means of them, civilisation has marched forward, and mercy and peace have kissed each other over the bloody graves of the victims.

Therefore even in my youth and inexperience I concluded that some ineffable purpose was at work through this horror, and that the lives of those poor men which had been thus sacrificed were necessary to that purpose. This may appear a dreadful and fatalistic doctrine, but it is one that is corroborated in Nature every day, and doubtless the sufferers meet with their compensations in some other state. Indeed, if it be not so, faith and all the religions are vain.

Or, of course, it may chance that such monstrous calamities happen, not through the will of the merciful Power of which I have spoken, but in its despite. Perhaps the devil of Scripture, at whom we are inclined to smile, is still very real and active in this world of ours. Perhaps from time to time some evil principle breaks into eruption, like the imprisoned forces of a volcano, bearing death and misery on its wings, until in the end it must depart strengthless and overcome. Who can say?

The question is one that should be referred to the Archbishop of Canterbury and the Pope of Rome in conclave, with the Lama of Tibet for umpire in case they disagreed. I only try to put down the thoughts that struck me so long ago as my mind renders them to-day. But very likely they are not quite the same thoughts, for a full generation has gone by me since then, and in that time the intelligence ripens as wine does in a bottle.

Besides these general matters, I had questions of my own to consider during those days of imprisonment—for instance, that of my own safety, though of this, to be honest, I thought little. If I were going to be killed, I was going to be killed, and there was an end. But my knowledge of Dingaan told me that he had not massacred Retief and his companions for nothing. This would be but the prelude to a larger slaughter, for I had not forgotten what he said as to the sparing of Marie and the other hints he gave me.

From all this I concluded, quite rightly as it proved, that some general onslaught was being made upon the Boers, who probably would be swept out to the last man. And to think that here I was, a prisoner in a Kaffir *kraal*, with only a young woman as a jailer, and yet utterly unable to escape to warn them. For round my hut lay a courtyard, and round it again ran a reed fence about five feet six inches high. Whenever I looked over this fence, by night or by day, I saw soldiers stationed at intervals of about fifteen yards. There they stood like statues, their broad spears in their hands, all looking inwards towards the fence. There they stood—only at night their number was doubled. Clearly it was not meant that I should escape.

A week went by thus—believe me, a very terrible week. During that time my sole companion was the pretty young woman, Naya. We became friends in a way and talked on a variety of subjects. Only, at the end of our conversations I always found that I had gained no information whatsoever about any matter of immediate interest. On such points as the history of the Zulu and kindred tribes, or the character of Chaka, the great king, or anything else that was remote she would discourse by the hour. But when we came to current events, she dried up like water on a red-hot brick. Still, Naya grew, or pretended to grow, quite attached to me. She even suggested naively that I might do worse than marry her, which she said Dingaan was quite ready to allow, as he was fond of me and thought I should be useful in his country. When I told her that I was already married, she shrugged her shining shoulders and asked with a laugh that revealed her beautiful teeth:

"What does that matter? Cannot a man have more wives than one? And, Macumazahn," she added, leaning forward and looking at me, "how do you know that you have even one? You may be divorced or a widower by now."

"What do you mean?" I asked.

"I? I mean nothing; do not look at me so fiercely, Macumazahn. Surely such things happen in the world, do they not?"

"Naya," I said, "you are two bad things—a bait and a spy—and you know it."

"Perhaps I do, Macumazahn," she answered. "Am I to blame for that, if my life is on it, especially when I really like you for yourself?"

"I don't know," I said. "Tell me, when am I going to get out of this place?"

"How can I tell you, Macumazahn?" Naya replied, patting my hand in her genial way, "but I think before long. When you are gone, Macumazahn, remember me kindly sometimes, as I have really tried to make you as comfortable as I could with a watcher staring through every straw in the hut."

I said whatever seemed to be appropriate, and next morning my deliverance came. While I was eating my breakfast in the courtyard at the back of the hut, Naya thrust her handsome and pleasant face round the corner and said that there was a messenger to see me from the king. Leaving the rest of the meal unswallowed, I went to the doorway of the yard and there found my old friend, Kambula.

"Greeting, *Inkoos*," he said to me; "I am come to take you back to Natal with a guard. But I warn you to ask me no questions, for if you do I must not answer them. Dingaan is ill, and you cannot see him, nor can you see the white praying-man, or anyone; you must come with me at once."

"I do not want to see Dingaan," I replied, looking him in the eyes.

"I understand," answered Kambula; "Dingaan's thoughts are his thoughts and your thoughts are your thoughts, and perhaps that is why he does not want to see *you*. Still, remember, *Inkoos*, that Dingaan has saved your life, snatching you unburned out of a very great fire, perhaps because you are of a different sort of wood, which he thinks it a pity to burn. Now, if you are ready, let us go."

"I am ready," I answered.

At the gate I met Naya, who said:

"You never thought to say good-bye to me, White Man, although I have tended you well. Ah! what else could I expect? Still, I hope that if I should have to fly from this land for *my* life, as may chance, you will do for me what I have done for you."

"That I will," I answered, shaking her by the hand; and, as it happened, in after years I did.

Kambula led me, not through the *kraal* Umgungundhlovu, but round it. Our road lay immediately past the death mount, Hloma Amabutu, where the vultures were still gathered in great numbers. Indeed, it was actually my lot to walk over the new-picked bones of some of my companions who had been despatched at the foot of the hill. One of these skeletons I recognised by his clothes to be that of Samuel Esterhuizen, a very good fellow, at whose side I had slept during all our march.

His empty eye-sockets seemed to stare at me reproachfully, as though they asked me why I remained alive when he and all his brethren were dead. I echoed the question in my own mind. Why of that great company did I alone remain alive?

An answer seemed to rise within me: That I might be one of the instruments of vengeance upon that devilish murderer, Dingaan. Looking upon those poor shattered and desecrated frames that had been men, I swore in my heart that if I lived I would not fail in that mission. Nor did I fail, although the history of that great repayment cannot be told in these pages.

Turning my eyes from this dreadful sight, I saw that on the opposite slope, where we had camped during our southern trek from Delagoa, still stood the huts and wagons of the Reverend Mr. Owen. I asked Kambula whether he and his people were also dead.

"No, *Inkoos*," he answered; "they are of the Children of George, as you are, and therefore the king has spared them, although he is going to send them out of the country."

This was good news, so far as it went, and I asked again if Thomas Halstead had also been spared, since he, too, was an Englishman.

"No," said Kambula. "The king wished to save him, but he killed two of our people and was dragged off with the rest. When the slayers got to their work it was too late to stay their hands."

Again I asked whether I might not join Mr. Owen and trek with him, to which Kambula answered briefly:

"No, Macumazahn; the king's orders are that you must go by yourself."

So I went; nor did I ever again meet Mr. Owen or any of his people. I believe, however, that they reached Durban safely and sailed away in a ship called the Comet.

In a little while we came to the two milk trees by the main gate of the *kraal*, where much of our saddlery still lay scattered about, though the guns had gone. Here Kambula asked me if I could recognise my own saddle.

"There it is," I answered, pointing to it; "but what is the use of a saddle without a horse?"

"The horse you rode has been kept for you, Macumazahn," he replied.

Then he ordered one of the men with us to bring the saddle and bridle, also some other articles which I selected, such as a couple of blankets, a water-bottle, two tins containing coffee and sugar, a little case of medicines, and so forth.

About a mile further on I found one of my horses tethered by an outlying guard hut, and noted that it had been well fed and cared for.

By Kambula's leave I saddled it and mounted. As I did so, he warned me that if I tried to ride away from the escort I should certainly be killed, since even if I escaped them, orders had been given throughout the land to put an end to me should I be seen alone.

I replied that, unarmed as I was, I had no idea of making any such attempt. So we went forward, Kambula and his soldiers walking or trotting at my side.

For four full days we journeyed thus, keeping, so far as I could judge, about twenty or thirty miles to the east of that road by which I had left Zululand before and re-entered it with Retief and his commission. Evidently I was an object of great interest to the Zulus of the country through which we passed, perhaps because they knew me to be the sole survivor of all the white men who had gone up to visit the king. They would come down in crowds from the *kraals* and stare at me almost with awe, as though I were a spirit and not a man. Only, not one of them would say anything to me, probably because they had been forbidden to do so. Indeed, if I spoke to any of them, invariably they turned and walked or ran out of hearing.

It was on the evening of the fourth day that Kambula and his soldiers received some news which seemed to excite them a great deal. A messenger in a state of exhaustion, who had an injury to the fleshy part of his left arm, which looked to me as though it had been caused by a bullet, appeared out of the bush and said something of which, by straining my ears, I caught two words—"Great slaughter." Then Kambula laid his fingers on his lips as a signal for silence and led the man away, nor did I see or hear any more of him. Afterwards I asked Kambula who had suffered this great slaughter, whereon he stared at me innocently and replied that he did not know of what I was speaking.

"What is the use of lying to me, Kambula, seeing that I shall find out the truth before long?"

"Then, Macumazahn, wait till you do find it out, and may it please you," he replied, and went off to speak with his people at a distance.

All that night I heard them talking off and on—I, who lay awake plunged into new miseries. I was sure that some other dreadful thing had happened. Probably Dingaan's armies had destroyed all the Boers, and, if so, oh! what had become of Marie? Was she dead, or had she perhaps been taken prisoner, as Dingaan had told me would be done for his own vile purposes? For aught I knew she might now be travelling under escort to Umgungundhlovu, as I was travelling to Natal.

The morning came at last, and that day, about noon, we reached a ford of the Tugela which luckily was quite passable. Here Kambula bade me farewell, saying that his mission was finished. Also he delivered to me a message that I was to give from Dingaan to the English in Natal. It was to this effect: That he, Dingaan, had killed the Boers who came to visit him because he found out that they were traitors to their chief, and therefore not worthy to live. But that he loved the Sons of George, who were true-hearted people, and therefore had nothing to fear from him. Indeed, he begged them to come and see him at his Great Place, where he would talk matters over with them.

I said that I would deliver the message if I met any English people, but, of course, I could not say whether they would accept Dingaan's invitation to Umgungundhlovu. Indeed, I feared lest that town might have acquired such a bad name that they would prefer not to come there without an army.

Then, before Kambula had time to take any offence, I shook his outstretched hand and urged my horse into the stream. I never met Kambula again living, though after the battle of Blood River I saw him dead.

Once over the Tugela I rode forward for half a mile or so till I was clear of the bush and reeds that grew down to the water, fearing lest the Zulus should follow and take me back to Dingaan to explain my rather imprudent message. Seeing no signs of them, I halted, a desolate creature in a desolate country which I did not know, wondering what I should do and whither I should ride. Then it was that there happened one of the strangest experiences of all my adventurous life.

As I sat dejectedly upon my horse, which was also dejected, amidst some tumbled rocks that at a distant period in the world's history had formed the bank of the great river, I heard a voice which seemed familiar to me say:

"Baas, is that *you*, *baas*?"

I looked round and could see no one, so, thinking that I had been deceived by my imagination, I held my peace.

"Baas," said the voice again, "are you dead or are you alive? Because, if you are dead, I don't want to have anything to do with spooks until I am obliged."

Now I answered, "Who is it that speaks, and whence?" though, really, as I could see no one, I thought that I must be demented.

The next moment my horse snorted and shied violently, and no wonder, for out of a great ant-bear hole not five paces away appeared a yellow face crowned with black wool, in which was set a broken feather. I looked at the face and the face looked at me.

"Hans," I said, "is it you? I thought that *you* were killed with the others."

"And I thought that *you* were killed with the others, *baas*. Are you sure that you are alive?"

"What are you doing there, you old fool?" I asked.

"Hiding from the Zulus, *baas*. I heard them on the other bank, and then saw a man on a horse crossing the river, and went to ground like a jackal. I have had enough of Zulus."

"Come out," I said, "and tell me your story."

He emerged, a thin and bedraggled creature, with nothing left on him but the upper part of a pair of old trousers, but still Hans, undoubtedly Hans. He ran to me, and seizing my foot, kissed it again and again, weeping tears of joy and stuttering:

"Oh, *baas*, to think that I should find you who were dead, alive, and find myself alive, too. Oh! *baas*, never again will I doubt about the Big Man in the sky of whom your reverend father is so fond. For after I had tried all our own spirits, and even those of my ancestors, and met with nothing but trouble, I said the prayer that the reverend taught us, asking for my daily bread because I am so very hungry. Then I looked out of the hole and there you were. Have you anything to eat about you, *baas*?"

As it chanced, in my saddle-bags I had some biltong that I had saved against emergencies. I gave it to him, and he devoured it as a famished hyena might do, tearing off the tough meat in lumps and bolting them whole. When it was all gone he licked his fingers and his lips and stood still staring at me.

"Tell me your story," I repeated.

"Baas, I went to fetch the horses with the others, and ours had strayed. I got up a tree to look for them. Then I heard a noise, and saw that the Zulus were killing the Boers; so knowing that presently they would kill us, too, I stopped in that tree, hiding myself as well as I could in a stork's nest. Well, they came and *assegaied* all the other Totties, and stood under my tree cleaning their spears and getting their breath, for one of my brothers had given them a good run. But they never saw me, although I was nearly sick from fear on the top of them. Indeed, I was sick, but into the nest.

"Well, I sat in that nest all day, though the sun cooked me like beef on a stick; and when night came I got down and ran, for I knew it was no good to stop to look for you, and 'every man for himself when a black devil is behind you,' as your reverend father says. All night I ran, and in the morning hid up in a hole. Then when night came again I went on running. Oh! they nearly caught me once or twice, but never quite, for I know how to hide, and I kept where men do not go. Only I was hungry, hungry; yes, I lived on snails and worms, and grass like an ox, till my middle ached. Still, at last I got across the river and near to the camp.

"Then just before the day broke and I was saying, 'Now, Hans, although your heart is sad, your stomach will rejoice and sing,' what did I see but those Zulu devils, thousands of them, rush down on the camp and kill all the poor Boers. Men and women and the little children, they killed them by the hundred, till at last other Boers came and drove them away, although they took all the cattle with them. Well, as I was sure that they would come back, I did not stop there. I ran down to the side of the river, and have been crawling about in the reeds for days, living on the eggs of water-birds and a few small fish that I caught in the pools, till this morning, when I heard the Zulus again and slipped up here into this hole. Then you came and stood over the hole, and for a long while I thought you were a ghost.

"But now we are together once more and all is right, just as what your reverend father always said it would be with those who go to church on Sunday, like me when there was nothing else to do." And again he fell to kissing my foot.

"Hans," I said, "you saw the camp. Was the Missie Marie there?"

"Baas, how can I tell, who never went into it? But the wagon she slept in was not there; no, nor that of the Vrouw Prinsloo or of the Heer Meyer."

"Thank God!" I gasped, then added: "Where were you trying to get to, Hans, when you ran away from the camp?"

"*Baas*, I thought perhaps that the missie and the Prinsloos and the Meyers had gone to that fine farm which you pegged out, and that I would go and see if they were there. Because if so, I was sure that they would be glad to know that you were really dead, and give me some food in payment for my news. But I was afraid to walk across the open *veld* for fear lest the Zulus should see me and kill me. Therefore I came round through the thick bush along the river, where one can only travel slowly, especially if hollow," and he patted his wasted stomach.

"But, Hans," I asked, "are we near my farm where I set the men to build the houses on the hill above the river?"

"Of course, *baas*. Has your brain gone soft that you cannot find your way about the *veld*? Four, or at most five, hours on horseback, riding slow, and you are there."

"Come on, Hans," I said, "and be quick, for I think that the Zulus are not far behind."

So we started, Hans hanging to my stirrup and guiding me, for I knew well enough that although he had never travelled this road, his instinct for locality would not betray a coloured man, who can find his way across the pathless *veld* as surely as a buck or a bird of the air.

On we went over the rolling plain, and as we travelled I told him my story, briefly enough, for my mind was too torn with fears to allow me to talk much. He, too, told me more of his escape and adventures. Now I understood what was that news which had so excited Kambula and his soldiers. It was evident that the Zulu *impis* had destroyed a great number of the Boers whom they found unprepared for attack, and then had been driven off by reinforcements that arrived from other camps.

That was why I had been kept prisoner for all those days. Dingaan feared lest I should reach Natal in time to warn his victims!

CHAPTER 20

The Court-Martial

One hour, two hours, three hours, and then suddenly from the top of a rise the sight of the beautiful Mooi River winding through the plain like a vast snake of silver, and there, in a loop of it, the flat-crested *koppie* on which I had hoped to make my home. Had hoped!—why should I not still hope? For aught I knew everything might yet be well. Marie might have escaped the slaughter as I had done, and if so, after all our troubles perchance many years of life and happiness awaited us. Only it seemed too good to be true.

I flogged my horse, but the poor beast was tired out and could only break into short canters, that soon lapsed to a walk again. But whether it cantered or whether it walked, its hoofs seemed to beat out the words—"Too good to be true!" Sometimes they beat them fast, and sometimes they beat them slow, but always their message seemed the same.

Hans, too, was outworn and weak from starvation. Also he had a cut upon his foot which hampered him so much that at last he said I had better go on alone; he would follow more slowly. Then I dismounted and set him on the horse, walking by it myself.

Thus it came about that the gorgeous sunset was finished and the sky had grown grey with night before we reached the foot of the *koppie*. Yet the last rays of the sinking orb had shown me something as they died. There on the slope of the hill stood some mud and wattle houses, such as I had ordered to be built, and near to them several white-capped wagons. Only I did not see any smoke rising from those houses as there should have been at this hour of the day, when men cooked their evening food. The moon would be up presently, I knew, but meanwhile it was dark and the tired horse stumbled and floundered among the stones which lay about at the foot of the hill.

I could bear it no longer.

"Hans," I said, "do you stay here with the horse. I will creep to the houses and see if any dwell there."

"Be careful, *baas*," he answered, "lest you should find Zulus, for those black devils are all about."

I nodded, for I could not speak, and then began the ascent. For several hundred yards I crept from stone to stone, feeling my way, for the Kaffir path that led to the little plateau where the spring was, above which the shanties stood, ran at the other end of the hill. I struck the *spruit* or rivulet that was fed by this spring, being guided to it by the murmur of the water, and followed up its bank till I heard a sound which caused me to crouch and listen.

I could not be sure because of the ceaseless babble of the brook, but the sound seemed like that of sobs. While I waited the great moon appeared suddenly above a bank of inky cloud, flooding the place with light, and oh! by that light, looking more ethereal than woman I saw—I saw Marie!

She stood not five paces from me, by the side of the stream, whither she had come to draw water, for she held a vessel in her hand. She was clothed in some kind of a black garment, such as widows wear, but made of rough stuff, and above it her face showed white in the white rays of the moon. Gazing at her from the shadow, I could even see the tears running down her cheeks, for it was she who wept in this lonely place, wept for one who would return no more.

My voice choked in my throat; I could not utter a single word. Rising from behind a rock I moved towards her. She saw me and started, then said in a thrilling whisper:

"Oh! husband, has God sent you to call me? I am ready, husband, I am ready!" and she stretched out her arms wildly, letting fall the vessel, that clanked upon the ground.

"Marie!" I gasped at length; and at that word the blood rushed to her face and brow, and I saw her draw in her breath as though to scream.

"Hush!" I whispered. "It is I, Allan, who have escaped alive."

The next thing I remember was that she lay in my arms.

"What has happened here?" I asked when I had told my tale, or some of it.

"Nothing, Allan," she answered. "I received your letter at the camp, and we trekked away as you bade us, without telling the others why, because you remember the Commandant Retief wrote to us not to do so. So we were out of the great slaughter, for the Zulus did not know where we had gone, and never followed us here, although I have heard that they sought for me. My father and my cousin Hernan only arrived at the camp two days after the attack, and discovering or guessing our hiding-place—I know not which—rode on hither. They say they came to warn the Boers to be careful, for they did not trust Dingaan, but were too late. So they too were out of the slaughter, for, Allan, many, many have been killed—they say five or six hundred, most of them women and children. But thank God! many more escaped, since the men came in from the other camps farther off and from their shooting parties, and drove away the Zulus, killing them by scores."

"Are your father and Pereira here now?" I asked.

"No, Allan. They learned of the massacre and that the Zulus were all gone yesterday morning. Also they got the bad news that Retief and everyone with him had been killed at Dingaan's town, it is said through the treachery of the English, who arranged with Dingaan that he should kill them."

"That is false," I said; "but go on."

"Then, Allan, they came and told me that I was a widow like many other women—I who had never been a wife. Allan, Hernan said that I should not grieve for you, as you deserved your fate, since you had been caught in your own snare, being one of those who had betrayed the Boers. The Vrouw Prinsloo answered to his face that he lied, and, Allan, I said that I would never speak to him again until we met before the Judgment Seat of God; nor will I do so."

"But I will speak to him," I muttered. "Well, where are they now?"

"They rode this morning back to the other Boers. I think they want to bring a party of them here to settle, if they like this place, as it is so easy to defend. They said they would return to-morrow, and that meanwhile we were quite safe, as they had sure tidings that all the Zulus were back over the Tugela, taking some of their wounded with them, and also the Boer cattle as an offering to Dingaan. But come to the house, Allan—our home that I had made ready for you as well as I could. Oh! my God! our home on the threshold of which I believed you would never set a foot. Yes, when the moon rose from that cloud I believed it, and look, they are still quite close together. Hark, what is that?"

I listened, and caught the sound of a horse's hoofs stumbling among the rocks.

"Don't be frightened," I answered; "it is only Hans with my horse. He escaped also; I will tell you how afterwards." And as I spoke he appeared, a woebegone and exhausted object.

"Good day, missie," he said with an attempt at cheerfulness. "Now you should give me a fine dinner, for you see I have brought the *baas* back safe to you. Did I not tell you, *baas*, that everything would come right?"

416

Then he grew silent from exhaustion. Nor were we sorry, who at that moment did not wish to listen to the poor fellow's talk.

Something over two hours had gone by since the moon broke out from the clouds. I had greeted the Vrouw Prinsloo and all my other friends, and been received by them with rapture as one risen from the dead. If they had loved me before, now a new gratitude was added to their love, since had it not been for my warning they also must have made acquaintance with the Zulu spears and perished. It was on their part of the camp that the worst of the attack fell. Indeed, from those wagons hardly anyone escaped.

I had told them all the story, to which they listened in dead silence. Only when it was finished the Heer Meyer, whose natural gloom had been deepened by all these events, said:

"*Allemachte*! but you have luck, Allan, to be left when everyone else is taken. Now, did I not know you so well, like Hernan Pereira I should think that you and that devil Dingaan had winked at each other."

The Vrouw Prinsloo turned on him furiously.

"How dare you say such words, Carl Meyer?" she exclaimed. "Must Allan always be insulted just because he is English, which he cannot help? For my part, I think that if anyone winked at Dingaan it was the stinkcat Pereira. Otherwise why did he come away before the killing and bring that madman, Henri Marais, with him?"

"I don't know, I am sure, aunt," said Meyer humbly, for like everyone else he was afraid of the Vrouw Prinsloo.

"Then why can't you hold your tongue instead of saying silly things which must give pain?" asked the *vrouw*. "No, don't answer, for you will only make matters worse; but take the rest of that meat to the poor Hottentot, Hans"—I should explain that we had been supping—"who, although he has eaten enough to burst any white stomach, I dare say can manage another pound or two."

Meyer obeyed meekly, and the others melted away also as they were wont to do when the *vrouw* showed signs of war, so that she and we two were left alone.

"Now," said the *vrouw*, "everyone is tired, and I say that it is time to go to rest. Good night, nephew Allan and niece Marie," and she waddled away leaving us together.

"Husband," said Marie presently, "will you come and see the home that I made ready for you before I thought that you were dead? It is a poor place, but I pray God that we may be happy there," and she took me by the hand and kissed me once and twice and thrice.

About noon on the following day, when my wife and I were laughing and arguing over some little domestic detail of our meagre establishment—so soon are great griefs forgotten in an overwhelming joy, of a sudden I saw her face change, and asked what was the matter.

"*Hist!*" she said, "I hear horses," and she pointed in a certain direction.

I looked, and there, round the corner of the hill, came a body of Boers with their after-riders, thirty-two or three of them in all, of whom twenty were white men.

"See," said Marie, "my father is among them, and my cousin Hernan rides at his side."

It was true. There was Henri Marais, and just behind him, talking into his ear, rode Hernan Pereira. I remember that the two of them reminded me of a tale I had read about a man who was cursed with an evil genius that drew him to some dreadful doom in spite of the promptings of his better nature. The thin, worn, wild-eyed Marais, and the rich-faced, carnal Pereira whispering slyly into his ear; they were exact types of that man in the story and his evil genius who dragged him down to hell. Prompted by some impulse, I threw my arms round Marie and embraced her, saying:

"At least we have been very happy for a while."

"What do you mean, Allan?" she asked doubtfully.

"Only that I think our good hours are done with for the present."

"Perhaps," she answered slowly; "but at least they have been very good hours, and if I should die to-day I am glad to have lived to win them."

Then the cavalcade of Boers came up.

Hernan Pereira, his senses sharpened perhaps by the instincts of hate and jealousy, was the first to recognise me.

"Why, Mynheer Allan Quatermain," he said, "how is it that you are here? How is it that you still live? Commandant," he added, turning to a dark, sad-faced man of about sixty whom at that time I did not know, "here is a strange thing. This Heer Quatermain, an Englishman, was with the Governor Retief at the town of the Zulu king, as the Heer Henri Marais can testify. Now, as we know for sure Pieter Retief and all his people are dead, murdered by Dingaan, how then does it happen that this man has escaped?"

"Why do you put riddles to me, Mynheer Pereira?" asked the dark Boer. "Doubtless the Englishman will explain."

"Certainly I will, *mynheer*," I said. "Is it your pleasure that I should speak now?"

The commandant hesitated. Then, having called Henri Marais apart and talked to him for a little while, he replied:

418

"No, not now, I think; the matter is too serious. After we have eaten we will listen to your story, Mynheer Quatermain, and meanwhile I command you not to leave this place."

"Do you mean that I am a prisoner, commandant?" I asked.

"If you put it so—yes, Mynheer Quatermain—a prisoner who has to explain how some sixty of our brothers, who were your companions, came to be butchered like beasts in Zululand, while you escaped. Now, no more words; by and by doubtless there will be plenty of them. Here you, Carolus and Johannes, keep watch upon this Englishman, of whom I hear strange stories, with your guns loaded, please, and when we send to you, lead him before us."

"As usual, your cousin Hernan brings evil gifts," I said to Marie bitterly. "Well, let us also eat our dinner, which perhaps the Heeren Carolus and Johannes will do us the honour to share—bringing their loaded guns with them."

Carolus and Johannes accepted the invitation, and from them we heard much news, all of it terrible enough to learn, especially the details of the massacre in that district, which, because of this fearful event is now and always will be known as Weenen, or the Place of Weeping. Suffice it to say that they were quite enough to take away all our appetite, although Carolus and Johannes, who by this time had recovered somewhat from the shock of that night of blood and terror, ate in a fashion which might have filled Hans himself with envy.

Shortly after we had finished our meal, Hans, who, by the way, seemed to have quite recovered from his fatigues, came to remove the dishes. He informed us that all the Boers were having a great "talk," and that they were about to send for me. Sure enough, a few minutes later two armed men arrived and ordered me to follow them. I turned to say some words of farewell to Marie, but she said:

"I go where you do, husband," and, as no objection was made by the guard, she came.

About two hundred yards away, sitting under the shade of one of the wagons, we found the Boers. Six of them were seated in a semicircle upon stools or whatever they could find, the black-browed commandant being in the centre and having in front of him a rough table on which were writing materials.

To the left of these six were the Prinsloos and Meyers, being those folk whom I had rescued from Delagoa, and to the right the other Boers who had ridden into the camp that morning. I saw at a glance that a court-martial had been arranged and that the six elders were the judges, the commandant being the president of the court.

I do not give their names purposely, since I have no wish that the actual perpetrators of the terrible blunder that I am about to describe should be known to posterity. After all, they acted honestly according to their lights, and were but tools in the hand of that villain Hernan Pereira.

"Allan Quatermain," said the commandant, "you are brought here to be tried by a court-martial duly constituted according to the law published in the camps of the emigrant Boers. Do you acknowledge that law?"

"I know that there is such a law, commandant," I answered, "but I do not acknowledge the authority of your court-martial to try a man who is no Boer, but a subject of the Queen of Great Britain."

"We have considered that point, Allan Quatermain," said the commandant, "and we disallow it. You will remember that in the camp at Bushman's River, before you rode with the late Pieter Retief to the chief Sikonyela, when you were given command of the Zulus who went with him, you took an oath to interpret truly and to be faithful in all things to the General Retief, to his companions and to his cause. That oath we hold gives this court jurisdiction over you."

"I deny your jurisdiction," I answered, "although it is true that I took an oath to interpret faithfully, and I request that a note of my denial may be made in writing."

"It shall be done," said the commandant, and laboriously he made the note on the paper before him.

When he had finished he looked up and said: "The charge against you, Allan Quatermain, is that, being one of the commission who recently visited the Zulu king Dingaan, under command of the late Governor and General Pieter Retief, you did falsely and wickedly urge the said Dingaan to murder the said Pieter Retief and his companions, and especially Henri Marais, your father-in-law, and Hernando Pereira, his nephew, with both of whom you had a quarrel. Further, that afterwards you brought about the said murder, having first arranged with the king of the Zulus that you should be removed to a place of safety while it was done. Do you plead Guilty or Not guilty?"

Now when I heard this false and abominable charge my rage and indignation caused me to laugh aloud.

"Are you mad, commandant," I exclaimed, "that you should say such things? On what evidence is this wicked lie advanced against me?"

"No, Allan Quatermain, I am not mad," he replied, "although it is true that through your evil doings I, who have lost my wife and three

420

children by the Zulu spears, have suffered enough to make me mad. As for the evidence against you, you shall hear it. But first I will write down that you plead Not guilty."

He did so, then said:

"If you will acknowledge certain things it will save us all much time, of which at present we have little to spare. Those things are that knowing what was going to happen to the commission, you tried to avoid accompanying it. Is that true?"

"No," I answered. "I knew nothing of what was going to happen to the commission, though I feared something, having but just saved my friends there"—and I pointed to the Prinsloos—"from death at the hands of Dingaan. I did not wish to accompany it for another reason: that I had been married on the day of its starting to Marie Marais. Still, I went after all because the General Retief, who was my friend, asked me to come, to interpret for him."

Now some of the Boers present said:

"That is true. We remember."

But the commandant continued, taking no heed of my answer or these interruptions.

"Do you acknowledge that you were on bad terms with Henri Marais and with Hernan Pereira?"

"Yes," I answered; "because Henri Marais did all in his power to prevent my marriage with his daughter Marie, behaving very ill to me who had saved his life and that of his people who remained to him up by Delagoa, and afterwards at Umgungundhlovu. Because, too, Hernan Pereira strove to rob me of Marie, who loved me. Moreover, although I had saved him when he lay sick to death, he afterwards tried to murder me by shooting me down in a lonely place. Here is the mark of it," and I touched the little scar upon the side of my forehead.

"That is true; he did so, the stinkcat," shouted the Vrouw Prinsloo, and was ordered to be silent.

"Do you acknowledge," went on the commandant, "that you sent to warn your wife and those with her to depart from the camp on the Bushman's River, because it was going to be attacked, charging them to keep the matter secret, and that afterwards both you and your Hottentot servant alone returned safely from Zululand, where all those who went with you lie dead?"

"I acknowledge," I answered, "that I wrote to tell my wife to come to this place where I had been building houses, as you see, and to bring with her any of our companions who cared to trek here, or, failing that, to go alone. This I did because Dingaan had told me, whether in jest or in earnest I did not know, that he had given orders that my said wife should be kidnapped, as he desired to make her one of his women, having thought her beautiful when he saw her. Also what I did was done with the knowledge and by the wish of the late Governor Retief, as can be shown by his writing on my letter. I acknowledge also that I escaped when all my brothers were killed, as did the Hottentot Hans, and if you wish to know I will tell you how we escaped and why."

The commandant made a further note, then he said:

"Let the witness Hernan Pereira be called and sworn."

This was done and he was ordered to tell his tale.

As may be imagined, it was a long tale, and one that had evidently been prepared with great care. I will only set down its blackest falsehoods. He assured the court that he had no enmity against me and had never attempted to kill me or do me any harm, although it was true that his heart felt sore because, against her father's will, I had stolen away the affection of his betrothed, who was now my wife. He said that he had stopped in Zululand because he knew that I should marry her as soon as she came of age, and it was too great pain for him to see this done. He said that while he was there, before the arrival of the commission, Dingaan and some of his captains had told him that I had again and again urged him, Dingaan, to kill the Boers because they were traitors to the sovereign of England, but that he, Dingaan, had refused to do so. He said that when Retief came up with the commission he tried to warn him against me, but that Retief would not listen, being infatuated with me as many others were, and he looked towards the Prinsloos.

Then came the worst of all. He said that while he was engaged in mending some guns for Dingaan in one of his private huts, he overheard a conversation between myself and Dingaan which took place outside the hut, I, of course, not knowing that he was within. The substance of this conversation was that I again urged Dingaan to kill the Boers and afterwards to send an *impi* to massacre their wives and families. Only I asked him to give me time to get away a girl whom I had married from among them, and with her a few of my own friends whom I wished should be spared, as I intended to become a kind of chief over them, and if he would grant it me, to hold all the land of Natal under his rule and the protection of the English. To these proposals Dingaan answered that "they seemed wise and good, and that he would think them over very carefully."

Pereira said further that coming out of the hut after Dingaan had gone away he reproached me bitterly for my wickedness, and announced that he would warn the Boers, which he did subsequently by word of mouth and in writing. That thereon I caused him to be detained by the Zulus while I went to Retief and told him some false story about him, Pereira, which caused Retief to drive him out of his camp and give orders that none of the Boers should so much as speak to him. That then he did the only thing he could. Going to his uncle, Henri Marais, he told him, not all the truth, but that he had learnt for certain that his daughter Marie was in dreadful danger of her life because of some intended attack of the Zulus, and that all the Boers among whom she dwelt were also in danger of their lives.

Therefore he suggested to Henri Marais that as the General Retief was besotted and would not listen to his story, the best thing they could do was to ride away and warn the Boers. This then they did secretly, without the knowledge of Retief, but being delayed upon their journey by one accident and another, which he set out in detail, they only reached the Bushman's River too late, after the massacre had taken place. Subsequently, as the commandant knew, hearing a rumour that Marie Marais and other Boers had trekked to this place before the slaughter, they came here and learned that they had done so upon a warning sent to them by Allan Quatermain, whereon they returned and communicated the news to the surviving Boers at Bushman's River.

That was all he had to say.

Then, as I reserved my cross-examination until I heard all the evidence against me, Henri Marais was sworn and corroborated his nephew's testimony on many points as to my relations to his daughter, his objection to my marriage to her because I was an Englishman whom he disliked and mistrusted, and so forth. He added further that it was true Pereira had told him he had sure information that Marie and the Boers were in danger from an attack upon them which had been arranged between Allan Quatermain and Dingaan; that he also had written to Retief and tried to speak to him but was refused a hearing. Thereon he had ridden away from Umgungundhlovu to try to save his daughter and warn the Boers. That was all he had to say.

As there were no further witnesses for the prosecution I cross-examined these two at full length, but absolutely without results, since every vital question that I asked was met with a direct negative.

Then I called my witnesses, Marie, whose evidence they refused to hear on the ground that she was my wife and prejudiced, the Vrouw Prinsloo and her family, and the Meyers. One and all told a true story of my relations with Hernan Pereira, Henri Marais, and Dingaan, so far as they knew them.

After this, as the commandant declined to take the evidence of Hans because he was a Hottentot and my servant, I addressed the court, relating exactly what had taken place between me and Dingaan, and how I and Hans came to escape on our second visit to his *kraal*. I pointed out also that unhappily for myself I could not prove my words, since Dingaan was not available as a witness, and all the others were dead. Further, I produced my letter to Marie, which was endorsed by Retief, and the letter to Retief signed by Marais and Pereira which remained in my possession.

By the time that I had finished my speech the sun was setting and everyone was tired out. I was ordered to withdraw under guard, while the court consulted, which it did for a long while. Then I was called forward again and the commandant said:

"Allan Quatermain, after prayer to God we have considered this case to the best of our judgment and ability. On the one hand we note that you are an Englishman, a member of a race which hates and has always oppressed our people, and that it was to your interest to get rid of two of them with whom you had quarrelled. The evidence of Henri Marais and Hernan Pereira, which we cannot disbelieve, shows that you were wicked enough, either in order to do this, or because of your malice against the Boer people, to plot their destruction with a savage. The result is that some seven hundred men, women, and children have lost their lives in a very cruel manner, whereas you, your servant, your wife and your friends have alone escaped unharmed. For such a crime as this a hundred deaths could not pay; indeed, God alone can give to it its just punishment, and to Him it is our duty to send you to be judged. We condemn you to be shot as a traitor and a murderer, and may He have mercy on your soul."

At these dreadful words Marie fell to the ground fainting and a pause ensued while she was carried off to the Prinsloos' house, whither the *vrouw* followed to attend her. Then the commandant went on:

"Still, although we have thus passed judgment on you; because you are an Englishman against whom it might be said that we had prejudices, and because you have had no opportunity of preparing a defence, and no witnesses to the facts, since all those whom you say you could have called are dead, we think it right that this unanimous sentence of ours should be confirmed by a general court of the emigrant Boers. Therefore to-morrow morning you will be taken with us to the Bushman's River camp, where the case will be settled, and, if necessary, execution done in accordance with the verdict of the generals and *veld*-cornets of that camp. Meanwhile you will be kept in custody in your own house. Now have you anything to say against this sentence?"

"Yes, this," I answered, "that although you do not know it, it is an unjust sentence, built up on the lies of one who has always been my enemy, and of a man whose brain is rotten. I never betrayed the Boers. If anyone betrayed them it was Hernan Pereira himself, who, as I proved to the General Retief, had been praying Dingaan to kill me, and whom Retief threatened to put upon his trial for this very crime, for which reason and no other Pereira fled from the *kraal*, taking his tool Henri Marais with him. You have asked God to judge me. Well, I ask God to judge him and Henri Marais also, and I know He will in one way or another. As for me, I am ready to die, as I have been for months while serving the cause of you Boers. Shoot me now if you will, and make an end. But I tell you that if I escape your hands I will not suffer this treatment to go unpunished. I will lay my case before the rulers of my people, and if necessary before my Queen, yes, if I have to travel to London to do it, and you Boers shall learn that you cannot condemn an innocent Englishman upon false testimony and not pay the price. I tell you that price shall be great if I live, and if I die it shall be greater still."

Now these words, very foolish words, I admit, which being young and inexperienced I spoke in my British pride, I could see made a great impression upon my judges. They believed, to be fair to them, that they had passed a just sentence. Blinded by prejudice and falsehood, and maddened by the dreadful losses their people had suffered during the past few days at the hands of a devilish savage, they believed that I was the instigator of those losses, one who ought to die. Indeed, all, or nearly all the Boers were persuaded that Dingaan was urged to this massacre by the counsels of Englishmen. The mere fact of my own and my servant's miraculous escape, when all my companions had perished, proved my guilt to them without the evidence of Pereira, which, being no lawyers, they thought sufficient to justify their verdict.

Still, they had an uneasy suspicion that this evidence was not conclusive, and might indeed be rejected *in toto* by a more competent court upon various grounds. Also they knew themselves to be rebels who had no legal right to form a court, and feared the power of the long arm of England, from which for a little while they had escaped. If I were allowed to tell my tale to the Parliament in London, what might not happen to them, they wondered—to them who had ventured to pass sentence of death upon a subject of the Queen of Great Britain? Might not this turn the scale against them? Might not Britain arise in wrath and crush them, these men who dared to invoke her forms of law in order to kill her citizen? Those, as I learned afterwards, were the thoughts that passed through their minds.

Also another thought passed through their minds—that if the sentence were executed at once, a dead man cannot appeal, and that here I had no friends to take up my cause and avenge me. But of all this they said nothing. Only at a sign I was marched away to my little house and imprisoned under guard.

Now I propose to tell the rest of the history of these tragic events as they happened, although some of them did not come to my knowledge till the morrow or afterwards, for I think this will be the more simple and the easier plan.

CHAPTER 21

The Innocent Blood

After I had been taken away it seems that the court summoned Hernan Pereira and Henri Marais to accompany them to a lonely spot at a distance, where they thought that their deliberations would not be overheard. In this, however, they were mistaken, having forgotten the fox-like cunning of the Hottentot, Hans. Hans had heard me sentenced, and probably enough feared that he who also had committed the crime of escaping from Dingaan, might be called on to share that sentence. Also he wished to know the secret counsel of these Boers, whose language, of course, he understood as well as he did his own.

So making a circuit up the hillside, he crept towards them on his belly as a snake creeps, wriggling in and out between the tufts of last year's dead grass, which grew here in plenty, without so much as moving their tops. At length he lay still in the centre of a bush that grew behind a stone not five paces from where they were talking, whence he listened intently to every word that passed their lips.

This was the substance of their talk; that for the reasons I have already mentioned it would be best that I should die at once. Sentence, said the commandant, had been passed, and could not be rescinded, since even if it were, their offence would remain as heavy in the eyes of the English authorities. But if they took me to their main camp to be re-tried by their great council, possibly that sentence might be rescinded and they be left individually and collectively to atone for what they had done. Also they knew that I was very clever and might escape in some other way to bring the English, or possibly the Zulus, upon them, since they felt convinced that Dingaan and I were working together for their destruction, and that while I had breath in my body I should never cease my efforts to be avenged.

When it was found that they were all of one mind in this matter, the question arose: What should be done? Somebody suggested that I

427

should be shot at once, but the commandant pointed out that such a deed, worked at night, would look like murder, especially as it violated the terms of their verdict.

Then another suggestion was made: that I should be brought out of my house just before the dawn on pretence that it was time to ride; that then I should be given the opportunity of escape and instantly shot down. Or it might be pretended that I had tried to escape, with a like result. Who, they urged, was to know in that half-light whether I had or had not actually attempted to run for my life, or to threaten their lives, circumstances under which the law said it was justifiable to shoot a prisoner already formally condemned to death?

To this black counsel they all agreed, being so terribly afraid of a poor English lad whose existence, although most of them did not know this, was to be taken from him upon false evidence. But then arose another question: By whose hand should the thing be done? Not one of them, it would seem, was anxious to fulfil this bloody office; indeed, they one and all refused to do so. A proposal was put forward that some of their native servants should be forced to serve as executioners; but when this had been vetoed by the general sense of the court, their counsels came to a deadlock.

Then, after a whispered conference, the commandant spoke some dreadful words.

"Hernando Pereira and Henri Marais," he said, "it is on your evidence that this young man has been condemned. We believe that evidence, but if by one jot or one tittle it is false, then not justice, but a foul murder will have been committed and his innocent blood will be upon your heads for ever. Hernando Pereira and Henri Marais, the court appoints you to be the guards who will bring the prisoner out of his house to-morrow morning just when the sky begins to lighten. It is from *you* that he will try to escape, and *you* will prevent his escape by his death. Then you must join us where we shall be waiting for you and report the execution."

When Henri Marais heard this he exclaimed:

"I swear by God that I cannot do it. Is it right or natural that a man should be forced to kill his own son-in-law?"

"You could bear evidence against your own son-in-law, Henri Marais," answered the stern-faced commandant. "Why then cannot you kill with your rifle one whom you have already helped to kill with your tongue?"

"I will not, I cannot!" said Marais, tearing at his beard. But the commandant only answered coldly:

"You have the orders of the court, and if you choose to disobey them we shall begin to believe that you have sworn falsely. Then you and your nephew will also appear before the great council when the Englishman is tried again. Still, it matters nothing to us whether you or Hernando Pereira shall fire the shot. See you to it, as the Jews said to Judas who had betrayed the innocent Lord."

Then he paused and went on, addressing Pereira:

"Do you also refuse, Hernando Pereira? Remember before you answer that if you do refuse we shall draw our own conclusions. Remember, too, that the evidence which you have given, showing that this wicked Englishman plotted and caused the deaths of our brothers and of our wives and children, which we believe to be true evidence, shall be weighed and investigated word by word before the great council."

"To give evidence is one thing, and to shoot the traitor and murderer another," said Pereira. Then he added with an oath, or so vowed Hans: "Yet why should I, who know all this villain's guilt, refuse to carry out the sentence of the law on him? Have no fear, commandant, the accursed Allan Quatermain shall not succeed in his attempt to escape to-morrow before the dawn."

"So be it," said the commandant. "Now, do all you who have heard those words take note of them."

Then Hans, seeing that the council was about to break up, and fearing lest he should be caught and killed, slipped away by the same road that he had come. His thought was to warn me, but this he could not do because of the guards. So he went to the Prinsloos, and finding the *vrouw* alone with Marie, who had recovered her mind, told them everything that he had heard.

As he said, Marie knelt down and prayed, or thought for a long while, then rose and spoke.

"*Tante,*" she said to the *vrouw,* "one thing is clear, that Allan will be murdered at the dawn; now if he is hidden away he may escape."

"But where and how can we hide him," asked the *vrouw,* "seeing that the place is guarded?"

"*Tante,*" said Marie again, "at the back of your house is an old cattle *kraal* made by Kaffirs, and in that cattle *kraal,* as I have seen, there are *mealie*-pits where those Kaffirs stored their grain. Now I suggest that we should put my husband into one of those *mealie*-pits and cover it over. There the Boers might not find him, however close they searched."

"That is a good idea," said the *vrouw;* "but how in the name of God are we to get Allan out of a guarded house into a *mealie*-pit?"

429

"*Tante*, I have a right to go to my husband's house, and there I will go. Afterwards, too, I shall have the right to leave his house before he is taken away. Well, he might leave it in my place, *as me*, and you and Hans might help him. Then in the morning the Boers would come to search the house and find no one except me."

"That is all very pretty," answered the *vrouw*; "but do you think, my niece, that those accursed vultures will go away until they have picked Allan's bones? Not they, for too much hangs on it. They will know that he cannot be far off, and slink about the place until they have found him in his *mealie*-hole or until he comes out. It is blood they are after, thanks to your cousin Hernan, the liar, and blood they will have for their own safety's sake. Never will they go away from here until they see Allan lying dead upon the ground."

Now, according to Hans, Marie thought again very deeply. Then she answered:

"There is a great risk, *tante*; but we must take it. Send your husband to chat with those guards, and give him a bottle of spirits. I will talk with Hans here and see what can be arranged."

So Marie went aside with Hans, as he told me afterwards, and asked him if he knew of any medicine that made people sleep for a long while without waking. He answered, Yes; all the coloured people had plenty of such medicine. Without doubt he could get some from the Kaffirs who dwelt upon the place, or if not he could dig the roots of a plant that he had seen growing near by which would serve the purpose. So she sent him to procure this stuff. Afterwards she spoke to the Vrouw Prinsloo, saying:

"My plan is that Allan should escape from our house disguised as myself. But as I know well that he will not run away while he has his senses, seeing that to do so in his mind would be to confess his guilt, I propose to take his senses from him by means of a drugged drink. Then I propose that you and Hans should carry him into the shadow of this house, and when no one is looking, to the old grain-pit that lies but a few yards away, covering the mouth of it with dead grass. There he will remain till the Boers grow tired of searching for him and ride away. Or if it should chance that they find him, he will be no worse off than he was before."

"A good plan enough, Marie, though not one that Allan would have anything to do with if he kept his wits," answered the *vrouw*, "seeing that he was always a man for facing things out, although so young in years. Still, we will try to save him in spite of himself from the claws of that stinkcat Pereira, whom may God curse, and his tool,

430

your father. As you say, at the worst no harm will be done even if they find him, as probably they will, seeing that they will not leave this place without blood."

Such then was the trick which Marie arranged with the Vrouw Prinsloo. Or rather, I should say, seemed to arrange, since she told her nothing of her real mind, she who knew that the *vrouw* was right and that for their own sakes, as well as because they believed it to be justice, the Boers would never leave that place until they saw blood running on the grass.

This, oh! this was Marie's true and dreadful plan—*to give her life for mine!* She was sure that once he had slain his victim, Hernan Pereira would not stop to make examination of the corpse. He would ride away, hounded by his guilty conscience, and meanwhile I could escape.

She never thought the thing out in all its details, she who was maddened with terror and had no time. She only felt her way from step to step, dimly seeing my deliverance at the end of the journey. Marie told the Vrouw Prinsloo nothing, except that she proposed to drug me if I would not go undrugged. Then the *vrouw* must hide me as best she could, in the grain-pit or elsewhere, or, if I had my senses about me, let me hide myself. Afterwards she, Marie, would face the Boers and tell them to find me if they wanted me.

The *vrouw* answered that she had now thought of a better plan. It was that she should arrange with her husband and son and the Meyers, all of whom loved me, that they should rescue me, or if need be, kill or disable Pereira before he could shoot me.

Marie replied that this was good if it could be done, and the *vrouw* went out to find her husband and the other men. Presently, however, she returned with a long face, saying that the commandant had them all under guard. It seemed that it had occurred to him, or more probably to Pereira, that the Prinsloos and the Meyers, who looked on me as a brother, might attempt some rescue, or make themselves formidable in other ways. Therefore, as a matter of precaution, they had been put under arrest and their arms taken from them as mine had been. What the commandant said, however, was that he took these somewhat high-handed measures in order to be sure that they, the Prinsloos and the Meyers, should be ready on the following morning to ride with him and the prisoner to the main camp, where the great council might wish to interrogate them.

One concession, however, the *vrouw* had won from the commandant, who, knowing what was about to happen to me, had not, I suppose, the heart to refuse. It was that my wife and she might visit me and give me food on the stipulation that they both left the house where I was confined by ten o'clock that night.

So it came to this, that if anything was to be done, these two women and a Hottentot must do it, since they could hope for no help in their plans. Here I should add that the *vrouw* told Marie in Hans's presence that she had thought of attacking the commandant as to this matter of my proposed shooting by Pereira. On reflection, however, she refrained for two reasons, first because she feared lest she might only make matters worse and rob me of my sole helpers, and secondly for fear lest she should bring about the death of Hans, to whom the story would certainly be traced.

As he was the solitary witness to the plot, it seemed to her that he would scarcely be allowed to escape to repeat it far and wide. Especially was this so, as the unexplained death of a Hottentot, suspected of treachery like his master, was not a matter that would have been thought worth notice in those rough and bloody times. She may have been right, or she may have been wrong, but in weighing her decision it must always be borne in mind that she was, and until the end remained, in utter ignorance of Marie's heroic design to go to her death in place of me.

So the two women and the Hottentot proceeded to mature the plans which I have outlined. One other alternative, however, Hans did suggest. It was that they should try to drug the guards with some of the medicated drink that was meant for me, and that then Marie, I and he should slip away and get down to the river, there to hide in the weeds. Thence, perhaps, we might escape to Port Natal where lived Englishmen who would protect us.

Of course this idea was hopeless from the first. The moonlight was almost as bright as day, and the *veld* quite open for a long way round, so that we should certainly have been seen and re-captured, which of course would have meant instant death. Further, as it happened, the guards had been warned against touching liquor of any sort since it was thought probable that an attempt would be made to intoxicate them. Still the women determined to try this scheme if they could find a chance. At least it was a second string to their bow.

Meanwhile they made their preparations. Hans went away for a little and returned with a supply of his sleep-producing drug, though whether he got this from the Kaffirs or gathered it himself, I do not remember, if I ever heard. At any rate it was boiled up in the water with which they made the coffee that I was to drink, though not in that which Marie proposed to drink with me, the strong taste and black hue of the coffee effectually hiding any flavour or colour that there might be in the herb. Also the *vrouw* cooked some food which she gave to Hans to carry. First, however, he went to investigate the old *mealie*-pit which was within a few paces of the back door of the Prinsloos' house. He reported that it would do well to hide a man in, especially as tall grass and bushes grew about its mouth.

Then the three of them started, and arriving at the door of my house, which was about a hundred yards away, were of course challenged by the sentries.

"Heeren," said Marie, "the commandant has given us leave to bring food to my husband, whom you guard within. Pray do not prevent us from entering."

"No," answered one of them gently enough, for he was touched with pity at her plight. "We have our orders to admit you, the Vrouw Prinsloo and the native servant, though why three of you should be needed to carry food to one man, I don't know. I should have thought that at such a time he would have preferred to be alone with his wife."

"The Vrouw Prinsloo wishes to ask my husband certain questions about his property here and what is to be done while he and her men are away at the main camp for the second trial, as I, whose heart is full of sorrow, have no head for such things. Also the Hottentot must have orders as to where he is to get a horse to ride with him, so pray let us pass, *mynheer*."

"Very good; it is no affair of ours, Vrouw Quatermain—Stay, I suppose that you have no arms under that long cloak of yours."

"Search me, if you will, *mynheer*," she answered, opening the cloak, whereon, after a quick glance, he nodded and bade them enter, saying:

"Mind, you are to come out by ten o'clock. You must not pass the night in that house, or we shall have the little Englishman oversleeping himself in the morning."

Then they entered and found me seated at a table preparing notes for my defence and setting down the heads of the facts of my relations with Pereira, Dingaan, and the late Commandant Retief.

Here I may state that my condition at the time was not one of fear, but rather of burning indignation. Indeed, I had not the slightest doubt but that when my case was re-tried before the great council, I should be able to establish my complete innocence of the abominable charges that had been brought against me. Therefore it came about that when Marie suggested that I should try to escape, I begged her almost roughly not to mention such a thing again.

"Run away!" I said. "Why, that would be to confess myself guilty, for only the guilty run away. What I want is to have all this business thrashed out and that devil Pereira exposed."

"But, Allan," said Marie, "how if you should never live to have it thrashed out? How if you should be shot first?" Then she rose, and having looked to see that the shutter-board was fast in the little window-place and the curtain that she had made of sacking drawn over it, returned and whispered: "Hans here has heard a horrible tale, Allan. Tell it to the *baas*, Hans."

So while Vrouw Prinsloo, in order to deceive any prying eyes if such by chance could see us, busied herself with lighting a fire on the hearth in the second room on which to warm the food, Hans told his story much as it has already been set out.

I listened to it with growing incredulity. The thing seemed to me impossible. Either Hans was deceived or lying, the latter probably, for well I knew the Hottentot powers of imagination. Or perhaps he was drunk; indeed, he smelt of liquor, of which I was aware he could carry a great quantity without outward signs of intoxication.

"I cannot believe it," I said when he had finished. "Even if Pereira is such a fiend, as is possible, would Henri Marais, your father—who, at any rate, has always been a good and God-fearing man—consent to work such a crime upon his daughter's husband, though he does dislike him?"

"My father is not what he was, Allan," said Marie. "Sometimes I think that his brain has gone."

"He did not speak like a man whose brain has gone this afternoon," I replied. "But let us suppose that this tale is true, what is it that you wish me to do?"

"Allan, I wish you to dress up in my clothes and get away to a hiding-place which Hans and the *vrouw* know, leaving me here instead of you."

"Why, Marie?" I said. "Then you might get yourself shot in my place, always supposing that they mean to shoot me. Also I should certainly be caught and killed, as they would have a right to kill me for trying to escape in disguise. That is a mad plan, and I have a better. Vrouw Prinsloo, go straight to the commandant ad tell him all this story. Or, if he will not listen to you, scream it out at the top of your voice so that everyone may hear, and then come back and tell us the result. Of one thing I am sure, that if you do this, even if there was any thought of my being shot tomorrow morning, it will be abandoned. You can refuse to say who told you the tale."

"Yes, please do that," muttered Hans, "else I know one who will be shot."

"Good, I will go," said the *vrouw*, and she went, the guards letting her pass after a few words which we could not hear.

Half an hour later she returned and called to us to open the door. "Well?" I asked.

"Well," she said, "I have failed, nephew. Except those sentries outside the door, the commandant and all the Boers have ridden off, I know not where, taking our people with them."

"That's odd," I answered, "but I suppose they thought they had not enough grass for their horses, or Heaven knows what they thought. Stay now, I will do something," and, opening the door, I called to the guards, honest fellows in their way, whom I had known in past times.

"Listen, friends," I said. "A tale has been brought to me that I am not to be taken to the big camp to have my case inquired of by the council, but am to be shot down in cold blood when I come out of this house to-morrow morning. Is that true?"

"*Allemachte*, Englishman!" answered one of them. "Do you take us for murderers? Our orders are to lead you to the commandant wherever he may appoint, so have no fear that we shall shoot you like a Kaffir. Either you or they who told you such a story are mad."

"So I thought, friends," I answered. "But where is the commandant and where are the others? The Vrouw Prinsloo here has been to see them, and reports that they are all gone."

"That is very likely," said the Boer. "There is a rumour that some of your Zulu brothers have come across the Tugela again to hunt us, which, if you want to know the truth, is why we visited this place. Well, the commandant has taken his men for a ride to see if he can meet them by this bright moonlight. Pity he could not take you, too, since you would have known so well where to find them, if they are there at all. Now please talk no more nonsense to us, which it makes us sick to hear, and don't think that you can slip away because we are only two, for you know our *roers* are loaded with slugs, and we have orders to use them."

"There," I said when I had shut the door, "now you have heard for yourselves. As I thought, there is nothing in this fine story, so I hope you are convinced."

Neither the *vrouw* nor Marie made any answer, and Hans also held his tongue. Yet, as I remembered afterwards, I saw a strange glance pass between the two women, who were not at all convinced, and, although I never dreamed of such a thing, had now determined to carry

435

out their own desperate plan. But of this I repeat the *vrouw* and Hans only knew one half; the rest was locked in Marie's loving heart.

"Perhaps you are right, Allan," said the *vrouw* in the tone of one who gives way to an unreasonable child. "I hope so, and, at any rate, you can refuse to come out of the house to-morrow morning until you are quite sure. And now let us eat some supper, for we shall not make matters better by going hungry. Hans, bring the food."

So we ate, or made pretence to eat, and I, being thirsty, drank two cups of the black coffee dashed with spirit to serve as milk. After this I grew strangely sleepy. The last thing I remember was Marie looking at me with her beautiful eyes, that were full—ah! so full of tender love, and kissing me again and again upon the lips.

I dreamed all sorts of dreams, rather pleasant dreams on the whole. Then I woke up by degrees to find myself in an earthen pit shaped like a bottle and having the remains of polished sides to it. It made me think of Joseph who was let down by his brethren into a well in the desert. Now, who on earth could have let me down into a well, especially as I had no brethren? Perhaps I was not really in a well. Perhaps this was a nightmare. Or I might be dead. I began to re-member that there were certain good reasons why I should be dead. Only, only—why should they have buried me in woman's clothes as I seemed to wear?

And what was that noise that had wakened me?

It could not be the trump of doom, unless the trumping of doom went off like a double-barrelled gun.

I began to try to climb out of my hole, but as it was nine feet deep and bottle-shaped, which the light flowing in from the neck showed, I found this impossible. Just as I was giving up the attempt, a yellow face appeared in that neck, which looked to me like the face of Hans, and an arm was projected downwards.

"Jump, if you are awake, *baas*," said a voice—surely it was the voice of Hans—"and I will pull you out."

So I jumped, and caught the arm above the wrist. Then the owner of the arm pulled desperately, and the end of it was that I succeeded in gripping the edge of the bottle-like hole, and, with the help of the arm, in dragging myself out.

"Now, *baas*," said Hans, for it *was* Hans, "run, run before the Boers catch you."

"What Boers?" I asked, sleepily; "and how can I run with these things flapping about my legs?"

Then I looked about me, and, although the dawn was only just

436

breaking, began to recognise my surroundings. Surely this was the Prinsloos' house to my right, and that, faintly seen through the mist about a hundred paces away, was Marie's and my own. There seemed to be something going on yonder which excited my awakening curiosity. I could see figures moving in an unusual manner, and desired to know what they were doing. I began to walk towards them, and Hans, for his part, began to try to drag me in an opposite direction, uttering all sorts of gibberish as to the necessity of my running away. But I would not be dragged; indeed, I struck at him, until at last, with an exclamation of despair, he let go of me and vanished.

So I went on alone. I came to my house, or what I thought resembled it, and there saw a figure lying on its face on the ground some ten or fifteen yards to the right of the doorway, and noted abstractedly that it was dressed in my clothes. The Vrouw Prinsloo, in her absurd night garments, was waddling towards the figure, and a little way off stood Hernan Pereira, apparently in the act of reloading a double-barrelled gun. Beyond, staring at him, stood the lantern-faced Henri Marais, pulling at his long beard with one hand and holding a rifle in the other. Behind were two saddled horses in the charge of a raw Kaffir, who looked on stupidly.

The Vrouw Prinsloo reached the body that lay upon the ground dressed in what resembled my clothes, and bending down her stout shape with an effort, turned it over. She glared into its face and then began to shriek.

"Come here, Henri Marais," she shrieked, "come, see what your beloved nephew has done! You had a daughter who was all your life to you, Henri Marais. Well, come, look at her after your beloved nephew has finished his work with her!"

Henri Marais advanced slowly like one who does not understand. He stood over the body on the ground, and looked down upon it through the morning mists.

Then suddenly he went mad. His broad hat fell from his head, and his long hair seemed to stand up. Also his beard grew big and bristled like the feathers of a bird in frosty weather. He turned on Hernan Pereira. "You devil!" he shouted, and his voice sounded like the roar of a wild beast; "you devil, you have murdered my daughter! Because you could not get Marie for yourself, you have murdered her. Well, I will pay you back!"

Without more ado he lifted his gun and fired straight at Hernan Pereira, who sank slowly to the ground and lay there groaning.

Just then I grew aware that horsemen were advancing upon us, a great number of horsemen, though whence they came at that time I did not know. One of these I recognised even in my half-drunken state, for he had impressed himself very vividly upon my mind. He was the dark-browed commandant who had tried and condemned me to death. He dismounted, and, staring at the two figures that lay upon the ground, said in a loud and terrible voice:

"What is this? Who are these men, and why are they shot? Explain, Henri Marais."

"Men!" wailed Henri Marais, "they are not men. One is a woman—my only child; and the other is a devil, who, being a devil, will not die. See! he will not die. Give me another gun that I may make him die."

The commandant looked about him wildly, and his eye fell upon the Vrouw Prinsloo.

"What has chanced, *vrouw*?" he asked.

"Only this," she replied in a voice of unnatural calm. "Your murderers whom you set on in the name of law and justice have made a mistake. You told them to murder Allan Quatermain for reasons of your own. Well, they have murdered his wife instead."

Now the commandant struck his hand upon his forehead and groaned, and I, half awakened at last, ran forward, shaking my fists and gibbering.

"Who is that?" asked the commandant. "Is it a man or a woman?"

"It is a man in woman's clothing; it is Allan Quatermain," answered the *vrouw*, "whom we drugged and tried to hide from your butchers."

"God above us!" exclaimed the commandant, "is this earth or hell?"

Then the wounded Pereira raised himself upon one hand.

"I am dying," he cried; "my life is bleeding away, but before I die I must speak. All that story I told against the Englishman is false. He never plotted with Dingaan against the Boers. It was I who plotted with Dingaan. Although I hated him because he found me out, I did not wish Retief and our people to be killed. But I did wish Allan Quatermain to be killed, because he had won her whom I loved, though, as it happened, all the others were slain, and he alone escaped. Then I came here and learned that Marie was his wife—yes, his wife indeed—and grew mad with hate and jealousy. So I bore false witness against him, and, you fools, you believed me and ordered me to shoot him who is innocent before God and man. Then things went wrong. The woman tricked me again—for the last time. She dressed herself as the man, and in the dawn light I was deceived. I killed her, her whom I love alone, and now her father, who loved her also, has killed me."

By this time I understood all, for my drugged brain had awakened at last. I ran to the brute upon the ground; grotesque in my woman's garments all awry, I leaped on him and stamped out the last of his life. Then, standing over his dead body, I shook my fists and cried:

"Men, see what you have done. May God pay you back all you owe her and me!"

They dismounted, they came round me, they protested, they even wept. And I, I raved at them upon the one side, while the mad Henri Marais raved upon the other; and the Vrouw Prinsloo, waving her big arms, called down the curse of God and the blood of the innocent upon their heads and those of their children for ever.

Then I remember no more.

When I came to myself two weeks afterwards, for I had been very ill and in delirium, I was lying in the house of the Vrouw Prinsloo alone. The Boers had all gone, east and west and north and south, and the dead were long buried. They had taken Henri Marais with them, so I was told, dragging him away in a bullock cart, to which he was tied, for he was raving mad. Afterwards he became quieter, and, indeed, lived for years, walking about and asking all whom he met if they could lead him to Marie. But enough of him—poor man, poor man!

The tale which got about was that Pereira had murdered Marie out of jealousy, and been shot by her father. But there were so many tragic histories in those days of war and massacre that this particular one was soon quite forgotten, especially as those concerned in it for one reason and another did not talk overmuch of its details. Nor did I talk of it, since no vengeance could mend my broken heart.

They brought me a letter that had been found on Marie's breast, stained with her blood. Here it is:

My Husband,

Thrice have you saved my life, and now it is my turn to save yours, for there is no other path. It may be that they will kill you afterwards, but if so, I shall be glad to have died first in order that I may be ready to greet you in the land beyond.

I drugged you, Allan, then I cut off my hair and dressed myself in your clothes. The Vrouw Prinsloo, Hans and I set my garments upon you. They led you out as though you were fainting, and the guards, seeing me, whom they thought was you, standing in the doorway, let them pass without question.

What may happen I do not know, for I write this after you

439

are gone. I hope, however, that you will escape and lead some full and happy life, though I fear that its best moments will always be shadowed by memories of me. For I know you love me, Allan, and will always love me, as I shall always love you.

The light is burning out—like mine—so farewell, farewell, farewell! All earthly stories come to an end at last, but at that end we shall meet again. Till then, adieu. Would that I could have done more for you, since to die for one who is loved with body, heart and soul is but a little thing. Still I have been your wife, Allan, and your wife I shall remain when the world is old. Heaven does not grow old, Allan, and there I shall greet you. The light is dead, but—oh!—in my heart another light arises!
Your Marie

This was her letter.

I do not think there is anything more to be said.

Such is the history of my first love. Those who read it, if any ever do, will understand why I have never spoken of her before, and do not wish it to be known until I, too, am dead and have gone to join the great soul of Marie Marais.

Allan Quatermain

LEONAUR

ALSO FROM LEONAUR
AVAILABLE IN SOFTCOVER OR HARDCOVER WITH DUST JACKET

TROS OF SAMOTHRACE 1: WOLVES OF THE TIBER *by Talbot Mundy*—When his ship is taken and his crew slaughtered Tros of Samothrace is captured by Imperial Rome.

TROS OF SAMOTHRACE 2: DRAGONS OF THE NORTH *by Talbot Mundy*—Tros of Samothrace burns for vengeance and has declared himself the implacable enemy of Rome.

TROS OF SAMOTHRACE 3: SERPENT OF THE WAVES *by Talbot Mundy*—Tros, his allies and the forces of Rome have drawn apart to prepare for the conflict to come.

TROS OF SAMOTHRACE 4: CITY OF THE EAGLES *by Talbot Mundy*—As Tros of Samothrace continues in his attempts to confound Caesar's plans for the invasion of Britain, he journeys to the Eternal City to seek the aid of its great leaders—and Caesar's opponents—Cato, Pompey and the Vestal Virgins themselves!

THE ILLUSTRATED & COMPLETE BRIGADIER GERARD *by Sir Arthur Conan Doyle*—As Tros of Samothrace continues in his attempts to confound Caesar's plans for tThese are the adventures of Conan Doyle's incomparable French hero-the finest swordsman in the Light Cavalry-Etienne Gerard. Arranged for the first time in historical chronological order, his many enthusiasts can now properly appreciate his colourful career as he fights, loves and blunders his way through the Napoleonic epoch-from his earliest adventure as a young blade determined to reach his lady love despite the unwelcome attention of her fathers bull-through many campaigns and special missions-to the bloody field of Waterloo, the downfall of his beloved Emperor and beyond. This is the complete collection of these classic stories. What makes this edition exceptional is the inclusion of nearly 140 illustrations-mostly by the famed military artist William Barnes Wollen-which accurately portray the spirit of the stories and the uniforms and scenes of the events they portray.

THE APACHE ADVENTURES *by Edgar Rice Burroughs*—*The War Chief & Apache Devil* two tales of the battles of the decline of the Apaches way of life.

THE COMPLETE MUCKER *by Edgar Rice Burroughs*—*The Mucker; The Return of the Mucker & The Oakdale Affair* Billy Byrne is the Mucker. Born and brought up on the tough streets of Chicago, Billy is familiar with the hard and seedy side of life in the big city, where only the strong survive and it is a good idea to be able to terminate a disagreement with your fists. A must for all ERB collectors—all the Mucker stories in one volume.